Darkenheight

War is imminent among the three lands of the Watershed.
A dark lord flexes his muscle, sending forth his minions
to destroy any city that stands in his way. Humans and
Faerines alike perish in the onslaught. Their only hope lies
in the one who is known as the Man of Three Waters. In
his hands, he holds the fate of the Watershed. And in his
soul flow the powers of all three realms . . .

*Second in the brilliant epic fantasy of wonder
and terror,
of magic and heroism,
and of good versus evil . . .*

The Watershed Trilogy
by
Douglas Niles

And coming in August 1997 . . .
The War of Three Waters
The epic conclusion of the Watershed Trilogy

A trade paperback from Ace Books

Ace Books by Douglas Niles

THE WATERSHED SERIES

BREACH IN THE WATERSHED
DARKENHEIGHT
THE WAR OF THREE WATERS

DARKENHEIGHT

DOUGLAS NILES

ACE BOOKS, NEW YORK

This Ace Book contains the complete text of the original trade edition. It has been completely reset in a typeface designed for easy reading, and was printed from new film.

DARKENHEIGHT

An Ace Book / published by arrangement with the author

PRINTING HISTORY
Ace trade edition / September 1996
Ace mass-market edition / July 1997

The Putnam Berkley World Wide Web site address is
http://www.berkley.com

Make sure to check out *PB Plug*, the science fiction/fantasy newsletter, at
http://www.pbplug.com

ISBN: 0-441-00456-3

ACE®
Ace Books are published by The Berkley Publishing Group, 200 Madison Avenue, New York, NY 10016.
ACE and the "A" design are trademarks belonging to Charter Communications, Inc.

PRINTED IN THE UNITED STATES OF AMERICA

10 9 8 7 6 5 4 3 2 1

To Mike Wesling,
Johnny Mac,
Pat "Mountain Man" Seghers,
and the valley of the *real* Stonehammer Lake.

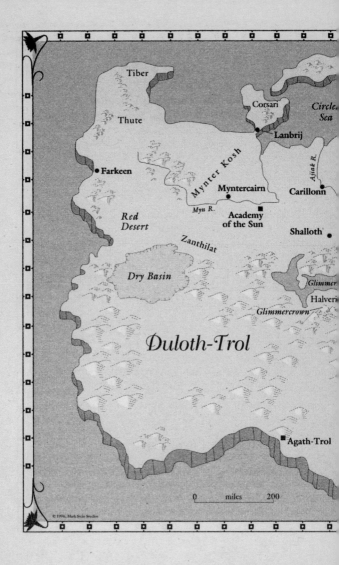

Andaram

Dalethica

Galtigor

North
Shore
Wayfarer's
Lodge

Taywick Pass

Auron R.

Faerine
Sea

• Shalemont

Faerine

Bruxrange

Darkenheight
Pass

N

The Watershed

DARKENHEIGHT

DAYBREAK

PROLOGUE

The gods contest a broad canvas, spanning the
Watershed and unknown reaches beyond.
Mortals, naturally, squabble within a much
more intimate framework.
—CODEX OF THE GUARDIANS

In the waning years of a generous life I can only hope to
complete these pages before my inkwell of time runs dry.
There are so many parts of the story still untold—and so many
of the prospective tellers, sadly, are gone. Although I strive
to weave their memories into these words, to speak through
their voices, I must inevitably fail. Still, certain events no one
observed from a better vantage than I, and, in utter frankness,
there is no one more properly suited to relate the story.

The first of these tales I have already recounted—how I
came to know Rudgar Appenfell and his companions, how
the battle at Taywick averted war between Faerine and human, and how this war had been a scheme of the Sleepstealer's to divert our attention from the real threat. That
realization came at a cost in blood paid by human and Faerine
alike—yet in the end that knowledge forged bonds of deep
friendship, and many kinds of love.

Following the bloody strife in the saddle of Taywick Pass,

I stood with the Man of Three Waters in the midst of destruction. Rudy knew by then that he was a being of magic—and yet, still very much a man. It was his gift, or curse, to mingle the powers of Aura and Darkblood with the mundane water of Dalethica. Now we perched upon a cusp of history, facing a future of unknown dangers—victors in one skirmish, of a war not truly begun.

And though Rudy is the one I dreamed about as a child, loved as a woman, and who burns brightest in my memory now, we had true and brave companions. Some were Faerines—a digger, a sylve, and a twissel. Others were humans: noble and common, a mountain girl and the king of a forest realm. It is fitting, perhaps, that our story resume with a tale I told to the companions, around a waning campfire on the night after Taywick's battle. It was a legend that I had learned as a girl, studying under Pheathersqyll at the Academy of the Sun. There, on the divide of the Watershed, it seemed to have portent for us all.

The fire settled and we stared pensively into the embers. Doubtless we all shared memories of the battle, and fears of the trials ahead. We had seen a Lord Minion of the Sleepstealer, and though he had returned to his master's realm, Nicodareus had not been defeated. Nor did we see any prospect of assailing him in the future. We knew, too, that the Watershed had been breached in at least one place—in Rudy's homeland of Halverica, where a crack in the mountainous ridge had allowed a trickle of Darkblood to befoul Dalethica. And humans, too—such as the late Prince Garamis of Galtigor—had been corrupted by the taste of the Sleepstealer's venomous elixir.

I am no bard, but I knew that it was my place to speak. I began with the tale of the Watershed's creation, when the three gods divided the world into their own realms—Dalethica, of pure water, beholden to Baracan, the God of Man; and glorious Faerine, home of magical Aura and the enchanted children of the goddess Aurianth; and finally Duloth-Trol, home to Dassadec the Sleepstealer, and polluted by the effluence of his Darkblood.

The results of that tale are known in basic form to all who live in the world, but my human companions were most intrigued by the vivid legend of the Watershed's inception. The taming of chaos I have described elsewhere in these *Recollections*, and thus I shall not do so again. But it was the latter part of the legend, the story of the Great Betrayal, that seemed to have the greatest import for our future lives. These were events lost in the fog of history, yet full of meaning for the shaping of the world. Because of Pheathersqyll's diligent instruction, I knew the story, and as the fire burned low I began to speak.

When the gods formed the Compact of the Watershed, each agreed to leave the world in favor of existence in another place, beyond the touch of the physical plane. Baracan prepared for his departure with deep and solemn meditation, giving humans the example of prayer; through the faith of his followers he would rise from the world. Aurianth, of course, wove her magic through music, melodies growing to an enchanted crescendo, a climax powerful enough to vault her into the ethereal heavens. She, like Baracan, was content to shed the bonds of mortality, leaving the tangles of the world in the pursuit of a lofty and serene existence. Dassadec, in turn, fueled his power through the sacrifice of countless captives taken by his minions. Blood flowed freely from the summit of his palace, the mountain Agath-Trol, and the other gods turned their faces aside lest their grieving at his butchery stay their power and bar ultimate transcendence.

Yet when the preparations of the three gods reached a mutual climax, only Aurianth and Baracan departed the world. Dassadec, soaked in the gore of his sacrifices, sank instead into the black stone fundament of Agath-Trol. The mighty mountain became his flesh, and his spirit filled the cavernous voids within the obsidian massif. Instead of flight, the Sleep-stealer used the immortal power of the Compact to create mighty servants—six Lord Minions, awful beings who would work their master's evil in every manner he desired. Tarclouds rolled forward from that great, dark mountain, and an army of minions—led by their sextet of lords—surged over the mountains to bring corruption to all the world.

Aurianth, thankfully, retained one eye upon her brother, witnessing his evil. She was enraged, but neither she nor Baracan could reverse the course that had carried them forever beyond the bounds of the mortal world. Between them they could only speak in warning to their mortal children. At the same time, they knew that admonitions would not be enough—there was no power on the Watershed that could stand against the Lord Minions.

To repair this potentially fatal weakness, Aurianth and Baracan taught their peoples to work together, weaving strengths of man and Faerine into mighty creations. In this fashion were the Artifacts created—tools that mortal warriors could wield to battle the armies of evil, dangerous talismans that threatened even Nicodareus, Reaper, and the other Lord Minions.

Like the spawn of Dassadec, the Artifacts numbered six: the legendary Sword called Lordsmiter, the Shield, the Spear, the Helm, the Belt, and the Cape. The wielders of these mighty tools utilized powers beyond any ordinary mortal's— proof against injury, capable of fantastic feats on the battlefield, or blessed by other mystical abilities. Most of the details have been lost in the ages, though ancient songs describe Lordsmiter's gilded, emerald-studded hilt and glowing blade of pearly white. Armed with their Artifacts, standing at the brink of the Watershed, the combined forces of Dalethica and Faerine met the onslaught of the Sleepstealer's evil. Many died on both sides, but after long years of striving, the minions had been stayed from forcing their way over that lofty barrier.

Only one phase of the climactic struggle was recorded in detail: the attack of Lord Minion Darkenscale. This goatheaded being reached the crest of the Watershed and began to descend into Faerine. A spring of Aura emerged from the heights above the Sleepstealer's subcommander, and diggers channeled the liquid into a plunging canal. When the Aura doused the Lord Minion, a tremendous force of destruction was released—an explosion so great that it obliterated a high barrier of the Watershed, creating the pass known ever since as Darkenheight. The violent eruption destroyed the Lord Minion absolutely and utterly, yet also tore at the very fabric of the world.

And still, five Lord Minions remained, and they pressed attacks in many places—including a major offensive through Darkenheight Pass. In the end it was an intervention unplanned by any god, born of the Watershed and rising from the stones of the mountains themselves, that brought a halt to the War of Betrayal.

The Guardians were not created by Baracan or Aurianth,

and indeed it is likely that the brother and sister gods were as surprised as Dassadec when the peculiar beings emerged into daylight. The Guardians' bodies were as rock, their will as irresistible as an avalanche, and they claimed the highest places of the world as their own. The High Guardians took the mountain peaks and ridges. Deep Guardians wormed into the rock-bound tunnels and caves that served as passage beneath the surface. Together, they drove the warring sides apart, and brought the War of Betrayal to an end.

The Artifacts were lost—many said destroyed. The five surviving Lord Minions each claimed a lofty throne in Agath-Trol, where they could pay obeisance to their master—and beg his forgiveness for their failures. Centuries and millennia would pass before Dassadec again gathered his forces for war. When he next attacked, however, the Sleepstealer War swept much of Dalethica, and came close to bringing all the world under Dassadec's brutal thumb—though that war cost the Nameless One two more Lord Minions, both slain by Guardians. Legends tell of omnipotent Nicodareus pressing forward, striving to avenge the deaths of his fellows.

In our gathering at Taywick Pass, the knowledge that the world again stood imperiled by the Nameless One was heavy on our minds. Our tasks were unclear, yet we knew that we, of all the peoples in Dalethica and Faerine, must do something. We were the ones who had seen the awakening threat, who had some appreciation of its imminence and its power. Our numbers included the Man of Three Waters, and even then we all sensed that Rudgar Appenfell formed an anchor of strength against the Sleepstealer's onslaught.

I knew, too, that it was my destiny to help him, and in that I was as content as I had ever been. My life had been guided by the dictates of prophecy, by scholarly or priestly masters— or a mistress who, in times past, had focused my concerns on matters of her own comfort and appearance. Perhaps I remained a prisoner of Fate, but for the first time the dictates of destiny compelled nothing less than the decisions I would have taken of my own free will.

Rudy—at least, then—did not sense the depth of my commitment. I had hopes that he would, but that was not the reason for the strength of my love. I had begun to sense the truth about the goddess Aurianth, the one key to releasing her power in the mundane world of humankind. We felt that strength among us, in the warmth of good friends and lovers. In that swelling truth, I would be strong.

And in our small group we gathered the hope of the world, and the mystery. Could the forces of two realms, of Aura and water, prove strong enough to resist the corrosive evil of the Sleepstealer's Darkblood?

We had no choice but to try.

From: *Recollections*, by Lady Raine of the Three Waters

ONE

The Iceman

A small stone tumbles from the mountain crest,
enticing other bits of rock and ice until,
ultimately, the power of the avalanche exceeds
its initial impetus by a factor of millions.
—CREED OF THE CLIMBER

— 1 —

The spire of stone jutted into the air like a needle, piercing
the heavens, leaving the mist-blanketed lowlands in a murky
haze of distance. Above, half the sky was black with night,
stars winking like diamonds from the arching vault; the other
half was the pale blue of a mountain sky in daylight, observed
from lofty vantage.

Rudy couldn't remember climbing the pillar of stone, but
now he stood at its top, on a narrow platform of shale. At
first he was alone, and then his brothers were there—Beryv,
who had been his surrogate father; and Donniall and Coyle,
teachers and friends. One by one the Appenfell brothers fell,
plummeting soundlessly, fatally, into the abyss. Rudy tried to
move, to grasp or extend a hand, but he was utterly powerless.

Then Garamis was there, foxlike face twisted into a sneer
of triumph. The Prince of Galtigor, servant of the Sleepstealer,

embodied everything that was vile, treacherous—and deadly.
The Iceman wanted to kill, to avenge the murder of his brothers, but his feet remained fixed to the platform, frozen im-
movably. Garamis laughed derisively waving his blade the
color of Darkblood. Again the Iceman strained unsuccessfully
to break free.

Now Kalland, tail lashing back and forth, crouched beside
him. The snow lion was loyal and brave, but seemed as helpless to intervene as Rudy—and doomed to perish as certainly
as the Iceman's brothers. Rudy fought a terrible sadness,
knowing he had brought the regal animal here, had led him
to places the great cat had not been meant to go.

And then Kalland was gone—not fallen, but vanished just
the same.

Raine appeared from somewhere, springing past Rudy to
kick the treacherous Prince of Galtigor in the face. Again and
again she attacked, and finally he fell, following the Appenfell
brothers to doom. But the victorious woman slumped as
though in defeat, and when she looked at the Iceman he saw
an intense sorrow in her eyes. Emotion surged; Rudy suddenly
knew that he loved her more than life itself. He sensed the
return of her love, even as he wondered why she should feel
such devotion. Didn't she understand, couldn't she *see* that
he was unworthy?

But the Sword of Darkblood remained nearby, and as Rudy
watched in horror it rose of its own volition, twisting in the
air to stab Raine through the heart. As soundlessly as the men,
she, too, toppled over the edge of the spire and vanished into
the mists below.

Only then did Rudy look down, see his own hand clenching
the hilt of the black-bladed sword, the cold weapon still slick
with Raine's blood. Darkness fell around him, as if the indigo
heavens had suddenly descended in a vast and smothering
cloak. Gradually, however, he discovered that the darkness
did *not* smother him; instead, it was a warm and comforting
presence. Somewhere in that timeless, spaceless cloud he saw
twin spots of red, glowing like embers of coal under the
breath of the bellows. He recognized Nicodareus, though the
Lord Minion's body was obscured by matching darkness.

And for the first time in his life, the image of that being,
the Eye of Dassadec, caused him no fear.

Rudy knew now that he could kill, and as he stepped forward the blade became a pale sliver of gleaming whiteness. It penetrated the Lord Minion's breast, stabbing again and again, but Nicodareus died very slowly. As he perished, a strange metamorphosis took hold, and by the time the Lord Minion was gone the Iceman felt an unfamiliar stretch of muscle behind his own shoulder blades. He reached back, then recoiled at the touch of a leathery membrane. Finally he screamed, the first sound to rip from his throat on this eerie promontory.

His back had sprouted wings, as dark black and powerfully supernatural as the Lord Minion's own.

— 2 —

Rudy awakened in a pool of sweat, squirming from his tattered bedroll in a desperate effort to shake off the lingering horror of the dream. Panting, he knelt and gasped for air, wiping the slickness of perspiration from his forehead. Around him slumbered his companions, while the night sky over Taywick glittered with a deceptively peaceful array of stars.

The battlefield was not in view, but Rudy felt acutely conscious of the torn, bloody ground nearby, of the many lives ended there since the last dawning of the sun. Forcefully he turned his back on that direction, on that memory.

His eyes fell upon Raine. She slept lightly, curled beneath a fur traveling blanket, with just the short brown curls of her hair visible. Though she was only two or three paces away, Rudy felt a gulf of distance between them. The strength of his love, burning fresh from his dream and carried over to wakefulness, ached within him, and he wanted to go to her, to lie beside her and enfold her in his arms.

But he couldn't do that. Instead he walked away from the camp, stepping past the lightly snoring Anjell. He looked down at his niece for a moment, tenderness bringing tears to his eyes, before he continued into the darkness beyond. Kalland padded almost silently beside him, and the Iceman allowed his fingers to trail through the snow lion's mane.

At last they reached a low rise on the edge of the pass. The

Tor of Taywick rose overhead, and Rudy remembered the perilous climb, the battle atop the pillar of rock. He thought of Garamis' sword, left up there by his and Raine's decision, and hoped that the deadly weapon would remain there, safe from mankind.

Kalland snuffed, laying his heavy head on the Iceman's thigh, and for a long time Rudy scratched between the tufted ears. His heart was filled with melancholy, but he knew what he had to do.

"Go back to the hills, big fellow," he said softly, gesturing to the rising ground beyond the pass. "We're going into the places of man now—cities and courts where you don't belong, where you'd be lost. Your place is here."

Rudy looked to the heights, to the snowy elevations where glaciers and snowfields stood out in luminous contrast to the indigo sky. He wanted to walk across those icy slopes, to climb the cliffs and stand atop the summits. He tried, without great success, to swallow that longing.

He remembered the story Raine had told, wondering about the Artifacts of the gods. Perhaps he *should* stay here, spend his life seeking those potent tools . . . but in truth, he knew this was a fruitless wish. His course was clear—the leaders of Dalethica needed to hear that the forgotten menace of the Sleepstealer was in fact an imminent threat, and Rudy and his companions were uniquely positioned to tell them this.

Kalland's yellow eyes blinked in comprehension. Finally he turned, huffing once in farewell before trotting across the boulder-strewn ground. Rudy watched as the big cat loped easily up the slope, until the white tuft of tail disappeared around a rocky knob.

Only then did the Iceman turn back. From high on the side of the pass, he could see the twin encampments of human and Faerine armies—linked in peace now, the scars of yesterday's battle mending. Purple fingers of dawn groped into the sky, and activity stirred among the warriors. As he reached his companions Rudy saw a man approaching, leading five horses, and the Iceman recognized Takian, Prince of Galtigor—and now heir to the throne, following the death of his treacherous brother Garamis.

"These are all good mounts, three of them sired by my own Hawkrunner," the sandy-haired nobleman said. "They'll see you to Carillonn, and beyond. The two ponies are sturdy and fast, as well—I thought Anjell and Danri would have an easier time with smaller steeds."

"Thanks, my friend—and I think you're right about that," Rudy replied. "We owe you a—"

"Don't even think that," Takian said firmly, raising a hand. "It's *myself* who carries the debt—to you, and your friends, who have helped me save my kingdom."

"And to earn you a throne," Bristyn Duftrall said proudly. The duchess came up behind the prince, and slipped her hand through his arm.

"Are you going to stay with the army?" Rudy asked her, amazed at how—despite the grime of the camp—Bristyn had managed to comb her golden hair into silken coils around her shoulders. Even in the dim light of dawn, her beauty was the brightest feature of the encampment.

"I'll return to Landrun for Takian's coronation," the noblewoman replied. "But I'll be going on to Carillonn, too."

"Good—we'll see you there later in the summer," Rudy declared.

"There's much to do in Landrun—my brother's treachery has left many scars in my late father's realm," admitted Takian.

"You'll go a long way toward healing those wounds," the Iceman replied sincerely.

"I hope so. I've already banished his Black Mantle warriors—those few of the traitorous wretches who survived the battle. My own men are loyal and true, and most of these fellows who followed Garamis are just misguided. Still, it's a time of changes—I've even decided I need a new banner when I take the throne. In fact, I was thinking of Kalland—the sigil of the Golden Lion, perhaps?"

"I like it—a herald worthy of a proud king," Rudy said. "I hope you bear it to the High King's court."

"And you'll join us there, in Carillonn?" asked the prince, running his fingers through his short straw-colored beard.

"Yes, by way of the North Shore Wayfarer's Lodge. Anjell's not going to like it, but I'm going to have to send her home."

"Good luck," said Takian with a chuckle, watching as the girl sat up in her bedroll and stretched. Anjell looked around, at the vista of mountainous summits and the verdant, rolling hills of Faerine, and smiled contentedly.

"I'll need it!" Rudy admitted. "And I can only hope her mother understands why she came this far with me."

Raine was one of the last companions to rise, but she stretched with feline grace and quickly strapped her bedroll and spare clothes into a bundle. Dark eyes glowed as she smiled at the Iceman, shaking her short brown curls and raising her sun-bronzed face to the dawn. Rudy, realizing he was staring, forced his eyes away from her lithe, wiry form. He remembered her skill yesterday, when they had scaled the Tor of Taywick together; and he thought with a warm thrill of the prophecy that had tied her life to his so strongly.

A girlish figure rose from the bedroll next to Anjell's, fluttering into the air on gossamer wings. Kianna Kyswyllis looked at Rudy and Raine, at the horses. The fairy saw Danri and Quenidon rolling their trail kits together, and her lips curled into a pout. Sniffling, she gave Anjell a hug, then floated over to Rudy and Raine.

"I'll *miss* you," she said, biting back tears. "But I can't go back to Dalethica—not now!"

"Of course not," Rudy said, giving the fairy a gentle squeeze. "You're at the edge of Faerine—it's time you were going home."

"I know," Kianna said sadly. "All the same, I can't help thinking that the Eternal Spring is going to be pretty boring after all I've been through!"

"Boring can be nice," Danri said seriously, clumping over. "A part of me still can't believe I'm this close to Shalemont, and instead I'm heading back to the world of humans!"

"Coming to Carillonn with us is the best thing you can do—it will help a lot if the Kings of Dalethica see the Sleepstealer as a threat to Faerine and mankind together," Rudy reminded him, acutely glad that he would have the pleasure of the stolid digger's company for the next few weeks.

"He's right," Takian agreed. "I can speak to my fellow rulers, but they distrust me as a rival monarch. Rudy can speak as a Halverican, and the Man of Three Waters; that should carry some weight. But you Faerines—*that's* how we'll get them to see this is a problem that spans the Watershed!"

"It's well worth a try," Quenidon Daringer put in, strapping his sword to his waist. The sylvan warrior stood tall, ready to ride. He smiled tightly, gesturing toward the human encampment. "A war is won more often with the right choice of allies than with the right choice of tactics."

"I'll see you when I get back home, little one," Danri said to Kianna, his tone unusually gruff. He blinked, and cleared his throat, patting the fairy on the back as she sobbed against his shoulder. Finally, sniffling bravely, she settled to the ground and watched the travelers mount their eager horses.

"We'll see you in Carillonn!" Takian declared, as he and Bristyn Duftrall saw the riders off. Anjell shouted and kicked her heels, urging her pony into a ragged trot, while Danri and Quenidon adjusted slowly to the unusual mode of transportation.

Rudy and Raine, riding from the camp at an easy walk, turned and waved to the noble pair. The Iceman looked beyond, to the green hills and distant lowlands of Faerine. For the first time in his life, he had seen the enchanted realm, only to turn back at its border.

He knew beyond any doubt that he would return.

— 3 —

The throne room of Agath-Trol was a chamber more immense than any other cavern or hall across the full breadth of the Watershed. Its shell was the massive black mountain that rose from the plain at the heart of Duloth-Trol; the lofty massif cloaked countless lesser chambers and a network of tunnels in addition to the vast cavern of the throne room.

Within that lofty vault numerous streams of black liquid spilled from niches high on cliff-like walls, the effluence collecting in a vast pool of perfect blackness. Huge galleries were paved in broad swaths of gleaming obsidian, while between the waterfalls cavern mouths marked tunnels leading to other parts of the massive palace. From the great chamber's three central thrones, around the lake of Darkblood, and to the far walls of the cavern stretched a distance that a man might need an hour to walk, an expanse like a plain of icy blackness under a midnight sky.

The three Lord Minions of Dassadec entered the chamber simultaneously, each advancing from a different access tunnel toward his throne.

Reaper, the great wyrm, spread his mighty wings and flew, gliding to the spire of obsidian that marked his perch. With regal hauteur he coiled onto the high pedestal, Darkblood-slick scales overlapping in snaky coils of neck, serpentine body, and tail. Blinking contentedly, crocodile teeth glinting in the flash of a smile, the Talon of Dassadec awaited the other two lords.

Nicodareus, emerging from his own entry tunnel, resisted the urge to spread his own wings, knowing that his awkward, lurching flight couldn't match the perfection of Reaper's serene glide. Instead, the Eye of Dassadec strode purposefully, long legs spanning the ebony floor with tireless haste. His skin of coal black was slick from a recent Immersion, and he felt the power of his lord coursing through his body.

Only Phalthak lagged behind, lumbering along, a bloated and bulbous body lurching atop stumplike legs. Extending like snakes from the gaping aperture of his neck, Phalthak's many heads leaned forward, straining toward the final throne. The Fang of Dassadec rolled his knuckles along the floor, aiding his gait, while the snake-mouths hissed and leered about the cavernous chamber. Yet even the Fang advanced with pride, a sense of purpose, that could only gall Nicodareus, reminding him of a fact he desperately wanted to forget.

He, the Eye of Dassadec, had failed.

True, Reaper and Phalthak had not yet had the chance to prove themselves—not since the last war had ended, a thousand years before. More recently, Dassadec had sent Nicodareus to prepare the way, to kindle strife between Faerine and human so that the tide of Duloth-Trol could advance into a vacuum of chaos. For the first time in that long millennium the minions of Darkblood would surge forward again, bringing annihilation to Dalethica and Faerine. Yet the Eye of Dassadec had failed to ignite the diversionary war.

Nicodareus came here fully prepared to beg, to plead and to obey. But would faith and craven obeisance be enough? Or would the Sleepstealer's rage at his servant's failure only be assuaged by the Lord Minion's agony—perhaps even his disfigurement or death? Brutally forcing his doubt aside, Nicodareus climbed the spiraling stairs leading toward the lofty perch of his own throne.

My children . . . you have come. The greeting entered the minds of the Lord Minions, borne by the all-seeing power of the Sleepstealer. Each fell to the floor before his throne, groveling in the face of that unseen presence. No sound was audible, but Dassadec's commands were clearly known to the trio.

Rise, Phalthak, Reaper. Resume your seats.

The omission of his name was a knell of doom to Nicodareus, and he clawed at the shiny stone of the floor as if he would scratch himself a hiding hole. The Eye of Dassadec remained prostrate, hearing the words his master directed to the other Lord Minions.

Reaper, your legions stand along the Dry Basin, ready to move into Dalethica. I bid you attack at once. Bear the wagons of Darkblood across that desert, and know that the elixir of Duloth-Trol will sustain you. Do not cease your onslaught until all of mankind has been brought to heel. Use the mighty bovars to dam the streams and rivers as you advance, so that in your wake the realm of man becomes a desert. Nowhere will your minions face the obstacle of open water—they will strike across the bovar dams, and the humans will be helpless to stand against you.

"Aye, lord," hissed Reaper, forked tongue flicking between massive jaws. The wyrm stretched his broad wings, flapping them proudly, anxious to be aloft.

And Phalthak, my Vile One—your minions have gathered below the slopes of Darkenheight Pass. The Sturmfleet awaits beyond the walls of Agath-Trol. You will board the Dreadcloud and fly to that gap, where you must commence the attack on Faerine. The cost will be high, for the pass is narrow and steep—but do not spare the lives of your minions and you shall break through!

"As you wish, master," burbled Phalthak, his snakelike heads bobbing and seething anxiously. "I will attack with all haste—and if ten thousand of my minions die in the first wave, their bodies shall pave the way for a hundred thousand more!"

For this task I grant you a new member, Vile One—the head known as Drackanbiter. Phalthak writhed backward, suddenly gagging. His shoulder pulsed obscenely, pressure building within the apelike torso. The bulge grew outward and the Lord Minion's other heads hissed and snapped, flailing wildly. Abruptly the moist wound between Phalthak's shoulders ripped wider, spilling black blood down the hairy, bulging gut. A new snake writhed upward, cloaked in a filmy membrane—but the serpent tore through that cloaking gauze, thrashing about a silver head, jaws gaping to reveal two long, dripping fangs.

With this head you shall make powerful allies in Faerine, just as we have corrupted the men of Dalethica. Seek the mightiest of creatures, the brown drackans. Drackanbiter shall bestow the kiss of Darkblood, and the great wyrms will aid your campaign. Go then, my loyal Lord Minions—go and commence your attacks!

Nicodareus shuddered miserably as the Fang and Talon of Dassadec departed the vast throne room, delaying only long enough to relish the sight of their rival, still bound by terror, groveling like a kroak before the power of the Sleepstealer.

Now, Nicodareus—rise!

Immediately the Eye of Dassadec stood.

You have failed me. I granted you the Power of Three, and each of those journeys was wasted!

"My lord—there were—!" Nicodareus groped for excuses, knew that none of his words could avert the imminent punishment.

Silence! roared that awful presence.

Then the agony began. Rivers of pain hissed across Nicodareus' skin, burning like acid, eating away at the stuff of his life. For time immeasurable his existence became a focus of suffering, unspeakable punishment inflicted by a ruthless and uncompromising lord. The Eye of Dassadec fell, rolled across the platform, then tumbled down the steps from his lofty throne. His back arched, and then he was rigid, locked in the grip of consummate anguish.

Yet with the pain came a measure of redemption, for as Nicodareus was punished, he knew that he could be absolved. The sun might have risen and set a hundred times while the Eye of Dassadec cowered on the floor; alternately, the time elapsed might have been mere minutes. In any event, when Nicodareus was at last free to move, he crept back to the lofty perch of his throne and awaited his master's command, relieved to know that he would be allowed to live, even to retain intact this powerful, magnificent body.

Deep, bitter fury flamed within the Lord Minion's breast—but his rage was not directed at the one who had delivered his punishment. Fear, awe, devotion, even the shame of abject debasement, were the feelings he expended on the Sleep-stealer, and these were emotions that no other being in all the Watershed could trigger within him. His rage was reserved for lesser creatures—his minion slaves, Lord Minion peers, or, as now, the mortals inhabiting the realms beyond the world's great divides.

Fuel that hatred, my Eye, my furious one. Know that you shall have the chance to gain vengeance on those who thwarted you. At the same time, you will be granted the opportunity to vindicate yourself in my presence.

"Thank you, Great One," Nicodareus growled, trembling with a mixture of relief and fury.

Always the barriers of the Watershed have held my agents back, prevented your powers from acting fully in Dalethica and Faerine. Now, my Eye, I believe there is a way. . . .

"Speak, master—and I obey!"

I shall grant you the power of Darkslayer. With this, you can stalk, and kill, our enemies among the humans.

"How does this power work?"

You will go to the Well of Agath-Trol, the deepest of the Darksprings below my palace. There, stalkers will treat you with a protection. It is made from the blood of humans, and when you are thus guarded you will be able to survive, and to remain strong, though you wander far from the realm of Darkblood.

The notion sent a thrill of power through the Lord Minion. On each previous journey across the Watershed he had needed to hasten back to the realm of Duloth-Trol. Hour by hour he had felt his strength wane, and the farther he had gone from the Watershed, the more pronounced had become his spiritual malaise.

"I will do your bidding wherever you command. Name the tasks—"

Your task is simple: You are to find the Man of Three Waters, and kill him.

A flush of pleasure brought renewed trembling to the limbs of Nicodareus, for there was no task that he desired more.

"I will travel among mankind and find this Iceman, this Man of Three Waters. I will bring about his death with praises to your name!" *And an ecstasy of pleasure*, Nicodareus added to himself.

There is a thing about the power of Darkslayer, continued the abiding, telepathic voice. *The power will sustain you long—perhaps even for a full year. But for all the time you are beyond the borders of Duloth-Trol, you shall need blood sustenance in order to maintain your strength.*

"Human . . . blood?" guessed the Lord Minion, with another thrill of anticipation.

Yes. You must slay a human every day, and consume the victim's blood. By that nourishment shall your power remain great, and your endurance be sustained.

"This killing is no less than the humans deserve. The taking of their lives shall be child's play."

I know that you will obey me. And each time you feed, my blessings—and my vengeance—shall be made known to you. Your powers remain unabated—you shall change the shape of your body so that you can walk among mankind without being noticed, save only for the bloodfire of your eyes.

"A blind man—I shall disguise myself with rags, so that none may see my eyes," Nicodareus decided. He pictured the terror of his daily victims as, when the moment—and the hunger—peaked, he whipped aside his screening mask and allowed the mortal to gaze into those crimson orbs. It would be the last image many humans would know, and it pleased the Lord Minion that it would be a picture of consummate horror and awful, inevitable doom. He also enjoyed the irony—that he, the farthest-seeing being in all the Watershed, would masquerade as a blind man!

Now go—Stalkers await you at the well, in the depths of Agath-Trol. Follow their bidding absolutely, or the power shall be incomplete.

"Of course, master. And my journey to the Watershed . . . ?" Nicodareus dared to hope for a great, black cloudship to fly him to that perennial border.

Fly under your own power—take the shape of a terrion, or a condor when you cross into Dalethica. And remember, Ni-

codareus—you shall not fail me again. Once more the shock
waves of pain swept through the Lord Minion, bringing him
crashing down from his throne. As before, he had no concept
of how long he writhed on the floor. The duration of his
suffering was eternal, so long as it lasted, and then it was
complete.

"You are all-knowing, lord," he gasped, when the spasm
had ceased. "I shall never fail you again!"

Despite the lingering memory of humiliation, Nicodareus
descended the steps, once more stalking regally as he crossed
the vast floor of the throne room. His punishment was forgotten as he sought the deep well of Darkblood, his master's
stalkers, and the magic called Darkslayer.

— 4 —

For a month Rudy and his companions rode hard for the North
Shore Wayfarer's Lodge, avoiding the settled lands of Galtigor in favor of a more direct route through the foothills. When
they could, they stayed at remote farmsteads or the occasional—and tiny—inn. Most nights they slept out of doors,
and even Anjell grew tired of the wearying routine as the
midsummer weather remained warm but soaked the companions with daily rain showers. By the third week of the ride,
everything they owned was sodden, and it was a weary and
uncomfortable group of travelers that finally reached the River
Ariak and the border of Halverica. As they crossed on the
ferry, the sun broke through the brooding overcast like a welcoming omen, and the woods steamed under refreshing
warmth as the riders ambled forward on the last miles before
the Wayfarer's Lodge.

"How much farther? Is this the last hill?" Anjell asked,
for the hundredth time in the hour since the ferry-crossing.
Golden braids flying, the girl twisted this way and that,
stretching upward in her stirrups to see around the next bend
of the forested trail. Rudy and Raine rode beside her, while
the two Faerines, Danri and Quenidon, brought up the rear.
All of them relished the warm sunshine, looking forward with
high spirits to the lodge.

"I thought that the North Shore Wayfarer's Lodge was

surrounded by meadows—Doesn't it seem like there are still too many trees around here?" Anjell chattered, ignoring the fact that Rudy whistled aimlessly, apparently uninterested in replying.

"Why couldn't we bring Kalland along?" she went on. "He liked it here last time, remember? Why did you have to let him go?" Anjell was petulant now, perhaps because she realized the reason that Rudy had brought them to the lodge.

Rudy sighed. "He needed to return to the mountains. Snow lions are not meant to live with people, after all."

"But Kalland *liked* us, didn't he?"

"I think he did—but Kalland is a wild animal. When he started into the mountains, there wasn't any way I could hold him back." Rudy didn't feel inclined to tell his niece that it had been his own decision to send the magnificent animal back to the wilds.

"Well, *I* would have thought of something," Anjell huffed. She looked up the gradually climbing roadway, trying to see past the edge of the forest. "How much farther is it *now*?" Thankfully, they reached the edge of the woods at that moment, sparing Rudy the need to repeat his "Any minute" answer.

"There it is!" squealed the girl, spinning around to call out to the two riders following a short distance behind. "Danri—Quenidon! It's the lodge! Isn't it absolutely *beautiful*?"

Still a mile distant, the vast chalet was indeed spectacular. Flower gardens surrounded the sprawling wooden wings of the massive inn, blossoms drooping from myriad terraced patios and roofed, shady verandas. Ornately carved, brightly painted boards framed clean tile roofs; and if the first impression of the lodge's sprawling appendages was chaos, the reflective observer had to admit to a remarkable symmetry in the overall picture.

The road curved gently up the slope, but even so, the structure was not high enough to block the view of the mountains beyond. Perhaps the peaked roofs of the inn attempted to mimic the jagged, whitecapped crest of Halverica forming the far horizon—but if so it was a mimicry in homage, not in any sense an attempt to match the majesty of nature.

The mountain peaks jutted like the upturned edge of a deep-toothed saw. Between the summits, swales of lush green bloomed in the height of late summer, while patches of evergreens mixed with pastureland for sheep and cows. Yet on the crags looming above, winter always reigned—glaciers and cornices of purest white reflected the sun brilliantly.

Rudy sighed, suddenly overwhelmed by a wave of homesickness. He wanted, at that moment, to turn toward those mountains, cross the Glimmersee and seek solace in the deep, forested valley of Neshara. Then Raine met his eyes, smiling easily, and his mood lifted. She could do that for him, with a word or a look, and he felt the gratitude—and wonder— that had grown within him during their long weeks on the trail.

"I was remembering the other time I came here," Raine said. "There was a young man, very forward fellow, who spoke to me at the saddle-makers. . . ."

"And he's glad, to this day, that he did." Rudy laughed briefly, but the wave of melancholy rose again. "I wish we could stay here, Raine—or even better, go up into the mountains. There are a dozen peaks within a day's walk of Neshara—we could climb half of them before the autumn snows!"

Raine smiled, but her happiness did not dispel the concern in her dark eyes. "Do you really want to do that?" she asked.

"No—yes, by Aurianth! I want to, but I can't!"

As he spoke he felt a familiar thirst, and unconsciously reached for the waterskin at his side. Raising the nozzle to his lips, the Iceman let the pure liquid of Faerine wet his tongue and moisten his throat. Looking forward to the Wayfarer's Lodge with a growing measure of anticipation, he turned to smile at Raine, once again reassuring and calm.

Rudy savored the feeling of capability that infused him. He thought of the lessons his companions had been giving him— Quenidon Daringer patiently teaching the basic techniques of sword-handling, while Danri had extensively demonstrated lifesaving maneuvers with the buckler and shield. The Iceman could not approach these veteran Faerines in their battle skills, but he now felt a comfortable familiarity with his weapon. The slender blades worn by Raine and himself were forged of digger steel, precious gifts from the grateful defenders of Taywick Pass.

And more—he was the Man of Three Waters! Aura was a tool to him. With it he had woven a flying cloudship, had foreseen terrible dangers. Why could he not use that insight to penetrate the future, to be more certain of his destiny? Was it enough to speak to kings, to try and rouse the world?

The gates to the courtyard of the great lodge stood open, and several people gathered on the porches to observe the new arrivals. Hostlers came forward to take the horses as the companions dismounted. Rudy looked instinctively toward the door of the lodge's great hall, seeking Awnro Lyrifell, but the innkeeper was nowhere to be seen.

"Anjell!" A familiar voice, nearly hysterical with relief, surprised them from a smaller wing of the lodge.

"Mama!" cried the girl dashing toward the attractive, dark-haired woman who rushed out of the lodge's doorway. Dara all but leapt down the stairway from the porch, kneeling to sweep her daughter into a smothering embrace. For several moments she sobbed, until Anjell squirmed away.

"Mama—I saw *Faerine*! And there was a battle! And Uncle Rudy made this cloud—!"

Something in Dara's face stopped the cascade of words. Approaching behind his niece, the Iceman regarded his late brother's wife as she rose to confront him.

"How *could* you take her away!" his sister-in-law demanded, her tears vanishing into a mask of anger. "You had no right!"

"I know—I'm sorry." Rudy knew that he deserved her fury, but he was shocked by the full realization of her distress. "I told you in the letter—I didn't plan it this way. My first thoughts were to get her out of danger, and instead—"

"Instead she could have been . . ." Dara shook her head miserably, and again knelt to embrace her daughter—but again Anjell squirmed free. She stomped her foot in the determined gesture Rudy had come to know very well.

"He didn't take me away!" she argued. "I *followed* him—and then, when he was going to take me home, the kroaks were there and we had to run away to the Glimmersee. And when we got here, I simply wouldn't let him send me home!"

"The poisoned river—I wrote you about it," Rudy interjected. "What happened in Dermaat? Is Neshara safe?"

"Our village is safe," said Dara, sighing and shaking her

head at further evidence of events beyond their control. "Dermaat is a poisonous place, but men from all the cantons have surrounded it. Like myself, many women have moved down to the Glimmersee—the mountain villages have the look of army camps, I'm afraid."

"And I had to go with Rudy, Mama—he took me away from Dermaat the only way he could! Then, when we got here, I showed him that he couldn't get by without me."

"But you're a child!" Dara retorted. "Those aren't decisions for you to make!"

"Then, I'm the first child to see Faerine," Anjell declared proudly. "And I *helped*! They needed me! When Rudy and Raine rescued Kianna—she's a twissel, and she was with us for a while but she went back to Faerine after the battle—I'm the one who held her hand and made her feel better. And I thought up the disguises for Kianna—and for Danri. He's not disguised now, though, because we have to tell everybody about the war. People need to know that the Faerines are on our side!"

"Danri? Kianna?" Dara glared at the digger, who with Raine and Quenidon had ambled over. She blinked, noticing Danri's short, powerful legs, the long arms bracketing unusually broad, strapping shoulders.

"Greetings, ma'am," offered the heavily bearded digger, bowing formally. "It's true that your daughter has been a great help to us all—she's a lass of courage, and has better than the usual share of brains."

"Th-thank you." Dara turned her gaze to Quenidon Daringer, noticing the lean warrior's slender features and his long, elegant ears. His hair was the gold of dry straw limned in sunlight, and his stern face softened as he looked at Anjell.

The sylve, too, bowed. "Her ministrations, after the battle at Taywick, saved the lives of a hundred warriors—human and Faerine alike."

"A hundred lives—but that's not possible. . . ."

"With Aura it is, Mama. That's part of what I have to tell you. And Rudy didn't choose to be the Man of Three Waters, but it happened to him. Oh, and this is Raine."

Dara's expression softened as she greeted the companions, but her hands remained protectively on Anjell's shoulders.

"King Takian of Galtigor is sending more men to help

watch Dermaat." Anjell was anxious to share her knowledge. "And the duchess will ask the High King in Carillonn to send some of his Hundred Knights! We're going to go there next, Mama, to talk to him. Can you come with—"

"You are staying in Halverica with me!" Dara replied curtly, glaring at Rudy again. "Even if your uncle chooses to go back to the flatlands!"

The Iceman's eyes swept to the spectacle of peaks lining the far shoreline of the Glimmersee. The lake, an indigo-tinted turquoise that he now knew was unlike any lowland water, brought a palpable yearning to his heart. He met Dara's eyes, and perhaps the anguish showed in his face; in any event, her face eased into a frown of sympathy.

"It's not a matter of choice, anymore," Quenidon suggested, his quietly authoritative voice commanding attention. "There are events underway in the world that involve Rudy and all of us, whether we wish it or not. We *have* to go to Carillonn, to meet the High King himself if he will see us. Unless mankind understands the danger quickly, it will be too late!"

Rudy nodded, meeting Dara's eyes with a frank stare. "When I left Neshara, I sought only to avenge the murder of my brothers. Long before I met Garamis I understood that I had a different purpose—the destiny that touched me on the Glimmercrown is not a thing I can ignore."

The Iceman knelt before Anjell. "I'll miss you every day— but your mother's right. Your place is with her." He stood again, loosening a pouch from his belt, handing the heavy purse to Dara. "Garamis' brother—the *new* King of Galtigor—has honored the Palefee for the deaths of my brothers. There's enough gold here for you all to live comfortably."

Dara took the pouch, but once again raised a hand to her mouth. "The chalet was so empty . . . Beryv, Donniall, Coyle, perished on the mountain . . . then you returned, like one from the dead." Dara shuddered and Rudy stepped forward, drawing his brother's widow tightly to him. She cried for a moment, and then sniffled and pulled away. "None of this *is* your choice, is it? Starting with the climb on the Glimmercrown—it's a miracle, really, but I . . ."

"It's a miracle, and a burden," Raine suggested softly. For the first time, Dara studied the lithe, brown-haired woman, looking from Raine to Rudy with quick comprehension. "There's never been anyone like him before, you know."

"No—I didn't know."

"Mama, this is a war against the ones who killed Papa, and Uncle Coyle and Uncle Donniall. Not just Prince Garamis—he's dead, 'cause Raine pushed him off a cliff—but *all* the bad men, and minions, too. Rudy has to go—and I should go, too!"

"That's enough talk of this," Dara said quietly, wearied by the argument but underlaying her words with stubborn determination.

"Hello there! My good Iceman!" The hearty greeting signaled the sudden appearance of Awnro Lyrifell as their garishly dressed host swept from the doors of the great-room. Removing his feathered hat with a flourish, the former minstrel bowed deeply. "And the lady Raine, again—what a considerable pleasure. Not to mention the charming Anjell! This is a splendid coincidence."

"Your hospitality was the brightest part of our previous journey," Rudy said sincerely. "It's very good to be back."

"But why is it a coincidence?" asked Anjell. "You knew that we were traveling together, didn't you?"

"Whether I did or not, that isn't the point. No—the splendid thing is that I have a message for you—and for the honored digger and his elegant sylvan companion, as well. It arrived by courier just this morning."

"A message?" squealed Anjell. "From where? From who?"

"Why, the Duchess of Shalloth, no less. She has just arrived home, but is making immediate plans to journey to Carillonn," declared the bewhiskered bard, stroking slender fingers through the pointed tip of his beard. He winked slyly at Rudy and beamed conspiratorially as Anjell all but exploded with curiosity.

"There's to be a royal wedding, in Carillonn. The High King himself hosts the ceremony, and monarchs from across Dalethica will attend as the King of Galtigor marries the Duchess of Shalloth! They wed in a month's time—and the best news of all: You're all to be there! In fact *you*, my wee lass, were specifically named as the royal flower bearer!"

Anjell's cry of delight easily drowned her mother's groan.

Rudy shook his head in surprise, but couldn't hide a smile of real happiness. Bristyn and Takian, married. The thought seemed not only proper and right, but somehow profoundly hopeful for the future. Dara's knuckles whitened on Anjell's shoulders as she shook her head, overwhelmed by the onrush of fate.

"You'll come with us, of course?" Rudy invited his brother's widow, holding out a hand.

Dara sighed in initial reluctance, and when she finally assented, a sheen of wetness sparkled in her eyes.

TWO

Farkeen

Neither the warmth of a winter's hearth nor the
passion of a woman's embrace eases the soul of
a sailing man like a night on the open sea.
—SONGS OF THE SAILOR

— 1 —

Two hundred miles of uninterrupted cliff framed the north-western headland of Dalethica. Rising from the ocean in a precipitous slab of rock, a hundred feet high in some places, a thousand in others, the jagged shore offered no inlet, not a niche deep enough to shelter a small fishing dory. And even had there been a bay in the shoreline, any landing would have been fruitless—the land above was wild Tiberian jungle, home to savages who preferred torture and killing to trade.

The rocks on this barren coast marked the graveyard for countless ships and crews. As a consequence, the *Black Condor* coasted for days along the harsh shore without so much as a glimpse of another sail. The four-masted galyon, aided by a strong shoreward breeze, soared like her namesake along this rugged expanse, while her master, Kestrel Capemir, anxiously awaited the sighting of the verdant fringe that would once again mark a lowland shore.

The captain of the *Condor* had known some of the vessels destroyed along this coast, ships smashed to kindling by a sudden storm swirling toward shore. He knew, too, of other vessels carried far beyond land by driving winds off the deserts—blasts that could push even the most well-captained vessel far from the Watershed. Very few of these ships ever reached shore again; instead they were doomed to vanish mysteriously in the trackless nothingness over the horizon.

On a bad night Kestrel's dreams portrayed similar fates for himself and his proud ship. Yet if these were his nightmares, on other nights Kestrel's sleep was visited by pleasant dreams—visions of treasures, of riches, of plunder and highly profitable trades. In these fantasies he often returned to his hilltop villa in Lanbrij, ever surrounded by piles of gold and a multitude of naked—and very willing—girls.

"Greensward ahead!"

When the traditional and triumphant cry of the westward sailor rang from the masthead, Kestrel knew a wave of relief that would certainly last for many days—probably until the inevitable return to Corsari forced the *Condor* once again to skirt that havenless coast.

For now, Kestrel's thoughts turned back to profit, a topic that always cheered him. In the *Black Condor*'s hold were goods from the lands of the Circled Sea and farther east. The great galyon bore steel-edged weapons from the smiths of Carillonn, huge beams of mahogany from the coastal forest of Andaran, fine fleeces from the Corsari sheep of Kestrel's homeland, and rare works of gemstone and jewelry from the artisans of Halverica. The remainder of his hold space was filled with bales of fabric woven from the lush cotton grown on the shores of the Circled Sea, always desired here in the arid west.

Kestrel had no regrets about lawful gain—honest cargo generally proved less lively, but more predictable, than plunder gained by piratical deeds. Lately, in fact, the speedy carracks under Duke Dalston Beymont's command had made the taking of prizes risky work anywhere around Corsari or the Circled Sea. Though the galyon was a match for any single vessel, the aggressive duke had begun sailing his ships in squadrons of three. Even the *Black Condor* was forced to flee from those odds.

On this voyage the captain would unload honest cargo in Farkeen for great profit, since everything he carried was rare in this part of Dalethica. In return, he would barter for silks and perfumes from Zanthilat, spices from the Thutan highlands, and perhaps a few of the exotic birds captured in the Tiberian jungles. Kestrel knew that even allowing for failure in some of his more speculative ventures, his profits would probably quadruple the worth of the items he had embarked in Corsari.

With a little luck he would also have a splendid time in Farkeen, then return home with a tidy profit—after which he would take some time off. Kestrel saw nothing wrong with passing weeks or months in the shaded garden of his white-walled villa, or dining sumptuously at his well-appointed table. As one of Lanbrij's most eligible older bachelors, the sea captain never lacked dinner companions, nor was he often alone during the later hours of the night. Indeed, rarely did the same woman share his bed more than once or twice.

But that was his life ashore; now he focused on the sea. For three more days the *Condor* glided along a shore of palms. Coral reefs extended outward, but Kestrel's crew was skilled at avoiding these obstacles, while staying as close to land as possible. Whales spumed in the deep waters, and seals scampered around the shoals that marked so much of this verdant shoreline. During the fast run, with a following wind and calm seas, sailors mended torn sails, varnished planks, and made sure that the galyon fairly sparkled as she drew toward her destination.

Kestrel spent pleasant hours musing in the very bow of the ship, sheltered by the forecastle from the view of his crewmen, nothing but a welcoming expanse of smooth water before his eyes. Leaning against the huge trebuchet that was one of the galyon's primary weapons—the other was its twin, on the wheel deck astern—the captain meditated on the sea or reflected on memories of a hundred raucous ports and ten times that number of women. Only once during this three-day stretch were his private musings interrupted.

"Captain? Might I have a word?"

"Eh? What is it, Pader?" Kestrel looked around in annoy-

ance, seeing that Pader Willith, the priest of Baracan, had
sought him out. The youthful fellow, thin of frame and pocked
of complexion, had all the seriousness of an elder zealot, a
disposition that made the captain very nervous. Now Willith
palmed his heart devoutly and closed his eyes, as if com-
muning with his god. Kestrel scowled, impatient with all the
trappings of religion—he had no time for gods, and even less
for their mortal spokesmen.

In his other hand Willith held the small leather-bound book
that was the scroll of his deity's teachings. Kestrel knew that
the book was rare, a symbol of honor bestowed only upon
promising young priests. Doubtless Pader Willith's chosen
task—as a missionary of Baracan to the wildlands of the
west—had earned him a copy of the treasured volume.

"Make it brief—I'm busy!" urged Kestrel.

"Er, yes sir, of course." Willith was an inexperienced
cleric, yet much full of the God of Man's many glories. He
was technically a passenger, for he intended to stay in Farkeen
for a period of years, but—in the ancient traditions of the
sea—the crew had adopted him as a spiritual counselor. Now
the captain felt obligated to give the man his ear, if only for
a few minutes.

"The men tell me we're drawing near to Farkeen—we'll
land within a day or two."

"Tomorrow by sunset, if the wind holds," Kestrel acknowledged.

"I would like your permission, sir, to assemble the crew
for a brief sermon—that is, before they are released ashore to
the temptations of the west. It might be useful for them to
receive some spiritual guidance, lest they wander too easily
into sin."

Kestrel snorted in amusement. "These are men who've
sailed the Circled Sea all their lives. Many have gone east
and west along the Watershed, and they've all been ashore in
some of the wildest ports in Dalethica. What makes you think
that the temptations in Farkeen are going to be any different?"

"Well, isn't it true—that is, I've heard—that the women
of the west tend to be rather . . . how shall I say? . . . *un-
clean*?" The young priest spoke as if the word itself left a
bad taste in his mouth.

Now the captain laughed, all the louder as he saw the look of shock and hurt on Willith's pimpled face. "D'you think these men are anxious to find *clean* girls?" he demanded in exasperation. "They've been at sea for months! And Farkeen is a fabled town, full of delights they've been hearing about all their lives!" Only a few of the three dozen crewmen had been to Farkeen before, but those had spoken in detail of the exotic pleasures to be found there. These tales had become increasingly embellished as the long weeks of the voyage went by.

"But—Captain! Surely, with proper devotion, the men can experience the wholesome wonders of the place and still avoid its more unsavory aspects. Perhaps then they can escape Farkeen with souls intact!"

"I've escaped Farkeen a half dozen times before, with my soul intact and a smile on my face!" declared Kestrel testily. "And the wonderfully pretty—and *very* cooperative—girls of Farkeen are one reason for that smile! So forget your sermon—it would be a damned waste of breath on these men. They're sailors, and good men—but they know enough to take the pleasures of life when they're offered! Now, come back and talk to me when you've got something important to say!"

With that, Kestrel went back to his musings—though his thoughts turned from financial lust toward fleshly desires, which, with the profits of this voyage, he could satisfy a hundred times over. The priest, crestfallen, returned to his cabin, no doubt to pray for his captain's imperiled soul.

Finally the *Black Condor* entered the deep sound of Farkeen, with the city sheltered at the bay's southern terminus. The narrow spires of prayer towers sparkled into view under the noonday sun, and before sunset the great galyon coasted through the embracing arms of a stony breakwater. Kestrel himself took the wheel from Garson, his trusted helmsman, as the ship nosed up to a solid quay. A huge crowd of westerners watched as lines were tossed ashore, and the first crewmen debarked to rousing cheers.

High on his wheel deck, Kestrel took the time to look about the harbor. The galyon was the largest ship here—only blunt-hulled dhows and a few longships rested within the breakwater. Fishing dories trailed into the bay, following the galyon like ducklings swimming after their mother—though those fishermen who had met with success quickly tacked across the harbor to the waterfront smoke houses and cleaning yards.

A silver-helmeted harbormaster forced his way up the gangplank against the press of debarking sailors. Drooping mustache bobbing in enthusiasm, he saluted Kestrel briskly.

"Greetings, in the name of the sultan! May your stay in Farkeen lead to prosperity and happiness, and may the pleasures of our fabled city soothe and titillate you!"

"My sincere thanks," the captain replied dryly.

The officer proceeded to inform him of the docking fees and offloading procedures, pledging as well to keep a careful eye on the ship when the captain and crew were absent.

"I'll keep a mate or two on board just the same," Kestrel noted, after arranging to pay the fees by donations of goods to the sultan's coffers. Finally, he contracted for a crew of dockers to unload his cargo, storing it in a waterfront warehouse while Kestrel worked out his deals in the marketplace. Then he told the grumbling first mate that he was to stand the first day's watch on the ship.

Twilight had faded into full darkness by the time Kestrel had collected a few belongings and carried his duffel down the gangplank. The bag contained only a change of clothes and a few toiletries such as soap and razor—his money was concealed in a pouch beneath his belt. Kestrel remembered numerous raucous taverns from his previous visits to the port, and over the next few days he intended to visit them all. Tonight, however, he would seek the quiet comforts of a once-familiar saloon. He remembered the place as the White Dolphin, or some such name—an establishment of lovely girls, good food, cold ale, and a spicy variety of shalewirt, the smoking weed favored by the men of the west.

A crowd pressed around Kestrel as he made his way through the waterfront. He swung his duffel freely, driving back beggars. Several harlots teased him, dropping the bodices of their gowns to reveal plump breasts.

"Hey, handsome—how you get dat silver in yer hair?" teased one, reaching out to trail a fingertip through his long locks.

Kestrel simply grinned and moved on. "Maybe later, girls . . ." he said lightly, pushing away from the docks and recognizing the wide boulevard leading into the city.

"Take ya to de best smoke house?" offered a boy, stepping from the shadows to tug at Kestrel's elbow. Snaky plaits of hair bobbed around the youth's ears as he looked the seaman up and down.

"Off with you!" barked the captain, aiming a backhand blow that the youngster easily dodged.

"Don't be mistake!" cried the lad, following a few paces behind. "Some guys take your money right quick! No good smoke—even sleepy-kind, den pick yer pocket 'fore you wakes!"

"Thanks for the warning." Kestrel chuckled, relishing the bustle of Farkeen as the urchin vanished behind him into the milling crowd.

Other beggars pressed forward. A man without legs hopped on his knuckles, then reached to tug at the captain's trousers. A woman, her face disfigured by disease, pleaded for money, while several more children clustered before him, effectively blocking his way.

"Here, you—get out de mister's way!" The boy who had offered to guide him darted past, bulling a path through the beggars. The youngster was strong and wiry; he turned back to look at Kestrel with wide, serious eyes. His black hair was long, braided tightly to his scalp and trailing onto his shoulders like many flopping tentacles.

"How 'bout I keeps de road clean for ya?" the boy asked, walking backward and holding out a dirty palm.

"Sure—just get me off the dock," Kestrel agreed, dropping a copper into the outstretched hand. The lad spun about, shouting and gesticulating, and in moments the captain had made his unimpeded way onto the boulevard.

Carts and oxen trundled down the wide street, weaving between numerous dusky, bearded men in robes of cotton or silk. Women of all shapes, with skin ranging from dark brown to palest ivory, also pushed through the throngs. Matrons and respectable young women wore hooded gowns and heavy sandals, while harlots often appeared barefoot, cloaked in filmy gauze that left nothing to Kestrel's enthusiastic imagination. An occasional chariot driven by a liveried warrior pressed through, bearing a noble or wealthy merchant somewhere, perhaps on business or to a social gathering. The throng parted for them, but closed again as smoothly as flowing water when the eminent citizen passed.

Numerous side streets led into darker reaches of the city, but torches and lamps cast an almost daytime glow across the main boulevard. An auctioneer hawked fine horses at a large corral, while a barker shouted to passersby that his smoke house offered the finest shalewirt in all the west. The captain paused, then continued to push his way through the press of people, looking for a landmark. Where was the street to the White Dolphin?

More harlots called out to Kestrel, several leaning far out of second-story balconies, and he tipped his hat cheerily at the display of wares. Many of his men, he knew, would make it no farther than these first houses. The establishments would be expensive, but sailors ashore after an eight-week voyage were not known to be either frugal or patient.

But where was that side street? It was a narrow alley, called Roselane, or Ivy Court, or something—he couldn't remember exactly. Most of the warren-like passages looked similar, and Kestrel's buoyant anticipation began to give way to frustration.

Then he saw a large, familiar-looking flowering bush—frangibloom, the westerners called it. The plant filled the small courtyard of a tall house, and a shadowy lane led past it, away from the avenue and back into the tangle of the city's heart. The bush didn't look exactly right, but Kestrel reasoned that it must have grown or been pruned over the last decade. Heartened again, he turned into the street and picked up his pace. The surroundings were oddly quiet after the boulevard, and he wondered if he had made a mistake. The White Dolphin, he remembered, was several blocks off of the main street, so he resolved to look a little farther.

After passing a pair of side streets—narrow alleys, more accurately—he still saw no sign of any business establishment, much less the inn he remembered, and Kestrel decided that he must have guessed wrong. With a muttered curse, he spun about, intending to head back to the boulevard.

Two shadowy figures darted into the protection of an arched doorway, but not soon enough to avoid Kestrel's notice. A tingle of alarm ran along his spine, and the fingers of his left hand touched the reassuring smoothness of his bone-handled knife. The weapon was lashed to his right forearm, and he could drop it into his hand with a mere flick of his wrist. If the men intended trouble, Kestrel might surprise them with cold steel. In any event, it would not be the first fight in which he was outnumbered two to one.

Boldly he stepped forward, approaching the alcove where the men had disappeared. Then a whisper of sound from the rear froze him in his tracks, and he whirled, seeing a trio of men swaggering down the narrow alley. A quick spin showed him that the pair on the other side had also stepped out of their cover, and now Kestrel was trapped in the lane.

"Whatcha got in dat bag?" asked the largest of the three men, a leering thug who revealed splintered chips of teeth through his unpleasant sneer.

"My business, I guess," replied Kestrel, straining to hear the two men behind, allowing his eyes to dart from side to side of the alley. Buildings pressed close to either side, with shuttered windows and stout, closed doors.

The big fellow laughed, a sound that was even more unpleasant than his appearance. "Give it here—mebbe then we'll let you go."

An undercurrent of cruelty in the thief's voice suggested that this was an unlikely possibility. Still, Kestrel didn't know what else to do—besides curse himself for wandering like some naive youngster into this dangerous predicament.

"Hey—what's—?"

Kestrel heard the exclamation behind him, and whirled to see the two men bowled over by a tumbling barrel. The wooden cask crunched against the wall of the house, leaving the pair of thugs groaning heavily on the ground. Shouting angrily, the trio blocking the captain's forward path charged.

"Here, mister—run!" A small figure crouched over one of the fallen men, delivering a sharp kick as the thief struggled to his knees. Kestrel's rescuer turned and sprinted into the darkness, and the captain needed no prodding to race after him. As the slight figure disappeared around a dark corner, Kestrel had a vague sense of recognition, but hammering footsteps to the rear quickly overshadowed any attempt at recollection. Dropping the duffel, Kestrel flew after the youth, dodging around another corner and diving through an open doorway. He heard the heavy barrier slam, and blinked as a candle flared into life.

"You're the boy from the docks!" he declared, seeing the grime-streaked face, the braided hair, and wide eyes. The youth quickly led him down a filthy hall. Dodging around several corners, the boy descended a rickety stairway to burst through another door and back into the streets of Farkeen.

For a few more minutes they darted and dodged down one narrow alley after another. Kestrel gasped for breath, though the boy didn't seem to be suffering at all. Finally the young-ster skidded to a halt before a darkened stairway, a few stone steps that descended from street level to a black, smoke-stained doorway lurking like a cave mouth under an over-hanging mantle of gray stone.

"Well. Here we be," said the boy.

"Here? Where?" demanded the captain, bracing his hands on his knees as he drew ragged breaths.

"Smoke house I told ya 'bout. Old Kenrick's—good and straight guy, not like dem tiefs!"

Seeing a stone bench beside the stairway, Kestrel slumped down onto it and started to chuckle, shaking his head in amazement. "What's your name, lad?"

"Me? Call me Darret."

"Well, Darret, I thank you for helping me. Those 'tiefs' would have had me for dinner, I'm afraid—That was a brave thing you did!"

"Bad men. Not good, honest, straight guy like Darret. Hey, mister, you got a tip for me?"

"Sure—sure I do."

Kestrel fumbled into his pouch of spending money—which was separate from the funds bundled inside his belt—and fished out a silver coin. He flipped the disk to the boy, who caught it with a smooth backhanded grab and immediately raised it to his mouth. Biting down on the coin, Darret ap-parently satisfied himself as to its value.

"Tanks, mister—tanks a lot!"

"I owe you," Kestrel replied sincerely, finding himself lik-ing the brave little urchin. "You wouldn't know of a place called the White Dolphin, would you?"

"Nope—Ol' Kenrick's de one, like I said."

The captain chuckled easily, turning toward the shadowy

doorway. "Tell me—does Old Kenrick have something to eat?"

"Eats, smokes, girls—and boys! He gots it all! Come on, mister—I see he treats you right!"

Darret scampered down the stairs and, with an amused shake of his head, Kestrel rose to his feet and followed the lad into the dark, spice-scented smoke house.

— 2 —

"What do you mean you've got no silk? Then I'll find some vendor who does!" snapped Captain Kestrel Capemir, in no mood to hear the merchant's excuses. The captain's head throbbed, and his throat felt as though he had swallowed half the sand in the Dry Basin. Furthermore, he had overslept by hours, and now felt certain that he had missed the day's best trading opportunities.

"No good looking—you find no silk! Not in the entire market!" The berobed merchant, quivering righteously, gestured a stack of woolen mats. "You buy some rugs, mebbe—I got lots."

"I came for silk!" Kestrel repeated.

"Can't be found, good Captain. Caravans, dey not been comin' for two, three week now!"

The bright sunlight of noon washed through the great bazaar of Farkeen, and for the first time Kestrel noticed that the place was not nearly as crowded as he remembered from previous visits. Still adjusting to wakefulness, he barely heard the man continue.

"Zanthilat Road been empty for all dat time!" declared the merchant, pointed beard bobbing in indignation or, perhaps, fear.

"When is the next caravan due?"

"Any day, now—it be overdue, to tell de truth."

Kestrel turned in disgust, trying to force himself to be patient. Profit, he reminded himself, was always worth waiting for—and this was merely the start of what could prove to be a long and enjoyable visit to Farkeen. He stalked away from the tent, though the full brunt of sunshine on his head reminded him that he had been up too late the night before. In fact, he had felt none too alert when he awakened barely an hour earlier.

Shrugging off his discomfort, the captain was forced to admit that Darret had been as good as his word. Old Kenrick's smoke house proved to be a small but pleasant place, and Kestrel had enjoyed a richly spiced dish of rice and a savory fillet of fish, all washed down with the sweet wine that was so popular in the western realms. Afterward he had shared a smoke with the other patrons, enjoying the experience of the great, bubbling water pipe—though he could barely see through the haze in the dim, candlelit room. Then, later still, he had taken his choice of several girls, spending more delightful, if somewhat foggy, hours.

He had awakened on a low couch to find that his funds were intact, and that Kenrick's servers were waiting to provide him with fresh fruit and bread. Sating his surprisingly strong hunger, he then stumbled into the daylight.

Kestrel found that the inn was adjacent to the vast market bazaar, a dusty plaza on the inland side of the city. The huge marketplace was flanked by several prayer towers, and opened to the vast plains of the east. Caravan roads leading to Zanthilat and Thute, and to even more distant Myntar Kosh and Corsari, departed as a main highway through a watchpost manned by the city guards. In the near distance the road, now partially obscured by dust, diverged into a series of tracks. The air above the distant flatlands roiled and twisted, vaguely obscure, like the effects of a distant dust storm.

"Hey, Captain! How you like Kenrick's?"

Kestrel looked down to see Darret standing beside him; he was surprised by how glad he was to see the boy. "That was a fine place you showed me. Looks like I might be staying there awhile," he added.

"Whyfor?"

"Silk. I intend to fill my hold with it before I sail back to Corsari, and that means I have to wait for the caravans to arrive."

Darret's expression darkened, and he looked accusingly across the plain—as if he took the caravans' absence to be a personal affront to his friend. Then the boy's face brightened, and he looked back at the captain.

"Mister—you like a game? Mebbe make big money? I know where!"

"Make—or *lose* big money?" asked Kestrel with a chuckle. "Sure, show me!"

Leading the captain around the fringes of the great bazaar, Darret took a circuitous route. Kestrel noticed that the boy avoided the numerous posts of the city guards, and he wondered idly if Darret was perhaps known, unfavorably, to those protectors of the marketplace. Finally the agile youth ducked under the low awning of a nondescript tent. Kestrel followed, squinting against the shadows of the interior. He saw four men, three wearing the silk robes of a wealthy lord or merchant, and one in the fur cape of a Thutan trader, seated cross-legged on an ornate rug. Their complexions ranged from dark to almost as light as Kestrel's own skin. All were bearded, and one drew deeply on a bubbling water pipe, wafting the spicy scent of shalewirt through the tent in a purple, smothering cloud.

In the center of the rug was a ceramic platter on which four oblong cylinders rolled back and forth.

"Here—a good game, make you lotsa money!" Darret whispered, halting just inside the entrance.

The captain stopped beside the boy, observing as the seated men stared at the tumbling shapes. Finally the objects came to rest, to a chorus of muffled curses—and a loud exclamation of disgust. The fellow who had sworn vehemently threw a coin, clinking the metal disk onto a pile that Kestrel noticed for the first time. Darret had been right about the stakes—even in the dim light the captain could see the golden glint of the coins.

The loser lifted one edge of the platter, and set the cylinders rolling back and forth again. As Kestrel's vision adjusted to the dim light, he could see that the game pieces bore hieroglyphic images. Each had pictures in the same pattern as the others, but as they came to rest, several different symbols were typically displayed.

This time one of the gamblers croaked in laughter, while the other three spat and cursed. The lucky fellow drew two coins from the pile of gold, and at the same time Kestrel noted that two of the pictures showing on the cylinders matched, each displaying a horsehead upon a shield. Disgusted, the

losers each tossed an additional coin onto the stack and one
of them set the game pieces to rolling again.

"When this game over, den you join up, hey?" whispered
Darret. "Lotsa gold to be makin'!"

Kestrel nodded, intrigued. He had gambled in many ports
of Dalethica, using cards and dice and spinning wheels, but
he had never encountered this western game before.

"How does the game end?" he asked Darret, speaking
softly so as not to disturb the concentration of the players.

"When *all* pictures de same, a fella be the winner. Before,
keep bettin', and payin', and winnin' maybe a little bits. So,
Captain," the boy continued guilelessly. "You like dat game,
you mebbe give to Darret a tip when you win?"

Kestrel chuckled. "You've got it—one tenth of my winnings. Does that mean you'll chip in if I lose?"

Darret's eyes widened in surprise, then squinted as he tried
to decide if this foreigner was joking. Finally realizing that
he was being teased, the boy grinned broadly.

For several more minutes the men grumbled and paid, with
never more than a pair of cylinders coming up a match. Finally all four of the rolling objects came to rest, each revealing a symbolic image of a ship under full sail. One of the
gamblers, the fur-caped trader with the golden skin of a pure
Thutan, howled with glee, sweeping the pile of coins away
from the rug. Kestrel, impressed, guessed that the fellow must
have hauled in something like twenty gold coins.

"Hey, misters—got another gamer here," Darret called
out, then turned to Kestrel. "You sits down now—I get you
some drink, hey?" He ushered Kestrel toward a vacant place
on the large rug. The captain bent his legs awkwardly and
seated himself.

"Three golds to start," declared a long-bearded fellow, his
head half concealed beneath a sweeping cowl of silk. From
the man's slender fingers and bronzed skin, Kestrel guessed
him to be a Zanthilite.

"Here you go," the captain agreed, reaching into his pouch
for the opening bet. The Thutan merchant's eyes widened as
Kestrel carefully arrayed a few gold coins on the rug. Sensing
Darret at his back, the captain almost yielded to an instinctive
distrust—he should send the boy away, or at least put him
where he could be watched.

But in the end, he forgot all about Darret. The gambling was fast and tense, the tumbling cylinders creating gradual, yet suspenseful increases in the betting pool. Soon nearly three dozen coins were piled beside the platter. Remembering the Thutan's luck—and fondly picturing the *Black Condor*—Kestrel had frequently bet the matching of the four ship symbols. When three of these matched, he groaned aloud; on the next roll the four pieces matched images of a coiled serpent, and the Zanthilite cackled merrily as he gathered up the pot.

The next game spiraled to a smaller total, but Kestrel won, raking in slightly more than his previous losses. Having learned that a gambler could raise the stakes, he doubled the pot for the next round, wincing in mock pain as a turbaned horse-trader from Farkeen eventually collected a mound of gold. Then he shouted in fierce delight when the four ships entitled him to the next, and largest, pot of the day.

Hours passed with reckless haste, darkness shrouding the marketplace, leaving isolated pools of life around brightly flaring torches and lamps. Serving girls entered the tent, faces and torsos concealed by silken veils, while the naked skin of their hips and legs, oiled to a golden sheen, rippled in the soft light of the lanterns they lit.

Darret left around sunset, returning later with word that the haze in the distance seemed to be a sandstorm, apparently bearing down on the city. Kestrel knew there would be no caravans coming out of that mess, but by then the news didn't matter. His senses focused on the game, on the gleam of the gold coins as they collected beside the platter, then flowed into the welcoming embrace of the most recent winner.

For several hours that winner was not Kestrel, and he fed the hungry pool for game after game, exhausting his winnings and depleting the funds he had brought to the game. But another pile began to build, this one progressing for a long time without a victor. The Zanthilite fell asleep, overcome by too many hours of shalewirt, and eventually the horse-trader, the Thutan, and Kestrel were the only players in the game.

The coins beside the platter numbered sixty, then seventy or more, and still the cylinders refused to match. Bets were placed, odds laid, and more gold tossed onto the mound. Kestrel dropped in two of his last ten pieces, almost tempted to offer a healthy cut to Baracan if the God of Man would only

favor this next roll with the matched ships. At the thought of
the sanctimonious Pader Willith he cursed the god's name
instead, and rolled.

There they were, arrayed like a proud fleet on a sea of
velvet green: four ships under sail, set out as if in response
to Kestrel's profane demand.

The Thutan cursed and Kestrel watched surreptitiously,
flexing his wrist beneath the supple weight of the steel-bladed
knife. But the barbarian appeared more disgusted with himself
than with Kestrel—he shook his head, spat to one side, and
scratched his bare and very hairy belly.

The captain of Corsari was in an expansive mood as he
and Darret walked back to Kenrick's. He gave the lad six
gold pieces. From Darret's wide-eyed reaction, Kestrel felt
certain it was more than the boy had ever before held in his
hand. Back at the inn, he hired two girls for the night, but
fell soundly asleep before they could undress him.

— 3 —

"Captain—wake up! Somethin's comin'—you wake up,
now!"

Groggily Kestrel opened his eyes, groaning at the dim light
that seeped through the shutters. It was not yet dawn, but the
sky was growing light.

"Your breath stinks," he grunted, swatting at someone he
vaguely remembered was Darret. "What are you doing
here?" he growled after a moment.

"Somethin's comin'—people up everywhere, walkin'
around, lookin'. I thought you should know, too."

"Thanks, kid—but *what's* coming? And where?"

"Dat dust storm—it's not just wind. Ground be shakin' too,
an' it's still comin' closer."

Struggling, Kestrel sat up and pulled on his boots—the only
articles of apparel he had shed the previous night. "Where
can we get a look at this storm, or whatever?" Despite his
fatigue, he felt a stirring of alarm as he cinched his belt pouch
around him. The usually unflappable Darret seemed very
tense, and when Kestrel listened closely, he could hear a buzz
of worried conversation from the streets and courtyards be-

yond. It was doubly odd, he thought, to hear the sounds of such frantic activity during this normally tranquil hour.

"Up de tower, here at Kenrick's. Get a good look." Darret led him from the room, down the narrow hallway and up a narrow, winding staircase. They climbed dozens of steps before emerging onto an outside balcony. Another stairway crossed back and forth, leading to the top of a squat tower.

"Kenrick got to know about caravans and ships both, so he knows what to buy and when. Dat's why he build himself a tower," Darret explained.

"Smart man," Kestrel muttered, meaning it. A few hours' advance notice on the arrival of a silk caravan or trading galyon could provide a sharp trader with a very profitable edge.

But this morning the tower served a different purpose. The fat innkeeper, Kenrick, and two armored guards were already up here—and they were not looking at the sea. Kestrel, too, turned toward the desert, startled by the extent of the cloud billowing into the western sky. The sun was obscured by the murk, though the rays of dawn ignited the top of the massive dust storm with fiery hues, seeming to emphasize the constant, churning motion that lay at its heart.

That heart, Kestrel knew instinctively, lay on the ground. Incredible as it might seem, the storm was no more than a mile away, closing fast, advancing with an audible rumble that he felt through the trembling floorboards. The captain habitually carried his spyglass in his belt pouch; now he drew the instrument out, extending the telescope and placing it to his eye. He focused at the base of the cloud, at the dark line that quickly distinguished itself from the dirty ground and dusty sky.

"It's an army," he said, surprised that he could make the announcement without trembling. "Impossibly fast—and huge enough that the front rank seems to be two or three miles long—but I'd wager my ship and my house that it's an army."

"Dat's no army! Where from?" demanded Darret caustically. "Zanthilat? Dey never march an army across Red Desert! Look again, see what!"

Kestrel obliged, discerning individual figures at the base of the cloud. The warriors were dark, of an unvarying hue,

but he could see no more details—except that there were
thousands of them, and that Farkeen was their clear objective.

"I've got to get to the ship!" The notion was a clear plan,
etched firmly in Kestrel's mind. "Show me the way, Darret—
I'll take you with me!"

"I tol' you—" Darret seemed inclined to argue for a moment, but then he turned and stared at the cloud, watching its
inevitable approach. As he looked, some of the people along
the marketplace wall turned and fled toward the city proper.

"Let's go!" the boy declared abruptly.

Too late Kestrel noticed the innkeeper and his guards lunge
for the narrow stairway. The captain started behind—then
cried out in dismay as the rickety structure broke, carrying
the three men to the ground in a tangle of splintered boards.

"We're trapped!" Kestrel cried, ignoring the shrieks of
pain rising from below.

"Over here!" Darret hissed. Before Kestrel could object,
the boy stepped over the parapet and started to scamper down
a tile drainpipe to the roof of the inn. Small pieces of the tube
broke away, but it supported Darret's weight. Impatient as he
was, Kestrel didn't want to risk their combined weight on the
pipe, so he waited for Darret to descend. Anxiously the captain drew out his telescope and took one more look at approaching doom. In the first rank of the attacking force were
warlike figures, helms layered in dust, heavy boots stomping
cadence on the ground as they advanced at a shambling run.
The surging formation closed the distance to the city walls
with shocking speed, and Kestrel suffered a sensation of raw
panic—how could anyone flee such a fast, relentless onslaught?

"Hurry!" he bellowed, as Darret picked his way slowly
down the pipe.

Amid the surging warriors Kestrel saw even larger figures—
manlike, but tall as horses. He blinked in astonishment, certain that sparks had twinkled in the air around one of these
monsters; staring for a moment, he saw the crackling
illumination again. In the marketplace below, women
screamed, racing from the wall, then darting past the stalls
and tents of the plaza. Those who had gathered at the wall
became a frightened, hysterical mob. Carts, tables, and tents
toppled as fleeing people swept through the plaza, pushing,

trampling, shouting. The crowd thronged past Kenrick's inn on both sides. Kestrel wiped a sheen of sweat from his brow as Darret neared the inn's roof. Turning his eyes toward the approaching figures, the captain saw the first of them clamber over the low wall, raising dark-bladed swords.

"Over here!" Darret cried, finally dropping to the roof and crawling along the sloping shelf. Kestrel followed, scrambling recklessly, and in a few moments he had tumbled to the roof where the boy had landed.

A few of the city guards made a show of resistance at the wall, standing at the caravan gate or trying to defend the waist-high barrier of stone. Kestrel saw them fall with shocking speed, cut down by the first attackers. It occurred to the captain almost as an afterthought that these sword-wielding troops were not men, but monstrous abominations risen from humanity's worst nightmares. Except Kestrel knew this was no nightmare—the scent of blood was on the breeze now, too vivid and pungent to be anything other than real. Screams of terror and pain rang through the haze, solid and undeniable evidence of carnage.

The attackers were blunt, broad-shouldered creatures with animal-like snouts and large, bony knobs on their foreheads. Sneering grotesquely, they ran on two legs and bore weapons in their hands. Despite the fact that they had apparently run for miles across the wastes of the Red Desert, they pursued their victims tirelessly, killing with ruthless skill.

Mixed among these brutes were larger, tusked monsters, scowling ferociously and swinging heavy, talon-studded paws. Each of these swipes left a trail of sparks in the air, and Kestrel dimly realized that these creatures seemed as willing to strike at the backs of their own warriors as at the humans who scattered or cowered in panic throughout the marketplace. The knob-headed troops responded to these slashes with maddened frenzy, attacking even more savagely in an effort to escape the brutal blows of their own masters.

Panic rose as a palpable stench from the crowded plaza, as people ran in all directions. Kestrel watched, sickened, as a young woman carrying a baby ran screaming around a corner, full into the advance of a black-armored warrior. The dark sword slashed and the woman's head went flying; following a sharp stab on the backstroke the babe ceased its plaintive wails.

"Here!" Darret cried, scampering to the edge of the roof. The monsters spread quickly through the plaza, but Kestrel forced himself to look down. Darret had spotted a place on the ground sheltered from the terrified people still rushing past.

Immediately below the man and boy, the throng parted around several casks. Darret leaped onto the bare ground behind the makeshift barricade. He gestured to the captain, who quailed at the drop but then plunged resolutely after. Kestrel tumbled heavily to the ground, rolling against the wall of the building and cursing at a pain in his ankle. He scrambled to his feet, relieved that the bone wasn't broken—but wincing at the jolt that stabbed at his leg every time he put weight on the injured foot.

One of the barrels shattered, boards exploding in all directions from a massive force, and Darret screamed at the monstrous creature charging through the gap. Cruel jaws gaped, and tiny eyes glittered wickedly. The beast raised the sword it had used to shatter the cask, aiming a blow at the boy's head—but Darret's reflexes saved him, and he tumbled away, bouncing to his feet against the wall.

The monster bellowed, revealing short, pointed teeth and a black, slime-streaked tongue. Kestrel flicked his knife into his hand, conscious of how puny it was against that massive sword. The screams of wounded and dying people came to him, seemingly from a great distance, and he wondered momentarily if his own voice would soon add to the cacophony.

Darret picked up one of the barrel staves and swung it like a club, bashing the monster in the knee. With a howl of pain it went down, and Kestrel's reaction was instinctive—and murderous. He dove, driving his blade into the creature's neck, then tumbled away, gagging as ink-dark blood spurted from the wound. Soundlessly the monster fell, while the captain frantically wiped his knife clean in the dust of the courtyard.

Kestrel looked around in fear, sensing beyond any doubt that Farkeen was doomed. He had one overriding instinct: get to the ship, raise the sails, and let the *Black Condor* fly away from this nightmarish scene of carnage.

THREE

Inn of the Minstrel

Music whispers magic into even the most
mundane of ears.
—SONGS OF AURIANTH

— 1 —

Dark timber paneled the walls in the great-room of the North
Shore Wayfarers' Lodge, with rafters of chiseled beams soaring far overhead. Even before dinner the place was crowded,
with travelers lining the bar or gathered at several of the
long tables. A wandering fiddler worked his instrument beside
the fireplace, the strains of a mournful ballad accompanying
the soft pop and hiss of the banked hardwood coals.

Rudy chose a table in a corner, away from most of the
other patrons, and Anjell, Dara, and Raine took seats on the
wide bench. As Danri clumped over, however, the merchants
at a nearby table ceased their raucous laughter and studied
the digger suspiciously. Quenidon Daringer entered last, the
room falling silent as the wiry sylve came through the door.
He was only as tall as an average man, but the dignity in his
bearing, the loft of his firm chin, and his emerald eyes made

him seem more imposing. Though his golden hair concealed
the distinctive sylvan ears, the serene grace of his walk made
it clear to everyone that he was other than a human.

"I feel like I'm in a zoo!" Danri groused, staring at one
burly patron until the fellow coughed and looked away.

"Look at it as an exploration," Quenidon said dryly.
"We're discovering the territorial habits of the natives."

Rudy was acutely aware that everyone in the great-room
regarded their table with cool, even hostile, curiosity. Though
they had stayed in many small inns during their travels, the
companions had not mingled with this many humans since
their meeting at Taywick, and the Iceman found the sensation
irritating.

"Perhaps you would be more comfortable somewhere private?" Awnro Lyrifell appeared, seemingly from nowhere,
and cheerily escorted the party of travelers through a door
that perfectly matched the wood paneling of the great-room.

"We have a tolerant clientele, I daresay, but there have
been too many rumors lately," the innkeeper explained, ushering them down a short hallway to a small, private sitting
room. "Word of turmoil in Galtigor, with the new king and
all—"

"Takian's a *great* improvement over his brother—don't
they know that?" Rudy challenged.

"I'm certain they do. Nevertheless, what men know and
how they feel are two different—and not necessarily related—
concerns. I will have refreshments sent along immediately."

"This is better," Dara said to the Iceman. "We can talk
in peace—and there're many things I'd like to know."

"Aye-uh, the lady's right," Danri agreed with a hearty
chuckle. "Don't know how long I coulda held my temper
against those goggle-eyed fools."

Shortly servants arrived, bearing platters of sausage and
cheese, fresh loaves of hearty, grain-rich bread, and pitchers
of creamy milk, cold ale, and tart Halverican wine. Realizing
that he was famished, Rudy joined the others in setting upon
the food, enjoying a pleasurable repast unlike any he'd shared
in many months. The fireplace in the cozy room burned low,
though a bed of hardwood coals radiated steady heat. Many
smooth glasses of Halverican wine warmed Rudy's insides,
even as the residue of the fire's heat seeped through his limbs.

For the first time in the long, weary weeks since he had departed Neshara, he felt as though he had come home.

Of course, his real home was the village high above the Glimmersee, but he wouldn't allow his thoughts to dwell on the Appenfell chalet. He reminded himself that the house in Neshara would never be the same—he had seen three brothers perish on the mountain, and he knew that sharing quarters with their widows would only remind him of their loss, and of his irrational but real guilt at his own survival.

With growing acceptance he faced a future where "home" would have to be any place he could catch a few days comfort and respite, a stopping place on the road to . . . where? As if she had read his mind, Raine took Rudy's hand, and he realized that wherever he found his respite, she would be there as well. The knowledge warmed him more than the food, the wine, and the fire combined.

After eating, he poured fresh glasses for Raine and himself, content for the moment to savor the very dry white wine characteristic of the free cantons. The cheese, sausage, and bread on the table added the final, familiar touches.

"A fine place, this—friendly, warm. A hospitable stopping place on any journey," Quenidon Daringer mused, setting his wineglass down. The wiry sylve raised his eyes from the fireplace to regard the Iceman. "Perhaps we in Faerine have been too quick to condemn you humans."

"Oh, we condemn ourselves readily enough," Raine said with a wry chuckle. "And anyone else who looks a little different, I'm afraid."

"You mean the reaction in the great-room? Faerines are the same way—it's not that type of thing that gives me concern."

"What *does* concern you?" Rudy asked.

"Just . . . this task of ours, I suppose. All my life—which spans more than three centuries—I've trained, practiced, prepared as a warrior. It was not the legacy my parents would have chosen for me, but it became my path. And my preparation has been for war, not diplomacy!"

"I think all that makes you the perfect ambassador!" Anjell exclaimed.

"Perfect? For knocking sense into someone, perhaps—but for persuading? I have a terrible fear that I will speak, and that mankind will not listen, while at the same time Faerine is menaced by the Nameless One and I'm not there to do my duty!" Quenidon's face remained impassive, but an undercurrent of tension thrummed in his voice.

"I know your worries," Danri agreed. "At times like this, pleasant as the company and the setting are, I worry for Shalemont. I've been away a long time—years, most likely, though I don't know how long I was lost in the Digging Madness. Still, *somebody's* got to try and form some kind of alliance, and I think we're in the best position of any Faerines. Not to mention that since we started from Taywick Pass, we were already halfway to Dalethica—so to speak."

The digger didn't say any more, but as Danri took a long drink of ale Rudy saw the distant look in his friend's eyes, knowing that the burly Faerine remembered more than Shalemont. Her name was Kerri, the digger had once told Rudy, but Danri had never elaborated on the memory, and the Iceman had been unwilling to pry. Now, touching the embroidered waterskin at his waist, the digger gruffly cleared his throat.

"Life is too short for regrets," Dara said quietly. "It's a feast of food and drink, some sweet and some sour—and unless we make the most of what we're offered, we'll starve. When Beryv was lost on that mountain . . . I thought my *own* life was over, as well." She touched Anjell's head, running a hand through her daughter's hair. "Now I know there's a joy in life that can only come *after* loss."

"Wise words, madam," Quenidon agreed solemnly. "Even if life's banquet is not the menu one selects."

"Mama?" Anjell was curled up on a pillow beside Dara's chair. For some time the girl had been quiet, and now she spoke with uncharacteristic hesitancy. "We have the chance to make that feast better, to stop the evil that killed Papa. It's for more than just the wedding that we should go to Carillonn—it's to see if we can do some good!"

"You're right, child." Dara looked at Rudy with fresh understanding. "I still don't know what you can do, but I see that it's the proper thing that you try."

"Me, too?" the girl asked, rising on her elbows to fix shining eyes on her mother.

"You—and *me*," Dara agreed. "From now on, I'm not

letting you out of my sight! I grew up in Neshara, and you're talking about places I never thought to see—but you're *not* going without me!''

Anjell's delighted agreement was interrupted as the door opened to reveal Awnro Lyrifell. The innkeeper had donned a kilt of bright colors and wore his characteristic wide-brimmed hat, the band studded with many feathers. He removed the garish chapeau as he bowed, eyes twinkling.

"Has the service met with your satisfaction?" he asked Anjell, fixing her with a mock-stern glare.

"Quite, my good man," she replied primly.

They laughed easily as the innkeeper joined them and servants passed around tiny glasses of steaming chocolate—a drink of the same rich brown as Raine's hair, Rudy suddenly realized.

After the servants had left, the Iceman broached the subject of an earlier discussion with the bard. "Have you found a boat for the journey to Carillonn?"

"Indeed—the *Loonsong.* She's a stout river craft, captained by an old friend of mine and awaiting us at the ferry landing tomorrow morning. There's even room for your horses aboard."

"Tomorrow?" Rudy was surprised. He should have been pleased, but he realized that his time in this little corner of his homeland was slipping by too quickly. He would have liked a few days to stay at the lodge, just to absorb that mystical skyline across the Glimmersee—but apparently it was not to be.

"You said 'us,' " Anjell observed. "Does that mean you're coming too?"

"If you think the noble King Takian would be wed without my music in the hall, then your familiarity with the royalty of Dalethica is sadly feeble!" cried the former minstrel, appalled.

"No! I mean, yes, it is—but I'm glad you're coming!"

"What do you know about Carillonn?" Danri asked gruffly. "Aside from the fact that it lies somewhere down the River Ariak?"

"Ah—'tis a city of wonders, and these I shall expound upon in good time. For now, perhaps, it is best that you know that the High King has important guests—monarchs from across the realms of men. Every ten years he holds this Council of Peace over the warm solstice, and, fortuitously, this is one of those summers. Consequently, your timing is splendid. You will meet the Sun Lord of Myntar Kosh, as well as Kings Macconal of Corsari, and Halltha of Zanthilat. These, together with Takian of Galtigor, are most powerful among the rulers of men.''

"But what about the High King—is he the lord over them all?" Quenidon inquired.

"No—the title is mostly honorary. High King Dyerston is lord of his city—which, as you will learn, is a place unmatched across Dalethica. He has the fealty of his Hundred Knights, mighty warriors all, but he has no army that could stand against even one of his powerful neighbors.''

"It is much the same in Spendorial," Quen noted, his tone surprisingly bitter. "Our nobility is presided over by the Royal Scion—an accomplished Auramaster. He commands an elite battalion, the Royal House sylves, but doesn't maintain an army except for the garrisons at Taywick and Darkenheight. And all *real* power is in the hands of those who wield magic.''

"What about Shalloth? Duchess Bristyn's realm? Didn't she say that was part of Carillonn?" Anjell asked, chewing on a piece of sweetbread.

"Aye," Awnro said approvingly. "Shalloth and several other duchies owe fealty to the High King. Lady Bristyn's father was the king's most loyal retainer—and now, with her wedding to King Takian, Dyerston has secured himself a powerful ally to the east.''

"And they *love* each other!" Anjell insisted. "It's not just for alliances and armies and such!''

"I know," Awnro agreed. "Indeed, I had an inkling when the duchess passed through here on her way to Galtigor. I tried to suggest as much, but I fear she was skeptical at the time.''

"It takes a while to get to know her sometimes, but she's nice!" Anjell declared loyally.

"Quite right," the innkeeper agreed. He turned to Danri and Rudy, regarding them frankly.

"I'm sure that you will have a royal audience. But tell me, if you will, what you intend to accomplish by your embassy."

"We'll tell them all that the Sleepstealer is moving against Dalethica, and Faerine." Rudy spoke for the companions. "We know he has spies and agents among us—Garamis was just one of them—but we also have to be ready for a full-scale invasion. Another Sleepstealer War, if you will."

"The kings will have to unite," Danri added. "Raise an army quickly—a *large* army—and stand ready at the Dry Basin. That's the only place where the Watershed is low enough for the Nameless One to send his army on the attack against humankind."

"You seek cooperation?" the innkeeper asked. "At great expense and difficulty, against a foe they cannot see? Your task is indeed a challenge."

"Perhaps the invasion will start before we get there," Rudy said bitterly. "Then our persuasion will be done for us."

"Don't count on it." The bard shook his head grimly, then stood to face the travelers. "The legends say that in the first Sleepstealer War the minions came on so fast that towns, cities—even whole realms—did not learn of the peril until the evil army stood at their gates. At times the dark hordes traveled even faster than the news of their incursion!"

"But *how*?" Dara asked. "Surely a rider on a fleet horse could carry word ahead of them?"

"Even the fastest horse needs rest, and a man needs sleep. Minions need neither, nor must they pause to eat." Rudy remembered with a shudder the implacable determination of the kroaks he had fled in the Wilderhof.

"That's true—they require only an occasional sip of Darkblood," Awnro added. "Legends say that the minion armies were accompanied by huge wagons, drawn by beasts called bovars, massive creatures that hauled vats of the stuff from Duloth-Trol."

"How can they be stopped?" Dara asked, wide-eyed.

"They can be killed in battle, at least the minions can," Awnro said. "The Lord Minions are another matter, I'm afraid. Nicodareus you have seen; do you know of Phalthak, the snake-headed Fang of Dassadec? Or Reaper, his Talon?"

"Those are the three who remain," replied Raine with a somber nod. "Two more were slain in the Sleepstealer War—and one of the original six was destroyed by immersion in Aura."

"Ah—there you speak of Darkenscale, the Fist of Dassadec," Awnro declared in obvious pleasure, turning to Raine. "Your comment speaks well of your education."

"It is said that his death was a convulsion of nearly volcanic proportions."

"Indeed. The explosion was so violent that an entire mountain was destroyed, and a pass opened in the Watershed," Awnro explained. "Then there are stories of the Lost Artifacts, not to mention legends of other techniques—folk tales, almost—like trying to ward a Lord Minion with garlic."

"I'd not care to give that one a try," the Iceman said grimly, shuddering at the memory of Nicodareus, looming black and horrible before him. No plant, however pungent, could possibly hold back that awful presence.

It was some time later, after the other companions had retired to their rooms, that the Iceman stood with Raine outside the door to her own, private chamber. He was acutely conscious of her inviting presence, and of their seclusion—though they had traveled together for months, they had had very few moments alone together.

"I don't know where we'll go from here, beyond Carillonn," he said. "But having you with me is enough, even if the answers continue to elude us."

"Perhaps we won't find the answers with each other, either—but we can look." Raine took Rudy's hand, raised it to her breast. His breath caught in his throat, and he thought that her dark eyes, upturned to his, were the most beautiful, the most inviting place, he had ever seen.

"Life . . . 'life is short,' Dara said. We do have to make the most of it." A smile teased the corners of Rudy's lips. His arms went around Raine, pulling her close. They kissed, the Iceman's heart pounding as he crushed her to him, embracing them both in an onrush of warmth.

Somehow they closed the door behind them, stumbling together across the dark room to the bed. Rudy touched her everywhere, awed by her luminescent beauty, lost in the silken feel of her skin. He kissed Raine fiercely, intoxicated by the clinging tightness of her embrace, hearing her soft gasps—of pain or pleasure?—in his ear. And then wonderful heat enveloped him; joy, and love, were all that he knew. Some part of him wanted to look at her, to devour her with his eyes as well as with his lips and his hands—but somehow they never managed to light the lamp.

— 2 —

The stalkers wove the spell of Darkslayer around Nicodareus. The most intelligent of Dassadec's lesser minions, stalkers were nimble and dexterous. They could shift the shape of their bodies to suit the needs of the moment. But it was for their inherent powers of sorcery that the Sleepstealer used them to weave the spell around Nicodareus.

When at last the Lord Minion rose from the bath of Darkblood, the reptilian minions hissed their approval, bowing cravenly as their lord stood in the chamber at the depths of Agath-Trol. Allowing them to lick a layer of Darkblood from his skin, Nicodareus enjoyed the attentions of the stalkers for a few minutes—but he quickly grew impatient with the delay. Casting the minions aside, he rose and climbed the long passageways back to the surface. Ultimately he emerged under the dark, tarcloud-layered sky of the Sleepstealer's realm.

From the flat plain at the base of his master's mountain, Nicodareus looked up the steeply sloping flanks of Agath-Trol. The summit was lost in the distance, three miles or more overhead, and further obscured by the massive, floating bulk of the *Dreadcloud*. That huge sky-ship drifted at its tether, secured to a spume of gaseous Darkblood trailing steadily from the top of the obsidian peak. For a moment the Eye of Dassadec let his Sight caress the hull of the great cloud, lingering on the massive batteries. He longed to fling their lightning against an enemy on the ground, to command that awesome and mightily destructive barrage, but he forced himself to set that yearning aside.

Patience, Nicodareus counseled himself. He would perform one task at a time. Someday the *Dreadcloud* would answer to his own commands! For now, the Lord Minion leaned into the scouring wind, shifting to the shape of a terrion, taking to the air on long, leathery wings.

For days the great minion-body flew northward, bearing Nicodareus toward the lofty heights of the Watershed. The shell of the Darkslayer lay like the warmth of fresh blood on his skin, and he flew into the chilly reaches of mountainous air without faltering. As he soared higher along the mountain valleys, however, the cold penetrated that skin, draining strength and dulling alertness. He crossed the Watershed at the lowest notch along the great ridge of the West Range, and even here the cold threatened to drag him down, to sap his powerful body into a torpor so deep that he might lie here for a hundred years. The power of the Darkslayer, the potent magic laid on him in the well of Agath-Trol, was no match for the bitter winds, the Darkblood-freezing chill. He could collapse, so easily, and abandon all he knew, surrendering ultimately to the cold. Snarling, Nicodareus pushed his way through the heights, desperate to cross the ridge and once again dive into lower, warmer reaches. He was grateful that the terrion was a fast flier, for soon his wings would carry him beyond the danger.

Within Dalethica, he shifted the leather-winged terrion's body into the feathered shape of a soaring condor. On wings of black he soared through plunging, rock-lined valleys, swiftly gliding down past the timberline until he was shrouded by warmer air. He sensed his fatigue, and his hunger, and instinctively he knew what to do.

In a clearing among the alpine forests he saw the white specks marking a large flock of sheep, with several shepherds clustered around a fire that blazed nearby. The condor glided silently between the trees, settling like a falling leaf to the forest floor. Nicodareus quickly assumed a two-legged form, stalking toward the artificial but welcome warmth of the campfire. Just before he entered the clearing he remembered the value of disguise, and altered his body to the shape of a bent, wizened old human. Raising the cowl of a hood about his head, he hobbled forward, his crimson eyes downcast as he approached.

"Ho, grandfather," called a cheerful voice. "What brings you to these lofty vales?"

"Come, share our fire—and our wine," added another.

With a sidelong glance, Nicodareus saw three men squatting around the small blaze, and he was pleased. He needed but one of them to survive, yet he would relish the slaying of the additional victims.

Perhaps something in his manner made the men uneasy, for

the first shepherd spoke again. "Don't remember seeing you around here—fact is, thought we were the only folks in this part of the West Range. Where did you say you came from?"

The men rose to their feet as Nicodareus hobbled closer. He saw that one of them laid his hand, casually, on a stout limb of firewood. Another kept his right hand hidden, and the Lord Minion sneered at the idea of a concealed knife—as if any pathetic piece of steel could offer the shepherd hope.

"Who *are* you?" demanded one of the men, this time taking a step forward.

"Call me . . . *Death!*" Nicodareus growled, raising his head and fixing his ember-red eyes on the fellow's face. The man's expression sagged with horror as the Lord Minion's hand lashed out, tearing out the wretch's throat with claws that sprouted in an eyeblink of time.

The other two men scrambled away from the fire, racing after sheep that scattered, bleating frantically. Nicodareus assumed his true form, dropping to all fours and pouncing after one of the shepherds like a charging lion. He leaped, bearing the man to earth, crushing his head between the fangs of crushing jaws. Raising his gore-streaked face, the Lord Minion watched the third shepherd disappear into the woods. The blood of his victim was hot and sweet on his tongue, unspeakably tantalizing, and he knew that he would have to drink deeply. He almost yielded to the immediate temptation, yet he was an ageless and patient creature—he would gain sustenance from his final victim.

Padding into the woods, Nicodareus sent his Sight before him, following the gasping, staggering flight of the shepherd. The man tripped over fallen tree trunks, bounding back to his feet and continuing mindless flight. The Lord Minion followed slowly and deliberately, crushing sticks with his taloned feet, bashing stout limbs out of the way with blows from his rocklike fists. He made noise, knowing that the sounds of pursuit added to the human's consuming, hysterical fear.

That terror was a palpable scent on the wind, and Nicodareus relished the sweet aroma as he gradually closed the distance. Gibbering, pleading maniacally, the man cast horrified glances over his shoulder. Knowing death approached, he was unable to turn and face his fate with courage—instead, he continued his pathetic flight, which only heightened the Lord Minion's pleasure.

Only when the shepherd scrambled toward the bank of a shallow stream did Nicodareus hasten. Like all creatures of Darkblood, he abhorred the clear water of Dalethica, and had no desire to fish his prey out of some mountainous brook. He sprang, sinking his claws into the flesh of the man's calves, dragging his prey to earth several feet short of the stream. Savoring each wailing scream, he slowly pulled the squirming fellow closer, holding him in an almost tender embrace for several minutes. Only when the man's fear drove him utterly mad, when he collapsed like a limp weight, did the Lord Minion lower his head, tear open the flesh and bone of the man's torso, and drink greedily from the still-pumping heart.

After the corpse was drained to a husk, Nicodareus ceased his slurping feast. Tossing the body aside, he rose to his feet, vibrant and full of power. The awful cold of the mountain passage was well behind him, and the power of Darkslayer would thrum through his body, sustaining him until tomorrow, when he would need to feed again.

Yet the vitality of the blood pulsing through him was almost too intense. He strived to change his shape, to shift into the body of the bird, but found that he couldn't. He was taut, energized—yet at the same time he needed to collapse somewhere. Then the agony struck, awful and consuming pain, as searing as the torture visited upon him by Dassadec in Agath-Trol. Falling, he rolled and writhed on the ground.

And then he knew: This was the Sleepstealer's reminder of failure, the Lord Minion's punishment renewed. The racking pain lingered for an eternity, until abruptly the spasms passed to leave him spent and paralyzed.

The Lord Minion curled into a ball, slumping over the drained body of his victim, and mercifully sank into torpor.

— 3 —

The blue-green waters of the River Ariak would mark the stately progress of the *Loonsong*'s journey north from the Glimmersee. The channel was deep, bedded with gravel, and the water flowing from that vast lake glimmered with aquamarine purity past the ferry landing.

The riverboat was a long-hulled schooner, mastered by a one-armed sailor introduced by Awnro as "my old friend, Captain Rorkok." The bearded riverman smiled, revealing that he had lost teeth and arms in approximately equal proportions, but when he welcomed the companions aboard, the warmth of his greeting overcame any initial reaction to his appearance.

"The ladies can stay here," he declared with a gentlemanly bow, opening a door to reveal a surprisingly spacious cabin near the bow. Beside it was a similar compartment, albeit a trifle smaller, for Awnro and Rudy to share with the two Faerines.

The schooner had the advantage of the current and made good time. For the downstream run the mast was lowered and lashed to the cabin roofs, while four oarsmen guided the long vessel around the occasional sandbars and submerged boulders. Because of its gravel bed, the river remained relatively free of silt even though it curled and meandered through forested lowlands for many miles.

Anjell, with her mother hovering protectively at her side, spent hours at the gunwale, peering into the azure depths, crying out with delight when she spotted a lurking trout or huge river sturgeon. Virgin woods blanketed the surrounding hills, and Rudy found the oak and maple forests a lush and beautiful alternative to the more open pine timberlands of Halverica. Occasionally the hills closed in, but even the gorges were pastoral and serene by comparison to the rockbound canyons of his homeland.

Sometimes the forest became so thick that the winding river seemed to course through a realm unknown to man, where great, moss-draped boughs swayed far over the water. Knotty, massive boles lurked in the woods, so gnarled that Anjell often cried out in mock alarm, identifying this one or that as a witch's face, or the certain image of a kroak.

Occasionally the *Loonsong* passed a town or village surrounded by pastures, where wooden docks and stony quays flanked the Ariak. The sleek ship glided always with stately grace, and as the hills fell away to flatland the travelers knew that they neared the fabled city of Carillonn.

Awnro Lyrifell had been settled at the Wayfarer's Lodge for a decade or more, but he hadn't forgotten how to strum a lute. Each evening of the five-day voyage he beguiled his companions—and all the other passengers as well—with songs and tales.

"Marbled Carillonn—City of One Hundred Bridges, they call it," he proclaimed, on the last night of the river journey. He winked at Danri. "Those spans have stood for a thousand years—built by diggers, you know."

"I'm not surprised they still stand—though I didn't know my ancestors worked on this side of the Watershed," Danri admitted, sipping a mug in the ship's spacious upper deck saloon. Orange flames of sunset fired the western sky, and a vast expanse of rolling woodland had framed the river for the entire afternoon of travel.

"A peace gesture it was, after the Sleepstealer War," the bard explained. "When the minions fell back to Duloth-Trol, they didn't leave much behind. A lot of diggers returned that way after the battle at Glimmersee, and they decided they'd help fix up some of the damage. Of course, it didn't hurt that white marble could be quarried within a few miles of the city. Before long it got to be kind of a contest, each company of diggers trying to build a higher, more graceful bridge than the next."

"Are there really a hundred of them?" asked Dara.

"All stone, too. Carillonn's on an island—but it's an island with three steep hills. There are bridges that connect the city to both shores of the river, and many more that link places on the hills to others on the neighboring heights. Then, in Castle Carillonn itself, bridges join many of the high towers to other towers. Aye, my lady—it's a sight like you'll see nowhere else." The bard played a few notes, then hushed his strings and met the widow's eyes. "And there are reasons—*good* reasons—for you to see all of it."

"I really can't wait!" Dara nodded, her cheeks flushed. "To be traveling, going someplace so wondrous . . . makes me feel like a girl again!"

For a time Awnro reduced them all to laughter with a rollicking ballad about an adventurous fisherman and his determination to land a mighty sturgeon. The sturgeon turned out to be an enchanted king who had escaped from Faerine, and when the fisherman finally brought him to friendly shores, the human received a magical "reward"—he, himself, was forced to assume the sturgeon's form.

As the last notes of the song faded into the soft hiss of water against the hull, Dara sighed and took her daughter's hand. She gestured toward the full darkness that had settled over the river. "Come to bed now, Anjell—Captain Rorkok says we'll reach Carillonn in the morning, so you'd better get your rest."

"I thought of one more thing," Anjell said to Rudy as she stood and stretched. "When we meet the High King, we should give him some Aura. Kind of as a present, you know?"

"That's a good idea," the Iceman agreed. They had brought numerous containers of Faerine's elixir, in addition to the barrels that Takian's army would haul from Taywick. "Why don't you fill one of the silver flasks we brought for the wedding?"

The girl nodded, satisfied—and tired enough that she didn't complain as Dara accompanied her to the cabin. The silent, dark forest slipped past on either bank as the other passengers lingered a while, each lost in private thoughts.

Awnro strummed a series of melancholy chords, music that soothed—and at the same time saddened—his pensive listeners. Danri, Quenidon, and Raine sat in silence while Rudy rose from his chair and went to the railing, staring at the great arc of stars spanning the forested horizon. He had the feeling that his life rushed forward as inexorably—and as unalterably in its course—as this mighty river. Carillonn lay before them, and he thought of the current carrying them onward. Was it possible that he and his companions could have a similar effect, as mighty and timeless in its way as the course of the Ariak?

"Awnro, what can you tell us about the High King? Should we seek him out directly, try to enlist his support?" Rudy asked, turning to the dapper minstrel. "And do you think he'll see us?"

"Good questions," Awnro Lyrifell admitted, setting his instrument aside. "I knew Kelwyn Dyerston in his younger days, and he cut a dashing figure—quite a man of action and excitement. He's settled down a bit, of course. I think he'll see you, and probably even believe the tale of your own adventures.

"King Dyerston comes from a long line of monarchs—rulers who do not trace their roots to Carillonn, or anywhere in central Dalethica. They are the men of Andaran, which means "ancient king" in the Elder Tongue. Dyerston has a son who is being raised there, among the halls of those ancient kings. He will come to Carillonn when he is needed—or when his father sends for him."

"Isn't Andaran a land far to the east?" Rudy asked. "Why does it have such a link to Carillonn?"

"Like so many other things, that alliance goes back a thousand years, to the Sleepstealer War," the bard explained. "Andaran is far away, but more importantly, it's an *island*. And islands were the only truly safe places then—the horde of the Nameless One avoided boats, didn't even like to cross bridges. Anyway, the House of the High King took shelter there, and the family has retained royal grounds on Andaran for ten centuries."

"Somebody with such vast holdings should have a lot of influence," Rudy suggested.

"As I intimated earlier: Though the High King is honored by them all, he is not the most powerful of Dalethican rulers. Even if you convince him that the threat of the Sleepstealer is real, and imminent, you'll mainly get his support for carrying your arguments to the others."

"And about these other monarchs—can you tell us about them? Who are they?"

Awnro nodded his head. "Since the kings are there for the council, and Takian can vouch for you, chances are good that you'll get an audience. After that, your task gets harder—especially as you'll have to make selfish monarchs worry about a threat they won't be able to see. And you'll have to encourage them to raise armies—an expensive undertaking—on nothing more than the suspicion of imminent trouble."

"But the threat of the Sleepstealer is real!" Raine objected. "Surely there can be nothing more important than preparing for it!"

"You're right," Awnro agreed cheerfully. "But that doesn't make it any easier for them to believe you. As to the 'who' of these kings, I think I let on before: There are four

monarchs who between them rule the most populous king-
doms—and command the largest armies—of all the realms of
Dalethica.''

"Takian of Galtigor is one." Rudy remembered.

"Aye—and he is your ally. That should count for something. The other three, however, will be more problematic, for
each of them rules a realm that lies closer to Duloth-Trol than
does Galtigor, or Carillonn itself for that matter.''

"One would be the Sun Lord," Raine said deliberately.

"Naturally, my lady. The Good King Garand Amelius of
Myntar Kosh is the elder statesman of Dalethica, and has
prided himself on devoting his life to peace. Alas, much of
that lack of strife has come at the expense of his realm.''

"What do you mean?" asked Rudy.

"Fifty years ago, when he mounted the throne, Garand
Amelius inherited the largest kingdom in Dalethica. Many of
his holdings were coveted by neighboring rulers, and rather
than confront his challengers the Sun Lord consistently traded
away these fiefdoms. He signed dozens of treaties, all of them
ceding this or that part of his kingdom to some covetous
neighbor. Zanthilat, Corsari, even Carillonn, have gained ter-
ritory because of these arrangements.''

"What kind of human could become such a king?" Quenidon Daringer queried. "Did he have no warrior tradition in
his family?''

"There are famous warriors in his pedigree," Awnro said.
"How do you suppose Myntar Kosh got so big in the first
place? Still, whatever traditions supported that part of his nature, Garand Amelius seemed quite capable of burying them.
And he has prospered through peace, insofar as the realm he
still controls. But it's widely known that Amelius himself
hates the very thought of war.''

"And the other monarchs? The ones who may be important
to gaining some kind of agreement?" Rudy pressed.

"They would include King Halltha of Zanthilat, and King
Jamiesen Macconal of Corsari. I confess I know little about
the former, never having journeyed that far to the west. As
to Macconal, he hails from a long line of warriors and sea-
farers. The sailors of Corsari have frequently been a scourge
along the shores of the Circled Sea, and they serve their king
with devotion.''

"At least this king may be a warrior," Quen noted. "He should understand the need for action!"

"We've got to get *all* these human kings thinking about the danger—to raise their armies, get men posted on the frontier of the Dry Basin!" Danri was adamant, unwilling to admit that the companions' sense of urgency might not be shared by their royal audience.

Awnro chuckled, his tone sympathetic. "There's a chance that warning will fall on deaf ears—at least, until the Sleepstealer gives us something more definite to worry about." He looked directly at Rudy, eyes flashing with understanding that the younger man found unsettling. "And I suspect that you, my unique Iceman, will have important business to attend to long before that happens."

Despite Rudy's entreaties, Awnro would say no more about the matter that night. Later, the Iceman tossed and turned in his bunk, anticipating their arrival at the fabled city—and strangely agitated by the bard's words.

The following morning all previous considerations were forgotten as, shortly after breakfast, the *Loonsong* came around a wide bend in the Ariak, and an expanse of alabaster stonework gleamed in the sunlight before them.

FOUR

Reaper's Tide

Not until a man has wallowed in the greatest
depths of despair can his spirit soar to heights
of transcendent joy.
—SCROLL OF BARACAN

— 1 —

Kestrel limped around a corner, leaving the horror of the plaza
behind. Brute-faced warriors probed through the wreckage of
stalls and huts, cutting down survivors, while more of the
monsters rushed into the main boulevard. Grimacing against
the pain of his throbbing ankle, the captain followed Darret
away from the crowd, into the first side street. The boy stumbled along, burdened by the dead monster's sword—which
he'd had the presence of mind to pick up before taking flight.
Cradling the blade across his skinny chest, Darret led his companion through a maze of Farkeen alleys.

"Which way to the docks?" gasped the captain when they
reached a six-way intersection surrounded by tall buildings.

Without a word Darret darted into one of the lanes, and
now Kestrel labored to keep up. They encountered fewer and
fewer people as they ran, noticing that many of the doors

flanking the street had been slammed shut and presumably bolted. Remembering the timber-crushing force of the monster's blow, Kestrel pitied anyone who sought safety behind such tenuous protection.

Darret darted around another corner, and for minutes the two fled in a strange cocoon of silence, their gasping breaths louder than the din of panic and destruction in the eastern reach of the city. That noise abruptly swelled in volume, and when they staggered around another corner Kestrel saw why.

They intersected again, the broad boulevard linking Farkeen's waterfront to the marketplace. The avenue was packed with terrified humanity, swelling and rolling like an ocean surface. Screams and cries mingled, panic tearing families apart, trampling the small and weak to the ground. A wagon overturned in the center of the street, and a wave of people scrambled over it and spread to both sides, re-forming beyond. Horses whinnied and reared in terror, and the captain knew that many folk must be crushed in the mindless throng. Tumbling out of the crowd, a man and woman collapsed in abject fear before Kestrel and the boy. "It's the end of the world!" wailed the terrified wife, while her husband—his own face numb with shock—cradled her against his chest, gently rocking.

Kestrel heard the clash of steel, and for a moment thought that the attackers had already penetrated this far into the city. He grimaced in disgust when he saw that several city guards had raised their weapons against the fleeing populace. The panicking warriors hacked their way to a pair of rearing horses, chopping the riders from the saddles. The men-at-arms mounted and put spurs to the steeds' flanks, plunging through the crowd, trampling adults and children with equal unconcern.

"Come on!" cried Darret, reversing course and racing up a connecting alley. Kestrel judged that they again ran parallel to the wide street, but still very few people chose to flee through these back lanes.

A red haze filmed across the captain's vision, his lungs burning with each gulp of air. Every footstep was a fresh stab into his ankle, and he feared that he would collapse momentarily. Staggering, he lumbered along like a drunk, while the sounds of splintering doors, the clash of iron weapons, rang from the back streets, marking the steady advance of death.

A slight breeze bore the welcoming scent of salty air. Darret ducked down a tight passageway, a gap lined on both sides with timbers and canvas, and Kestrel turned sideways to follow. He pushed forward for just a few steps before they emerged onto the solid stone surface of the Farkeen wharf.

People poured onto the waterfront from the main avenue, and from many narrower lanes as well. Several fishing dories, sails raised to catch the offshore breeze, lumbered into the harbor. Some of these bore just a few passengers, while others were laden to the gunwales, panicked citizens clutching every handhold in frantic attempts at escape.

The *Black Condor* stood as Kestrel had left her, lashed to the quay nearby. She rode high in the water, and the captain cursed his lack of foresight in ordering the cargo unloaded— he would be abandoning a fortune in goods. At least someone had had the presence of mind to raise the gangplank—a good thing, for the mob had selected the great galyon as a focal point. Desperate people swarmed toward her from all directions. Canvas already drooped from the top spars, and Kestrel suspected that his mate had given orders for a swift departure—though the officer was nowhere to be seen. Indeed, as he looked across the deck Kestrel saw only men he didn't recognize.

"The watchers I hired—they're taking the *Condor*!" he gasped, suddenly understanding. Pushing forward angrily, Kestrel used his bulk to force through the crowd, ignoring those he shoved aside.

"Captain! Wait!" Darret's voice rose above the crowd, tugging at Kestrel's reluctant attention. "Take me wit' you!"

The crowd surged again and the boy disappeared, swallowed in the panicked throng. Kestrel looked longingly toward the ship, watching as awkward hands struggled to lower another sail from its lofty spar. He teetered at the brink of the dock, ready to dive.

"Captain! Help!"

Abruptly Kestrel's mind conjured the image of Darret standing over his bed in the dawnlight so long ago—by Baracan, it was only minutes! If the boy hadn't awakened him, the captain would no doubt be trapped somewhere in that distant throng, perhaps already gutted on one of those black-bladed swords.

Cursing against the unexpected constraint of conscience, Kestrel turned back from the dock's edge. He elbowed people roughly aside until he caught a glimpse of the dark, braided locks flopping from a boyish scalp.

"Darret—here!" he bellowed.

He saw the boy's eyes flare open, suddenly bright with hope. A small fist rose from the crowd, reaching, grasping toward Kestrel. The captain's hand clamped onto Darret's wrist, and when he turned back to the water the boy stumbled along behind, struggling to stay close.

— 2 —

Kestrel balanced at the edge of the wharf, looking at the water that lapped, mockingly placid, at the pilings below. Around him the mob surged, pressing and growing like a living entity in the limited space of the waterfront. On the galyon, another sail slipped loose, but only half the sheet unfurled. One of the piratic guards perched on the high yardarm, tugging at a line—but lost his balance and tumbled to the deck, his scream lost in the cacophony of wails and shouts.

Craning upward, looking across the crowd, Kestrel saw the helmsman Garson nearby, standing with a number of the crew in a pack near the ship's stern. The captain caught his sailor's eye, nodding meaningfully toward the empty notch where the ship's gangplank had rested. Garson tipped his head in acknowledgment and, with a dozen burly mates in tow, started wedging his way through the crowd.

Now smoke mixed with the stench of fear, and clashing metal joined the cries and screams of battle—or massacre, more accurately. The relentless attackers pushed their way down the city's main avenue, driving terrified citizens like cattle, packing more and more people onto the teeming waterfront. Beside Kestrel a man lost his balance and toppled into the harbor, dragging another with him in a frantic grasp at safety.

"Can you swim?" Kestrel asked, stooping and staring Darret in the eye.

"Sure."

"Let's go." Without a backward glance Kestrel leapt off the dock, springing far from the edge. Kicking back to the surface, he saw the bubbles where Darret had jumped, but he treaded water for several seconds without seeing a sign of the boy.

Frantically the captain dove, flailing with his hands toward a dark object he saw underwater. Grasping Darret's collar, he pulled upward, surprised at the weight; their heads came free and Kestrel kicked hard, holding them both afloat.

"I thought you could swim!" he sputtered.

"I can—but de sword's too heavy!" the boy gasped.

Kestrel groaned, realizing that Darret still clutched the slain warrior's iron weapon. "Drop it!" he shouted, but the lad stubbornly shook his head.

"Here, then," Kestrel sputtered, taking the hilt of the weapon and pulling it toward him. Kicking strongly, trailing the sword through the water, he led Darret to the far side of the *Black Condor*. Rungs bolted into the hull descended all the way to the water line near the stern, and he grasped the lowest of these, vague relief barely penetrating his exhaustion.

Darret seized the same metal rung, swimming easily now that he was no longer burdened with the heavy weapon. Kestrel, for his part, didn't regret the weight of the iron sword. Indeed, if, as he expected, the Farkeen guards proved stubborn, he would be grateful for the blade.

"Follow me." Thrusting the weapon through his belt, the captain of the *Black Condor* started up the rusted rungs. Pain shot through his ankle, but he forced himself to ignore the agonizing jolts. He heard Darret coming behind, but kept his attention focused on the railing over his head.

None of the guards showed his face on the seaward side of the ship—apparently they shared the logical fear that the threats lay toward the land. Atop the ladder Kestrel peered cautiously over the solid wooden gunwale. At least a dozen swordsmen, each wearing the chain-mail shirt of the city guard, stood along the opposite rail, regarding their fellow citizens on the dock with a mixture of pity and contempt.

"Hurry wit' de sails!" cried one, staring upward. Nevertheless, the men in the rigging crept with extreme caution toward the high spars—they had seen their companion's fatal plunge. Fortunately, these would-be seamen had climbed the two forward masts; there was no one directly over Kestrel's head.

With a smooth gesture the captain pulled himself over the railing and rolled onto the deck. Darret followed, darting behind a row of water casks near the galley door. Abruptly that hatchway opened and one of the guards emerged carrying three large loaves of bread. He stepped past the barrels, eyes widening as he saw the sodden, crouching captain. Kestrel froze, but Darret leapt at the mail-shirted pilferer, snatching one of the loaves as he dove for the galley door.

"Hey! What d'you think—''

The fellow barked in astonishment, instinctively turning to reach after Darret—but before he finished his outcry Kestrel leapt to his feet and stabbed him through the back with the heavy sword. Dropping like a felled tree, the man sprawled lifeless on the deck, blood spouting from his chest and back. Whirling back to the dockside railing, Kestrel was amazed to see that none of the other guards had noticed the brief clash.

"Thanks, kid—that was quick thinking," the captain muttered, crouching behind the barrels again. Kestrel had killed before, more than once in defense of his ship, and though in his own mind the pirate had gotten no more than he deserved, he watched for the boy's reaction. Darret stepped over the body, flashed Kestrel a grin, then bit off a large piece of the bread.

Peering between two of the barrels, Kestrel recognized the silver helmet of the guard captain who had arranged to "protect'' the *Black Condor*. The fellow stood back from his comrades, turning to shout upward, urging the novice sailors to hurry. Looking around further, Kestrel noticed that the door to the deckhouse was shut, with a bar in place to secure the latches.

"Find a place to hide," Kestrel whispered to Darret. "I'm going to talk to these fellows. When I have their attention, get over to that door and pull the bar."

"But—!"

"Do as I say!" the captain hissed. Without a backward glance, Kestrel drew the sword and rushed across the deck. Sprinting toward the leader of the guards, who still stared upward with his back to the captain, Kestrel seized the man by the neck, yanked his head backward, and placed the tip of the iron sword against the fellow's quivering throat.

"Get your men down from the masts—now!" growled Kestrel, digging sharp metal into the man's bobbing larynx.

"But—ulp!" A little more pressure turned the fellow's voice into a squeak.

"Do it!"

"You men—down to the deck, quick!" he shouted when Kestrel relaxed his grip.

"Hey! What's doin'?" demanded one of the guards at the rail, who finally noticed the intruder. The rest whirled to face the captain, hands going to the hilts of their own swords. Kestrel counted perhaps a dozen men on deck, guessed that an equal number made their way hesitantly down the rigging from the mastheads.

"Where'd you come from?" demanded another of the pirates, drawing his weapon—but holding back at his leader's squeal of pain when Kestrel pressed the iron tip of the sword to his throat again.

"Never mind that—we've got to get the crew on board, so we can set the sails properly." The master of the *Black Condor* jerked his head toward Garson and his mates, many of whom had forced their way through the crowd to the edge of the dock below the galyon.

"We'll sail anyway!" snapped the pirate. "And if you try to stop us, you'll get stuck through for your trouble!"

"Who among you knows how to sail the *Condor*?" Kestrel demanded. "If you'll let the rest of these men aboard, we'll *all* have the chance to get out of here!"

"How do we know you'll take us with you?" croaked the leader of the guards.

"The last thing we need is bloodshed among ourselves— the real problem is out there! Now—drop that plank!"

Kestrel's voice, tempered by two decades as a shipmaster, spurred the men to action; the gangplank slid out from the deck and Garson's men settled it onto the dock. At the same time Kestrel glimpsed Darret pulling the bar from the locked cabin. Another dozen of his crewmen stumbled out, blinking in the light. Several rubbed bruises, and one had his arm in a makeshift sling.

On the docks, Garson started up the plank, leading a score

or more of the crew—including Pader Willith, whose slight
form was swept along by the brawny sailors. Following after
the last seaman several Farkeen beggars scrambled onto the
gangplank, followed by a throng of men, women, and children.

"Stop those people!" Kestrel shouted to one of his men.
The fellow hoisted a belaying pin and stood at the top of the
plank, swinging the makeshift club casually. The beggars
cowered back, pleading with the sailor to let them aboard.

"What about these fellows?" growled Garson, when the
treacherous watchmen had been surrounded by a ring of angry
sailors.

"The way I see it, you're pirates," Kestrel said grimly.
"You can jump overboard, or get thrown!"

"You said you'd take us with you!" blurted their terrified
leader.

"You obviously have difficulty with words," the sea captain growled. "You said you'd protect my ship *for* me, not
from me. I, on the other hand, never said that I would take
you with me. It would seem that you're a liar *and* a fool."

The *Condor*'s crewmen stepped forward menacingly and
the men of Farkeen backed to the rail. A few hurled themselves toward the dock, while others plunged into the water—
and sank like stones, weighted by their mail shirts. Some had
the presence of mind to shed their armor before leaping, and
Kestrel gave these men a few seconds to do so.

"Now—to the spars!" he shouted to his own willing crew.
"Lift the plank!"

"Captain!" Darret cried, tugging at Kestrel's arm as he
started for the wheel deck. The boy pointed toward the wailing throng massed on the dock. "Those people—can't we
take 'em? Some?"

Kestrel looked at the lad in disbelief. "There's no time!"
he shouted. "Get out of my way!"

"The boy is right!" Pader Willith's voice reached the captain with startling force, and Kestrel whirled to confront the
priest. Ignoring the captain's rage, the cleric continued
sternly: "In Baracan's name we must extend a hand to our
fellow men!"

"Baracan be damned!" snarled Kestrel, raising a fist, ready
to strike.

"Look!" cried one of the sailors, his tone shrill with shock and terror.

The chaos of the dust storm and smoke from numerous fires filled the sky, but through that murk another menace became visible. Wings spread wide, fanged jaws agape, a monstrous creature soared above the attacking army. With a thunderous bellow, the massive beast swooped low, roaring again, then rising with powerful strokes of its huge wings.

The monster was as large as the galyon, with jaws that looked capable of crushing the hull in one bite. The invading soldiers were insignificant nits compared to this awful presence. Gleaming black scales coated the awful body, though the tongue that flicked from the great jaws was blood red. Eyes like hot coals glared hatefully from the massive, ridged sockets atop the flat skull. Even at this distance, the crimson orbs bored into the ship.

Kestrel felt the numbness of his own horror even as he stumbled toward the wheel. The creature soared closer, winging ahead of the rank of black-garbed soldiers, and the captain shuddered at a sudden, horrific image: a moment in the near future, when his beautiful galyon lay splintered and sunk beside this waterfront of doom.

— 3 —

The great head lay still, as it had for many decades, unaware of the soundless summons ringing through the deep cavern, probing at the scaly form. No flicker of recognition marked the massive body; neither ridged eyebrow nor dagger-sized claw twitched, and the leathery lids lay still and dormant over deep-set eyes.

Yet the intangible summons was persistent, filtering into the mountainous cavern with steadily increasing force. The message did not travel by sound exactly; it rode upon waves of deep, elemental magic. Though it remained inaudible, the communication was, ultimately, a force that would not be denied.

Eventually the drackan snorted, an exhalation of stale air from inert lungs. Over the course of an hour, the serpent inhaled a replacement breath, and only then did the eyelids twitch, gradually drawing back from orbs grown cloudy with disuse.

Grunting softly, Jasaren roused himself from a hibernation of some seventy-six years. Vaguely aware of a pervasive, debilitating weakness, he turned, creakingly, toward the back of the lofty cave. The tiny spring still trickled from the wall, and the pool of cool Aura had refilled itself many times in the decades since the drackan had last been awake—draining the pool had been his last act prior to long hibernation.

A spoonlike tongue rasped forth, immersing to scoop the precious liquid. For long minutes Jasaren slurped at the pool, and as he did his scales grew brighter, the earthen-brown burnished to a brighter, coppery hue. The cloudiness melted from his eyes until they became slitted golden pupils staring keenly from indigo circlets.

This craving for Aura satisfied an acute need, though Jasaren reflected that it was not like the overwhelming desire that had obsessed him during his Time of Thirsting, eight centuries ago. At that time he had been a youngster, wings dormant inside his dorsal cocoon, and the compulsive need for fresh sources of Aura had driven him across the mountains for several years before his wings burst forth at the end. Now, the elder drackan would be content with this large, deep spring.

Finally, the pool drained, Aura drooling in streams from his crocodilian jaws, Jasaren turned toward the mouth of the cave. Something compelled him to leave, though he was not consciously aware of the subtle urge that had brought him from dormancy. Revitalized by Aura, he moved with the supple grace of his kind, striding on his legs with his scale-covered belly and tail raised slightly off the ground, mighty wings folded against his back.

At the mouth of the cavern the drackan paused, allowing his great heart to swell with the grandeur of the Bruxrange. Beyond Jasaren's mountain the stony, treeless chaos of ridges, peaks, and valleys spilled like a stormy sea frozen in mid-gale. When he stepped onto the ledge outside the confining walls, the brown drackan stretched his wings outward, unfolding them from his ridged backbone. Like mighty fans they grew, arcing on either side into semicircular sails framing the long, serpentine body.

Leaning outward, Jasaren felt the Aura-scented breeze against his snout, allowed it to brush back his black-bristled mane. Anticipating freedom and flight, he twisted his wings to catch the wind, then hurled himself from the lofty shelf. The sheltered lower vales of the range, where flocks of Aurasheep thrived, beckoned him with the promise of meat.

Yet, surprisingly, the drackan found himself banking through a wide half-circle, flapping his wings with a tremendous expenditure of energy, struggling to *gain* altitude. There would be no game along the rugged crest, nagged a small inner voice—nevertheless his bizarre decision did not distress him. Jasaren concentrated instead on powerful wing strokes, climbing through thin air, not questioning the direction of his flight.

Above him, etched like a barrier where the world met the sky, extended the line of the Watershed. For a moment the ancient drackan felt the lifelong antipathy, knew the urge to turn away from here. Beyond lay only the wasteland of Duloth-Trol, and though Jasaren had observed that bleak realm from soaring vantage, and he had never seen anything to make him want to go there, or even to look at it again. Yet now he strained upward with the determination to do just that.

In no place along the divides did the realms of the Watershed meet in such a precipitous, knife-edge crest as marked the border of Faerine and Duloth-Trol to the east of Darkenheight Pass. Cloud-piercing ridges and summits crowned cliffs that plunged straight down into each realm. On the Faerine side were the valleys and aeries of the brown drackans, mightiest mortal creatures in all the Watershed. Dozens of dens were scattered through these heights, inaccessible to land-bound creatures, lofty and impregnable on the shoulders and crests of great mountains.

Now Jasaren approached the loftiest ridge, a place where there were no lairs. The drackan climbed through wide circles, each spiral passing close beside the looming gray wall. Occasionally patches of frozen Aura clung to small cracks, or draped a ledge in fanglike icicles, but for the most part the massive cliff was a seamless, unclimbable span of vertical bedrock. Finally Jasaren reached the level of the ridgetop, and he swerved to the Watershed, seizing the stone crest with powerful forepaws. Supporting himself with that grip and

strokes of his mighty wings, Jasaren studied the dark slate
mountains of Duloth-Trol.

Cornices of black ice draped the far side of the ridge, and
many of the mountains beyond appeared mired in a substance
that lay like snow in the swales and shaded slopes, but had
the appearance of dark, sticky tar. The drackan still didn't
know why he had come here, but the compulsion moved him
farther. Straining, Jasaren extended his long neck, reaching
over the crest and inhaling the air of Duloth-Trol—air which,
except for a faintly acrid taint, was not very different from
the air of Faerine.

The attack came from below, and the drackan didn't see
his assailant until a bright red, snakelike head, jaws spread
wide, darted from beneath a tarry cornice. Twin fangs punctured the drackan's throat, and Jasaren felt hot slivers of pain
slice through his neck, into his mouth and head.

The drackan bellowed a shrill challenge and twisted downward to bite the insolent snake—but the attacker dodged
away. Jasaren's jaws clamped shut on air as he fought an
unnatural stiffness, a paralysis that delayed his reactions. He
felt searing fangs puncture his skin again, near the base of his
throat, and when he tried to whip his neck away it was as
though he dragged a frozen limb through thick, slushy snow.

Again and again that viper of bright red slashed forward,
stabbing the twin prongs between the drackan's scales. Jasaren at first struggled to fight back, then to break away and
flee, but his jaws merely gaped soundlessly, his neck taut and
unbending. A dozen times those wicked fangs drove home,
and ultimately the mighty Faerine was paralyzed, fully im-
mobile at the crest of the Watershed.

He could see, however—and he could fear. From one slitted pupil he watched a grotesque creature creep into view.
The thing's lower portion was a massive, barrel-shaped torso
with two blunt, clumsy-looking legs. Each of those limbs was
tipped with sharp, spiraling talons, and the hideous beast
drilled these claws into the stone of the mountainside. Only
after one foot was securely mounted did the thing extract the
other, reach upward, and painstakingly bore another foothold.
Two long, apelike arms allowed it to seize handholds with
supple fingers.

The drackan kept his eyes fixed upon that slow, deliberate

climb, staring at the thing's body in order to avoid the horrific visage of its upper portions. Snakes seethed there, a nest of serpents slithering and writhing, scaly tentacles of many colors—absolute black, and cobalt-blue, and the ruby-like red that had paralyzed Jasaren, another of emerald-green—but they had this in common: They all grew out of this monster's raw, oozing neck!

Snakes strained and flicked forward with palpable urgency as the beast reached a perch at the lip of the Watershed. Jasaren could only watch in mute horror as a broad-headed viper of shimmering silver darted forward, sinking sharp fangs into the flesh of the drackan's shoulder. Immediately Jasaren's paralysis vanished—but with it, too, passed his fury and his desire for vengeance. A sensation of tingling, scintillating pleasure flowed through his body, and all thoughts of earlier delights in his long and eventful life were immediately, permanently snuffed.

Again that silver head slid forward, slowly this time, tracing tenderly along the drackan's belly until once again the jaws gaped, the twin fangs sank into flesh. The ecstasy came once more, an even stronger wave of sensuality that threatened to dim Jasaren's mind, to carry him into blissful depths of unconsciousness. Abruptly that benign fulfillment passed, and the world seemed bleak, a colder place. The drackan twisted from Duloth-Trol to Faerine, and neither held any promise of relief.

There was only that silver snake.

"What is your wish, my master?" the mighty drackan inquired, lowering his head humbly before the grotesque being—a being who was, Jasaren now knew, the messenger from a very powerful god.

"You will serve me, Drackan of Brownsteel," replied Phalthak, the Fang of Dassadec. "You will go among your brown drackan kin, in the dens and caverns of Faerine, and you will awaken them and summon them to my service. The power of Darkblood shall fill your belly and theirs."

"I hear—and will obey."

"Too, you are to find the lairs of your rivals, the greens. You are to enter those caves, and slay them where they slumber."

"The green drackans will die as you command, Mighty

One. But the browns are stubborn—they will not obey willingly.''

"No, my pet—they will not. That is why I shall provide
you with a means of persuasion.''

Once more the silver snake stroked forward, and again the
gleaming fangs drove home.

— 4 —

Kestrel stared at the horrific image soaring out of the dust and
smoke. Like a great flying lizard, far more huge than the
galyon's namesake or any other flying creature of Dalethica,
the monster glided above the city. The serpent's skin was a
scaly shell of purest black, and the wicked mouth drooped
open to reveal hooked, sword-sized teeth.

The captain and the priest scrambled up the ladder to the
wheel deck, Darret scampering after. A ripple of terrible
power rushed through the air, borne not by sound or sight but
by some intangible, overarching source of terror. Screams
arose from those still on land, and from some of the men in
the rigging overhead.

"By Baracan and the Watershed—it can be none other than
a Lord Minion!" declared Willith. "Spawn of the Sleepstealer
himself.''

Wisps of cloud and smoke again obscured the massive
creature, but Kestrel sensed its steady, inevitable approach.
For the first time he noticed other fliers, smaller creatures—
though still greater than any bird. These were hard to see, for
their skin reflected a rippling camouflage that perfectly
matched the backdrop of sky, smoke, or cityscape. The lesser
fliers soared and weaved in the wake of the great black monster.

Kestrel heard Pader Willith's words, wanted to meet them
with scorn and mockery, but he couldn't. He beheld clear and
deadly proof that gods—or *one* god at least—really existed.

"Cut the lines—shove off!" Raising his captured sword,
the captain severed one of the heavy cables himself. Again
he looked toward the sky, sensing the ponderous motion of
the *Condor* as the wind puffed out her sails, tugging against
the lines still lashed to the dock.

The smoke cleared, wafted by the rising wind out of the desert, and still Kestrel tried to deny the proof before his eyes. The thing soaring toward them was so massive, so unimaginably terrifying, that it couldn't possibly be real. Surely it was no more than some trick of vapor and light, an intangible mist that would be dispersed by the next gust! But he saw wings as broad as the galyon's sails, and a sinuous body that, despite impossible size, certainly cloaked a solid, living being. The wings drove powerfully, carrying the serpentine body inexorably closer—and with each passing second the monstrous visage grew more real, more menacing. The smaller winged monsters dove, scouring the waterfront, seizing some victims in talons or beaks, knocking others into the water. The nimble fliers stayed over the land, striking viciously back and forth at the humans on the docks.

The awful wyrm shrieked a mind-numbing challenge, jaws gaping to reveal the jagged row of teeth. The beast dove into the mass of refugees with a shrill, timber-rattling cry. A hundred people or more perished in the moment of the monster's landing, crushed under its massive weight or rent by claws and teeth more savage than the cruelest man-made blade. A few lucky survivors hurled themselves into the water; others were bashed to the ground, broken when the beast flapped its wings. Kestrel saw the scaly black head swivel, and he was rooted to the deck when twin eyes, glowing like volcanic fires, fastened upon the stern of the great galyon. As waves of hysteria swept through the terrified mob, hundreds of people leapt from the dock, trying to swim to safety—or, perhaps, choosing drowning over the merciless weapons, jaws, and talons of the monstrous attackers.

"To the masts!" cried Kestrel. "Hang all the canvas you can!"

Sailors scrambled into the rigging, bounding upward like monkeys, hastening to free lines and drop the huge sails. "Garson—take the helm," the captain shouted, and the reliable pilot quickly ran up to the afterdeck to take the wheel.

"This may be the end of the world—the coming of eternal darkness," Pader Willith declared through clenched teeth. "At the very least it is the end of the life mankind has known for centuries!"

Kestrel stared at the phalanx of attackers, which had now

emerged from the avenue and spread through the dock, butchering everyone in its path. The captain was numbed by the ruthless efficiency of the advance. A dozen or more of the smaller fliers circled the great serpent as it squatted on the gory street, still regarding the galyon with those baleful eyes of ember-red. Then the monster took to the air again, wings thrusting as it rose over the waterfront and banked toward the *Condor*. Wind whipped through the city, surging against Kestrel's face, and he felt the timbers of the ship straining—as if they, too, yearned to free themselves from this dock, sensing the imminence of doom.

"Cut those lines!" Kestrel snarled to his crewmen. Caught up in panic at the approaching horror, only a few of the men moved to obey. Jaws gaping, the winged monster swooped toward the stern of the *Black Condor*. Kestrel felt the hilt of his sword as a useless weight, a pathetic thing to raise against the relentless attack.

"Baracan, God of Man—show us thy mercy, and thy might!"

Pader Willith's impassioned voice somehow broke through the haze of the captain's focus. Kestrel turned, startled to see that the young priest had somehow attained a demeanor of absolute serenity. Now Willith stared intently into Kestrel's eyes.

"There can only be a single explanation, and you must carry the word: The Nameless One comes again. His army is commanded by a Lord Minion and it has broken through the Watershed. All Dalethica is endangered. Tell the peoples of the Circled Sea, of Corsari and Carillonn. Warn them of the menace! Else the rest of the world will fall as quickly, as completely, as Farkeen!"

"But how—?" The captain's despairing question died in his throat as he saw that Willith's attention had shifted. The young priest faced the railing at the rear of the wheel deck. In his hand was the small book of parchment sheets—the *Scroll of Baracan*. Kestrel had never paid much attention to that leather-bound volume before, and now it seemed like nothing less than madness to face death with only a book as a weapon.

The monstrous wyrm swept closer, winging over the dock-side. The massive jaws gaped, and Kestrel gagged at the streaks of gore trailing from the mighty fangs. Willith brandished his tome as the monster dove. Kestrel blinked, suddenly wondering if he saw a haze of light around the young priest—but surely it was his imagination!

When it seemed that the beast must strike the stern of the galyon and crush the transom, Pader Willith hurled himself off the rail, straight into the gaping maw. The jaws snapped shut, engulfing the priest, blanking out the gleam of light that was *more* than Kestrel's imagination. The monster's flight carried it into the *Condor*, and the captain fell, struck by a splintered section of rail. Men screamed, thrown free from the rigging, and the rear mast creaked and groaned dangerously. Several lines snapped free from the dock, but the galyon remained lashed at the bow—even as her stern bobbed slowly into the harbor.

The flying wyrm swept past, struggling desperately to gain altitude as it banked around the harbor. Watching it swerve toward land, Kestrel, who had risen to his feet, got the sense that it actually feared the water. The jaws opened to reveal a torn and bloody form, but even when the monster rattled its head violently it couldn't dislodge the body of the young cleric.

"Go! Cut the lines!" cried Kestrel, slashing at more of the heavy ropes. He spun back toward the shore, expecting to see the ghastly creature returning for another pass. Instead the beast soared beyond a waterfront warehouse and settled to the ground. For another moment Kestrel watched, but he saw no sign that the monster intended to immediately return to the air.

"It's a miracle—a miracle of Baracan," he whispered hoarsely, knowing that the priest's courage had been the catalyst for whatever power held the Lord Minion at bay.

"Cut that line!" shouted one of the mates, starting toward the bowline.

"Captain—all de folks . . ." Darret tugged at his sleeve again, looking toward the dock.

Kestrel couldn't listen—he wanted only to escape! But the reality came, unbidden, to his mind that any person trapped in Farkeen was doomed by these merciless invaders.

A light *had* flared around Pader Willith as the priest faced death—as bravely as any man Kestrel had ever seen. Willith's sacrifice *must* mean more than the simple chance for the *Black Condor* to escape. The decision came to him with such force that had his cargo still been aboard, he would have dumped it.

"Drop the planks and let 'em aboard," Kestrel shouted. "As many as we can hold. Open the hatches on the holds, get them moving down. Quickly, now!"

Numbed though they were, his crewmen obeyed. The gangplanks slammed to the dock and terrified folk of all ages swarmed on board. Several sailors stood at the forward hatch, raising the heavy barrier and urging people down the rope ladders leading into the hold. Driven by panic, the refugees of Farkeen were nothing loath to seek shelter in the shadowy compartment.

Kestrel looked again—there was no sign of the Lord Minion. Apparently the stinging reaction of Pader Willith's final prayer had dissuaded the monster for a few precious minutes. More and more people poured onto the *Black Condor*, while the remaining fishing boats and dhows—all wallowing, heavily laden—waddled toward the gap in the breakwater. The galyon was the only craft still lashed to the dock, and Kestrel knew that she would soon bear the brunt of the attackers' attention.

Finally they cut away the lines, and the offshore wind snapped the sails. Garson steered toward the gap in the sea wall and the ship picked up speed with stately grace. Even so, the screams of doomed thousands chased them over the water. Kestrel knew that those cries would haunt his dreams for a long time.

Then the breakwater was behind them, and neither the flying serpent nor its winged minions showed any desire to pursue the galyon or the smaller vessels scattered across the surface of the bay. The wind held, and for more than an hour Kestrel kept watch in agonized silence. Numbly, he ordered his men to see to the refugees, while he kept his own eyes to the rear.

A long time later the site of Farkeen remained visible, marked by a billowing, steadily growing column of black smoke.

FIVE

The City of One Hundred Bridges

Evil is a starkly violent force, often working in
an eyeblink of time. The beauty of goodness,
like love, must grow over years, yet when it
flourishes the bloom can last for ages.
—SONGS OF AURIANTH

— 1 —

"Carillonn! It's *Carillonn*!" cried Anjell, hopping up and
down on the foredeck.

"It's more beautiful than I ever imagined," Rudy whispered, awestruck.

Raine's hand slipped into his. "I know what you mean—
it's as fabulous now as it was on my first visit. You never
get tired of the magnificence." She looked at Rudy with a
sly smile that made his blood race. "Hey, fella, maybe I can
show you some of the sights?"

"You're the *only* one who can show me the sights I'm
thinking about . . ." he murmured, squeezing her hand.

"That's digger work all right," Danri declared admiringly,
clumping over to the couple. "Look at the height of those
arches—and the narrowness of the spans!"

Rudy, chuckling, looked up—and was in fact startled by

the elegance of the stonework. The hilly island occupied most
of the riverbed, forcing the water into a narrow, rapid channel
to either side. A sheer wall of white marble ringed the shoreline, rising high above the water, no doubt concealing a good
portion of the city's wonders. Towers, parapets, and tall stone
buildings rose beyond that wall, dotting the verdant slopes of
the three hills rising from the island. Elegant manors, gracefully curving streets, numerous small, neat houses clustered
in pastoral harmony, even many of the lesser buildings, were
made from the characteristic marble.

Atop the highest hill was Castle Carillonn, the fortress of
which the bard had sung. An alabaster curtain wall, studded
with turrets and towers, surrounded the royal compound. The
tall keep encompassed many halls, wings, and towers, occu-
pying the upper slopes and crest of that steep-sided hill. Towers rose like a forest of white spires, a multitude of colored
banners trailing from the pinnacles. White bridges linked
many of the towers, some of the spans so narrow that they
looked more like cables than constructs of stone.

Despite Awnro's descriptions, Rudy was stunned by the
sweeping grandeur of the white marble spans. One of the
bridges emerged above the city wall, curved toward them,
then veered toward the eastern shore in a series of arches
supported by footings anchored in the riverbed. The ferry
passed under the lofty curl, and Rudy saw that this bridge was
much wider than he had earlier speculated.

The boat curved into a sheltered harbor behind a breakwater of, naturally, gleaming white marble. Wide dockyards
lined the waterfront, divided by huge warehouses of whitewashed timber. Wooden piers extended into the water, and
watercraft ranging from tiny punts to seagoing carracks and
caravels bobbed at anchor, or hugged the docks with lines at
bow and stern.

The city rose beyond the waterfront, sweeping steeply upward through a series of terraced plazas. Marble retaining
walls covered much of the hillside, reminding Rudy of the
icy glaciers draping the Glimmercrown. Though the city and
castle were considerably smaller than that great mountain,
they projected the same sense of lofty grandeur, proudly
boasting that nowhere else in all Dalethica might one see their
equal.

"Isn't it the most fabulous thing you've ever seen? D'you suppose Takian is here yet? And Bristyn?" asked Anjell, crossing excitedly to Rudy.

"Yes—and I don't know, and I don't know," he replied, wrapping a long arm around her shoulders. He pointed toward the quay, where several trumpeters had just raised their instruments to blow a long, rousing blast. "But it looks like *somebody* is expecting us!"

"Can that carriage be for *us*?" demanded Anjell, pointing to a six-wheeled conveyance rolling along the waterfront street, drawn by an equal number of prancing white horses. Drawing up before the dock, the driver hauled in the reins and the carriage came to a halt. A footman leaped from the rear and opened the door, allowing a tall figure in an imperial coat of silk to emerge. The man went to the boat landing and stood there, waiting attentively.

"Is that Takian?" Anjell squinted. "No, it's not. But I bet he's here somewhere!"

The *Loonsong* drew up to the quay, amid another flourish of trumpets, and dock workers pushed gangplanks to the sleek-hulled vessel. Most passengers debarked at the stern, but Rudy and his companions were shown to the forward gangplank. Captain Rorkok grinned, displaying his lonely teeth, as he clapped the departing companions, one by one, on the shoulders. "Now you be lookin' careful not to make them noble ladies jealous!" he teased Anjell, who didn't even stop to blush as she raced up the gangplank to gawk, wide-eyed, at the wonders of Carillonn.

A crowd gathered, boatmen and pedestrians drawn by the arrival of the impressive carriage. They stared curiously as Danri clumped up the gangplank, followed by the dignified, serene Quenidon Daringer. Rudy and Raine, arm in arm, paused long enough to thank the captain, then joined their companions on the dock. The Iceman was acutely conscious of the stares that greeted their arrival, and—for perhaps the second time in his life—found himself wishing that his wardrobe included more than the travel-stained cloak and trousers he wore.

"Standarl, it's splendid to see you again!" cried Awnro Lyrifell, striding up to the tall, regal-looking man who had emerged from the carriage.

"Awnro—I dared not believe it when I heard you'd be returning to the city!"

"Did you think I'd stay away forever?" The bard laughed, stepping aside to usher his companions forward. The man called Standarl turned to the travelers and cleared his throat formally.

"On behalf of High King Dyerston, welcome to Carillonn!" he proclaimed. Standarl bustled forward to pump Rudy's hand, then bowed to Danri and Quenidon. "And you must be Anjell—and Raine," he continued, bowing again.

"And this is my mother, Dara Appenfell," Anjell said politely.

"Warmest welcome to you all!" the imperial representative said heartily. "Allow me to present myself: Standarl Drade—His Majesty's Chief of Protocol. I'm here to extend King Dyerston's greetings, and to see that your needs for lodging and sustenance are met. Perhaps clothing, as well?"

Rudy flushed, feeling Standarl's last comment acutely. "Have King Takian and the duchess arrived in the city?" the Iceman asked, after introductions were concluded.

"Indeed—they send their greetings. Both are meeting with the council of lords as we speak, but they will see you later. You are all to be given quarters in the castle—but first I have an invitation: If you are not too fatigued by your journey, the king wonders if you would consent to an immediate audience."

The Chief of Protocol cleared his throat, looking directly at Rudy. "His Majesty made it clear that if you needed time to prepare, you were to have it; yet he is most anxious to speak with you, and the two Faerines as well. He was really quite stern—to me, of course—when he insisted that I take care of every detail regarding your needs."

"We'll meet him immediately, of course!" Rudy agreed, to the willing nods of his companions.

"I've taken the liberty of arranging a carriage—"

"To the palace?" Anjell asked excitedly.

Standarl Drade smiled benignly. "Soon to the palace, of course—that's where you'll be staying. But the king maintains an audience chamber beyond the walls of yon castle, and it is there he currently awaits your pleasure."

The footman held the door as the seven travelers and their

royal escort entered the closed carriage. The mighty horses lurched in their traces, easing the big conveyance forward. Soft springs cushioned the ride up the steeply climbing street.

Anjell twisted in her seat, pulling back the curtains to stare at the city. "I can't see enough!" she complained. "Can't I get out and walk?"

"You'll have plenty of time for sightseeing!" Dara snapped, pulling the girl back into her seat.

"Besides," noted Standarl Drade with an easy chuckle, "we're almost there."

— 2 —

At the top of the hill they passed through a gate and drew up in an enclosed courtyard, within a wall that circled the entire crest of the rounded summit. Despite that barrier, the ground domed high enough that the companions, emerging from the carriage, could see over the wall to much of the city beyond. Rudy would have marveled at a new and spectacular view of Castle Carillonn, which occupied the neighboring height, had he been able to think of anything other than the upcoming meeting. Instead, he barely noticed the small, walled garden around them, or the paving-stones leading to the door in the base of a white marble tower. The spire occupied the crest of the hill, extending very far into the sky overhead. Emerging from the side of the tower high above, a narrow strand of bridge soared like the arc of a rainbow to meet one of the castle's towers perhaps a half mile away. Despite the length of the viaduct, it was supported by less than a dozen footings—including several standing in the valley between the two hills that were many hundreds of feet tall.

Danri could not let the surrounding workmanship pass unremarked. "Like the bridges, this tower was made by diggers, too—or I'll drop my hammer in the river. Look at the way those stones meet—not a crack you could stick a pin into!"

Rudy forced himself to listen, amazed at the grandeur of the lofty spire. Though the hilltop at his feet was lower than the castle's ground elevation, the Iceman guessed that the top of this tower was higher than any other place in the city.

The door opened and a royal attendant, attired in a red coat with a high collar, emerged.

"Ah—here is Pillotte, His Majesty's majordomo," Standarl said. "He shall see you to the king, while I prepare for your arrival in the castle."

Pillotte, a tall, slender man dressed in a bright crimson coat of the shiniest silk Rudy had ever seen, nodded with polite restraint. "His Majesty will see you immediately. Will you please come with me?"

Rudy was surprised when Pillotte led them into a small room in the base of the tower, the only obvious door being the one through which they had entered. There was no furniture, and the tiny chamber had barely enough room for the eight occupants to stand without rubbing elbows. Pulling a chain that dangled from the ceiling, the king's man rang a bell.

"Perhaps you'll wish to hold on?" he suggested, indicating a railing that ran around the inside wall of the chamber.

Mystified, Rudy placed a hand on the rail—and was grateful that he had when the floor lurched under his feet. Anjell squealed delightedly while the Iceman looked around in alarm.

"We're moving!" he gasped, then flushed with embarrassment as he saw Danri regarding him with amused, sparkling eyes.

"This lift is digger-made too, I'll wager," the bearded Faerine declared with a chuckle. "You signal the counterweights with the bell—somewhere nearby another cage is going down, right?"

"Correct, sir," the major-domo replied. "The High King maintains a staff of climbers who ascend the tower stairs and stand ready to ballast the lift, in order to bring his guests—and, occasionally, himself—more quickly to the top."

Nodding, trying to ignore the unsettling sensation of movement, Rudy realized that they went up very quickly. Picturing the operation of the lift, the Iceman found the notion quite ingenious—and he almost stumbled to his knees as the cage abruptly clattered to a halt.

They stepped from the compartment into a small antechamber, tastefully warmed by a rug of intricately woven threads of red and orange. Pillotte crossed to a large wooden door in

the far wall. As the majordomo knocked once and pushed the
barrier open, Raine pointed out the carved blossoms of inlaid
rosewood on the dark oaken panels. Rudy, still distracted,
barely noticed the remarkably detailed woodwork.

"Your guests, sire. They reached the docks not half an hour
ago." Pillotte stepped into the room, then ushered the companions through the doorway.

"Splendid!" came a hearty voice. The travelers entered a
room that was lit so brightly, Rudy had to suppress the feeling
they had stepped outside.

The Iceman, who had been picturing an elderly and bewhiskered monarch, was surprised as High King Kelwyn
Dyerston stepped from behind a cluttered table and advanced
toward the companions. The monarch's face was unlined and
cleanshaven, split by a smile of endearing warmth and accented by stone-gray eyes that sparkled like silver behind the
twin circles of steel-framed spectacles. His hair was full and
gray, cropped short, and his stride was strong and purposeful.
The companions knelt, but he quickly bade them rise, greeting
them with a surprising lack of formality. He warmly clasped
the hands of Rudy, Danri, and Quenidon in a sure, firm grip,
then turned to Raine.

"Raine, dear—welcome back to Carillonn. It has been an
emptier place since your departure to Shalloth."

"Thank you, sire," Raine replied, and Rudy was surprised
to see—for the first time ever—a flush of red creep up her
cheeks.

"And to you, bold ambassadors," the king declared to
Danri and Quenidon. "There will be few who understand the
depths of your commitment—all I can say is that I, myself,
am eternally grateful.

"And Awnro Lyrifell. I've already placed extra guards
around the wine cellar, so you, too, are welcome." The monarch laughed at his own joke, and when the companions
joined in, no one's hilarity was louder than the elderly minstrel's. The king's tone gradually became more serious as he
continued. "And to you all: I'm grateful that you could come
so quickly. Refreshments, Pillotte?"

"Of course, sire," the major-domo murmured.

"Your Majesty?" Anjell stepped forward and curtsied politely. "We've brought you a gift, sire, if you will. It's, well—

here it is.'' She extended a silver flask, which the monarch took with a grateful nod. He tilted the flask to the sound of sloshing liquid.

''It's Aura,'' the girl said helpfully.

''This is indeed a rare treasure, my child. Thanks very much—thanks to you all.'' King Dyerston was moved by the gift, and emotion thickened his voice. Slowly, reverently, he removed the cork from the flask and raised the neck to his nostrils. Inhaling slowly, he nodded as if in confirmation. ''No scent to speak of, but it has a presence just the same.''

''It has beneficent effects on anyone who drinks of it, Your Majesty,'' Rudy said. ''A drink can make aches, wounds, even illness, vanish.''

The king raised the flask to his lips and sipped. When he recapped the container and set it on the table, his eyes sparkled in a way that Rudy found strangely compelling.

''Now, please, won't you all take seats,'' urged King Dyerston, indicating several large, cushiony ottomans. The lone chair stood beside the table, but when the monarch sank onto one of the plush hassocks the guests followed suit. Rudy relaxed into the soft cushion and took a moment to look around the tower-top chamber.

The sensation of airiness remained, though not because they were out of doors. It seemed so, however, because the room was surrounded by lofty, arched windows—in fact, more of the wall area was covered by glass than by stonework. Several of these panes were actually tall, latticed doors, and Rudy saw that the outside of the tower was circled by a narrow balcony. The chamber occupied half the floor space of the tower, with the rest given to the anteroom and, presumably, the shafts for the two lifts.

Seen through the windows, the other hills of Carillonn rose in stately majesty. Tall trees—oaks, elms, maples, ironwoods—thrived throughout the city, shading many of the homes, forming verdant arches over the smooth, clean streets. Horses, chariots, and pedestrians all bustled about, though at an orderly pace that seemed unusually harmonious.

Within Kelwyn's chamber Rudy was surprised to see very little furniture. The lone table was huge, covered with a haphazard mass of loose papers and heavy tomes. Some of the books were opened, and others had pages marked with distinctive ribbons. On one corner of the table no less than a dozen books were stacked, leaning erratically this way and that. One nudge, the Iceman suspected, would bring them all crashing down.

He also noticed small tables beside the hassocks; these found use when Pillotte returned with bottles of warm beer and a pitcher of fruit juice, serving each of the companions and the king. Only when the major-domo quietly withdrew, closing the door behind him, did Kelwyn Dyerston break the silence.

"I count it a singular privilege to have the honor of making your acquaintance," the king resumed, speaking to the Faerines. "Communication between our peoples has been all too rare during the last centuries."

"The Watershed makes a pretty good border," Danri allowed. "Though there seems to have come the need for passing it, now."

"Never did I imagine I would find myself in the heart of Dalethica," Quenidon put in. "Though I admit that your city impresses favorably, even when compared to the crystalline beauty of Spendorial."

"High praise indeed," Kelwyn replied, his eyes twinkling. "Though no doubt you've observed that we have Faerines— diggers, most notably—to thank for many of our beauties."

"I *did* notice that, yes." Danri chuckled. "These bridges are a wonder such as the world has never seen."

"They have been a symbol, too, of the peace and spirit of cooperation that once existed between our peoples. Let us hope that it can be so, again."

"That's why we came all this way," Danri said. "To try and talk to some of these kings and such, so they see how dangerous the situation is likely to be."

"Good! I have known Takian of Galtigor for many years, and he has told me much of your experiences."

"Will the other kings listen?" Rudy remembered Awnro Lyrifell's warnings.

"That remains to be seen—and is one reason I wanted to speak to you before my fellow monarchs surprise you with recalcitrance, or send you stomping back to Faerine in disgust."

"I daresay that is unlikely," Quenidon noted, raising his eyebrows skeptically.

"I hope so—and we'll know soon enough. But as our time is short, let us take the discussion in a different direction."

"How did you know we were coming?" Rudy asked. "And why did *you* think it was important to talk to us?"

"The Duchess of Shalloth makes a strong and vocal champion," Kelwyn declared dryly. "I, for one, am inclined to believe some of the stories that others have greeted with frank skepticism."

"Such as . . . ?" Danri left the question uncompleted as he took a long drink of his beer.

"It is said that you created an Auracloud and carried your companions to safety through the air." Kelwyn met Rudy's gaze frankly, and once again those gray eyes sparkled with intelligence and understanding.

"I did—I used a small amount of Aura, and a great fire to make a cloudship that carried us from certain death."

"*I* was one of those companions," Danri acknowledged. "Aye-uh, the lad saved our lives without a doubt."

"Do you know that this is something no human in the history of the Watershed has ever been able to do?" The spark still flickered in the king's eye, but now it was harder, a hot, inquisitive probe trying to burn through to an explanation.

"I guess—that is, I hadn't thought about it in that way. I believe you're right," Rudy acknowledged.

"I am. And that is a thing of paramount importance—greater than whether the minions of Duloth-Trol attack this summer, or the next; or whether the onslaught should come from Zanthilat, or Halverica, or Faerine. Do you understand?"

"*Why*?" Rudy wondered momentarily if the High King was delusional, for his words made no sense.

"Have you heard of the Artifacts?" the king asked, with seeming irrelevance.

"I told my friends of that legend," Raine said. "Of the six mighty tools bestowed by the gods."

"Made at the dawn of the Watershed, to counteract the threat of the Great Betrayal," the king noted approvingly. "They gave mankind and Faerine some hope of standing against the Lord Minions—and yet, they were not enough to win the war.''

''What does that have to do with the lad—or with anything?'' demanded Danri.

Kelwyn continued as if he hadn't heard the digger. ''It was the *Guardians* who held the Watershed, insured that the realms would remain divided. Going back to the dawn of time, *they* were the force to remain unaffected by any of the waters.''

''Didn't the Guardians even kill some Lord Minions?'' Rudy asked.

''Yes, during the Sleepstealer War. That is a more 'recent' conflict than the War of Betrayal—but still it was waged a thousand years ago. I should be grateful that you, at least, know of it. Most of mankind has apparently forgotten.''

''I had the story from Awnro,'' Rudy replied softly. He remembered, vividly, the dark pantomime of warfare, enacted during his first visit to the North Shore Wayfarer's Lodge. That performance, too, had brought him together with Raine, face to face in the first hint of the destiny he still sought.

''During the Sleepstealer War, the Guardians slew a pair of the Nameless One's Lord Minions—Balzarac and Karthakan. Yet many Guardians perished in that strife, as well. And like the Lord Minions, the Guardians are a set and finite number—they do not procreate.'' Kelwyn paused, regarding the companions with eyes that glittered far more silvery than before—at least, to Rudy's newly speculative gaze. The king took a slow sip of beer, and it seemed to the Iceman that the words of their conversation settled around them like snowflakes, clearing the air for more speech.

''You, my young friend, are in a sense like the Guardians. You are of Three Waters, and it may be that you will provide the hope for some kind of victory against the Sleepstealer. And you have come to the world now, of all times.''

''But—how can I make a difference?'' demanded Rudy. ''True—certain things have happened to me. Aura gives me understanding, the ability to see things . . . and I have used it as you described, to create an Auracloud. In the presence of Aura I can see through darkness, like any Faerine. Yet I fail to understand how any of this can be seen as offering some kind of hope to save the world!''

"Of course not—though I admit, I should like to witness that business with the Auracloud, someday. As to the *how* of your question, I am sure I don't know. That knowledge will have to come to you from elsewhere. All I hoped to do was get the matter churning in your brain."

"If there's a clear purpose for my skills, I will seek it— but we have to look at other ways to combat the Sleepstealer as well. Don't you agree?"

"Naturally. There are those—King Takian and Duchess Bristyn, to name a pair—who are working actively to gather armies, to train troops and horses for battles that, whenever they occur, will come too soon."

"I'm intrigued by the legends of the Artifacts—were they all destroyed at the time of the Betrayal?" asked Danri.

"That is a very good question. It is known that the Spear and the Helm were consumed in battle, and the Cape was reputed to be cast away at sea. Of the Sword and the Shield, little has been written—save that they were used in Faerine, at the battles around Darkenheight. If they were not destroyed, it seems likely that they are irretrievably lost."

"So we have no real hope there," Rudy suggested.

The king nodded curtly, then frowned. "Do you know, too, that there are other legends about the Lord Minions, tales of heroes who have faced them. Surely you've heard the ancient rhyme:

> *Hush for the night flier,*
> *From the darken south,*
> *Three things may force him to stay:*
> *Mirror to trick him,*
> *Garlic to ward him, And*
> *Aura to hold him at bay.*

"I think I'd want, at the very least, my hammer," Danri said dryly. "Though I can see where Aura might be of some use, too."

"Ah, well—work with the tools you have, I always say," King Dyerston said with an easy laugh.

Rudy barely listened. He wondered about the king's earlier words, and about the power that might lie, untapped, within himself. Yet how could he discover the truth—or falsehood—

of that speculation? Suddenly the Iceman realized that the High King was speaking directly to him.

"Whatever happens in the next days, keep seeking, searching. You may have to leave much of your old life behind, but I urge you not to rest, not to abandon the trail, until you gain the knowledge you need."

"But *where*? *How*?"

"Seek, always seek," King Dyerston said, unhelpfully. "And now, my friends, you will no doubt desire to go to your quarters in the castle. You have had a long journey, and will certainly wish to speak with your friends. I know that young King Takian and his lady duchess have been anxiously awaiting your arrival."

"They've been meeting with the other rulers, haven't they?" Danri noted as the travelers and their host got to their feet. "Surely they've managed to convey a sense of urgency?"

The High King shook his head sadly. "Alas, the monarchs of the west suspect a trap to turn their attentions away from us. Jamiesen Macconal fears that the union of Carillonn and Galtigor bodes trouble for Corsari, and he is loath to shift his armies west."

"But that's ridiculous!" Dara declared, startling even herself with the outburst. Having the king's attention, she forged ahead. "I thought Bristyn and Takian's marriage was supposed to end a war that's lasted for fifty years. Why in all the Watershed would they want to start another one?"

"A ruler must examine every act for its effects upon his own realm," the king declared. "Sometimes those concerns can blind even a good monarch to necessities beyond his borders. I myself have issued orders to my warriors, the Hundred Knights. They patrol the distant reaches of my kingdom—to the west. At the earliest sign of trouble they will rally here, together with as many of my subjects who will bear arms.

"But more urgently, tomorrow some of you will have a chance to speak to the Kings of Corsari, Myntar Kosh, and Zanthilat. If that is acceptable, Takian will no doubt provide you with the time and place."

The companions readily agreed to an audience for the following day. "We'll change their minds, if we have to knock their skulls together to do it!" Danri growled, his hand touching the head of the hammer that never left his side.

"I trust you're speaking figuratively," the king said with an easy laugh. He clasped Danri on the shoulder, then indicated the view across the valley to Castle Carillonn. The high bridge that they had seen before commenced slightly below the level of this room, curving toward the alabaster walls of the palace.

"That's the Highbridge," Kelwyn explained. "The loftiest, and to my mind most elegant, span, of all the One Hundred Bridges. If you would like, you can take it to the castle."

"I would," the digger replied without hesitation, and Rudy agreed wholeheartedly. The turrets seemed so close he could practically touch them from where he stood, and he believed that—once within those encircling walls—the companions' message must be received by the western kings with more attention than Kelwyn had predicted.

"I bid you farewell, and good luck," said the monarch as he accompanied them down a flight of stairs and led them to the balcony from which the bridge embarked into space. "I am afraid you'll need it."

Dara and Anjell, with Awnro, started across the span. Rudy and Raine followed, while the two Faerines lingered for final words.

"It has been interesting to share your observations regarding your people. But are you always this much of a pessimist?" inquired Quenidon, cocking an eyebrow curiously.

"Realist, my friend—a realist. It's just that I know my fellow rulers very, very well," the spry, bespectacled king replied.

The bridge surface was solid as bedrock underfoot, though the wind whipped the companions' garments to the side. Still, it was with a sensation almost like flying that they started along the lofty span, seeing all the city and the aquamarine waters of the River Ariak encircling them below. The only disquiet came from a snatch of wind that carried Kelwyn's final words, murmured in a voice that should have been inaudible at this distance.

"Sometimes, I fear . . . I know them *too* well."

— 3 —

Prince—*King* Takian, Rudy reminded himself—came forward with his arms outstretched. His handsome face, framed
by a straw-colored beard, was split by a smile so warm that
the Iceman's troubles melted at the sight of it. The golden
crown on Takian's head rested amid a lush tangle of sandy
hair.

"My friends! Welcome to Carillonn—our wedding would
have been an empty formality without your presence here!"

Accompanying the young monarch was Bristyn Duftrall,
elegant in a blue gown and matching slippers, with a tiara of
gem-studded silver crowning her magnificently coiffed tresses
of gold. Remembering the mud-splattered woman who had
slogged through the heart of Galtigor with them, hiding in
waterlogged ditches and camping under the stars, the Iceman
found the transition utterly astounding. Her beauty, indeed,
was a thing that could take a man's breath away.

"Raine!" cried the duchess, embracing her former serving-
maid with fervor. The two women clung to each other for
several moments, while Takian clapped Rudy, Awnro, and
the Faerines on their shoulders, hugged Anjell, and was introduced to Dara.

The royal couple had found the companions in their opulent
chambers of Castle Carillonn—which the chief of Protocol
had provided immediately upon the conclusion of the royal
audience. They had a large sitting room, an area for dining,
and a number of luxuriously furnished bedchambers.

"We've arranged for a meeting with the other kings tomorrow morning—a private audience, immediately after
breakfast," Takian told them. "Quenidon and Danri, of
course, should be there—and Rudy as well." He looked in-
quiringly at Awnro and Raine.

"I suggest the kings hear from the three you named," the
bard said. "I fear that the rest of us would only serve to
confuse the issue—and, too, no monarch likes to have a great
many people giving him advice."

"Wise words," Raine agreed. "We'll pray for your success, and wait for you here."

For hours the reunited friends shared the tales of their travels and reminisced about their adventurous trek to Taywick Pass. Bristyn had journeyed to Carillonn overland via her own duchy, subsequently spending more than a week in the city making wedding preparations. The ceremony was now slated for a little more than a fortnight hence, the duchess informed them breathlessly.

Takian had arrived in Carillonn just a few days ago, accompanied by a company of his personal guards. "I formed the Golden Lion Regiment," he told Rudy, "and recruited the best men in Landrun. Their leader, Captain Jaymes, is a fellow I've known all my life."

"Did you put Kalland on the banner?" Anjell asked.

"Here it is!" The king removed a silken kerchief and, to murmurs and whistles of delight, proudly showed them the regal lionhead, emblazoned in golden thread over a shield of blue. "It flies over Castle Landrun, and from the mast of the *Searunner* as well." Takian went on to assure Rudy the many casks of Aura gathered at the border of Faerine had also accompanied them, and remained safely stored aboard the king's carrack at the city's waterfront.

Evening became night, and would have gently merged into dawn without an interruption in the reunion—save that the companions were acutely conscious of the importance of the next day's early meeting. With reluctance, they bade each other good night and parted for the evening.

Later, Rudy lay beside Raine in the bedchamber that Standarl, without any word, had given them to share. The Iceman's body was relaxed, sated, but a flurry of thoughts raced around his mind, preventing sleep. Finally he verbalized his agitation.

"What I least understand—even if the High King spoke the truth—is *how* I can learn any more about this . . . *thing* that's happened to me! It never occurred before, so how can anyone know anything about it?"

Raine was silent for so long that he wondered if she was asleep. Finally she rolled to her side, curling in the warmth of his long arm.

"There's a man I know—knew, once. He was my . . .

teacher, I suppose, though he was more than that. I think he's the wisest person I've ever met—and he gave me the first of the prophecies that seemed destined to rule my life. We could seek him, ask his advice.''

"Who is he—and where could we find him?"

"His name is Pheathersqyll, and he is the master at the Academy of the Sun, in Myntar Kosh.''

"Maybe we should go there,'' Rudy agreed. He kissed Raine slowly, grateful in the knowledge that wherever he went she would be there too. And when he thought of the man who had raised her, who had helped to prepare her for her destiny, he realized that he very much wanted to make Pheathersqyll's acquaintance.

His arm curled around Raine, cupping her breast, and she moved closer, molding her small form perfectly into the curve of his lanky body. A sense of drowsy content settled around the Iceman, drawing a blanket of darkness across his concerns. Finally he fell asleep, dreaming about a dusty, endless road. It seemed that he was lost, and no one could tell him how to find his destination. He sought Myntar Kosh, he thought momentarily, but he knew that he really journeyed toward someplace else—someplace much farther away.

But he was content because Raine was there, too.

SIX

A Council of Kings

There are but three truly impenetrable objects:
the black granite at the heart of the Watershed;
a shield of digger-forged steel; and the mind of
someone who doesn't want to hear what he's
being told.
—DIGGERSPEAK PROVERB

— 1 —

Nicodareus emerged from torpor slowly, shaking his head, groggily lifting himself from the mud to rest on hands and knees. Gradually he rose, dragging himself with talons raking through the armored bark of a stout ironwood trunk. Baring his fangs, the Lord Minion snarled soundlessly at the sky.

His vision cleared and he estimated from the advance of the stars that perhaps two hours had passed since his feasting on the shepherd. Soon, equilibrium and vitality restored, he stalked imperiously through the forest, cloaked in his magnificent body. Nicodareus once again focused on his mission and his victim, relishing the stillness of the woodland floor, the small animals quivering in terror nearby, helpless in the glare of Sight. He could have killed dozens or hundreds of these pathetic creatures, but he was uninterested in wasting time on mundane prey.

In the post-midnight hours he paced like a woodland predator, following the course of the valley. Before dawn, urgency drove him once again to the skies. Though his Sight allowed him to navigate easily, regardless of light or darkness, he chose to fly in the body of an owl, feeling the silent hunter a natural choice for this time and place.

Nicodareus knew that he had entered Dalethica in a relatively uninhabited region of mountains and foothills. The realm of Myntar Kosh lay to the north and west, while Carillonn, the heart of mankind's realms, stood off to the east.

As sunrise colored the horizon he came to rest high in the branches of a tall tree, allowing his omnipotent vision to roam across the realms of man. He growled in momentary frustration, remembering previous experiences in which he had learned that Sight could not locate the Man of Three Waters. The touch of Aura masked the Iceman's presence, as it did all things of Faerine, from the vision of the Lord Minion. Still, Nicodareus could see much, and from this treetop vantage he scanned the realms of Dalethica, seeking the place where he should begin his search.

Soon his potent vision fell upon a multitude of alabaster bridges, and the Lord Minion recognized the island capital of Carillonn. Nicodareus remembered the city, for he had been instrumental in its sacking ten centuries earlier. Now the soaring bridges and lofty spires mocked the blood-drenched success of that long-ago campaign, but the Eye of Dassadec took grim pleasure in the expectation that these stoneworks would tumble into ruins sometime in the very near future. Observing the lords gathered in the hilltop castle, Nicodareus saw the tension on their faces, perceived voices raised in acrimonious debate. Beyond all these behaviors, seeing deep into mortal souls, he sensed the overriding *fear*: In Carillonn, the humans who held power were afraid.

This was interesting news to the Lord Minion, for it suggested that the Sleepstealer's plans were, if not known, at least suspected. Carillonn was the greatest seat of power in Dalethica, and would be central to any resistance against Dassadec's minions. Since the Sleepstealer believed the Iceman to be a key component of the enemy's defenses, it seemed likely that the Man of Three Waters would go to the marbled city.

Wrapped now in the body of a falcon, the Eye of Dassadec made Carillonn his destination. For five days he flew across the realms of Dalethica, and each night around dusk he settled to the ground. Assuming his true form, he waylaid humans where he found them: a family at a remote farmstead; travelers staying at a small inn; or, as on his first feeding, herdsmen huddled at a remote campfire. If possible he killed every person in the area of the attack. Sometimes five, ten, or more died simply for the pleasure of the Lord Minion's bloodletting—that, and his desire to leave no witnesses who could describe his attack.

But sometimes he couldn't wait—the hot blood running over his fangs and slicking his talons drove him to a feeding madness, leaving one or two human survivors to flee in terror. Always after he nourished himself the Lord Minion sank into the daily agony of his punishment, until torpor again soothed his pain and restored the Darkslayer's strength.

Twice during his journey he was delayed by rain. The first drops of water hissed into his skin with scalding force, and each time he took shelter in a barn until the showers passed; on both occasions he was able to fly again within an hour or two. Ultimately he soared onward, crossing many miles with each day's flight, or racing along forest trails and over grassy steppeland on tireless feet. Always, by wing or hoof or paw, he drew closer to marbled Carillonn.

— 2 —

Rudy awakened early, acutely conscious of Raine's warm body, her measured breathing, beside him. Rising gently, dressing without making a sound, he left the sleeping chamber, anticipating the imminent meeting with the kings. Still, when he found that a breakfast of fresh fruit, bread, and sweet rolls had been brought to the apartments, he allowed the food to distract him. No sounds emerged from behind the doors of the other sleeping rooms, so Rudy deduced that his companions still slumbered. Taking an apple and a roll, the Iceman strolled into the early morning sun, appreciating the view from the wide flagstone balcony extending from their rooms.

Loons dove into the aquamarine waters of the River Ariak.

Rudy was impressed by the length of time the birds remained underwater—and amazed to see them pop back to the surface, far from where they had disappeared. Swans glided past, riding the current with serene dignity, and it was easy to imagine those regal birds sniffing down their beaks at the antics of the loons.

Raine, barefoot and wrapped in a bright smock, came to stand beside him, and for a time they shared the tranquil morning in silence. Standing well above the nearest courtyard, they looked upon a succession of lower enclosures, each buried like a well among the castle's many high ramparts. Even within the crenelated battlements trees thrived, and numerous fountains and pools reflected the morning's growing brightness with cheerful gaiety. Holding Raine close to his side, Rudy saw with perfect clarity how incomplete his life had been before.

"My lord, where would you like these—oh, excuse me," stammered a female voice behind them.

"Oh, hello—and I'm no lord!" Rudy turned, smiling at a serving-maid who brought several bouquets of flowers into the chambers. He recognized her as the same woman who had first welcomed them to the castle. "What's your name?" he asked, as she arranged the blossoms in a pair of vases.

"Nellidyn, my lord—and lady," replied the young woman with a deep curtsy. "I've been assigned your chambers for the length of your stay. If there's anything that you need . . ."

"We'll be sure to ask. And thank you," the Iceman replied.

"Hi, Nelli!" Anjell said brightly, emerging from her own bedroom. "You met my Uncle Rudy? And Raine?"

"Yes, my lady," replied the maid with a quick dip—and a playful wink at the girl, before hurrying from the chambers.

Soon Danri and Quenidon came out of their rooms, and Dara joined them in the pleasant morning air. Awnro Lyrifell was the last to awaken, but he emerged with his long hair neatly groomed, the pointed beard waxed into an elegantly upcurved tip. The bard barely had time to wish the trio of messengers "good luck" before the Chief of Protocol knocked at their chamber door.

"If you will be good enough to accompany me, the kings are preparing for the audience." Standarl Drade bowed low as Rudy and the two Faerines crossed to the door.

"Good luck, Rudy," Dara whispered, her hands tightly clutching Anjell's shoulders. The girl, for once, remained silent, looking up at her uncle with somber comprehension of the council's significance. The Iceman squeezed her arm, reassuringly he hoped, and hastened after the others.

They passed through a maze of castle corridors, up a grand staircase, along a balcony extending above a formal garden, then down a winding stairway and through several wide, tapestry-adorned halls. Intricate marble statues of a variety of human figures—men and women, warriors and babes— glowed almost magically in the morning light; many windows of stained glass filtered the golden rays into every color.

Finally they entered a surprisingly cozy chamber. Breakfast dishes had been cleared away, though the smell of bacon lingered, and four men, including Takian and King Dyerston, sat at a massive table; a fifth place remained vacant. A fire crackled above a massive hearth, and the room was quite warm.

The High King rose from the head of the table and, without formality, beckoned the companions forward. "My fellow sovereigns, like myself, enjoy the occasional opportunity to talk without the trappings of office." He presented the companions to the two men Rudy hadn't met. "King Jamiesen Macconal, monarch of Corsari, has journeyed by carrack across the Circled Sea and up the Ariak to Carillonn."

Macconal was a hawk-faced man with the swarthy, weather-beaten skin of one who has spent much of his life outdoors. He regarded the travelers impassively, his dark eyes hooded beneath heavy gray brows.

"And His Majesty Garand Amelius, the Sun Lord of Myntar Kosh!"

This portly fellow smiled pleasantly, nodding as the companions bowed. Garand Amelius was an old man, hearty of girth, with plump cheeks and puffy fingers suggesting a tendency to overindulge. His thin beard could not conceal ripples of fat beneath his chin, nor the pasty nature of his complexion. Still, his benign expression seemed far more welcoming than Jamiesen Macconal's impassive stare.

"Lord Halltha of Zanthilat, alas, will not be joining us." King Dyerston indicated the vacant place at the table. "He started for his realm last night in response to some distressing economic news."

Rudy knew that Zanthilat lay close beside the Dry Basin, and he wanted to ask about that bad news—but before he could form the words Macconal of Corsari began to talk.

"My fellow monarchs of Carillonn and Galtigor suggest that I should prepare my armies for an attack from the west," King Macconal said bluntly. "Can you offer proof that this is not merely a ruse to weaken my eastern borders?"

"I cannot," Quenidon Daringer replied with equal forthrightness. "Except insofar as my own knowledge as a warrior suggests: If I am about to attack a foe, I would not cause him to take up arms, even if I could deceive him into suspecting a strike from the opposite direction. Would it not be better to attack an enemy who is lulled by peace rather than one who is alert and ready for war, however misguided as to its source?"

Jamiesen Macconal chuckled, his fierce visage softening with genuine amusement. "You argue well, sylve! But tell me: What is there to fear from Duloth-Trol? The Sleepstealer was defeated for all time a thousand years ago. Fifty generations of mankind have come and gone since—how can you expect us to disperse treasuries and armies, to panic our people because of your words?"

Now Rudy spoke, describing the breach in the Watershed that the minions had excavated in Halverica, destroying the village of Dermaat and polluting the upper reaches of a pristine brook. "Only after Danri tapped a spring of Aura, allowing it to also flow into Dermaat Creek, was the pollution abated from there downstream. The breach still exists—and it could be the site of attack against Dalethica."

"And have a care not to forget the first Sleepstealer War," King Dyerston added. "The minions came from the Dry Basin, moving so swiftly that a place might be conquered before men in the neighboring realm even heard of the attack. Though it was a thousand years ago, it is not a memory that should be lightly discarded."

"These are ancient and tragic legends, stories that were old when I was born," the Sun Lord demurred softly. "I have lived for eight decades, and throughout those years I have striven always to expand peace. I am reluctant, now, to consider the prospect that it has all been in vain. No, my earnest young messengers, this is not a sense of alarm that I can share. Even a breach, as you describe, cannot be taken as proof of an imminent invasion."

"My own brother was taken by the Nameless One!" Takian declared passionately. "We *saw* the Lord Minion Nicodareus join him at Taywick Pass—what more proof do you need?

"That was a Faerine matter," the Sun Lord declared with maddening lack of emotion.

"It was *war*—between the realms of the Watershed!" Rudy railed against the monarchs' refusal to act. "It was a campaign ordered by the Sleepstealer, to distract us from an invasion that could be imminent! What other purpose could move him to such a bloody diversion? And when the attack comes, it will be lightning fast—for all we know, it could have begun already!" Abruptly the Iceman remembered his earlier fear. "What are the rumors, the distressing economic news from Zanthilat?"

"A simple matter of a missing supply caravan, bearing treaty payments owed to myself," the Sun Lord declared dismissively. "It was probably taken by bandits. I daresay a shipment of perfume and spices would be of precious little use to the Sleepstealer!"

"When the minions came the first time, they destroyed everything," Rudy pressed. "Spice and gold, people and lands—whatever stood in their path was doomed!"

"Yet in the end, the Sleepstealer's defeat was assured!" Garand Amelius rebutted illogically.

"That recent Faerine war was a defeat for Galtigor, I am told," Jamiesen Macconal noted, speaking to Takian bluntly. "Your army was weakened in that campaign, which makes it all the more necessary for you to divert other potential enemies."

"You are not my enemies!" the King of Galtigor declared, though the anger in his tone came near to denying the words. "We're trying to warn you, to take steps that will help us all! I'm doing what I can alone—I've formed a new regiment under my own banner, and sent a detachment of my army to Halverica. Other, larger formations are marching to Shalloth and even Carillonn."

"And you wonder why we fear for our *eastern* borders," King Macconal said dryly.

"These are *defensive* deployments," Takian shot back. "If you wish to see them as threats, the mistake will be yours alone!"

"What will it take before you recognize the danger?" growled Danri, exasperated. "Kroaks marching down the main streets of your cities? Terrions flying over the palace walls?"

"Those are legendary foes." Garand Amelius chuckled, apparently taking no offense. "I prefer to devote my energies to more realistic objectives. A lasting treaty, perhaps, between the five of us—a legacy for our children. What do you say, my lords?"

"The treaty will be forced on us by necessity—and only signed by those who survive!" Takian protested.

"The foes Danri describes are real, and deadly." Despite his raging frustration, Rudy forced his voice to remain level. "They move so fast that if we're not prepared, we'll have no time left when the danger can't be ignored. That's why it's so important to take action now. You need to raise the militia, gather troops and position them on your western borders. We have to stand together!"

"We are not so complacent as you might suspect," Macconal said stiffly. "We have in fact sent scouts to guard the approaches from the Dry Basin—Garand Amelius has been kind enough to allow my riders passage."

"Kind enough?" huffed the Sun Lord. "I had little choice in the matter!"

Macconal went on, ignoring the interruption. "Those scouts will provide warning, should any attack commence. We will redeploy troops if danger is conclusively indicated. But in any event, it would be very poor form to disrupt this council, and this city, in the midst of the signal alliance our fellow monarch is about to make with Shalloth." The King of Corsari nodded, with a tight smile at Takian. "I doubt your lovely bride enjoys all this talk of war during such an auspicious season."

"The Duchess Bristyn, soon to be my queen, knows the perils all too well. She saved my life and risked her own when agents of the Nameless One sought to kill me."

"Such dangerous involvement, on the part of a woman?"
Garand Amelius remarked. "My goodness, I should never
have mistaken Bristyn Duftrall for a warrior!"

"I do not know much of the warrior tradition among your
people," Quenidon declared stiffly. "I *do*, however, understand practical labors and idle conceits—and I fear that mankind suffers a surfeit of the latter. Perhaps, my lords, there
are too few like Bristyn Duftrall."

"It is well to cement a peace with marriage vows," observed Jamiesen Macconal. "However, I fear that we elder
monarchs must be a bit more pragmatic. And as I said before,
we will do nothing to distract from the magnificent ceremony
planned for a fortnight hence. This should be a time of celebration and festival."

"*Then* you might see if you're under attack?" replied
Danri sarcastically. He turned to Takian. "Seems like they
think a lot of your wedding."

"The Duchess of Shalloth is more precious than survival
to me—and this marriage to her is the most profound act of
my life. Yet I tell you this, my lords: As of now, that wedding
shall take place tomorrow! We will rush the ceremony and
the celebration so that, on the following day, I can embark
for the west!" Takian turned to King Dyerston, speaking in
a rush. "With Your Majesty's permission, I'll take several of
your pigeons. My stallion, Hawkrunner, will carry me faster
than the wind. Then, if an alarm must be sent—if there *is*
trouble—the birds will bring word back here faster than any
messenger can ride."

The King of Galtigor's stunning pronouncement lay heavy
on the air. Even the monarchs of the west seemed taken aback
by the abrupt change in plans.

"Very well," Jamiesen Macconal said, regarding Takian
from behind a carefully neutral smile. "If you are going to
disrupt Her Grace's timetable with such cavalier abandon, it
would seem that the least we can do is attend the festivities.
Until tomorrow, gentlemen?"

Garand Amelius lifted himself to his feet with alacrity that
belied his bulk, and Rudy knew that the council was over.

— 3 —

With the ease of a natural sailor Darret slipped through the rigging and over the galyon's forward cabin, finally sliding down a rope to the tiny foredeck. Here he found Kestrel leaning on the rail beneath the great trebuchet. The ship's master had spent most of the last weeks here, unable to confront the suffering that was everywhere evident on the *Black Condor*.

"Captain—I saved you bread and soup. Come eat now, okay?"

Kestrel didn't reply for a moment. The boy's dark eyes stared at his friend, concern showing in the drooping of his wide mouth. "You got to *eat* somethin'!" he declared.

"Twenty-four of them left," muttered the captain, waving at the ragged sails scattered to port and starboard across the gray, rolling sea.

Darret didn't need to see Kestrel's gesture to know what he meant. Two dozen dhows and fishing boats plodded along in the galyon's shadow, trailing behind or surging beside, mostly straining to keep up with the big ship as she coursed along the stormswept northern coast of Dalethica.

"Twenty-four boats fulla people who'd be dead now if you hadn't helped—"

"There were eleven more of them a fortnight ago—and how many more will we lose before Lanbrij?" demanded Kestrel, so sharply that the boy turned away, hurt. The captain took no notice. Instead he remembered a stormy night, when four of the boats had vanished into the darkness—gone, like the people of Farkeen were gone, obliterated as if they had never existed!

Only this small flotilla had escaped the doomed city. The day after fleeing the wracked port, they made a brief stop on the shore of Farkeen Bay, taking on water and as much food as they could forage in the face of the inexorable minion onslaught. The enemy advance had been easy to track—as soon as the monsters reached the forests of the western coast, they relentlessly felled trees and set fire to the wasted woodland. That blaze cast a pall of smoke into the sky visible for many miles.

What would the motley refugees find in Lanbrij? Kestrel tried to picture his villa in the Low City, its multitude of airy rooms surrounded by the sculpted garden, the graceful statuary arrayed beside the reflecting pool. Were the minions coming? Had they arrived already? Of course, the First Wall stood as defense of the Low City, and the Second Wall blocked the High City and all Corsari; but how long could mortal troops man those, or in fact *any* barrier, against the tireless warriors of Duloth-Trol?

"You stop this!" Darret's voice cut through the captain's morose introspection. "Whyfor you save people, den wants to jump offa ship?"

"I don't want to jump off the ship!" snapped Kestrel, thinking of the teeming main deck, the crowded holds and cabins—including his own berth, which had been converted to nurseries for the very young. Two babies had been born aboard since the *Black Condor* had departed Farkeen, and the knowledge of those new lives gave the captain a momentary flicker of hope. He remembered Pader Willith's sacrifice, the priest's demand that Kestrel carry the alarm back to the Circled Sea, and he felt a growing resolution within him.

"Thanks for coming to get me—maybe you could take my food up to the wheel deck. I'll meet you there in a few minutes."

Mollified, Darret nodded and left, cocking a skeptical eye backward as if to evaluate the truth of Kestrel's acquiescence. Apparently satisfied, he seized the rope and scampered upward and away.

Kestrel smiled through his bleak mood as he watched the boy bounce through the rigging. Of course, the foredeck could be reached by catwalks to port and starboard of the forward cabin, but during this overcrowded voyage there were usually a half dozen people or more gathered on each narrow walkway. Darret had taken to swinging through the overhead lines, and Kestrel was certain that the youngster could get about the ship faster than anyone who tried to make his way through the throng on deck.

The captain's moment of amusement passed as quickly as it had come, and again he found himself looking at the limitless expanse of sea. A single-masted longboat plowed through the swell nearby, and he tried to picture life for the passengers aboard that vessel—and the numerous, even smaller boats in their pathetic fleet. Constantly washed by spray, tossed about like corks in a storm, the unfortunate refugees must be suffering extreme discomfort. Still, every one of them was grateful for the chance to escape. So why wasn't he, himself, more elated with their successful flight?

He found himself, as he did frequently, thinking about Pader Willith's last moments. The mere memory of the Sleep-stealer's Lord Minion soaring down upon the ship was enough to bring trembling to Kestrel's limbs and loosen his bowels. Yet the priest of Baracan stood up to that horror, challenged it and—at the cost of his own life—bought the *Black Condor* enough time to bring aboard hundreds of refugees and escape the dying port. The captain was grateful he had stayed long enough to save some lives, though the abrupt change in his intentions had stunned him at the time. Finally, after days of meditation, he was beginning to understand the cause of his reversal.

"Baracan . . ." He said the word softly, as if cautiously tasting it. He had never thought much about the god of his people, Lord of Dalethica and father of humanity. Indeed, he realized that he had never truly believed in Baracan's, or any god's, existence. Yet the minions of Duloth-Trol had confronted Kestrel with the concrete and deadly proof of another god—a deity of unspeakable darkness, of monstrous and limitless evil. In the face of that might, Pader Willith had shown him the strength of the God of Man—a deity who had already saved Kestrel's life, his ship and crew, and these many, many others.

"Baracan . . . God of Man, thank you," the captain said, lowering his head briefly to his white-knuckled hands. He looked out to sea again, across the rolling swells, wondering what Lanbrij held in store for them. But he was no longer content to remain here, alone and brooding, in the bow.

Starting along the starboard catwalk, Kestrel stepped over several young people huddled together under tarpaulins. He had noticed that many of these were couples, always the same pairs. He felt a flash of envy, considering his own penchant for discarding women after a night or two. Truly, there seemed to be something warm and compelling in the bond that a man might share with a beloved partner.

Finally, and with some relief, he felt hungry again.

— 4 —

The slender blade of gleaming steel snaked toward Rudy's right shoulder. His own weapon slashed in a frantic parry, a moment too late. Quenidon smiled grimly, the tip of his sword pressing against the Iceman's chest for a split second before the human's blade clanged it aside in a powerful slash.

"That would have been a lung, at the very least," chastised the sylve as the pair sheathed their swords. "Though I'll admit, you made me work for it. You're showing some anticipation now, in addition to technique."

"Thanks for not drawing blood," Raine put in with a laugh. "I'm getting to kind of like him."

"Besides," added Danri, rising from the bench in the corner of the castle weapon room. "*I* haven't had a chance at him yet."

The four were the only people in the large, stone-walled chamber. The practice had been going well, but now they were content to rest for a moment.

"We still have some time before we need to get ready for the wedding," Quenidon noted. "Enough for another round of drills."

"Great," Rudy said, groaning. He was aware that his skills developed quickly, but invariably found it frustrating to be constantly bettered by his three teachers.

"I'm surprised Bristyn agreed to get married so quickly," Raine commented.

"Aye-uh. She didn't look any too happy about the notion, but I give her credit for being practical," the digger replied, tossing Rudy a shield and nodding to the sylve and Raine. "My turn. Let's do some shieldwork before we fancy up."

The digger hoisted a similar shield while Rudy slipped his hand through the straps of his own metal circlet and drew his sword. Danri used a wooden mallet instead of his steel-headed hammer; even so, Rudy had emerged from many previous training sessions with an assortment of hammerhead-shaped bruises. His skill in the shield had improved rapidly, motivated by his sincere desire to avoid pain, and over the next ten minutes he deflected a barrage of blows low and high, suffering only a slightly smashed toe as the result of a too-deliberate retreat.

For another hour the two Faerines and Raine alternated, continuing the training begun in earnest after the Battle of Taywick. Quenidon was a master swordsman, and Danri, for his part, knew a great deal about a variety of tool-type weapons, such as hammers, axes, picks, and poles. The digger was also skilled with the shield, and Rudy suspected that the defensive moves he had learned would save his life some day. Raine specialized in showing the Iceman maneuvers with the knife, and tumbles and rolls useful for evading an attacker. She added refinements to his swordsmanship and Rudy listened willingly—he had seen that, with her own blade, Raine was nearly a match for Quenidon in a sword fight.

Finally, sore and sweaty, they suspended the practice, returning through the lofty corridors to their apartments in the castle. The wedding feast would not begin for a few hours, but they wanted plenty of time to bathe and dress. "No sense sweatin' up the nicest thing I've ever worn," was the way Danri put it, and he voiced the opinion of them all. King Dyerston had provided the services of several tailors, and enough material for each of the companions to have an extravagant outfit created. Now they found the completed ensembles waiting in their chambers.

"Her ladyship is already dressing," the maid Nellidyn informed them. Rudy smiled privately, imagining how Dara would blush at the title. "Anjell's not back yet—she said she needed to go to the kitchen for something. I gather her mother is getting a trifle worried."

"Anjell's not about to miss the wedding," said the Iceman with certainty. As if to support his remark, the door to their chambers burst open and the girl darted into the room.

"Rudy—Danri, there you are! You'll never believe what happened!" Her pigtails bounced as she rushed forward, cheeks flushed with excitement.

"What is it?" asked the Iceman, turning to his sister-in-law as Dara came running out of her own room. "Where did she go?"

"I don't know," Dara replied, her brow furrowed in concern. "I was combing my hair, and Anjell went down to the kitchens for some more bread. What happened?"

"War!" The word exploded from Anjell and hung in the air for several heartbeats before she amplified. "Well, rumors of war anyway. The cooks were talking about it, and they didn't pay any attention to me—you know how some grownups are about children, like we don't have *ears* or something."

"What did they say?" asked Rudy tersely.

"Well, it's supposed to be in the west somewhere. One of 'em heard that Zanthilat was invaded by somebody, that there were no caravans coming out of there anymore. Another said that Myntar Kosh was going to war, but they didn't know who with!"

"And beyond Zanthilat lies the Dry Basin." Rudy felt a prickle of alarm run along the back of his neck.

"Where the Sleepstealer invaded Dalethica a thousand years ago," Raine concluded numbly. "Is it coming so soon?"

"Those old windbags will just pass this off as another rumor!" Danri growled.

"But surely they'll believe you now!" Dara argued.

"Not until they have a couple of kroaks standing on their faces, ready to chop off their empty heads!" snapped Danri with real bitterness.

"No bloodshed at the wedding, I hope!" Awnro Lyrifell cried in mock horror. The sartorially resplendent bard emerged from his room, proving that he had outdone himself. A long coat embroidered with gold and silver thread swirled dashingly around his white leggings and gleaming black boots, while feathers in scintillating shades of red and green adorned his hat, the floppy leather brim of which had apparently been burnished for the occasion. New strings of gleaming gold winked from the minstrel's lute as he bowed low before the companions.

"Now, you get into our room, young lady, and get yourself ready!" Dara demanded, as Anjell circled the bard, admiring the detailed threadwork of his coat.

"But—what about the *news*?"

"It's not *terribly* surprising," noted Rudy. "The same kind of rumors we've been hearing. We'll see the Sun Lord and King Macconal at the wedding—perhaps they'll have a little more information."

"For now, your mother's right—you and I are supposed to get there early, remember?" Awnro chided.

Despite her excitement, the girl dressed quickly, squirming under the ministrations of Nellidyn, and her mother. Awnro, Dara, and Anjell soon departed for the palace hall, while Rudy, Raine, and the two Faerines took their time getting dressed.

"How do these buttons work?" Rudy wondered aloud, after fifteen fruitless minutes trying to match the two sides of his shirt.

"Beats me—I'm just making sure that mine stays tucked in," Danri declared.

"Savages!" cried Quenidon Daringer, who quickly saw to it that at least the Iceman was properly put together.

Rudy finally decided that he looked quite dashing in his black silk shirt and trousers, over which he wore a yellow tunic and black cape trimmed in gold—but when Raine emerged from her dressing chamber, he felt completely unworthy to appear as her escort. A gown of blue satin, trimmed with gauzy lace, fell about her bare shoulders like a cascade of deep ice, its close-fitting bodice accentuating her small breasts and tiny waist before billowing out in a wealth of flowing material.

Rudy gaped at her, overwhelmed as she smiled and pirouetted, allowing the liquid satin to float around her legs in graceful swirls. Even Danri whistled, while Quenidon Daringer bowed deeply, declaring himself humbled in the presence of such unparalleled beauty.

The digger and sylve were themselves resplendent in long coats, with gleaming boots of black leather and ruffled white shirts. They each wore a squared silk hat adorned with a single arched plume—white for Danri, and black for the sylve. Finally they were ready to depart. Rudy hesitated, thinking of the Aura in his waterskin, but then shrugged and left it behind—in Carillonn he had not been afflicted by the acute thirst that had nagged him on the journey.

The companions made their way to the royal balcony, where King Dyerston had promised seats would be waiting.

Here, joined by the Sun Lord and Jamiesen Macconal together with an entourage of courtiers, ladies, and nobles, they looked down upon the huge formal garden that would be the scene of the nuptials. Harpists and pipers played, while drums pounded a beat. His Majesty, King Takian of Galtigor, came forward trailing a long purple robe, ultimately to stand rigid beside the altar.

"Look—there's Boric," Raine whispered, squeezing Rudy's hand. They saw Takian's genial brother standing stiffly beside the king—for a moment. Presently, Boric's attention wandered, and the round-shouldered fellow looked with childlike delight about the gathering, waving unabashedly at Anjell.

"And that's Captain Jaymes, commander of his Golden Lions," noted the Iceman, pointing to a handsome warrior with long dark hair and a gleaming silver breastplate. The officer took a position of honor beside Takian. Other officers of the Golden Lion Regiment, resplendent in gilded robes and shining black boots, stood as an honor guard behind their king. Awnro Lyrifell played his lute and recited a ballad of love, while forty knights of Carillonn in silver plate mail marched forward, twenty to each side raising their swords to form an arch over the path leading to the altar.

Anjell came next, scattering blossoms of yellow and white along the grassy path. Her gauzy white dress floated like mist, and Rudy was reminded poignantly of Kianna Kyswyllis. His niece might have been the twissel's sister to judge from the rhythmic grace of her skipping walk.

When Bristyn Duftrall, Duchess of Shalloth, appeared, the wedding guests gasped collectively in awe. Gowned in white silk, with a silver circlet upon her head, the bride advanced serenely beneath the canopy of swords. Her beauty was borne with an inherent grace that seemed to suspend her several inches above the ground—and commanded the rapt attention of everyone present. Bristyn's golden tresses were coiled about her tiara, then cascaded in ringlets over her shoulders and down her back. Her eyes, fastened upon the breathless Takian, were radiant.

An elder priest of the city, Paderon Dyllrand, performed the ceremony, remarking in stentorian tones about the somber responsibilities implicit in such an historic bond. Raine squeezed Rudy's arm once, as Bristyn tilted her head, winking mischievously at her groom while the priest expounded on the virtues of a politically pragmatic union.

Finally the couple exchanged vows, pledging a lifetime of love, loyalty, and respect. Awnro played an achingly beautiful love ballad, the knights of Carillonn cheered heartily, Boric picked flowers off the ground and threw them exuberantly into the air, and the priest declared the ceremony complete.

When the dancing began, Rudy was astounded to find himself whirling about with Raine, trying to match the intricate steps she taught him. "Did Old Pheathersqyll teach you to dance, too?" he teased once, when they paused for breath.

"No—the Academy of the Sun has *lots* of teachers," she replied in the same light tone. He was about to reply, when she leaned close and whispered: "And *some* things I've had to figure out on my own."

She laughed gaily at the crimson flush creeping up to Rudy's ears. Moments later they were back on the floor, the Iceman flailing madly to keep up—and wrestling with the completely unfamiliar, and decidedly unpleasant, sensation of jealousy as he contemplated Raine's nameless dance instructor from some distant year. He tried to get her to tell him more, but she smiled with a teasing glint that nearly made him crazy—until she pulled him close and kissed him, hard.

Rudy caught a glimpse of Dara's radiant face as she spun past in Awnro's arms. The Iceman realized, with warm pleasure, that this was the first time the young widow had looked truly happy in a long time. Anjell and Boric clomped past next, whooping and whirling, the girl shrieking in delight as the beaming, uninhibited prince spun her wildly around the floor.

Despite the fact that the cooks had been forced to move their dinner plans up by two weeks, the trays that began to emerge from the kitchen were laden with such an array of splendid foods that Rudy's mouth immediately started to water. Stuffed peacocks, tails arrayed as centerpieces, were the focal point on each of a hundred tables. Brandied fruits were presented on beds of shaved ice, while numerous loaves of bread had been assembled into a single cone, making a passable replica of the solitary King's Tower on the nearby hill. Whole sturgeons, seven feet long and arrayed on platters of equal length, drew expressions of awe from the guests as they realized that each great fish was stuffed with a pig—and each pig stuffed with the black eggs of the sturgeon!

Still later, after the splendid banquet and endless glasses of excellent wine, Rudy found himself deep in discussion with the Sun Lord. That monarch, still smiling benignly, seemed now to be somewhat less skeptical of the companions' warning, confiding that he had become rather alarmed by some of the rumors flying eastward from the distant fringes of his realm. Messengers from Myntar Kosh had carried to him a series of vague stories; nothing had been confirmed, but people were afraid.

Even the hawk-faced King Macconal of Corsari relaxed his imperial suspicion enough to commend the Faerines on their determination to come this far to aid humankind. "It's to our own interests, as well, to draw mankind into an alliance against the greater foe," Quenidon reminded the dour monarch.

"Aye—and as a fact, that is the only thing that makes me inclined to believe some of these warnings. Indeed, I have sent Captain-General Arrante, commander of my armies, a message ordering him to be prepared, and to act quickly in the event of sudden developments."

Rudy was somewhat encouraged by this news, though he vigorously urged the King of Corsari to dispatch his troops immediately. Past midnight the celebration continued, though Takian—mindful of his pledge to ride to the west on the morrow—retired early with his bride.

Some time later the Iceman was intrigued when King Dyerston took him aside. "These festivities always put me in the mood for thinking—and for talking. Perhaps you'd do me the honor of an unusual audience?"

"Of course, Your Majesty!"

"Come across the bridge and meet me in the King's Tower, say at dawn. I think we shall have some interesting things to discuss—before you leave."

Thoroughly curious, the Iceman could get no more information from the monarch. Naturally, he agreed to cross to the lofty spire on the neighboring hill. Only after he had started back to Raine did a thought occur to him: He'd never said anything to anyone about leaving Carillonn.

— 5 —

At last Nicodareus swept into view of the marbled city, be-
holding walls, bridges, and towers gleaming whitely even in
the faint light of the crescent moon. Sounds of laughter and
music rose from numerous enclaves, torchlight flaring from
even the meanest hovels as the humans apparently celebrated
some kind of holiday. The Lord Minion settled to the ground
on the far bank of the Ariak, for he hated to fly over open
water. Instead, he adopted the guise of a human beggar and
hobbled unnoticed across one of the fabulous bridges—a
wide, solid span that led straight toward the heart of the city's
central markets.

As hunger racked his body with a craving he could no
longer ignore, Nicodareus turned into the twilit shadows of a
back alley. For now, he decided that the assumption of his
true form would be too dangerous—a panic among the populace would only make his search that much more difficult.
Instead, he retained the shape of the wrinkled beggar—the
body he had envisaged when Dassadec had first told him of
the gift of Darkslayer. In the guise of this wretch he limped
through the darkened waterfront district, until he passed a lone
house where his Sight showed but a single person asleep.

The Lord Minion entered the dwelling by the simple ex-
pedient of wrenching the door from its hinges, slowly and
deliberately enough that he did not attract a great deal of
attention. He found the human, an old woman, hobbling indignantly from her bedroom. She stared at the elderly man
who had bashed in the door to her house, demanding an explanation even as that body changed shape. Before she could
scream, cruel fangs ripped out her throat.

The old woman's blood proved thin and savorless, but Nicodareus drank greedily. Then, as always, came the pains; for
a long time he lay insensate across the body of his victim,
caught in the grip of his master's vengeance.

— 6 —

The City of One Hundred Bridges might have been called the
City of One Hundred Opinions on that waning-summer's

night. As the wedding swirled by in a collage of colors and sounds, all the nobles in the city seemed possessed by a celebratory frenzy, perhaps in an effort to prove that no danger loomed on the horizon.

The wedding guests listened to our tales politely enough. Still, I had the feeling that we might have been so many arcane fortunetellers, uttering warnings to titillate primitive fears—fears that vanished into the ether with the coming of day.

But we tried, talking to everyone who would listen, and hearing in turn those who bade us not to be alarmists. For a few hours we even tried to fool ourselves into complacency, pretending it was a fallacy, trying to believe that we lived in a world of future peace and harmony.

That illusion, sadly, would not last beyond the dawn.

From: *Recollections*, by Lady Raine of the Three Waters

SEVEN

Darkslayer

One need not immediately destroy a hated
enemy. Indeed, great satisfaction can be derived
from the destruction of that adversary's friends,
lovers, possessions, and so forth. Frequently the
torment caused by such secondary executions
is infinitely more gratifying than the foe's quick
extermination.
—TOME OF VILE COMPULSIONS

— 1 —

The High King took a drink from the silver flask and set the
container on the edge of the cluttered table. Tingling alertness
pervaded every one of his senses, heightening the bright, star-
speckled sky, the torches and lanterns still flaring throughout
the city of white marble. Many celebrations had faded but
raucous laughter and the strains of music for dancing still
marked a few outposts of continued revelry.

This sensory acuity had seized Kelwyn Dyerston two days
earlier, upon his first taste of Aura. The power of magic had
pulsed through his veins since then, sustained by the small
sip he took every few hours. There was no doubt in his mind
but that he would continue to do so until the enchanted liquid
was gone.

Although the High King had seen and done much during
a long and well-traveled life, *this*—the power of the Water-

shed's magic—was remarkable beyond his every other memory. Kelwyn had discovered that his reaction to the precious elixir was unusual and acute. Pillotte had indulged his liege by drinking some Aura, reporting no noticeable effect except the dramatic easing of a vexing lumbago. Yet while the king drank he remained vividly awake, incapable of drowsiness or fatigue, and infused by a nervous tension that brought him constantly to his feet and set him pacing about his chamber.

After dark on the first night, he had sprinkled some of the liquid on the floor, and when he discerned no visible illumination, he knew that the magical water was not producing in him the effects suggested by Rudy. This was the reason Dyerston had invited the Iceman to the tower—he wanted to compare his own response to Aura with Rudy's experiences.

Dyerston took another sip of Aura, considered the upcoming conversation—and was suddenly shot through with a chilling bolt of alarm. Danger approached—a terrible, deadly menace that bore down on the city of white marble, hunting, seeking, riding on wings of night. And in an instant of clarity the king saw the intended victim of this evil stalker, and knew that the monster had to be stopped. If the malignant creature was not somehow vanquished, it would seek out the Man of Three Waters and exterminate him with cruel pleasure—and disastrous import for the Watershed.

Perhaps there was still time to warn the Iceman, to get him out of the city. An abrupt thirst seized the king. He took another drink from the silver flask—and the imminence of danger prickled along his skin. There *was* no time!

He reacted immediately, snatching up a walking stick and charging toward the nearest of the windows encircling his chamber. With a single swing he smashed the pane, sending shards of glass tinkling to the ground far below. Kelwyn sensed more than heard the stirring of the guard detail in the courtyard; he ignored the shouts that followed, had no time for explanations. One by one he knocked out the panes of precious glass, until the night breeze wafted into the high tower room, and out the opposite side.

Then he uncorked the Aura, shaking the flask, spraying the stuff wildly across the room. The wind gusted harder, sweeping papers from the table, carrying the mists of magic into the city—

And acting as a beacon, and a decoy, for the horror that lurked without.

— 2 —

Nicodareus rose groggily, kicking aside the dried husk of the old woman's corpse. He emerged from the house to find the city lost in early morning quietude—though in a few places music and revelry marked pockets of hardy celebrants. The Lord Minion, in his beggar's guise, cocked his head to the side, crouching in the shadows like a dozen other pathetic wretches. His Sight probed through streets and houses, along walls, even into the castle and the high towers.

It was not his potent vision that gave him the first clue, however. His nostrils caught the vile stench of Aura, a surprisingly powerful stink on the night breeze. Following the wind, sniffing as he shuffled up the street, he fixed the source of the reek at the top of the nearby hill. Only then did he probe with his Sight, seeking the upper reaches of a lofty tower. Aura was everywhere, but Nicodareus perceived a man, sensed the nearness of his victim. The Lord Minion quivered with anticipation as he changed shape. Once again the barreled body of the owl cloaked him, wings lifting even before the taloned feet touched the ground. Nearby, another beggar saw a hint of the transformation, gasped in astonishment, then snatched up a nearly empty bottle and guzzled desperately. When he looked up, the owl had disappeared.

But it had not vanished. The thick-bodied bird came silently to rest in the courtyard at the base of the King's Tower. A dozen guards, startled by the shower of breaking glass, suddenly found the Lord Minion among them, clawing, rending, and biting. In seconds the fight was over, the entire detachment bloodily slain.

Climbing again with sweeps of his powerful wings, Nicodareus circled that lofty tower, seeking the suggestive image within, the human cloaked in the fumes of Aura.

The potent liquid suggested one thought, persuasively, and this hope became a conviction in the Lord Minion's mind: Here he would find the Man of Three Waters.

— 3 —

Perhaps the Lord Minion could be defeated, could be warded
away. There were the legends, tales that Kelwyn had heard
from his earliest days—songs sung beside his cradle, in the
Hall of Kings on Andaran. He could remember some of those
ditties, act upon them, pray that they were more than empty
phrases.

The monarch hurried around his chamber, pulling a large
reflecting glass off the wall and setting it beside his writing
table, then lifting out of a basket the bulbs of garlic he had
sent for the day before. His memory of an ancient verse had
prompted the request at the time, though Pillotte had looked
askance at the notion. Still—and as Kelwyn had expected—
the major-domo had procured the bulbs within the hour.

The High King hummed the remembered verse as he put-
tered about his chamber, making ready:

> Hush for the night flier,
> From the darken south,
> Three things may force him to stay:
> Mirror to trick him,
> Garlic to ward him,
> And Aura to hold him at bay.

Kelwyn looked toward the broken windows, sensed evil
drawing nearer by the second. Obviously the Lord Minion
had taken to the air, for only by flight could he approach with
such speed.

Too late the High King remembered Pillotte, who was
sleeping faithfully in his chamber below, near the bridge
doors. Before Kelwyn could raise his voice in even a brief
shout of alarm, those solid doors were rent from the entryway,
a splintering crash from two floors below signaling the violence of the assault. The king heard Pillotte's single shout of
alarm, but the major-domo's cry was cut off with a brutal,
tearing sound followed by utter silence.

The king sat in his chair behind the cluttered table, sensing
the power that drew closer with each padded footstep. He

looked at the mirror he had placed beside him, fingered the bulbs of garlic dangling from his neck. As he picked up the half-empty flask of Aura, the certainty came to him: He had made a terrible, fatal miscalculation.

Quickly the High King snatched up his quill—perhaps there was time to write a note, to warn the Iceman to leave . . . ! Then the door to his sanctum shuddered under a heavy blow and he knew that the Lord Minion stood without.

Time had run out.

Even with that foreknowledge, Kelwyn was unprepared for the awful visage revealed when his oak-paneled door splintered inward. Nicodareus ducked beneath the high lintel, crunching over the pieces of broken paneling to loom before the unflinching king. Crimson eyes glared like living fire, and when the ink-black face parted to reveal a fanged mouth, the tongue that slithered forth was as red as fresh blood.

"The Aura stink is powerful, human." The voice rumbled like a landslide, engulfing the High King in sweeping power. "Who are you?"

"Should not the Eye of the Nameless One know the answer to such a simple question?" Somehow the High King kept his voice calm, watching grimly as the Lord Minion stepped casually over the ring of wetness on the floor.

"You are not the one I seek."

Even as he sensed impending doom, Kelwyn Dyerston's heart thumped to a flash of hope. As he had suspected, it was the Man of Three Waters who was important, who must be saved! His own death mattered not—indeed, he saw now with detached clarity that it would be the most, the *only*, effective way of alerting his fellow monarchs to danger.

"I am the one you have found," the monarch stated, rising from his chair. "I see the rumors are true—your master once again works his evil in the realms of man."

Nicodareus laughed, a bark of thunder that boomed through the semicircular chamber, rattling outward through the broken windows. "There is nothing you can do about my master's intentions—but perhaps you can serve *me*, mortal, before you die!"

"I am accustomed to accepting the service of others," King Dyerston demurred. The Lord Minion's crimson eyes followed him closely as the king, moving sideways, suddenly stepped behind the mirror set beside his table.

"Fool—you seek to deceive me with parlor tricks, or children's rhymes?"

Slashing talons reached out, smashing the mirror to the side and seizing the king by the throat. Kelwyn grunted as the monstrous fist crushed the bulbs of garlic strung around his neck—one more line of the verse grimly disproved.

The High King snatched for the silver flask, but Nicodareus was too fast. With a wrenching twist he snapped Kelwyn's shoulder loose in its socket, watching impassively as his victim writhed in anguish.

"Where is the Iceman? Where can I find the Man of Three Waters?" growled Nicodareus, lifting the monarch and smashing into his stomach with a gut-rupturing blow.

The High King groaned, twisting deliriously in the grip of doom. Pain distorted his features, but his eyes were clear and focused, fastened on the fiery orbs of the monstrous intruder.

"*Where?*"

It was just an involuntary flicker, a turn of those pain-racked eyes toward the lofty castle rising on the next hill. Kelwyn Dyerston died fearing that his last reflex had answered Lord Minion's question.

But when the talons ripped the skin of the High King's throat, when the thick, sweet blood ran over his hands and arms, hunger claimed Nicodareus again. Greedily he swilled the rich stuff of the High King's life—blood so much more invigorating than the old woman's.

Nicodareus barely had time to lunge from the high tower, feeling the grip of his punishment cloak him in agony. He glided downward, thudding heavily into the courtyard, changing shape just before the torpor claimed him.

Finally, concealed in the body of a black snake, the Lord Minion huddled in a storm sewer. The blood of the High King was leaden in his belly, far more sustaining than his feeding from the old woman. Consciousness faded with grim contentment, as Nicodareus knew that he was near the end of his quest.

Before sunset, the Man of Three Waters would die.

— 4 —

Rudy strolled across the marbled surface of the sweeping bridge. All around—and so very far below—the city of Carillonn slumbered toward sunrise. The last of the celebrators had departed the wedding feast an hour before, but the Iceman had remained uninterested in sleep. Raine's teasing removal of her gown had aroused his passion, but afterwards, when she lay drowsing, he had risen to pace restlessly on the balcony.

Realizing that it had been a long time since he had taken a sip from his Auraskin, Rudy had reached for the leather sack. He shrugged the carrying strap over his shoulder but for some reason had decided not to drink; instead, he had quietly reflected, barely conscious of his lofty vantage over the city. Finally a tinge of brightness had shaded the eastern horizon, indicating that it was time to answer the High King's summons. Still, the Iceman felt no particular urgency; he paused at the middle of the bridge to look around for a while, in solitary enjoyment of the marbled city. The pleasure of solitude was a sudden, surprising sensation. Rudy began to realize how draining the royal council, the wedding, everything about these days in Carillonn, had been. For the first time he wondered if their attempts to persuade the kings of Dalethica had been a waste of time—whatever the solution to the problems of the world, it seemed likely to exist somewhere else.

Perhaps Rudy had acquired some of his Faerine companions' glumness. Danri had groused all the previous day about the "wasted trip" to Carillonn. Quenidon hadn't been so vocal, but the sylve, as well, had been disappointed in their failure to sway the council of lords. The Faerines both missed their homelands, and worried increasingly about the dangers menacing the enchanted realm.

The Iceman didn't notice that he had started across the bridge again until he drew near to the King's Tower. He felt vibrant, and powerfully moved by the fading starlight and gently reflecting river. The spire rose before him, pale and almost fluorescent against the heavens. Rudy's eyes searched those lofty windows, looking for the flicker of light that would indicate the monarch was awake and expecting his visitor. Oddly, the array of windows was as black and lifeless as a dead man's eyes.

It might have been that sinister image, insinuating itself, unbidden, into Rudy's mind—or perhaps it was the subtle, sickening stench that drifted past on a wisp of night breeze. The Iceman's pulse quickened, his mind focused entirely on the bridge, the doors, and the tower. Closer, he could see the shattered windows, then crunched through glass on the bridge. He ran toward the entryway, remembering the heavy wooden doors closing with a solid thud when he had departed that tower two days earlier. Why, then, would they stand open through the night? Rudy shivered as he saw that the great barriers had not merely been left ajar—something terribly powerful had smashed them inward. Splinters dangled where the lock had been ripped out, and one of the heavy doors sagged tiredly, supported by only a single hinge. The other lay cracked and broken on the marble floor inside the tower.

Stepping across the threshold, Rudy entered a region of utter darkness—there were no windows on this level, and the half-standing door screened the pale sky. The Iceman drew his waterskin from his side, splashing a few drops of Aura across the floor, allowing the magical liquid of Faerine to cast its glow through the darkened entry. The wet places brightened the entire passageway in the Iceman's eyes—and he recoiled from the images revealed.

He recognized the body of the major-domo Pillotte by the black waistcoat, which had apparently been thrown hastily over a sleeping-robe. The corpse, which lay in a broad pool of blood, was so grotesquely positioned that it took the Iceman a minute to realize that the man's head had been ripped from his shoulders. Rudy's hair prickled on his scalp and he grimaced at the smell of sticky blood. Sprinkling more drops of Aura before him, he illuminated the circular marble stairway leading up to the king's chamber.

The Iceman froze at the foot of that stairway, spine tingling at the sight of a footstep outlined in dried blood. It had not been left by a boot—instead, the imprint was that of an unshod, taloned paw. Nearly twice as long as Rudy's own foot, the outline had a manlike shape: heel narrower than ball, five toes extended at the front. Yet the claw marks protruding from each toe, and the massive size of the print, all suggested a thing infinitely more horrible than a human killer—a fact that spoke to Rudy with brutal, indisputable clarity.

Nicodareus was here, in Carillonn. The realization was not a complete shock—in the last minutes the Iceman had come to suspect as much. Still, it was a cruel piece of knowledge. With a sickened, heaving stomach Rudy continued up the stairs. At the upper landing he saw the carved roses gouged from the door to the king's chamber, that stout barrier also smashed in.

The floor of the semicircular room was littered with papers, many of them shredded. Pale illumination washed through cracked and broken panes of glass, and the wire-rimmed spectacles on the floor immediately caught Rudy's eye. Bent flat, both frames cracked, they lay pathetically beside the High King's chair. The sight of a boot jutting from under the table caused Rudy's breath to catch in his throat, but he immediately knelt and brushed the debris of paper away to reveal first a pair of frail, almost sticklike legs, and then the High King's torso and head.

"By Aurianth!" he gasped, recoiling from the skull-like visage that stared sightlessly upward from the floor. He retched, heaving convulsively for a moment before he clenched his teeth in an effort at self-control.

The body of the king had not been mutilated in the same way as that of the major-domo. Instead, it looked as if the blood and flesh had been sucked from the vessel of Dyerston's skin. That membrane was drawn tightly over his skull, revealing jaw line and cheekbones. Sunken eyes rattled in deep, dry sockets, and when the Iceman inadvertently bumped the corpse it moved easily, weighing little more than a bag of clothes filled with straw.

Rudy sagged back on his haunches, grief-stricken—and terrified. Why had the Lord Minion slain the High King?

Only then did the Iceman notice the wetness all around the chamber, the bright liquid that coated the papers and pillows and walls. Aura—Kelwyn Dyerston must have sprayed the precious stuff everywhere. The potent enchantment would surely have lured the Lord Minion here, and away from his real target . . .

The Man of Three Waters.

— 5 —

Standing tautly on a balcony outside the castle apartments, Rudy watched another column of guards troop across the bridge toward the wreckage of the High King's tower. More men-at-arms formed a cordon around the base of the tower, where the detail of royal guards had been found slain to the last man. As the sun crested the eastern hills, golden rays fell upon a scene of confusion, consternation, and hysteria.

In the brief hour since the Man of Three Waters had sounded the alarm, gates throughout the castle had been closed and barred. The Chief of Protocol had spoken to Rudy, accepting the Iceman's assertion that the assassin was a Lord Minion of the Sleepstealer. Standarl Drade had then gone to inform the visiting kings of the assassination.

Rudy felt a numbness that was worse than fear, a hundred times more agonizing than mere pain. Once before Nicodareus had come for the Iceman. That time the Eye of Dassadec had barely been thwarted—and many innocent people had died, an entire inn crowded with travelers razed. Once again Rudy was a terrible danger to everyone around him—in this case, to the whole city. Half-expecting to see the bat-winged horror of Nicodareus sailing into view from the cloudless sky, he recalled the last words he'd heard from Kelwyn Dyerston: "I think we shall have some interesting things to discuss *before you leave*." The phrase had made no sense a few hours before, but now it seemed coldly prophetic. The Iceman knew that he must immediately depart the city of white marble.

"Come inside," Raine said, stepping beside him and slipping her hand into his. "You can't do anything more."

"If only I'd gone sooner!"

"Then you'd be dead, too," she replied bluntly.

In the sitting room of their castle apartments, Danri, Quenidon, Awnro, Dara, and Anjell waited for him. Rudy felt profound affection for his old friends, and a deepening sorrow at the prospect of parting from them.

"I—I can't stay here," he began, "for the same reason I had to leave Neshara, six months ago. This . . . monster"—

he couldn't bring himself to call it a Lord Minion, though there was no doubt about the killer's identity in his own mind—"came here looking for me. As long as I stay in the city, I put thousands of innocent people in danger. I'm leaving within the hour."

"But where will we go?" asked Anjell.

The Iceman sighed. "This time, little one, I have to leave you behind. I've decided to go to Myntar Kosh, to the Academy of the Sun. Raine knows a man there who might be able to give me some information."

"I'm going with you," Raine declared, but Rudy shook his head forcefully.

"You can tell me how to find old Pheathersqyll, but it won't be safe for you to travel with me. Perhaps I can send for you later, or come—"

"*Send* for me?"

Raine's voice cut like a whip, and her eyes flashed with a burning anger Rudy had never seen before as she continued relentlessly. "I'm going with you—now, if not sooner. Make your farewells while I have the hostlers ready our horses."

"I won't take you!" the Iceman retorted firmly. "There's—"

"You *will*, by Aurianth! Don't you think I know who killed the High King? Who's pursuing you? Do you think you'd last two minutes if he finds you alone?"

"At least you won't have to share my fate!" He was shouting now, furious at her stubbornness.

"How can you say that? The High King is dead, and there was nothing you could do about it! Now stop arguing—I'm coming along, and I'm not asking your permission!"

"Why don't you understand?" demanded Rudy. "I *can't*—"

"*You* understand, dammit. It's not your decision! Now stop acting like a gallant fool and get ready to go!"

Rudy's intense anger melted in a rush of relief, tempered by guilty shame, and he nodded mutely. Then even this new emotion paled, overwhelmed by the need to move. He rose and gave Dara a long hug, then knelt to embrace Anjell.

"You'll be coming back soon, won't you?" she asked, bravely stifling her tears, sniffling into his shoulder.

"I hope so," he said, before turning to the pair of Faerines. "My friends, you too must leave here now. I know that your own realm has need of you both—and I can only thank you for embarking this far with me.''

"Aye-uh," Danri said, shifting uncomfortably. "But it's not right taking off now—I feel worse than bad, leaving you."

"If there were any doubts about what lies ahead, the death of the High King will put them to rest," Rudy replied, clapping the stout digger on the shoulder.

"And at the very least you have to take word to Faerine," Raine declared, embracing Quenidon. "I'll try to see that our Iceman doesn't forget how to hold a sword."

"Good—I fear he'll need it." The normally serene sylve blinked back a tear of emotion, then turned to Rudy. "And good luck to you. I wonder, someday, if you'll appreciate the irony—that I became friends with a human Auramaster." Quenidon abruptly took the Iceman's hand, then turned away before Rudy could ask what he meant.

"Now make haste, my friend," Raine said, patting the flushing Danri on the back. "I hope you can get home in time."

"And pray that it's not already too late," Quenidon said grimly. He turned to Raine. "Perhaps you could have them saddle our horses, as well?"

She said that she would.

"And we're going back home," Dara said firmly, taking her daughter by the shoulder, squeezing hard enough to halt Anjell's anticipated protests. Dara looked at Rudy, fear tightening her face. "Be careful—and come home soon!"

"I will," he agreed, to her first request. As for coming home soon . . . it was best that he made no promises.

A knock on the door indicated the arrival of Takian and Bristyn, married now for less than twelve hours. Concern lined the young king's face. "I spoke with Standarl Drade—by the gods, it's horrible!" Takian declared with a groan. "Was it—?"

"Nicodareus? Yes," the Iceman replied. "Have you heard from the other kings?"

"The Sun Lord departed immediately. He's frightened—so much so that he embarked for home and left his servants to pack up behind him!" Takian paced back and forth, pounding his fist into his palm.

"Things are starting to happen—fast," Rudy said. "I have a feeling that Garand Amelius doesn't have much time."

"I know that!" Takian snapped. "And I'm *still* going to Myntercairn—with the carrier pigeons. That's where the minion army has to gather, whether it intends to strike to the east or the north. I have to see for myself, to be there when the trouble starts. With the pigeons I can send warning to Carillonn and Shalloth—and maybe stiffen Garand Amelius' resolve a little bit while I'm there!"

"We're riding west, Raine and I," Rudy said. "We'll take the back roads, I think, but we're going almost all the way to Myntercairn. We seek a scholar at the Academy of the Sun."

"That's it, then—I'll ride along," Takian declared. "I'll be traveling light—only my loyal sergeant, Randart, and three trusted men as bodyguards—so we can make good time."

Rudy wanted to protest against the young king's putting himself in danger, but when Takian and Raine exchanged a determined glance the Iceman knew that, too, was a fight he would lose. He felt another twinge of shame, admitting that he was tremendously relieved to have companions on his journey.

The king turned to his bride, who had stood by impassively while her husband planned his immediate departure. "There will be matters to handle in Carillonn . . . King Dyerston's son and heir is in Andaran, and won't be able to get here for months. Of course, Standarl Drade is a capable man, but there's bound to be some confusion."

"I know what you have to do—and myself, as well," said Bristyn, holding her chin firm. "But be careful—please!"

"I will. I'll try to come out through Lanbrij, travel seaward from Myntercairn. I can take ship from Inport and get back here as soon as possible."

"I'll send *Searunner*, with the Golden Lion Regiment," Bristyn promised. "They can meet you in Lanbrij."

"Your carrack?" Rudy remembered something. "You said those casks of Aura are aboard, in Carillonn?"

Takian nodded.

"Can you leave them on the ship, bring them to Lanbrij as well?"

"Aye," the king agreed.

"I'll take care of all the details immediately," Bristyn

promised. She took the Iceman's hand, bidding him good luck with tears in her eyes, then embraced Raine with a sob.

The maid, Nellidyn, stood near the door and cleared her throat diffidently. "I've taken the liberty of having the kitchen staff prepare some parcels of food—cured ham, bread, and the like. They'll be waiting for you in the courtyard." The maid's eyes teared, and Anjell came over to give her a hug.

"Thanks—thanks very much," Raine replied, answering for all the travelers.

Rudy took another glance out the window, saw the cloudless blue sky beyond the city. Yet somehow the horizon seemed closer now, the air dense, oppressive . . . even menacing.

He knew that it was time to go.

— 6 —

Jasaren glided through dark skies, soaring from the icy swales of the Bruxrange toward greener, warmer valleys. He flew restlessly, bored by the routine that had occupied his last few weeks. True, his master, Phalthak, would be pleased by his accomplishments, but the drackan yearned for the immediate praise of the Lord Minion—and, too, he increasingly longed for the tender kiss of those sweet fangs in that venomous silver head. Nothing else in his life could hold much interest by comparison.

Sunlight glinted from a sheltered pool. The reflection vanished abruptly, obscured by a sudden eruption of steam, and the brown drackan banked downward to investigate. He settled to an outcrop of rock, peering into a narrow grotto bordered by stony walls. The steam rose from a pool in the base of the niche, where liquid emerged from the ground in muddy bubbles.

Hot springs were uncommon in the high mountains, though Jasaren remembered many in these lower reaches. Still, he was curious, especially when he saw the rippling, prismatic patterns swirling across the surface of the steaming pool. Recognizing Aura, the drackan crept down the steep, rocky cliff, extending his neck to the hot spring. He ignored the sulphurous fumes, lapping at the enchanted liquid tentatively, and then with more enthusiasm.

Pressure rose in his belly and Jasaren clamped his jaw to restrain the explosion. Burning pain seared his throat as the Aura mingled with the Darkblood that had become a part of his being. The drackan's vision burned red, tinged by rising, uncontrollable fury. He twisted his head in an unsuccessful search for some worthy foe. Spreading his jaws, he expelled a searing blast of steam, scalding lichen and moss on the cliff face, withering the leaves of the few bushes huddled in cracks between the rocks. The cloud of killing heat expanded, a lethal swath that left Jasaren drained, yet exultant. Leaves burned away, and the rock steamed and sizzled in the wake of the searing breath.

No drackan had ever exhaled such a lethal blast! Although any of the Faerine serpents could turn a drink of Aura into a puff of soothing gas useful for putting prey to sleep, that attack caused a victim no real hurt. If a mature drackan devoured snow of Auraice, the resulting blast of frost was enough to inflict serious damage upon a foe.

But this! Prior to Jasaren's receiving the kiss of Phalthak, the taste of such hot Aura would have scorched his mouth and throat. Now, the drink caused little discomfort, and the scalding temperature, the huge size of the gas-cloud, dwarfed the most deadly blast of frostbreath. When a drackan of Darkblood drank Aura from a hot and sulphurous spring, his breath would become the scourge of any battlefield!

Flushed with the pleasure of his discovery, Jasaren took to the air, soaring through verdant valleys with predatory intensity. Thus far his activities in his master's name had been devoted to polluting the lairs of other brown drackans, insuring that, when they awakened, they would drink Aura tainted by the nectar of Duloth-Trol, and thus be bound to the will of Phalthak. Yet now he did not seek the lair of a brown drackan—his cousins, in any event, dwelled in the higher, remote regions of the Bruxrange. He recognized a cave mouth, tucking his wings into a shallow dive and coming to rest before a dark gap in a rough limestone wall.

He remembered this place, for it had been the scene of one of his most passionate matings—the only time he had coupled with a green. As Jasaren crept beneath the dripping ceiling he saw that Meamare slumbered within, a massive emerald form curled against the far wall of the cavern. The brown drackan stepped forward, briefly remembering a long-past year filled with exquisite pleasures. Then Darkblood surged, and the instinctive antipathy of brown for green twisted into violent hatred. Lashing forward, Jasaren ripped a great bite out of the sleeping drackan's neck.

Meamare thrashed, extending a wing, struggling to raise her head, but Jasaren struck again. His talons pressed the huge body to the floor while he ripped away at her gouged and bleeding throat. Afterward Jasaren crossed to the pool of Aura at the rear of the cave. He drank deeply, for a long time, but he couldn't cleanse the taste of blood from his tongue.

EIGHT

A Captain-General of Corsari

The violence of a day-long gale often lurks
behind a most beautiful dawn.
—SONGS OF THE SAILOR

— 1 —

Kestrel stood on the wheel deck of the *Black Condor*, more
hopeful than he had been in all the weeks since departing
Farkeen. A score of fishing boats scattered to the horizon,
plucking along in the galyon's wake. Though more than a
dozen of the smaller craft had been lost on the long passage
around the Tiberian Head, the surviving ships brought hundreds of people toward the safety of the Corsari coast.

And now, perhaps, they would make it. The captain's heart
swelled at the sight of a telltale cloud bank on the horizon.
In his mind's eye, he contemplated the remembered views
from his villa gardens, the towering walls rising on the Land
Bridge.

"How much farther?" Darret asked, bounding up the ladder to the helm.

"Did you get my quarters cleaned?" huffed Kestrel.

"Aye, Captain!" Darret replied with a grin. The ship's master never doubted the youngster, who had proved such a remarkably able cabin boy that Kestrel found himself wondering how he had ever sailed without him. "So, how much farther?"

"See that ridge of cloud there," Kestrel said, pointing to the horizon beyond the bow. "That's sitting over land. We should make Outport by tomorrow dawn."

"What kinda name is Outport?" demanded the lad.

Kestrel chuckled. "It's because of the nature of Corsari. You see, it's a realm that's *almost* an island—just linked to the mainland by a rocky ridge, fifteen miles long but no more than a mile or so wide. We call it the Land Bridge."

"But you can't sail under it?" Darret scowled, suspecting a tall tale.

"Not in the *Condor*, no. There's a port on either side of the Land Bridge—Outport, which leads to the Great Ocean; and Inport, which opens onto the Circled Sea. The docks are just a mile apart by land, but it's better than five hundred miles for anyone who wants to sail from one to the other, 'cause you have to go around all Corsari."

"You said *Black Condor* can't sail under de bridge—somebody else *can*?"

"There's a canal tunnel—made by the diggers of Faerine, a thousand years ago. It's a real ride on a fast-ebbing tide."

"Never saw nothin' like dat," Darret allowed, squinting into the distance.

"There isn't anything else like it—not in all Dalethica," Kestrel agreed with a laugh. His tone grew more serious as he clapped a hand on the boy's shoulder. "I'm glad you're going to get a look at it," he noted soberly.

True to the captain's prediction, the galyon dropped anchor in the sheltered waters of Outport by the following dawn. A rocky ridge encircled the bay, while the city walls looked as lofty and impregnable as any barrier on the Watershed. Kestrel was relieved to see no signs of war—in fact, it looked like word of the Sleepstealer's invasion had not even reached this part of Dalethica. The gates were still open, and the seaman knew those portals took the better part of a day to pull shut. When he squinted toward the Low City—the part of Lanbrij nestled on the hilly ridge between the two walls—he could see the whitewashed adobe of his own villa, high atop its brush-covered hill and undisturbed by any visible threats. Another wistful thought took him by surprise: If he had a wife, she would be there now, awaiting his return. The notion was pleasant, and startling.

The *Black Condor* and her flotilla had drawn the attention of people on shore, and Kestrel was met at the dock by a beribboned official of the king's guard. "His Majesty's captain-general desires your presence in the palace," the officer declared, ushering Kestrel—and Darret, who showed no signs of letting the captain out of his sight—into a waiting chariot.

"What about the others?" Kestrel objected. "We've been short of provisions—at sea for weeks! These people need to get ashore, to get some fresh food and water!"

"They'll be taken care of—but for now they have to remain on the ships!" barked the officer.

"Why?"

"Orders. Now, hold on."

The driver put a lash to the horses, and the little chariot rolled quickly through the city, climbing steep streets toward a blocky stone fortress that occupied a height overlooking the port.

They rolled past columns of troops marching toward the waterfront, and Kestrel was heartened by this evidence of the king's readiness—silver breastplates gleamed, and each of the men wore a long, wickedly curved scimitar at his side. The men-at-arms marched in neat formation, and several more columns were visible moving through the city's streets. As the chariot reached the top of the rounded ridge line, an expanse of blue water came into view beyond—the Circled Sea, placid and inviting compared to the slate-gray ocean.

"And there are the Walls of Lanbrij," the captain pointed out as they climbed. "They guard Corsari against any attack from the mainland.

Darret tried to accept the sights with aplomb, but his eyes widened as he stared at the wonders around him. The walls indicated by the captain were two tall barriers, each stretching from the cliffs along the ocean coast toward the lower terrain flanking the shore of the Circled Sea.

"Whatsat?" asked the boy, pointing to the rolling brown horizon of continental terrain.

"Myntar Kosh."

"Who de walls were made for, to stop 'em comin' here?"

Kestrel shook his head. "The walls were built at the same time as the canal—in case the minions of the Sleepstealer ever came again." He had seen the lofty barriers all his life, but for the first time he wondered if they would actually see use against their intended foe.

The chariot trundled through a lofty, arched gateway, where twin portals of heavy wood opened onto a wide courtyard. When the conveyance came to a halt inside, Kestrel and Darret were ushered out. Corsari Castle sprawled around them, walls of sand-colored stone, with squared corners—each guarded by a squat tower—and a stone-toothed battlement extending completely around the top. A troop of silver-armored guards flanked the captain and the boy, marching them through vast halls, between rows of ivory columns, across floors of gleaming marble in black, gray, and gold. Incense wafted from one hall, and then they passed through another courtyard where sleek black horses were being trained to carry riders in formation. Finally they entered another hall, wider than any other they had seen, ringed by pillars at the periphery, and here a tall figure looked up from a table.

"His Excellency Arrante, the Captain-General of Corsari," intoned one of the guards.

Kestrel, who had never been in the palace before, bowed before the thin-faced man who rose and approached them. He knew Arrante by reputation: the king's closest advisor, commander of all the ground forces serving the Corsari Crown. Reputedly the second most powerful man in the realm, his appearance was suitably imposing. The Captain-General wore a long robe of crimson silk lashed at the waist with a belt of braided gold, draped over a breastplate of shining steel. The narrow features of Arrante's face were augmented by a black beard that covered only his chin, but swept upward to frame his mouth in a curling mustache.

"Greetings, Captain," said Arrante in a tone far softer than his forbidding features suggested. "I am told that you have returned from a voyage to Farkeen."

"Aye, Excellency—and I bring news."

"I had hoped as much. His Majesty is unfortunately absent, attending the Council of Peace in Carillonn, but we have heard distressing rumors of war from many parts of Dalethica. The king sends word that there are those in the council who warn of a threat posed by the Sleepstealer himself—rumors of another great war.''

''It's true!'' Darret piped up. ''Farkeen was burned down, and everybody kilt—'cept those Captain Kestrel got away on his ship!''

''Indeed?'' Arrante's black eyebrows arched. ''And who are you?''

''Darret's a lad who served me in Farkeen,'' Kestrel explained. ''When the minions attacked, he helped me reach my galyon and get her away.''

''Tell me about this attack.''

''I have more than rumors, Excellency. An army of minions has marched from Duloth-Trol. It seems inevitable that they will come to Lanbrij.''

Kestrel described the events in the west, beginning with the absence of caravans. Going on, he told of the attack that swept through the city with such brutal efficiency, and gave an account of the horrific fliers, with a description of the monster Pader Willith had called a Lord Minion. Arrante listened carefully, eyes half closed, as the sea captain finished his tale.

''Distressing . . . quite distressing,'' murmured the royal advisor. ''And you feel that no one else escaped Farkeen to carry this alarming news?''

''Quite certain, Excellency. The attack cut off all approaches by land, so no one could get out on foot. Fact is, I suspect the caravan routes had already been closed by the minions—could be that there's another wing of the army, already on its way toward the east.''

''And these fishing vessels . . . you are certain that all of those who survived the voyage entered Outport in the wake of your galyon?''

''Sure as I can be. Many a man on those boats'll be willing to take up a sword against the Sleepstealer, I'm sure.''

''Quite—though I don't think that will be necessary.''

''What do you mean?'' Kestrel didn't understand the captain-general's lack of concern.

''Just that, perhaps, the arrival of the minions will not be the tragedy that you believe it to be.''

"*What*? I told you—they killed everyone! I've never seen such butchery, such destruction!"

"Silence!" snapped Arrante, his tone edged with iron. "Guards—take these two to the dungeons! I want them to speak to no one—do you understand!"

Kestrel only comprehended what was happening as the captain-general's men-at-arms stepped forward, clasping the seaman's arms behind his back and swiftly removing the dagger from its sheath in his sleeve.

"Darret—run!" he cried, while directing a look of cold fury at Arrante. "Get away!

The boy grasped the danger immediately. Misjudging the speed of his youthful charge, a guard seized the lad by the shoulder—then shrieked as his knee was smashed by a swift and accurate kick. Other guards leapt toward the boy, but Darret ducked and tumbled away, leaving another guard groaning from a painful bite in the leg.

Bouncing to his feet, Darret darted around the clutching arms of one guard, kicking again, twice, with the speed of a striking snake. Then he tumbled backward, reeling from another guard's punch. Two of the men dove after him, but Kestrel, turning swiftly, tripped one of them, knocking him into the other so that both men-at-arms crashed heavily to the floor.

By the time Arrante's men had disentangled themselves, the boy from Farkeen had vanished into the mazelike corridors of Corsari Castle.

— 2 —

Darret dashed through an open doorway, panting in a shadowy alcove as guards pounded past. Everywhere in the great keep torches flared, and men shouted back and forth, seeking the boy who had escaped the captain-general's snare. "What's in here?" asked one man, sticking his head into the room. But Darret had moved and was now crouched motionless behind a marble pillar.

"I been watching the gate—he didn't get out that way!" came a shout from another guard.

Creeping from column to column, Darret silently skirted

the huge empty chamber, thankful for the shadows shrouding the aisles beyond the lofty pillars. Though he had tried to follow Kestrel and his captors, the boy had been forced to hide from the numerous and aggressive searchers. Now he had no idea where the sea captain had been taken.

Darret slipped toward the door, then hid in a corner as a pair of guards ambled through. The men carried torches, and stood just inside the portal, effectively barring Darret's escape route.

"Seen anything?" The cry came from the far end of the chamber.

"Nope." The torchbearers took a few steps forward, leaving a gap between themselves and the darkened doorway.

Darret seized on a desperate idea. Taking from his belt pouch one of the precious coins Kestrel had given him, he tossed the silver disk against the far wall.

"Hey!" cried one of the nearby guards. The two men advanced cautiously toward the sound, and Darret scuttled behind them, diving through the door and finding himself in another huge chamber surrounded by stone columns. With luck he could dart into the hallway on the other side, perhaps catch up to Kestrel—at least he might see where the guards were taking his friend.

He crossed much of the dark room before the torch-bearing guards returned to their post, arguing in subdued tones. The great doors in the near wall drew closer with each of the boy's heart-pounding steps.

Abruptly he heard boots thumping on the wooden floor and the clanking of metal shoulder-plates—more guards! Darret crouched in panic, using a nearby pillar to screen himself from the men-at-arms. Unfortunately, the column couldn't also conceal him from the guards at the far end of the room, so he tried to squirm into the shadows near the floor, forcing himself to remain absolutely motionless.

Three men entered the great chamber, passing the pillar and walking quickly toward the center of the room. Darret edged backward, observing that these men-at-arms walked with a noticeable swagger and wore tall cavalrymen's boots. Their leggings were splattered with mud.

"Halt."

The order came from the far side of the room and Darret's

heart pounded in sudden fear. The trio stopped immediately, and the boy breathed a sigh of relief when he realized that the command had been directed at them. A tall—and all-too-familiar—figure stalked into the chamber.

Captain-General Arrante, escorted by two of his attendants, approached the fidgeting horsemen with measured dignity. When he drew near, each rider dropped to one knee and bowed; the leader quickly leapt to his feet.

"Excellency—we were sent by King Macconal to guard the southwestern approaches to the kingdom. We've ridden hundreds of miles in the last days to bring reports of unspeakable destruction to the south; I myself have talked to witnesses who tell tales of invasion from the east as well. An army of killers marches with terrible speed, butchering everything in its path. I urge you to order the City Gate closed—if this force is moving as quickly as they say, Lanbrij must be protected!"

"This is alarming. Have you told anyone else of this, anyone in the city?"

"Certainly not—we came here directly," replied the officer stiffly. "When we learned that His Majesty had not returned from Carillonn, we came to you."

"Splendid. As you should. Indeed, you must proceed at once to the gate and order that it be sealed."

"Very good, Excellency!" The two kneeling men stood and all three saluted, before spinning back to the door. Darret, leaning along the floor for a better look, froze, aware of the riders approaching.

One of the men met his eyes and opened his mouth in surprise—ready to demand an accounting from this skulking youth—when the captain-general's voice barked.

"Gentlemen!"

The riders stopped in surprise, turning in time to see Arrante's two attendants each toss a tiny object. The pair of small, dark vials struck the hard floor and shattered with a tinkle of glass. Darret gawked in surprise as a dark cloud billowed upward, enveloping the three horsemen in a foggy embrace.

The cavalrymen toppled to the floor, kicking reflexively, gagging and choking horribly. The officer extended a clawlike hand toward the serenely smiling captain-general, but in another second the stricken man grew still, utterly rigid. By the time the cloud dissipated—carrying a bitter, stomach-churning scent to Darret's nostrils—it was clear that the three horsemen were dead.

"Splendid work," Arrante declared as he and his attendants stepped forward to inspect the corpses. The lingering fog didn't seem to bother them, Darret noticed, though a much more diluted sample had been enough to cause him to retch.

"Now, spread the word to the guards—that young thief is still loose in the castle. He may be killed; if he is captured, he is to be brought directly to me. Describe the little wretch so they'll know who to look for."

"Yes, Excellency!" declared one of the attendants.

"Your performance was indeed flawless," the captain-general declared. His voice was casual, but Darret sensed that the two men hung on his every word. "A reward, perhaps, is due."

Immediately the attendants dropped to their knees, turning their faces upward. Arrante removed a small metal flask from a pocket of his robe, uncorked it, and placed a drop of its contents on the extended tongue of each lackey. They closed their eyes and sighed, swaying dizzily, giving every appearance of momentary ecstasy.

"Now rise, and do my bidding!" declared their master, and the servants hurried from the vast chamber. The captain-general departed more slowly, and only then was Darret able to scoot out the door into the gathering shadows of the courtyard.

Guards marched everywhere in this vast open space, and he heard the measured tread of more boots within the great audience hall. In despair he whirled through a circle, wondering where to run. Clopping hooves nearby startled him, and he ducked low in the shadow of the wall as an overloaded wagon creaked past, drawn by a sag-bellied mare, listlessly steered by an elderly stablehand. The cart was piled high with dirty straw, the stench suggesting that the stables had been cleaned and that the waste was being carried out of the castle.

Without stopping to think—or he would surely have changed his mind—Darret dove into the back of the pile of straw, holding his nose and worming his way under the moldering stuff. Gasping for breath, pressing his nose to a crack in the floorboards, he waited only until the wagon had trundled across the drawbridge and started down the streets of Lanbrij before he rolled out, darting into the shelter of an alley and brushing himself off as thoroughly as possible—which, unfortunately, was not very thoroughly at all.

— 3 —

Nicodareus awakened slowly after the killing of the High King. Still cloaked in the body of the black snake, he slithered undetected from the storm grate, coiled beneath a bush, and then slid under the courtyard gate. In a tiny alleyway the Lord Minion shifted his shape, rising again into the body of the cloaked, ragged beggar that had served him so well during his sojourn into Dalethica.

The time was nearly noon, the sun high in the sky, and Nicodareus realized that he had remained torpid for an unusually long time. He shuddered with memories of the consuming agony that always preceded torpor, fearing the need that would drive him to feast again. At the same time, the Eye of Dassadec knew that he deserved that horrid pain, for he had failed his master.

Now that the sluggishness of the kill had worn off, Nicodareus moved toward the castle eagerly. His fear fed his hunger, making him that much more desperate to kill. And he knew where to look for his real victim. High King Kelwyn Dyerston had not spoken willingly in response to the Lord Minion's probing questions, but as the life had been crushed from him he had inadvertently looked toward Castle Carillonn. That had been enough for the Eye of Dassadec, and now he approached that lofty fortress, prepared to seek out—and, to slay—the Man of Three Waters.

The gates of the mighty fortress were sealed, for the humans knew now that an enemy lurked within their lofty capital. Judging that the beggar might attract undue attention among the nobles and courtiers of the castle, Nicodareus changed shape again, adopting the appearance of a castle guard in a full-visored helm. It was a simple matter to fall into step with a returning patrol and pass through the cautiously opened portals into the palace.

For the remainder of the day he wandered the halls of Castle Carillonn seeking something, any clue as to his victim's whereabouts. He got his first information by overhearing the words of a servant girl.

"They took off of a sudden this morning—surprised me, it did!" The lass was hanging sheets on a clothesline just outside a door. She didn't notice the helmeted guard standing within, listening as her companion, another maid, replied.

"And the wedding only last night? Did they always do things so fast?"

"Not that I noticed. They were friendly folk," the first girl replied. "And those Faerines—the nicest people you could imagine!"

Gathering up her empty basket, the young woman went inside, nodded to the guard, and started along the castle corridor. Intrigued by her words, the Lord Minion followed the maid into the darkened halls of the laundry quarters, waiting until she started down a long passageway. No one else was in sight.

Quickly, soundlessly, Nicodareus rushed behind the girl, who started to turn in alarm. He clasped a powerful hand around her shoulder, pulling her into an empty room and slamming the door behind them. He still retained the form of the castle guard, keeping his eyes shielded with the lowered visor of his helm.

"How *dare* you!" she spat, knocking a fist into his helmet. "Unhand me—or I'll scream!"

"It will do you no good—there is no one to hear," said the Eye of Dassadec, his voice rumbling with menace, deeper than the sound born of any human throat. The maid clamped her jaw shut in the face of the threat.

"I seek the Iceman of Halverica—the one they call the Man of Three Waters. You are the maid of his quarters?"

"I was, yes. But he's gone." Apparently relieved to hear that her captor wanted only information, the maid spoke, albeit reluctantly. Her body trembled and her eyes darted fearfully toward the door.

"Where did he go?" Rage coursed through the Lord Minion's body, and he had to forcefully resist—for now—the urge to rip open the girl's throat and guzzle her blood.

"He—he and the lady Raine—journey to Myntar Kosh,"

stammered the girl, looking wildly around as she sought help, or escape.

"Why? Why did he depart?" demanded Nicodareus.

"Th-they seek someone at the Academy of the Sun!" The maid was sobbing, wriggling in the Lord Minion's iron grip. "She had a schoolmaster there they wished to consult. Will you let me go, now?" The quaver in the girl's voice suggested that her fear was growing.

"That is all I require of you."

She had begun to breathe a sigh of relief, when Nicodareus let her see his eyes. The girl had barely gulped the air for a scream before his jaws tore into her arteries, and greedily he gulped the crimson stuff of her life.

Again came the bliss, but now it passed with maddening quickness. Unspeakable suffering locked Nicodareus in its talons, bearing him down, driving him to the cold stone floor. The Lord Minion, again as the black snake, slithered to a castle storeroom, coiling in a shadowy corner.

He learned another thing about his torpor while he lay there, when a human entered the remote storeroom. The Lord Minion's trance was shattered by the intrusion, and though pain racked his body, Nicodareus had the speed and strength to rise, to strike out and slay the intruder. A clever safeguard of his master's, he saw—insuring that the necessary revitalization of torpor did not give an enemy the chance to find and slay the helpless Lord Minion.

For a time afterward he sent his Sight across the world, seeking the Iceman or his companions. He scoured the roads west, but saw no group of travelers that included either Faerines or a child—the two most recognizable of the man's earlier companions. Doubtless the Iceman continued to consume his Aura, which made his very presence unidentifiable to the far-seeing Lord Minion.

Still, Nicodareus had learned where Rudgar Appenfell was going, and that information would prove sufficient for the task—requiring only that the Eye of Dassadec display somewhat more patience than would otherwise be necessary.

But the Lord Minion was an immortal creature, one used to measuring time in centuries. Waiting was something that he could do.

— 4 —

The settled lands between Carillonn and Myntercairn were crossed by many roads, dotted by numerous villages as well as the castles, keeps, and manors of assorted fief-holding nobles. A wide highway ran directly between the two cities, but the party of fleet riders had elected to take less-traveled roads. Even these lanes proved smooth and, to judge by the well-grazed shoulders and frequent inns, usually bore a great deal of traffic. However, a day out of Carillonn the seven riders had encountered very few travelers. By the third day of the ride it seemed that the country byways were virtually empty of traffic.

Myntar Kosh was far away—impossibly distant, on the scale of the Iceman's earlier life—but Takian declared that they would likely reach it in a fortnight's hard riding. Randart, the king's burly sergeant-at-arms, set a hard pace every day, but Rudy and Raine rode the same fleet geldings, sired by Takian's Hawkrunner, that had borne them from Taywick. They matched the pace of the veteran horsemen, though not without a daily variety of blisters and cramps.

Rising before dawn, moving as fast as the steeds could go, the travelers galloped westward with few pauses for rest, pushing their exhausted horses until there was no longer enough light to see the roadway before them. If an inn was handy, they slept indoors; at other times they accepted the hospitality of a local lord. Always they sought information from their hosts, but each time they found that the folk along their way—though without exception nervous and afraid—knew nothing specific about any threat.

One mid-morning the riders stopped at a water hole. Randart fed and watered the homing pigeons, who rode in a pair of wicker cages behind Hawkrunner's saddle. Rudy and Raine dismounted, stretching, intending to splash down their faces and hands, when the Iceman spotted an old woman tottering down the road on bony legs, heading eastward.

"Hello, grandmother!" called one of the men-at-arms cheerily.

"Beware!" she cried, hurrying past and wagging a knobby

finger. "Beware—the bringer of nightmares is abroad!"

"Wait—what do you mean?" cried Takian, stepping into the road as she wobbled by.

"Beware!" she cried again, without a backward look.

Unsettled, Rudy took his lover's hand as they approached the clear pond. Had the woman meant Nicodareus? Or other minions of the Sleepstealer? In any event, it was a grim omen.

The pressure of Raine's hand in his finally drew the Iceman's attention. She bent down and drank, and the supple grace of her movement, the brightness of her laugh as she turned to splash him, filled him with a profound joy. He seized her in his long arms, wrapping her to his chest as she struggled—albeit halfheartedly.

"By the gods and the waters—you're beautiful!" he whispered, burying his face in the brown curls of her hair.

"You're not so bad yourself," she retorted, giving him a coy look. "It's too bad we don't have time for a swim . . . or something."

He felt a powerful rush of arousal, and drew her close again. "Someday . . . someday we'll have plenty of time," he promised, not allowing himself to wonder when, making himself content with Raine's presence, for now.

The travelers soon made ready to ride, and by habit the Iceman took a small sip from his Auraskin. He probed with sudden acuity, seeking some indication of Nicodareus—and staggered backward, struck by the raw strength of evil. The Lord Minion's presence was a burning poker driven into his mind, terrifyingly near.

"What is it?" From somewhere, Raine was talking, but Rudy couldn't reply. He felt the Eye of Dassadec reaching out, seizing his mind, locating him.

Then Raine's arms were around him, her lips against his ear. "I love you!" she whispered fiercely. "You're mine!"

"I . . ." Rudy's throat was dry, his tongue paralyzed as he pulled Raine close. In the next instant the darkness was gone, and he breathed a long, shuddering sigh of relief. Somberly they mounted and returned to the road, though the bright daylight and verdant forest seemed a quieter, more sinister place.

Frequently they were forced to halt in the depths of a wooded valley or along a barren stretch of scrubland and plains. Then they camped, curling in bedrolls for a few hours—and praying that the skies would stay clear, or at least rainless. More often than not the latter hope was granted, as a late summer of unusual dryness unfolded across Dalethica. They entered lands falling under the banner of the Sun Lord, though the people looked the same as those who owed fealty to the High King, and the language was only marginally accented.

Only once during their first week of travel did the clouds shed their watery burden, pouring a day-long drizzle through temperatures cool enough to bring the companions to their earliest halt of the ride. At sunset, the shivering, sodden riders came to a large inn at the edge of a new stretch of woodland. Takian's suggestion that they stop was greeted by a weary assent from Rudy, and a few minutes later the travelers gratefully warmed themselves beside the hearth while a pair of young hostlers looked to the comfort of their horses.

As he had since departing Carillonn, Rudy took a sip from his flask of Aura as they ceased their day's ride; likewise, he had begun each day with a taste of Faerine's precious liquid. Since the menace at the water hole he had gained no indication that the Lord Minion was near. Still, his conviction that he had been the target of the creature's murderous mission had never wavered—he only wondered how long it would be before his imagined fears became real danger.

On the twelfth night of the ride, they crossed a ferry on the mighty River Myn and stopped for the evening at a quiet forest inn on the opposite bank. The great-room of the way-stop was empty except for the bored innkeeper, who sat morosely behind the bar after providing the travelers with refreshments. A pair of traveling merchants came in later, but all they did was complain about the lack of business up and down this once-bustling road.

After learning that they were merely three or four days' ride from Myntercairn, Rudy and Takian asked the innkeeper the usual questions. The man was recalcitrant and frightened; when pressed, however, he told a story he had heard of a farmstead some distance away. The teller had been a traveling smith who had seen the evidence, and was hastening to his own home along the coast. The traveler had been pale with fright, and the trembling in his hands had persisted through many glasses of ale.

Finally the innkeeper had pried forth the story: Several days earlier the smith had stopped at a comfortable farmstead, only to find the family brutally slaughtered. The slain farmer had been a big man, but his body was left a frail, empty shell, drained of blood and life. His wife and children had been butchered in ways that echoed, to Rudy, the horror of Pillotte's death. With a shiver of apprehension the Iceman knew that the Lord Minion remained abroad, now moving westward from Carillonn. Rudy lay awake for hours, wondering about his enemy's plans; he took several sips of Aura, but could gain no inkling about the whereabouts of Nicodareus.

Raine slept fitfully beside him. It was well past midnight when the Iceman felt her arms around him, sensed the yearning—and the comfort—offered by her warm body. Their coupling was fierce and passionate, draining and exultant. Yet even in the intimacy of Raine's arms, where all the outside cares in the world should have faded away, Rudy remained aware of a dark and powerful presence, lurking somewhere beyond the horizon.

Seeking always, searching for him . . . perhaps, even now, waiting along the road.

— 5 —

The flight to Myntar Kosh was long, but Nicodareus traveled more quickly than any human—even one mounted on a fleet horse. Pausing only to kill and eat as required by the power of the Darkslayer, the Lord Minion chose lonely farmsteads for his feasting, leaving none alive who could tell of his arrival.

Ten days after his departure from Carillonn, he reached the Academy, where he took up his blind beggar's disguise and sought alms from the school's gullible apprentices. It took but a short day's conversation to discover the whereabouts of the woman's teacher—the sage called Pheathersqyll. That night Nicodareus flew far from the Academy for his feasting, so as not to raise an alarm, but the next day he returned before dawn.

Pheathersqyll did not see the Lord Minion enter his chambers in the hours of waning darkness, nor did he know that his decanter of water had been tampered with. Nicodareus departed with stealth, assuming the comfortable guise of the owl in a tree where he could observe the Academy's comings and goings.

When the elderly sage awakened and took his morning drink, he did not know that it was a taste of Darkblood that brought the blackness closing through his mind, felling him in the midst of shattered crystal and treacherous, transparent liquid.

— 6 —

Darret ducked around the corner, by habit looking up and down the side streets before taking another step. Buildings crowded the narrow byways of Lanbrij's castle district, forcing many twists and turns in the narrow streets, and the boy never knew when a sudden corner might bring him stumbling into one of the ubiquitous patrols commanded by Captain-General Arrante.

The hour was late afternoon, and he saw many women doing the shopping for the evening meal. They bickered and bartered in the food stalls packed tightly along the street. Longingly, Darret looked at a stack of apples piled before a sharp-eyed fruit vendor, but he resisted the impulse to steal. He already had the enmity of the guards—he couldn't afford to antagonize the local merchants as well.

He reminded himself that he had eaten a few times since his escape from the castle. Fortune had been kind, giving him the chance to cut loose the purse of a young dandy—though that daring theft had yielded all of four miserable coins. Darret had encountered the victim in a different part of the High City, at the only time in the last week that he'd left the immediate vicinity of the castle.

From here on the hilltop dominated by Castle Corsari, surrounded by teeming streets and stalls where merchants offered all manner of goods, he could see much of the rest of Lanbrij—and its twin ports, gateways to the Circled Sea and the Great Ocean. The *Black Condor* lay at anchor beside a barren rock at the outer rim of the harbor. The passengers had been allowed to embark on that bleak islet, but none had come to the city since Darret had been watching.

In his twelve years of life Darret had seen a fair degree of treachery, trickery, and betrayal—he had worked his own share, and been the victim of many others'. He thought he understood what had happened: The captain-general was determined that no one in Lanbrij should think themselves threatened, and the inevitable attack would hence be that much more disastrous. Furthermore, when Darret searched his memory, he realized the stench released by the shattering of that black vial had been vaguely familiar. Some days afterward he abruptly identified the smell as the same that had lingered on the hilt of the black-bladed minion sword.

A stench he had come to know as Darkblood.

Darret wasted no time wondering why the captain-general was in league with the Sleepstealer's minions. In fact, the boy prided himself on remaining unsurprised by any example of humanity's evil. Nor did he feel inclined to tell anyone his story—who knew which among these greedy merchants, stealthy pickpockets, miserable beggars, and swaggering nobles might be in Captain-General Arrante's pay?

"Hey!" A burly hand clapped Darret on the shoulder before he even knew that the guard was there. Another chain mailed man-at-arms stepped in front of the boy, planting his hands on his hips and leering unpleasantly.

"You look like the thief-boy I been told about. Seems there was some gold mentioned for the fellow that brings you in."

"Not me!" Darret protested. His eyes flicked over the guard's shoulder, then widened in shocked surprise. Alarmed, the fellow quickly glanced behind him.

In that instant Darret's foot lashed out to the side, jabbing into the second guard's knee. With a howl of pain the man fell, while the first whirled back, diving to wrap his burly arms around the boy. But Darret was no longer there—he leapt sideways, tumbling under the table of apples, spilling the fruit in the dust.

A chorus of curses followed him as he ducked past the canvas flap that served as the back of the stall. So much for staying on good terms with the merchants, the boy thought with a grimace. Darting down the narrow aisle, he turned into the first alley he saw, sprinting around several more corners until he had left the frustrated guards—and the infuriated vendor—far behind.

NINE

Pheathersqyll

A monarch is only as secure as the foundation
and floor supporting his throne.
—SCROLL OF BARACAN

— 1 —

"Do you know that I *really* love you?" Rudy whispered, gradually emerging from sleep, acutely conscious of Raine's naked back against his chest. "And I'm glad you made me take you along to Myntar Kosh."

"Mmm-hmm," Raine murmured from the depths of the downy mattress. With a curl of her shoulder and a twist of her hips she turned to nuzzle the hollow of his neck. "Smartest thing you've ever done, even if I had to do it for you. As to really loving me, I think you showed me again last night."

Looking through the room's large window, Rudy saw that darkness still shrouded the sky over this crossroads inn; they had a little time before rising to get back on the road. For blissful moments the Iceman lay still, relishing the touch of Raine's fingers, the kisses and caresses that trailed along his body, finally compelling him to reach for her. With a soft laugh she straddled his belly, trapping him between her muscular thighs—and then they were together until the lavender glow of dawn tinged the east.

By the time that brightness had spread across half the sky, the horses were saddled, and the riders had breakfasted on bread and bacon. The inn was miles behind them when the first rays of the sun filtered through the morning mist.

The road was a forest-fringed track, and they met no other travelers until mid-morning, when a heavily laden ox cart lurched into view coming toward them. The riders pulled their mounts under the trees to give the wagon room to pass on the narrow lane. A strapping man of middle age walked beside the ox, while a weary-looking woman and several squirming children rode in the cart. A lanky hound had been trailing the family, but at the sight of the riders the dog rushed forward, barking.

"Ho, my good man," Takian said breezily, with a wave and a smile. Hawkrunner kicked once at the dog, which ceased barking to retreat and growl fiercely from between his master's legs. "It's been an empty road today."

"Would that it was empty of us!" growled the man, clearly in a foul humor. "We left a crop in the fields, packing since midnight, on the road at dawn!"

"You don't want to be traveling?" Raine asked the woman, as one of the children reached up to stroke the muzzle of her horse.

"*I* do—it's Hanc don't believe me!" the farm wife retorted, glaring at her husband.

"Believe a *dream*?" Hanc's voice was tired. "She has this dream. She won't tell me about it, just gets up and says she's taking the young'uns and moving east. All the way to Carillonn, she says! And I can come too, if I want."

"What kind of dream?" Raine probed gently.

The woman shook her head in response, but before her expression grew blank the riders saw a flash of real horror cross her face. "Can't talk about it," she said, with a glance at the children. "But you, too, might want to think about traveling east. The west . . ." She pulled her shawl over her face, but Rudy saw that her eyes were filled with tears.

"We understand," the Iceman said. "Only necessity carries us this way."

"Your wife is a wise woman, unusually so," Takian said to the farmer. "And Hanc—you are a very lucky man. I urge you both to make haste." With that the riders were off, leaving the man scowling suspiciously after them and the woman sternly suggesting that Hanc get moving.

The horses loped for hours, sensing the riders' compelling need for haste. The land had gradually changed from the thick forests of central Dalethica to the open, flat steppeland of the west. They began to catch increasing glimpses of the River Myn, Raine remarking on a familiar riverside village or a grove of ironwoods atop a hill that she remembered from her childhood. They all shared her anticipation as the day crossed into afternoon.

Finally the road descended nearer to the bank of the Myn. "The Academy of the Sun stands upon those heights," Raine explained, indicating the tree-lined bluffs that commanded the opposite bank of the pastoral waterway. At the top grew a fringe of oaks and maples, while the terraced slopes were interspersed with placid ponds. Several splashing brooks connected the little lakes, leading to a laughing cataract that plunged down the bluff to the great river.

"There!" Raine's voice rose with barely contained excitement as she pointed to a crest of low hills, nearly opposite the riders. Rudy saw a series of stone buildings, great halls, and rambling, compartmented lodges. Three massive pyramids rose beyond the summit of the ridge, arranged in a regular triangle atop a low, rounded hill. The structures dominated the grounds of the Academy, looming over buildings and trees. Many ancient oaks and elms shaded the ground between the structures, and sweeping, marble stairways led past fountains down to a manicured riverbank garden.

"There's the landing," she added, pointing to a small inn on the near side of the river. A boatman dozed in his craft, which was secured to the inn's pier by a line while the current tried to tug the ungainly flatboat downstream.

"We'll try to reach you in Myntercairn," Rudy promised, as he and Raine turned into the narrow lane leading toward the inn.

"Leave word at the palace of the Sun Lord," the king

replied. His eyes met Rudy's, and the Iceman saw the hope there. "And good luck!"

The king and his four guardsmen galloped off, while Raine rode down the lane to the river bank, kicking the flanks of her gelding, forcing the Iceman to gallop after. Soon they passed under an ivy-draped arch of carved stone and halted before the dock.

"We have a fare for the river!" Rudy called, dismounting and shouting to wake the boatman—who still lay motionless, a battered felt hat shading his eyes.

"Can't go yet—waitin' for another fella," drawled the man, pulling his hat lower over a sun-darkened face.

"It's urgent," pressed the Iceman. "We'll pay for haste."

"Won't be long, anyway," replied the man, without lifting his hat.

"We can wait—for a little while, anyway," Raine said quietly, taking Rudy's hand. "Life has a tempo of its own around here." She looked across the river at the lofty buildings, at the marble facades and domed roofs. The Iceman, sensing her pleasant nostalgia, forced himself to be patient.

"Those pyramids look ancient," Rudy observed, studying the massive structures with interest. "Almost like man-made mountains."

"They are ancient, older than the bridges of Carillonn. They were raised before the Sleepstealer War—in fact, they're some of the few human constructs to have survived the minion horde."

"Were they built as monuments?" Rudy was moved by the pyramids' air of serenity.

"No—actually, the Lord Astronomer uses them for his studies of the stars, and for observing the cycles of the moon. Pheathersqyll's hall is on this side of the nearest one, at the far end of the hill," she declared breathlessly. Her cheeks were flushed and her eyes bright, giving Rudy a soft, pleasing impression of the young Raine who had pursued so many studies here.

Rudy looked absently at the building she had indicated, preoccupied by his own desire to get over there, to talk to the man inside. Noticing a strangely dark bank of cloud in the western sky, he wondered if the murky haze was the precursor of a thunderstorm. In a few minutes another rider entered the dockyard astride a swaybacked mare. At his arrival, the boat-man rose and began freeing his lines.

"Lord Wendeth!" cried Raine delightedly, running toward the newcomer. "He's the Lord Pilferer," she called over her shoulder to Rudy. "His classes were some of the most fun I ever had!"

"What kind of academy teaches pilfering?" Rudy asked, before Raine seized her elderly teacher in an enthusiastic em-brace.

"Raine!" cried Wendeth, clearly delighted. "This is a splendid occasion—the Girl Born Under Three Stars Rising returns!" The lord's expression saddened then, and he looked into Raine's eyes as he gently held her shoulders. "You have heard about Pheathersqyll, then? Even so, you got here re-markably quickly."

Raine's face tightened. "Heard—heard *what*?"

Rudy was deeply apprehensive as he came up to her, touched her shoulder, felt her body trembling under his hand. The old teacher shook his head sorrowfully. "Forgive me— I thought that you knew, that you had come . . ."

"What's wrong with him?" demanded Raine.

"It's—that is, the physicians think it was a stroke, more than a week ago. He still lives, so far as I know, but he hasn't awakened in all that time."

"No!" Raine's voice was a moan, and Rudy held her as she fought against a wave of grief. "Where is he? I must go to him!"

"Yes—yes, of course. He's in his chambers, the same apartments he's always had, overlooking the river."

They hurried the horses onto the flatboat. "Remember— we have Aura," Rudy said urgently. "There's hope—*good* hope!" Raine made no reply, but held his hand in a bone-crushing grip.

Though the boatman seemed to take an agonizingly long time to pole his barge, Rudy paid him with a silver coin when they finally reached the far bank. The man stammered a sur-prised "Thank you, milord!" but the two travelers had al-ready mounted and ridden their horses off the flatboat, leaving Wendeth to plod slowly behind. Raine led the way up a long, curving road, until at last they galloped under a granite arch and drew up before a huge, rambling stable. The riders sprang from the saddle as several hostlers advanced. Only as they drew close did Rudy notice the long hair flowing from beneath their head scarves, and he saw that the livery workers were girls. Dressed in leather breeches, woolen shirts, and gloves, they took the reins of the horses with easy familiarity, promising that the animals would be well-tended.

Before trotting after Raine, Rudy removed the two extra Auraskins from his saddlebags, slinging them over his shoulder with the half-full sack he already carried. Raine led him between high hedges, pointing out landmarks in a tight, cold voice—the massive oak she had climbed as a youngster; the statue of the Academy's founder, Sun Lord Dalric I; and the pool where she involuntarily learned to swim when winter's ice had proven unexpectedly thin. All the while her tone was grimly furious, as if she accused each landmark of some sort of betrayal.

Finally they passed through the doors of one of the Academy's greatest halls. Running down the flagstoned corridor, Raine did not slow her pace until she approached the door at the very end. Here sat a youth, who looked up from a page crowded with symbols to squint curiously at the man and woman who paused to catch their breath.

"Old Pheathersqyll—I have to see him!" Raine announced without preamble.

"He's . . . well, he's still resting. You can't go in," declared the boy. "He wouldn't know you, anyway."

Raine's body trembled but she held her voice firm. "Whether he knows me or not, I'm going to see him. I've traveled across Dalethica to come back here, and you'll not stop me at his door."

The lad blinked, surprised. "Were you a student of his?" he inquired hesitantly, looking past the pair as if he expected help from some other quarter.

"I was his ward for the first seventeen years of my life."

Raine stepped to the door and turned the latch, the youth making no move to stop her. Rudy followed her through the portal, pulling the door softly shut as she approached the long, low bed.

Giving her a moment of privacy, the Iceman allowed his eyes to roam around the cluttered yet spacious chamber. A vaulted ceiling of dark wood matched the paneling on the

walls, but numerous windows—many extending from just
above floor level almost to the rafters—gave the room a
bright, airy feel. Comfortable chairs faced a deep fireplace,
and numerous shelves were buried under the weight of countless books, scrolls, and boxes. Huge rugs, dyed in bright and
intricate patterns such as the Iceman had never seen, layered
nearly the entire floor.

Rudy counted at least four desks, and one wall of the sage's
room was covered with maps. On one of these he recognized
the outline of the Glimmersee, and guessed that another
charted the drainage of Dalethica's major rivers. Still others
were not true maps at all, unless one could map the heavens—
they illustrated arrays of the night sky, diagramming the cycles of the moon and the stars of the various seasons.

Raine knelt motionless beside the bed, and when Rudy
stepped behind her, he was shocked by the appearance of the
man who had been so much a part of her life. There was no
other way to put it: Pheathersqyll looked dead. Pale wisps of
hair surrounded the wrinkled scalp, and the pinched features
of his face were furrowed with deep lines. His hands, crossed
formally on his chest, might have been claws coated with
pocked, spotted skin.

Only the faint motion of the chest, rising and settling
slightly with each inaudible breath, belied the image of a
corpse. Disturbed, Rudy looked away from the bed, surprised
to see that the tall windows of the room stood open to admit
a warm summer breeze. He would have expected the windows
of the sickroom to be tightly closed—although perhaps the
vista of nearby gardens, grass, and the tree-lined riverbank
was presumed to offer some healing benefit.

Yet Pheathersqyll showed no sign of opening his eyes for
vista or visitor. Raine reached up to clasp her strong hands
over the frail fingers. For long moments she said nothing, and
Rudy couldn't tell if she was offering up a prayer, or seeking
to commune with her ancient tutor.

"I can't—I *won't* be too late," Raine said, her voice strong
as she finally broke the silence. "To travel all the way to
Faerine, to come back here just a week too late . . ."

"We haven't tried the Aura," Rudy said gently. "Perhaps
it will be enough to awaken him, even to help him heal."

"Yes—try it!" She seized at the hope, turning to Rudy with desperation in her eyes.

Uncorking one of the skins, the Iceman held the nozzle to the old man's lips, which were parted slightly. Rudy felt acutely conscious of the learning and knowledge, the insight and wisdom, trapped within that motionless figure. He allowed a drop of the liquid to emerge, followed that with a slow trickle. Fearing the unconscious man might choke, he pulled the waterskin away after a few seconds. Raine kept Pheathersqyll's hands in hers while Rudy waited for some reaction. After a minute or so, he dribbled out a little more Aura, adding a third dose after another period of waiting.

"It doesn't seem to—" Rudy was interrupted by Raine's upheld hand. The Iceman looked at Pheathersqyll's frail hands, wondering—then certain!

Two of the fingers had moved.

He trickled more of the Aura into the man's mouth, heartened to see the lips part slightly. When the tutor swallowed, the Iceman gave him more. Then Pheathersqyll opened his eyes, and they were so clear, so startlingly blue and vital, that Rudy entirely forgot the man's appearance of a moment earlier. With a contented sigh, Pheathersqyll turned his head and looked around, beaming at the view through the windows, and the glorious blue sky over Dalethica.

Puffing, the elderly sage tried to sit up. Raine gave him a hand, then placed several cushions behind his back.

"Raine . . . the Girl Born Under Three Stars Rising," said the tutor with a kindly chuckle. "Aurianth granted that I should behold you one more time while I still breathe!"

"Don't try to talk," Raine urged, brushing the wisps of hair back from his forehead. "Just rest—"

"Rest? I've had enough of that, I should say, to last for quite some time! Though I'd have another drink, if I may make so bold as to ask?" Pheathersqyll's eyes twinkled as he looked at Rudy.

"Of course!" The Iceman handed the waterskin over, and the sage, nodding his thanks, drank deeply. After returning the skin to Rudy, he swung about on the mattress and dropped his feet to the floor. With a push from his arms he stood, tottering alarmingly.

"Sit down!" cried Raine, leaping up to take his elbow.

The sage paid no attention. Instead, those blue eyes, sparkling with amusement, fastened upon Rudy's face. "A tall man, brown-haired and lanky. Sort of a shy smile . . . reminds me of a certain description I heard, from a ten-year-old girl. The fellow who visited her dreams, if I make my guess."

"This is Rudy Appenfell," Raine said, blushing.

"The Man of Three Waters," Pheathers completed, chuckling at the astonished glance that passed between Rudy and Raine. "Oh, yes—I, too, have had some vivid dreams. I'm glad that you have sought me, for I have important information."

"Information?" Rudy asked excitedly. He had hoped for nothing less!

"Yes—you must leave here, as soon as possible." The elderly scholar sighed and sat on the edge of his bed, looking sympathetically at the two young people.

"You seek the answers to many questions, don't you?" he asked.

"I—that is," Rudy stammered. "I had hoped you would be able to help me understand."

"I have no answers for you—only a suspicion."

"Suspicion of what?"

"A feeling that before we are through, the Watershed will be contested between you and the god; and the victorious one will lay his stamp on the world in a mark that will endure forever."

Rudy sagged backward, thunderstruck. Surely the old man was delusional! "Wh-what do you mean?" he demanded.

"Just that you are an important bit of history—and of hope. The rest of us might as well be pawns, for all that we matter to the future of the world. But *you* . . ." Pheathersqyll's words trailed off cryptically.

"But enough prattle—I know you're in danger here, and you must travel far to gain the answers to your mysteries."

"Travel—to where?"

"Why, Faerine, of course. Where did you think?"

"Faerine? But—well, I thought . . . I thought that maybe I should come here!" Rudy retorted, taken aback. He had thought that his mind was numbed to impossible beliefs, but one of Pheathers' statements punctured that insentience: *The Watershed will be contested between you and the god!*

"Here? Whatever for?" the old man was saying. "This place is finished, or it will be in a matter of days. Oh, and be sure to travel by water—he can't follow you there."

"He? *Who?*" Rudy's head was spinning, but he suddenly noticed that the sage's eyes were grimly serious. Pheathersqyll gestured to the waterskin that the Iceman still clutched in his hand, and Rudy raised it to his lips, allowing a swallow of the water to splash into his mouth. Immediately he spun toward the window, staring at the pastoral scene of riverside and field—and he knew that danger was real, and close. He started toward the open window, then recoiled as a looming shadow filled the frame. Shaking his head, he saw nothing out of the ordinary—

Until a black, wedge-shaped head rose above the low sill. Darting forward, a dark, thick-bodied viper slithered into the room like a curl of perfect blackness, coiling against the wall—and then changing shape very quickly. The snake body grew, rising, twisting to loom manlike and larger. Black wings sprouted to either side, and ember-red eyes glared at Rudy with an absolute hatred that he had seen only once before.

"The Lord Minion!" Raine gasped, stepping to Rudy's side. Each of them drew their swords, extending the slender steel blades toward the horrific being.

"Nicodareus himself comes for you," Pheathersqyll remarked in a tone of remarkable detachment. "This means that Dassadec knows of your power, your destiny."

"Your destiny is to die!" declared the winged black creature, advancing on two talon-studded paws. Its forepaws, also tipped with wicked claws, reached toward the Iceman.

Raine's sword lashed out, the keen tip scoring a scratch across the Lord Minion's wrist. Nicodareus snatched the limb back, roaring so loudly that the door of the room rattled on its hinges.

"We bear the weapons of Faerine," Rudy declared, heartened. He lunged forward with a thrust of his own. "It seems even a Lord Minion can feel the cut of digger steel!"

"Impudent human!" bellowed Nicodareus. His forepaw lashed out, knocking the sword from Rudy's hand, sending the blade skidding across the smooth floor. The bestial face curled into a gloating sneer. "Your resistance only increases my pleasure!"

Rudy's hand stung as he stared at the sword, his rash optimism forgotten. The Lord Minion took a step toward him and the Man of Three Waters retreated, sensing Raine moving sideways away from him. He wanted to tell her to run, to save herself, but he knew she wouldn't listen.

"Why do you seek the Iceman?" asked Pheathersqyll conversationally. "It seems that your master has sent you a long way to deal with one mere human."

Nicodareus ignored the ancient scholar, continuing to advance, backing Rudy toward a corner of the large, high-ceilinged room. Desperately the Iceman looked around for some avenue of escape, seeing the lofty windows as his best hope—but to reach them he would have to pass within easy reach of the looming monstrosity.

Steel flashed as Raine charged in. The Lord Minion swiped at her, but with lightning-quick reflexes she ducked the blow, lancing forward to slash the flesh of the creature's bulging thigh. With a roar Nicodareus spun and leaped; only Raine's astonishing agility allowed her to roll out of the way, tumbling across the floor to bounce to her feet before the tall windows.

"Go!" she spat at Rudy, sending him a pleading glance. She tilted her head toward the door, and he knew that she would sacrifice herself to give him time to escape. But he also knew that, like her, he couldn't leave. Instead, he dove toward his own sword, sliding across the floor to seize the weapon's hilt.

The Lord Minion pounced, catlike, and the Iceman collided with a body as solid as iron. The wind exploded from his lungs and he felt himself lifted, groaning as cruel talons tore through his shoulder and plucked him off the floor.

Then Nicodareus shrieked, a sound like a mighty tree splitting under the assault of a mountain storm. He cast Rudy against the wall, and as the Iceman slumped to the floor, he saw Raine skipping away, the tip of her blade smeared with steaming black liquid. Ignoring his intended victim, the monster leapt after the woman, quickly backing her into the corner of the room where he had tried to trap Rudy.

Numbly the Iceman tried to rise, but his body wouldn't respond to the commands of his brain. Seeking to grasp the hilt of his sword, he found that he could barely curl his fingers. His legs would do no more than feebly bend, kicking without effect at the stones of the floor.

Across the room Nicodareus towered menacingly over Raine. "It pleases me to destroy your wench," he growled, turning to glare wickedly at Rudy. The woman lashed out, but this time the Lord Minion twisted away, then smashed a backhand blow across her face, sending her tumbling across the floor—though somehow she maintained the grip on her sword.

Rudy found the strength to gather his legs beneath him, to rise to his knees and get a firm grip on his sword, but he moved with agonizing slowness. "No!" he grunted, dismayed as the word came out sounding like nothing more than a croak of despair.

Raine groaned, and the Iceman was shocked to see blood spilling from her mouth, to recognize cruel claw marks across her cheek. She tried to raise her weapon and Nicodareus plucked it from her hand like a vexsome thorn. With another brutal paw he reached down and wrapped his fingers around her throat. More blood trickled out as talons pierced her skin, and though she kicked at the monster's belly, her struggles only made him chortle with cruel amusement.

Pushing himself to his feet, lurching like a drunk, Rudy stumbled toward the Lord Minion's broad back. He saw the leathery wings flapping in cruel deliberation, heard the sounds of Raine's choking gasps for air. Then he drove the blade of digger steel forward with all the power of his fury and despair. The tip of the weapon gouged one of the monster's wings, tearing the leathery skin—and again Nicodareus roared. The sound alone made Rudy stagger, but he pressed forward, brandishing the sword.

Nicodareus turned, batting the blade aside and dangling Raine before Rudy. Swinging the woman about by her neck, the Lord Minion used her as a shield. Raine, soaked with blood, flopped limply, and the Iceman's anguish drove him to a frenzy. He charged, slashing at the monster's knee, cutting slightly through the black skin—but then the taloned foot lashed out, catching Rudy in the hip, bashing him against the map-lined wall.

"I call you by your name, Nicodareus," declared Pheathersqyll, his voice strong enough to cut through the chaos.

"You who are the Eye of Dassadec—you who are also the greatest failure among the Sleepstealer's minions! No miserable kroak has committed greater derelictions in your master's name!"

The monster dropped Raine, who collapsed senselessly to the floor, and turned to regard the scholar with the fiery hatred of his malignant eyes.

"Who are you to say this, human?" he growled—and there was more than menace in his tone. Now Rudy sensed an undercurrent of fury that had been lacking in the Lord Minion's earlier, gloating remarks.

"Was it not you who was tricked by the Guardians a thousand years ago?" demanded the sage forcefully. He pointed an accusatory finger at the monster. "*You* who caused the deaths of two Lord Minions—the deaths of Balzarac and Karthakan—with your ambition, your lack of caution!"

There was a light, singsong quality to Pheathersqyll's voice that made Rudy wonder if the old man had gone mad. But in fact it was the Lord Minion who was apparently seized by madness, for Nicodareus took a step forward, trembling with almost palpable fury.

"Who *are* you?" the monster demanded again.

"Simply a human who remembers history—one who knows the truth about the Sleepstealer's greatest failure!"

"I am not a failure!" The voice had dropped to a rumbling growl, deeper than that of a huge bear—and infinitely more dangerous. Rudy scrambled toward Raine, cradling her blood-soaked head, trying to stem her deep wounds with his hands, his shirt, anything at hand. Through one horrid cut he saw her jugular pulsing with the beat of her heart. He sobbed, recognizing that another fraction of an inch would have been fatal. Yet she had lost *so* much blood. Uncorking another Auraskin, Rudy spilled the precious water over her face, pouring some into her mouth and more over the wounds themselves. A detached part of himself listened to the sage's taunts while he desperately struggled to save his beloved.

"This is a thing that all humans soon will know—that the one who would raise himself above all the Sleepstealer's minions is none other than a fool, a creature whose own ambition carries the seeds of his master's destruction!"

"Silence!" The word thundered through the room, stunning Rudy's ears.

"Your ambition, your greed! You saw the Lord Minions die, did you not? You knew that they perished because of your stupidity. Even if your master hasn't learned the truth, in your own heart of Darkblood you know it!"

Pheathersqyll startled Rudy—and Nicodareus—by throwing back his head and laughing, a sound that was shrill, almost hysterical with amusement, but completely free.

Nicodareus took another step toward Pheathers while Rudy, still grasping for cloth to stem Raine's bleeding, continued to drain the waterskin of Aura. Frantically he pressed the nozzle to her lips, spilled the enchanted liquid over her face, ignoring the excess that mingled with the blood still flowing from her torn cheek and lips.

"I call thee Nicodareus, Fool of Dassadec!" cried the sage again, his voice vibrating with a rich, triumphant declaration of victory. "Your arrogance—and your stupidity!—will be your master's undoing!"

The taunts were finally too much for the Lord Minion. He pounced forward, seizing the ancient sage in both of his forepaws, sweeping him hard against that rocklike chest. With a vicious snarl he bent his muzzle downward, brutally tore away the flesh of Pheathersqyll's neck, and allowed the blood erupting from the academic's throat to splash over his own bestial face.

Rudy watched, breathless, as Nicodareus struggled to turn his head away, to bring his attention back to the two humans cowering against the far wall of the room. But there seemed to be something compelling in those gouts, and the monster turned back to the corpse with a groan, lowering his muzzle to the gory wound. Nicodareus struggled visibly to twist away, to fight the craving, but the lure of blood was too strong. His fangs reached downward until black lips touched, almost tenderly, the gushing slash in the human's neck.

And he drank. The Lord Minion suckled on blood as an infant desperately consumes mother's milk. In horror Rudy watched the monster swill Pheathersqyll's life, raising the corpse over his head so that all of the blood could drain, could nourish his monstrous hunger.

Raine groaned feebly, and Rudy poured more of the Aura

into her mouth, relieved to see her eyes flutter open. She tried
to turn her head but he blocked her with his body, unwilling
to let her see the grisly communion occurring across the room.
Finally Nicodareus threw the husk of the sage's body to the
floor, where it bounced like a stick figure. Rudy was reminded
of the empty visage of Kelwyn Dyerston, and only his grief
prevented him from gagging anew at this proof of how the
High King had died. The Iceman's hand closed around the
hilt of his sword, and he laid Raine as gently as possible
against the wall, ready to stand and fight this beast to the end.

But now it was the Lord Minion who staggered like a
drunkard, lurching toward the window through which he had
entered. That bestial face swung groggily about the room, and
the Iceman saw the hellish fire of the eyes dim. Rudy couldn't
tell whether the monster saw him or not. Nicodareus fell toward the open window, head and arms dangling over the sill.
Scarcely daring to breath, Rudy watched as the awful body
shifted and lurched, shrinking back into the sinewy viper that
had first slithered into the room. Appalled, sickened, Rudy
cradled Raine with one arm, his free hand still clenched
around the hilt of his sword.

The snake was far from perfect—great lumps marred its
body, and it slithered with desperate, sickly haste over the
sill, as if the transformation had been completed only as far
as the Lord Minion's abruptly weakened state could manage.
Sensing vulnerability, Rudy broke from his stupor to dash
after the monster. He chopped at the inky tail, but the grotesque viper whirled with shocking speed, lashing with mouth
agape, needlelike fangs extended. The Iceman tumbled backward, barely escaping the deadly bite, and by the time he
scrambled to his feet the monster was gone.

— 2 —

The days were long and lonely, Anjell thought, as she wandered around Castle Carillonn. Since the death of the king,
gates were closed and locked throughout the great edifice.
Usually she couldn't get where she wanted to go, even when
she had a particular destination in mind.

Not that she *wanted* to do much, anymore. Since Nelli had

been killed by that awful thing (which, though nobody had told her, she knew was Nicodareus), the world seemed a grimmer, scarier place. She had seen that Lord Minion once before, and knew how awful he looked and acted. Yet the killing of the friendly servant girl seemed so absolutely unfair!

She missed Nellidyn a lot, but also Rudy and Danri and all her friends who'd gone off traveling. Bristyn and Awnro were nice to her, but they were also busy tending to things like the High King's funeral, and meetings with lords and ambassadors from seemingly everywhere. At least one good thing had happened: Although Dara had been determined to depart for home immediately, Awnro Lyrifell—who had been spending a great deal of time with the pretty widow—persuaded her to remain in the city for a while longer. And as boring as the castle was, Anjell was certain that going back to Halverica would be worse.

In fact, Dara had become very interested in things about Carillonn, and the history of Dalethica. She read books, some of which she shared with Anjell, in the royal library, or pried information and songs from the bard. Since the girl had always enjoyed Awnro's stories, she was glad that her mother now took such delight in hearing them.

As far as Nicodareus was concerned, Anjell wasn't so much scared by the monster that had killed her friend Nelli as she was mad at it! And anger, naturally, required action. To that end, she decided that she needed to devise a plan.

In matters such as this, the girl had found that Bristyn's counsel was much more inspirational than her mother's. Anjell came upon the young queen pacing in her quarters, wringing her hands and turning back and forth in agitation. The girl entered the parlor and sat primly in one of the cushioned chairs as Bristyn smiled briefly at her, then resumed pacing.

"What's wrong?" asked Anjell.

"Jamiesen Macconal has invited me to accompany him to Corsari," Bristyn explained. "And I'm not sure if I should go—but I think I will, anyway."

"Why?" asked the girl, intrigued.

"Well, for one thing, Takian's going to Lanbrij—that's the capital of Corsari—from Myntar Kosh. And Standarl Drade seems to have things well in hand in Carillonn—at least, the militia captains report many volunteers, and the formalities of the funeral have been dealt with. The Hundred Knights are prepared—Captain Dennimar has them making patrols to the east, while he organizes the defenses of Carillonn. And finally, Awnro has agreed to come as my escort.

"On the other hand, the ship leaves tomorrow. I don't know if I can be ready, and I'm still not sure if I *should* go!"

"Of course you should!" Anjell declared. "Takian will be really glad to see you! And you're right—there's really not much to do around here."

Bristyn sighed, then smiled with firm determination. "All right—I will go."

"Can I come too?" Anjell asked instantly.

The noblewoman looked at Anjell, smiling kindly. "I'd be grateful for your company, and Dara's—if your mother agrees."

"Oh, yes!" Anjell squealed. Naturally, her mother would go too—it only remained for Anjell to figure out a way to inform Dara.

Then she had an idea: She would enlist Awnro's aid! Anjell found the minstrel tuning his lute in the castle music room—a chamber containing an array of harps, pipes, drums, harpsichords, horns, and other instruments Anjell couldn't name.

"Are you going to Corsari with Bristyn?" asked the girl.

"Indeed I am—'tis too many years since I have seen the Circled Sea."

"I'm coming too, and my mother. I just have to come up with a way to tell her," Anjell explained seriously.

"Aha! And you wondered if I might be of some help?"

The girl nodded. The bard was obviously a fellow of keen perception, and she was pleased with her selection of him as an ally.

"It should be as safe a journey as anywhere else—considering the times," declared Awnro, musing to himself. "Let me talk to Dara. She's been interested in stories of the Circled Sea—and 'tis true, Lanbrij is a wonder, in a very different sort of way than Carillonn. It could be that she will see this trip as a good idea."

And in the end, of course, Dara did—not that Anjell ever had any serious doubts.

— 3 —

Rudy spilled more Aura into Raine's mouth, over her motionless, pale body. He pressed his ear to her breast, and barely heard the fluttering heartbeat.

"*Please*, don't die!" he begged, taking her face in his hands, trying to penetrate her closed eyes with his will. Her skin was cold to the touch, and no flicker of recognition showed in her face.

"Aurianth, Mistress of Magic—I'll promise anything!" he prayed, squeezing his own eyelids shut in concentration. "If I have to face the Sleepstealer himself, if that's my destiny—I accept it willingly! But don't let her die!"

Anguish choked off any further words. He cradled his beloved's body, rocking back and forth, trying to stop his own violent, involuntary sobs. In the back of his mind the challenge of Pheathersqyll lay smoldering—*The Watershed will be contested between you and the god!* Of course the notion was mad, but if madness would save Raine, the Iceman would leave sanity behind.

The wounds inflicted by the Lord Minion's claws were cruel and jagged, seemingly resistant even to the healing power of Aura. In some places scabs had started to form over torn flesh, but in others the gouges looked red and angry. The Iceman trickled the last Aura from his waterskin over the most dangerous-looking wounds.

Where was Nicodareus? The question slowly but firmly pressed its way through Rudy's grief. The Lord Minion had disappeared for the present, but the Iceman knew that his enemy would return, possibly very soon. Leaving Raine for the moment, he went to the window, scrutinizing the dense hedges where the viper had disappeared. It would take him hours to search that greenery, even if his quarry was still there—and then he had no guarantee of victory if he should find him.

It made far more sense, Rudy thought, to flee. Pheathersqyll had said to go to Faerine—and: "Travel by water." The former suggestion seemed nearly as mad as the notion that the Man of Three Waters was supposed to battle Dassadec himself; but the latter seemed to indicate a realistic course of action. Only then did the Iceman think of calling for help. He dashed to the door, flinging it open to find that the boy posted outside earlier had disappeared. He shouted, but heard no answering cry.

Returning to Raine, he bandaged the worst of her wounds with strips torn from some of Pheathersqyll's spare robes. Then he lifted her, frightened by the lightness of her once-solid body. Carrying her easily to the opened window, he stepped over the low sill, turning away from the garden to the grassy sward leading down to the river.

As he looked around the grounds of the Academy, the Iceman thought it strange that no one seemed to have noticed the noise of the fight—indeed, the great university seemed strangely deserted. Only as he moved away from the building, carrying Raine down the long slope to the river, did he begin to understand why. Great columns of smoke billowed into the air, rising like unnatural clouds to the west. The wind tugged the vaporous pillars sideways, increasing the illusion that they were actual mounds of dark cumulus—but so thick was the base of the clouds that it could have no other origin than the ground itself.

With awful surety, Rudy pictured the destruction occurring below those smoldering clouds. The war had reached Myntar Kosh, he knew, and would soon sweep beyond. Students and their instructors alike had apparently gathered at the western end of the sprawling estate, seeking a better look at the approaching storm. Rudy felt no such urge—all his energies were focused on the need to flee.

The source of the smoke seemed to be on the south bank of the Myn—the same side occupied by the Academy. Rudy remembered the haze he had noticed this morning, and wondered if that cloudiness had been a more distant precursor of this smoke. If that was the case, the fires had advanced very far in a single day. Cradling Raine in his arms, the Iceman bore her with ease as he made his way toward the river, his eyes probing through the reeds on the shoreline.

"This place is finished." Another of Pheathersqyll's phrases rang through Rudy's mind. With a look at the billowing clouds—weren't they closer than they had been ten minutes ago?—he had no trouble believing the old scholar's statement. As he had hoped, Rudy found a boat tucked among the long cattails of the river's edge. The craft was long and slender, with a half dozen short benches straddling the hull. He lowered Raine between two seats, bending her legs gently. Finding a canvas sail in the bow, he made a makeshift blanket for her; because he intended to go downstream, they wouldn't be needing the wind.

Then he took one of the two long shafts doubling as oars and poled away from the shoreline. The sluggish waters of the Myn tugged first at the stern, then along the length of the hull, as the graceful craft slipped free of the reeds. Poling with urgency, Rudy pushed them toward deeper water. Finally he sat down to row, using the oar like a paddle, stroking from alternate sides of the boat. They moved steadily along the shore, leaving the Academy buildings behind as the river passed between two forested banks. Before the next bend took them out of sight, the Iceman cast another look behind. He was chilled to see that his earlier suspicion had been correct.

The ominous clouds of smoke had moved much, much closer in the course of the last hour.

TEN

Myntercairn

When confronted by crisis, almost any course
of action is preferable to complete paralysis.
—SCROLL OF BARACAN

— 1 —

King Takian and his guards rode into the city of Myntercairn
on lathered horses. As his eyes fixed on the looming cloud of
blackness rising in the west, urgency drove any suggestion of
fatigue from the king's muscles and mind—he had to see the
Sun Lord!

Myntercairn, like so many cities of Dalethica, was defined
by its river. The Myn was a much larger flowage than the
Ariak, longer and far more placid. A well-silted bed insured
that the waters remained a murky, eternal brown, but this did
not deter the peoples of Myntar Kosh from bathing and doing
laundry along the flat, muddy banks.

The city itself was a sprawling collection of wood buildings, some of them grand villas, the vast majority squalid
hovels extending in a vast slum along the riverbank. It was
obvious that most of the business and population of Myntar

Kosh existed on the north side of the great waterway. There were no bridges, though numerous ferries offered passage to southern farmlands and forests—regions that, at least in the west, lay under the pall of the darkened, angry sky.

Throughout the town unique towers of wood marked the residences of the wealthiest nobles, as well as the Sun Lord's palace. Unlike the stone spires of Carillonn, these structures rose in a series of separate levels, each smaller than the one below. Curving roofs and encircling balconies distinguished each story—and some of the towers stacked a dozen or more levels into the sky. The largest cluster of high roofs marked the palace of the Sun Lord, and Takian guided Hawkrunner toward the gates, pushing through the crowded streets, blocked now by a large flock of sheep, then by a tangle of pedestrians who showed no inclination to get out of the way of even well-armed horsemen.

The pigeons cooed and fluttered in the baskets on the king's saddlebags, nervous among the throng of people. Takian was conscious of many frightened glances, and noticed several merchants packing their stalls with frightened looks at the western sky. Counseling patience from his retainers, Takian proceeded at a walk to the wide, wooden stockade that surrounded the Sun Lord's palace. A gate of stout wooden timbers blazed with bright patterns of yellow and red paint stood half-closed, and the somber expressions on the many warriors posted there belied the welcoming colors.

"Halt!" shouted a swarthy, muscular man-at-arms. The fellow's drooping mustache added a sinister touch as he swaggered forward. "You can't come in here!"

"I come to see His Majesty Garand Amelius, the Sun Lord," Takian said stiffly. "I am King Takian of Galtigor—and he will want to meet with me."

"You? A king?" scoffed the guard, scowling at the small, mud-spattered party. He reached out to pull the gate shut, but something in Takian's bearing made him hesitate. The monarch reached behind him, pulling the golden crown from his saddlebag. Setting the gleaming circlet on his head, he glared icily at the guard—who hastily stepped back and swung the gate wide.

"His Majesty will be told of your arrival immediately!" pledged the fellow, bowing low as other guards advanced to escort the riders toward the stables. Hostlers came to take their horses, and several of the men-at-arms promised to show Takian's men to comfortable quarters.

"Randart—keep an eye on the pigeons." The king looked grimly at the sky. "We may be sending a message to Carillonn very soon."

"Aye, sire," pledged the sergeant-at-arms.

The warriors of the Sun Lord wore their black hair long, and their faces were often distinguished by drooping mustaches. Lightly armored, many wearing mere strips of metal-studded leather, the men displayed a hardiness suggesting they would be equally comfortable with a long overland march, or in battle against any foe of their king.

Takian himself was led to a lofty pagoda rising from the center of the vast palace compound. He crossed arched wooden bridges over pools where goldfish flicked between lily pads. The fragrance of lush blossoms wafted through each courtyard, every garden exuding a subtly different scent. Many towers rose from the palace grounds, and Takian saw dusky maidens leaning over several balconies, dangling tresses of black, silken hair. In other places the king smelled the acrid smoke of a smithy, or heard the snorting of proud horses, and he knew that the royal grounds must also serve as the garrison housing a great portion of the Sun Lord's army.

Finally they reached the grandest tower in the palace grounds, a sprawling structure with broad wings, stairways, and balconies, framed by many artfully pruned trees. Takian's escort led him up a wide stairway of gleaming planks. Doors that were little more than screens of parchment slid open, and the King of Galtigor stepped onto a vast floor of smooth, waxed wood. Pillars of carved mahogany—each apparently made from the trunk of a very large tree—circled the periphery of the great room, which was otherwise empty except for a tall throne and its portly, smiling occupant.

"Greetings, my cousin from the east," declared Garand Amelius, descending from the throne to take both of Takian's hands in his own. The pudgy ruler, still holding Takian's hand, led him through a side door of the throne room and into a small, walled garden. "Let us talk here—the serenity will help us to think, don't you agree?"

"Certainly, Your Majesty." Takian looked about the tiny enclosure, which was surrounded by a stone wall higher than his head. Each flowering shrub, each boulder, seemed to have been placed with precise care, and the Sun Lord sighed contentedly as he looked about this agreeable refuge. Seating himself on a stone bench, he invited Takian to join him. A pool of clear water, ringed by nearly identical white stones, formed a curve around part of the bench. Garand reached downward, his blunt fingers tracing a circle on the placid surface.

"Tragic . . . about Kelwyn Dyerston, I mean," said the Sun Lord sadly.

"And portentous," Takian replied. "We know it was a Lord Minion of the Sleepstealer, abroad in Dalethica!" Garand Amelius didn't seem to hear. "Have you had a chance to speak to your garrison commanders in the west?" asked the King of Galtigor, mindful of the ominous cloud he could still see over the palace wall. "What do they tell you of the danger?"

"Danger? They tell me nothing, really," said Garand, with a dismissive wave. "In truth, most of them haven't even responded to my messengers."

"Doesn't that indicate something's wrong?"

"Oh, bosh. We do things more slowly here than in the east. Certainly they would have replied if there was any matter of urgency to report."

"Have your messengers returned?" Takian pressed.

The Sun Lord merely shrugged.

"That's a grim sign of its own!" asserted the younger monarch. "Surely you'll at least want to muster your army, to have it stand ready for a threat? Even if you suspect me of treachery, what benefit would I gain in encouraging your troops to prepare for war?"

"You are shrewd, my young cousin. By turning the eyes of my generals to the west, placing them on that border of my kingdom, I would leave myself terribly vulnerable to the east."

"Keep them here, then—in the city! I fear, in any event, that it may already be too late for your western border. This business of sending out messengers and having them disappear—doesn't that make you suspicious? And have you looked at the sky today? Has it occurred to you that black cloud might be *smoke*?''

''There are many things that make me suspicious,'' Garand replied lightly. ''The shepherds from the west should have brought their flocks to the landings a week ago, yet they, too, have failed to appear. And you, with your stories of corruption in Galtigor, threats to Faerine . . . these are distressing reports, of course. As to smoke or storm cloud, I cannot say—though I will soon learn.''

''You must *act*!''

The Sun Lord sighed and shook his gray head. ''What is there to do? If the Sleepstealer chooses to come, who am I— and what is my army—to stand before him? His minions will go where they please, and the gods will settle the score in the end.''

''But the gods have forever used mortals as their tools!'' Takian argued.

''I am too old for another war. No, it shall be as Fate decrees . . .''

The younger monarch might have said something else, but a commotion in the great pagoda distracted Takian. He rose to his feet, hearing shouting men, running footsteps pounding across that vast wooden floor. Surprisingly, Garand Amelius remained seated, his eyes upon the clear waters of the reflecting pool. The doors to the palace slammed quickly open and a mustachioed captain of the royal guard, his chest adorned by a bronze breastplate, hurried forward to kneel before the bench.

''Excellency! Scouts have just crossed on the ferries, carrying word to the city—the kingdom is under attack!''

The Sun Lord said nothing, merely hummed softly to himself and continued to stare at his reflection in the clear pool.

''Out of the west?'' Takian demanded, maddened by Garand's lack of concern. ''Who are the invaders?''

''The west, yes—the scouts tell us they could barely outride the enemy horde, though it marches on foot. None of the men who reached the city could get close enough to see the nature of the onslaught—all who faltered in their flight were slain!''

''Your Majesty—this is the proof!'' cried Takian, turning to the Sun Lord. When Garand carefully avoided his eyes, the

King of Galtigor reached down and shook the man's rounded shoulders, trying to provoke some kind of reaction. The guard was appalled to see the Sun Lord thus handled, but his fear was strong enough that he made no move to stop Takian.

"It is as the gods have willed," declared Garand Amelius. "Much as they have willed the purity of this water, the perfection of that lily. Have you ever seen such a magnificent bloom?"

Now the Sun Lord looked up questioningly at Takian, clearly waiting for an answer. With a shock, the young king realized that his counterpart actually was more interested in this elegant pool than in the fate of his kingdom.

"You!" snapped the King of Galtigor, confronting the equally aghast captain. "Summon all the troops that you can—you'll have to stand at the river! Go!"

The guardsman cast one despairing look at his ruler, but the Sun Lord's eyes had returned, dreamily, to the reflecting pool. With an anguished groan the captain spun and raced back through the throne room. Takian followed on his heels, sprinting through the maze of courtyards, trying to remember the way to the stables. Arrived there at last, he found his horse freshly groomed and contentedly devouring hay.

"Send for Randart and the rest of my guards!" the king shouted, his intensity spurring one of the stableboys into action. "Tell them to meet me at the riverbank—and to bring the pigeons!"

Quickly he saddled Hawkrunner, who pranced eagerly at the prospect of another run. Leaping onto the stallion's broad back, Takian kicked hard, charging at a gallop through the stockade's wide-open gates. He heard sounds of commotion through the sprawling palace, and could only hope that the Sun Lord's warriors would have more heart than their demented monarch.

Pushing through increasingly crowded streets, Takian let the stallion bull his way forward. Confusion reigned; mobs fought to reach the waterfront, while others struggled to flee in the opposite direction. No one named any threat out loud, but the king noticed many men buckling on swords, or seizing up pitchforks, fishing spears, anything that would serve as a weapon. Takian spared a glance at the sky, seeing that the pillars of smoke were much closer than they had been earlier.

The docks of Myntercairn extended for more than a mile along the river. Takian emerged from an alley between two boatyards, relieved to see many of the Sun Lord's bronze-plated men forming ranks there. The river was broad, but he could see a multitude of the shining breastplates reflecting along the far bank—a huge regiment was lined up immediately opposite the city docks.

Nearby, Takian spotted a man astride a prancing white horse. The fellow wore a golden helm with a plume of black feathers, and he barked commands with the tone of one used to being obeyed. "Bring those casks of oil up! And clear people back from the docks. We need more boats—you men, take those at the end of the dock, and get them on the water!"

Numerous boats already dotted the river, most occupied only by an oarsman and a pilot; Takian decided they must be standing by as emergency ferries, should a shift in the Myntercairn force become necessary. He was relieved that someone had had the presence of mind to act. Impulsively the monarch urged Hawkrunner forward, dropping his hood to reveal the golden crown and raising a hand to the officer on the white horse.

"Your Majesty!" cried the man. "This is likely to be a dangerous place—I urge you to seek safety!"

"Thanks—but I need to see what's happening. It may be that I can get you some help. You are in command?"

"General Wazier, Your Highness. You're welcome to watch, then, along with the rest of us."

"What do you know of the threat?" Takian looked westward, where the opposite bank was lined with a dense fringe of cottonwoods. Nothing moved in that wood, but the pillar of smoke originated from the unseen ground immediately beyond.

"People have been arriving at the river in a panic, begging to cross, telling tales of an invasion. They talk about monsters, lots of folks dead, how they had to ride as fast as they could to escape."

Takian's heart felt like a block of ice in his chest, but he tried to suppress any visible appearance of fear. "Use the river," he urged. "They won't like the water!"

"What do you know of these troops?" demanded the general.

"I've never seen them before," the king replied truthfully. "But I'm certain they don't like water. And don't be afraid of their appearance—they can still be killed."

General Wazier scowled, then turned back to his troops. "More boats!" he cried. "I want enough to bring that whole regiment back here!"

"Sire—there you are!" At the sound, Takian turned, relieved to see Randart and the three other guardsmen struggling through the crowds to find him. The wicker cages and their agitated pigeons were lashed to the sergeant's saddle.

Abruptly, the huge regiment of Myntercairn's men began to march. Takian saw many ranks of warriors peel away from the river bank, forming blocks on the flat plain beyond. They took a position perpendicular to the river, so the king could see the nearest block clearly, but he had no idea how many more of the defensive formations extended the line.

"You men in the ferries—stand ready now! Move toward the far bank!" General Wazier shouted from the dock, and the rowers immediately pulled to obey.

"Look, sire!" cried Randart, pointing beyond the fringe of cottonwoods.

A dark, solid rank of attackers emerged into view, the wide front of the army vanishing into the distance. The ground seemed to shake under the impact of heavy boots—though that effect certainly came from his imagination, Takian chided himself. Still, the wave came on with stunning speed, sweeping toward the men of Myntercairn.

"Are those *horse*men?" asked one of Takian's guardsmen, astounded by the quickness of the charge.

"No—they're not men of any kind," the king replied, getting a clearer look at the creatures. They were manlike, but too bulky, and their gait—for all its speed—was an awkward, rolling motion. Yet the hideous warriors moved upright, bearing lethal weapons in their hands.

The horde swept around the regiment of Myntercairn's soldiers like a wave encircling bumps of sand on a beach. Within two minutes of the first clash there was no longer any possibility of the bronze-armored men reaching the boats or the safety of the near bank—each of the formations was surrounded by the dark, hulking beasts. The men of Myntercairn must have fought bravely, for the clash of weapons rang across the river for more than an hour. The watchers on the docks could see nothing of the battle, but they witnessed its aftermath finally, when the minions formed ranks and marched on, leaving a field stained with blood and bodies. More of the monstrous invaders gathered along the far bank, and Takian estimated that the front rank alone outnumbered his kingdom's entire army.

Then that massive block parted in the middle, revealing creatures larger than any Takian had ever seen. These were four-legged monsters with blunt, wedge-shaped plates growing back from their skulls. Two-legged overseers, crackling and glowing amid the sparks that cascaded from their bodies, lashed the behemoths forward. One by one the massive beasts lowered their heads into the ground and began to push.

Great scoops of the river bank fell forward, toppling into the water. More of the monsters pushed, ripping up balls of soil, straining to push the dirt forward. Gradually the mound of earth extended outward from the bank, a solid dike creeping into the current. The laboring monstrosities continued to pour more dirt onto the pile, building it higher—and still pushing farther into the placid river.

Beyond the troops on the opposite bank Takian perceived a great movement—more like a migration than an army on the march. Clouds of dust billowed upward from the plain, extending farther and farther eastward. Occasionally he saw large wagons, apparently drawn by teams of creatures similar to those goring the river bank. These trundled past on massive, solid wheels. The king tried not to think of Rudy and Raine, presumably still at the Academy of the Sun, but he knew those grounds were on the same side of the river as the advancing horde of monsters.

At one point Takian saw a huge shape flying above the enemy horde. The creature looked like some sort of monstrous lizard, with broad, leathery wings; it landed among the minions and Takian lost sight of it in the smoke. For another hour the King of Galtigor watched, wanting to learn as much as possible before he carried the news back to Carillonn. Yet it was clear that his speculations had been correct, as the massive beasts brought more dirt from an unseen quarry, hauled it to the bank, and dumped it in the river.

The monstrous invaders were building a bridge of earth,

damming the flow of the Myn—and establishing a route of attack from the far bank directly into the city of Myntercairn.

— 2 —

Nicodareus plodded along the south bank of the River Myn, scarcely taking note of the massive destruction surrounding him. The swath carved by Reaper's army marred the land on this side of the wide flowage for as far as one could see, but the Lord Minion didn't make an effort to look. The enormity of his own failure wrapped him in a cocoon of fury. Could he blame it on the two humans' surprising possession of digger steel? Nicodareus winced at the memory of wounds inflicted by weapons no man could forge—yet he understood that his intended victims' armament was not the reason they had escaped.

The Lord Minion stalked over burned, brittle ground; he marched straight through a formation of kroaks, forcing the minions to scatter like mice in order to avoid their menacing lord. Even a rank of brutox captains ceased whipping their subordinates long enough to stand at attention, saluting with spark-trailing talons. Only the stupid bovars didn't know enough to fear Nicodareus, as he came upon several teams of the beasts, guided by brutox drivers, hauling huge, iron vats of Darkblood. With deft snaps of their whips, the minions halted their teams long enough for the Eye of Dassadec to pass.

Looking longingly at the gigantic iron vats, imagining with relish the sweet nectar in each, Nicodareus forced himself to continue walking. The vats reminded him of his own power—and its attendant punishment. He felt the familiar hunger, but now he longed for a different succor, the Immersion in Darkblood that would restore and revitalize him without the crushing pain of the Darkslayer's aftermath. The thought of that pain was unbearable, unthinkable, when the balm of his master's blood was this close. But these vats belonged to Reaper's great army, so there was a cost to this option: Though it galled him bitterly, Nicodareus would have to seek his fellow Lord Minion's permission for the luxury of Immersion.

Where would he find the Talon of Dassadec?

For the first time since awakening from his torpor amid the
ruins of the Academy, the Eye of Dassadec took an interest
in his surroundings. He saw that all but the marshy ground
had been scorched to ashes. Tree trunks lay everywhere, scattered like spilled matchsticks.

As Nicodareus came to a stream he was pleased to see the
dry bed. A series of dams between here and the mountains
had created a swath of dry land extending to the Dry Basin
and the borders of Duloth-Trol. This had been the most important tactical lesson of the Sleepstealer War: The drying of
the land created dry air, which minimized the risk of rain and
allowed for unimpeded movement by the minion hordes. The
dams were sited at the exits from gorges and long valleys,
places where such water as did flow would collect for years
before eroding the barriers.

Yet the mighty river to his right continued to flow, and
would form an obstacle until the waters could be halted and
dammed. Nicodareus probed with his Sight, quickly locating
the massive encampment opposite the city of Myntercairn. He
saw that the river was already partially dammed, with more
than a hundred bovars filing back and forth, bearing great
loads of dirt.

On the charred steppeland beyond, he saw dozens of Darkblood wagons. Minions lolled across the plain for as far as
he could see, tens of thousands waiting for the completion of
the huge dam. Neither eating nor sleeping, subsisting on nothing more than a tiny ration of Darkblood every day, the creatures would nevertheless be ready to attack relentlessly all the
way to the ocean.

The *ocean*—the very thought gave Nicodareus a tremor of
nausea. Yet at the same time it quickened a suspicion, triggered by something the Lord Minion had heard before he
slithered into the sage's room. The Eye's intended victim, the
Man of Three Waters, had been there for the killing, and yet
Nicodareus had allowed an aged human's taunts, reminders
of memories long buried, to drive him into an irrational
frenzy.

But the old man had said more than this—something . . .
Go by water. The Iceman would flee not only the Eye of
Dassadec, he would be forced to avoid Reaper's army as well.
And that flight must lead him down the River Myn to the sea.

If Nicodareus allowed himself to be freed by the power of the Darkslayer, he could cross that broad river and continue north.

Yet first he needed to find his fellow Lord Minion. Even as Nicodareus made his decision, a shadow darkened the ground and he saw the massive form of Reaper, gliding downward. The Talon, black scales gleaming, came to rest before the Eye of Dassadec, a crocodilian smile twisting his fanged snout.

"Greetings, Eye of our master ... Have you come to inspect my progress, to report to Dassadec?" Reaper inquired, mocking.

Nicodareus stiffened. "No, Talon of the Mighty One, I do not come to observe, nor to spy—though if I did, I could report only that you have met with splendid success. It seems, however, that our separate tasks have drawn us to the same location."

"Indeed. Your task is accomplished, then?"

The Eye of Dassadec suspected that the nature of his mission was not entirely known to Reaper, so he shrugged. "I have made progress—but this time in Dalethica is taxing. I ask you, fellow lord, to grant me Immersion before I continue."

The serpent huffed, flexing his wings as he scowled in concentration. "As you know, my Darkblood is precious—it is the stuff of life to my minions. Though I allow them but a tiny sip each day, I shall be hard pressed to reach Carillonn with the wagons I have."

"Naturally," replied the Eye dryly, leaving unspoken an obvious fact: His immersion in Darkblood, while tremendously revitalizing for himself, would scarcely deplete the army's supplies—the vat would remain nearly full even as Nicodareus departed. Nicodareus spread his own wings in response, straining from the effort to control his temper.

"Too, I must divide my army here," Reaper continued, in somber tones of regret. "A strong force awaits this crossing—they must march on Lanbrij and conquer Corsari. I myself shall be required for the main assault on Carillonn. I understand that city is considered by humans to be a thing of unique beauty; it will please me to reduce it to rubble."

"Another in a proud series of victories," Nicodareus allowed. "I presume you have sacked, already, the Zanthilites and Thute?"

"For the most part. Northern Thute has proven vexingly wet—the forest won't take to the torch, and it's intermixed with swamps too vast to dam. Still, the humans living there are little more than savages. There will be time to deal with them when our greater victories have been won." The serpent snorted derisively, twisting his tail into a tight coil.

"Indeed. And the weather has favored you?"

"Very much. As the land burns and the rivers dry, so does the air—it seems that there is no moisture for rain."

"May Dassadec see that your good fortune continues," Nicodareus murmured coolly.

Reaper's eyelids drooped thoughtfully. "I think that you might be of some small service to me," he suggested cautiously.

Nicodareus wrinkled his obsidian brow in silent inquiry.

"The greatest obstacles are the walls of Lanbrij—two massive barriers, raised since our victory ten centuries ago." Reaper snorted through his serpentine nostrils—clearly, he didn't expect any human obstacle to bring his advance to a halt.

"The bovars can bear a ram powerful enough to batter any gate. But there is another advantage we have—a traitor, charged with holding the gate in the First Wall open. However, I have questions about his effectiveness—this crossing of the Myn is taking longer than I had planned. And, as I have told you, my own presence is needed to support our advance against Carillonn."

"My own mission takes me in the direction of Lanbrij," Nicodareus suggested, also cautiously, sensing the bartering power that might gain him the balm of Darkblood.

"Your presence would hearten the minions, to be sure," Reaper acknowledged. "Yet even more so, if you were to reach the city early, you could hold the gate against the humans' worst efforts. Then, when my army arrives, you will have gained them passage through the first obstacle."

"True—Darkslayer will allow me to travel ahead, and I would be there to meet your minions. I *could* hold the gate for days, if need be. The humans will be helpless against me."

"And I *could* grant you Immersion." Reaper's fangs showed in a tight, wicked smile.

"We have an arrangement, then—I will seize, and hold, your gates . . . with your lordship's permission."

"A good plan," Reaper agreed. "Let us arrange the final details after your Immersion."

— 3 —

High bluffs flanked the north bank of the Myn, and the roadway that rolled along the crests gave travelers a wide vista to the south. King Takian followed that well-paved route for many miles from Myntercairn before he reined Hawkrunner to a halt. Nearby stood a public well, and his bodyguards started to draw water for the horses and themselves while their king scribbled several notes, fixed them to the legs of the pigeons, and set the birds free.

"Back at Myntercairn they'll cross the river to this bank soon enough," Takian muttered, to himself as much as his men. He remembered the massive dam and knew that, even if they had to flood half the city, the minions would extend their rampart to the high ground on the opposite bank.

The five riders sought momentary rest on the bluff overlooking the Myn, allowing their horses to graze while the men ate hardtack and watched, with narrowed eyes, the inexorable advance of the minion army. The blot of darkness extended as far as they could see to the south, and expanded inexorably to the east as well. From this distance they could not discern individual troops, but the columns of smoke marked the backtrail of the invading horde, a foul stain spreading across the Watershed.

Some of the sprawling formations had already passed over the horizon to the south and east, marked only by their trailing pyres, but two of these massive corps were visible across the river. One followed the Myn, destroying vegetation up to the river bank, still nearly matching the speed of Takian's mounted party. Amid the swirling dust and smoke, the king guessed that this force numbered at least ten thousand warriors—larger than his entire army!

Takian had hoped to ride quickly along the river bank,

outdistancing the advance of the minions until they could find a place to cross. Randart was to have raced for Carillonn, carrying additional details about the monstrous force, while the king continued on to Lanbrij. Now, however, the scope and speed of the Sleepstealer's attack made the plan seem virtually suicidal.

"How can they move so damned *fast*?" demanded the sergeant.

"If you don't have to stop to eat or sleep, or even to rest, I guess you can make pretty good time," Takian declared bitterly. "It's no wonder they've struck with such surprise—survivors of a battle would have to move like the wind to carry the alarm to the next city!"

He shuddered at the sudden recollection of an earlier horror: An hour's ride beyond Myntercairn they had reached the bank opposite the Academy of the Sun, where Rudy and Raine had visited. Already the stone buildings had been reduced to rubble, the great trees felled and tossed together in monstrous pyres. Only the pyramids still stood, apparently impervious to the destruction wrought by the horde. Takian agonized over the fate of his friends, hoping they had crossed the river—or gained passage in one of the many boats that dotted the broad waterway.

"There are no other great rivers between here and Carillonn," he declared, thinking aloud. Doubtless the many small streams could be easily dammed by the shovel-headed beasts he had observed opposite Myntercairn. Or could the monsters cross on bridges? He pictured the marbled city on its island, linked to the mainland only by those tenuous spans. Suddenly the question seemed terribly important.

"Back to your saddles!" he announced abruptly. Takian led the party at a gallop, eyes searching the far bank, looking for the sign that might help him answer his question. The army remained in view along the opposite bank of the river, but slowly the racing humans pulled ahead. An hour later Takian saw a notch in the embankment on the far side of the river, a fringe of cottonwoods trailing across the steppeland. Sunlight reflected from rippling waters, confirming that a small side stream entered the Myn on the far bank.

The bluff provided a good vantage, so once again the king indicated a halt. "Time to get some sleep," he told his men.

"We might be here for a few hours—but then I'll want to ride all night."

Takian himself was too tense to close his eyes. Instead he stared intently, following the relentless advance of the minions. In no time the force drew even with them. The advance companies halted at the stream bank, quickly dragging down the cottonwoods. The snapping and splintering of tall trunks echoed across the river, and the King of Galtigor fumed powerlessly in the face of the destruction. Through the plumes of dust, Takian watched the blunt-headed creatures advance. They looked like giant lizards, moving with a ponderous air of patience. Jabbing their heads into the stream bank, powerful hind legs driving, the monsters pushed wedges of dirt into the creek. Sparks sizzled beside them, and the creatures backed up to repeat the procedure.

The advancing elements of the minion army continued to concentrate, as more and more of the bulky regiments caught up. Takian saw again the huge freight wagons, each drawn by a team of eight monstrous lizards. The black color of the oblong cargo beds suggested iron tanks. When the elephantine monsters had finished filling in the stream bed, minions scrambled over the loose earth, laying a bed of planks hewn from the cottonwoods. About three hours after reaching the stream, the first minion companies marched across the dam and continued the advance down the Myn.

"Shouldn't take too long before that thing washes out," one of the guards suggested hopefully. "That water's got to go somewhere."

"Look—up the streambed," snapped Takian. "It's almost dry. I'll bet they've built another one of these dams—who knows, maybe three or four of them!—upstream. They're drying up the whole plain!"

"How're we going to get ahead of them?" asked Randart tentatively. Already the first companies had marched a half mile down the bank.

"We're not—at least, not to Carillonn." Takian had reached this decision reluctantly, while observing the stream-crossing of the minion army. "Our only choice is to continue down the Myn. We'll all go to Lanbrij, and take *Searunner* back to Carillonn."

Again they mounted, this time urging their horses to a canter that Takian insisted they maintain for hours. At nightfall they slowed to a walk, but continued onward. The long hours of darkness were framed by the hellish conflagrations that remained in view, scattering to the far horizon of the plains. At dawn the horses staggered along, and Takian looked at the drawn, haggard faces of his men. He himself felt strong enough to continue on foot, but he recognized that short-term solution for the foolish fancy that it was—a rested horse would carry him farther in a few hours than he could walk all day.

"Sire—what's that, by the river bank?" asked Randart.

Takian looked down, startled by a winking reflection—the sun was glinting off of a mirror, or perhaps highly reflective steel. "Seems to be signaling us—that's too regular to be accidental," he observed.

"Two people in a boat," the king said, realizing. He led the little company down the grassy surface of the bluff, switching back and forth to even the grade. The tired horses stumbled, moving slowly, but avoiding a fall. By the time Takian neared the river bank he recognized Rudy standing in the boat; the Iceman had caught his attention by waving his digger blade in the sunlight. Raine lay still in the bow of the slender craft, which Rudy had lodged in the reeds of the shoreline.

"How did you know—?" Takian reached his friend, saw the waterskin hanging at Rudy's side and didn't need to finish the question. "I'm glad you found us."

The king's eyes widened in alarm as they fell on Raine. Bandages encircled her neck, shoulders, and face; in several places, crimson stains had soaked through the cloth. "By Baracan, what happened?"

"Nicodareus," Rudy said, with an icy edge to his voice. His eyes were hard and black as coal. "She's still alive." The Iceman knelt beside Raine, pouring a few drops of Aura between her lips and then easing one of her bloody bandages, washing a cut on her shoulder. Takian stared, horrified by the red, angry wound—and the contrasting pallor of the woman's skin.

"We're taking the river to Lanbrij," Rudy declared abruptly. "The current is swift—do you want to come?"

"Certainly!" Takian agreed, seizing at the chance to continue moving. "Randart, take Hawkrunner with you—get to Lanbrij as soon as you can."

His sergeant saluted unquestioningly. "Aye, sire—and good luck!"

"To you, as well." Takian climbed into the boat, took up the second oar, and aided Rudy in pushing away from the bank. The current took them quickly as the king took a seat, working like a galley slave to hurry their journey to Lanbrij.

— 4 —

I learned, later, that I rode the river for four days with Rudy and, later, Takian—four days down the Myn, on a course for the Circled Sea. The sun beat down on my face, cold air surrounded me at night, mist and fog certainly dampened and chilled me to the core—and I never knew any of it.

To Rudy I was gone, insensate and, he thought, at the brink of death. And though I may have been close to dying, I was *not* unconscious. My blood raced, fueled by more Aura than I had ever drunk before, and my mind traveled a wide and varied path. Indeed, a state of insensibility might have been a blessing, but instead I was very much aware, and very much afraid.

At times I was a little girl again, in vaguely recognizable surroundings where nothing was truly familiar. Things hinted at normalcy—a pyramid of the Academy looming overhead, or the golden wheels of the Sun Lord's carriage rolling past— but my world for the most part was obscured by smoke. Burning in that murk, everywhere I turned, lurked a pair of glowing, hellish eyes. They moved closer, always before me, and I sensed their hunger as a primitive force of greed.

Then I became a young woman, virginal again, and those eyes bored forth from the face of a man. His presence frightened me, but what frightened me even more was that a part of me wanted, indeed *craved,* his touch. He entered me and I was shot through with pain, a burning, killing agony that should have ended my life—yet for an interminable time I was not granted the release of death. Still the man tore at my flesh, rending, piercing, taking, claiming . . . using.

And then at last Rudy was there, his love showering like

water and Aura around me. I rose toward the light, felt the sun and air beckon me to the world. I saw the Iceman, my love, reaching out, offering hope and sustenance and life.

But I recoiled in terror when he smiled at me, when he looked at me with eyes that should have been brown—but instead glowed crimson red, as furious as all the embers of hell.

From: *Recollections*, by Lady Raine of the Three Waters

ELEVEN

City of the Land Bridge

Stay to the land, human—he who sails beyond
the horizon is condemned to wander the
oceans of the world.
—CODEX OF THE GUARDIANS

— 1 —

"Is that it? Is that the *Gullwind*?" Anjell asked delightedly
as she and Dara joined Bristyn and Awnro on the white marble quay of Carillonn.

The three-masted ship flew the crossed-scimitars flag of
Corsari. Anjell knew this must be King Macconal's flagship,
for it looked every bit the royal seacraft. The planks of deck
and hull gleamed, rich with dark grain, and brass fittings
glowed like gold upon railings, masts, and hatches.

"The *Gullwind* indeed, my lass," declared Awnro, as the
travelers ambled toward the gangplank. "Ready to take us to
the balmy waters of the Circled Sea!"

"Remember your manners," Dara reminded Anjell as she
was about to charge toward the gangplank. Biting her lip, the
girl held her pace to a measured walk. She knew that King
Macconal was being nice to them by taking them aboard his

ship, so it was only right not to make him upset. In truth, the hawk-faced monarch frightened the girl a little, so she didn't find it hard to watch her behavior. Of course, she had long known adults to maintain all kinds of silly rules and restrictions, about everything from eating and dressing to talking. Lately, however, she had learned that these rules—when applied to the noblemen, ladies, and courtiers of a castle—were even worse!

Meekly Anjell allowed the ship's steward to lead her, Bristyn, and Dara along the deck. Two cabins forward of the mainmast were provided for the ladies—one for the queen, and the other for Dara and her daughter. King Jamiesen Macconal and his party, together with Awnro, established themselves in the stern—though Anjell soon learned that everyone kept fairly close quarters during the day. For all its size, the carrack carried some twenty passengers and an equal number of crew; there always seemed to be folk about when Anjell went looking around.

Riding the River Ariak, the *Gullwind* made stately progress for several days. A fresh wind aided the current, hastening them past many of the great stone citadels of Carillonn's fiefdoms. Anjell gawked at castles upon high spires of rock, and quaint villages tucked in the hollows of river bends. Much of the time they meandered through reaches of ancient forest or lush, rolling pastureland, while the girl watched the scenery and stayed out of the king's way—which was easy, since the monarch spent most of *his* time in the cabin.

As on the *Loonsong*, Awnro entertained passengers and crew. He even showed Anjell a secret weapon he had designed for his lute—a small crossbow, built into the body of the instrument. "I keep it loaded," he said with a wink. "The tension on the spring bar helps to keep the strings in tune."

The bard told her also of fabulous Lanbrij, with the two lofty walls that barred passage from the mainland into Corsari. The city itself lay in two parts, the Low City between the walls, and the High City on the Corsari side of the inner wall. Upon the elevation of the High City, Awnro declared, stood Castle Corsari—a structure even bigger, if not half so elegant, as Castle Carillonn.

Dara asked as many questions as Anjell—How old was the castle? What kind of clothes did Corsari people wear? When had Awnro last been to Lanbrij? At first, the girl was a little disgruntled by her mother's eager interest, but soon she decided it was good. In fact, Dara seemed happier than she had been in a long time—kind of like she had been when Papa was still alive.

As the carrack passed between the twin towers rising at the Ariak's mouth, Awnro told Anjell that they were now sailing on the Circled Sea. The girl had at first been impressed by the vast expanse of water, featureless to all horizons. She watched the land sink out of sight astern, and trusted Dara's words—that, since they were in an enclosed sea, the captain would be able to tell in which direction they sailed by the sun and the stars, so they wouldn't get lost.

By the second day, however, Anjell decided that the expanse of water, azure and sparkling though it was, was also rather boring. For the first time she noticed the lack of other children on the ship. Then there was the irritable predilection of the adults to be occupied with matters that held no interest for Anjell. To make matters still worse, she found herself missing her uncle a great deal. She worried that Rudy would get into no end of trouble without her steady guidance—and she didn't even know when she was going to see him again!

After about a week at sea the carrack ran into a blustering storm—not a gale, according to the captain, but a "goodly blow" nonetheless. That experience was certainly interesting, even if Dara insisted that her daughter spend altogether too much time in the cabin.

"Land ahoy!"

The long-awaited cry finally punctured the bubble of Anjell's ennui. She joined her mother and Bristyn in rushing to the bow, where they saw a dark smudge of color along the horizon. The storm clouds had broken during the night, and sunlight again sparkled from the waves.

"It's Lanbrij, all right!" proclaimed the captain, pleased with himself. "We're barely ten miles up the coast from where I thought we'd make landfall!" The bewhiskered master turned his attention to the signalman. "Run up the king's pennant—let the city know he returns!"

For hours the *Gullwind* tacked toward Inport. The dark line of the horizon took on additional detail, growing into the spine of rock that connected Myntar Kosh on the mainland to

Corsari. Eventually Anjell could even see the two great walls. On the heights of Lanbrij, north of both walls, loomed the squat, squarish block of the fortress-castle.

As they drew closer to the city, passing into the bustling, crowded harbor of Inport, Anjell squirmed at the rail, anxious to be ashore and exploring. The port bustled with ships, including other carracks as big as the *Gullwind*. The city even *smelled* like an exotic place—the offshore wind carried a hint of spices the girl had never sniffed before.

A huge coach, paneled in dark wood embossed in waves of silver wire, awaited the royal party as they debarked onto a waterfront far more extensive than Carillonn's. A huge seafood market filled a nearby square, sending an overpowering, fishy stench through the air. The waterfront in the other direction was occupied by a huge shipyard, where Anjell counted no less than a dozen vessels in various stages of completion. One of these was to be a four-masted giant, even bigger than the *Gullwind*; Awnro told her that the vessel would be called a galyon.

The king invited Awnro, Bristyn, and the Appenfells to accompany him, nodding to a uniformed footman standing beside a portable stairway. The man bowed low, holding open the elegant mahogany door. Anjell remembered the curtained coach in Carillonn, and couldn't bear the thought of climbing into that darkened cabin and missing all these new, exciting sights. "Can I ride on top? Please?" she asked, indicating a ladder leading up the side of the coach.

"What? Oh, that would be quite all right," the king declared. "There's a nice bench up there, protected by a railing," he reassured the girl's mother, who looked ready to object. Perhaps because Jamiesen looked noticeably relieved at the suggestion, Dara agreed. .

Anjell scrambled up the ladder and settled into a bench that was in fact very comfortable. The coachman seated below the level of her compartment turned and gave her a wink before devoting full attention to his team. The footman closed the door, then joined the driver; with a flick of his lash in the air, the coachman started the six huge horses moving easily along the streets.

Leaning forward, the girl saw a file of at least a dozen gleaming horsemen leading the way, one of them blasting a trumpet at regular intervals to announce the royal party. People emerged from shops and houses to line the streets and wave, and for a time Anjell enjoyed waving back, imagining that she was a princess—or even an empress!

Lanbrij was clearly a different sort of city than Carillonn. It lacked the lofty marble arches of the alabaster capital, but the city throbbed with greater vitality than any place Anjell had ever been. Every street corner was a marketplace, and merchants scooted carts of jewelry, roasted meats, candy, and beer out of the way of the procession. Looking behind, the girl saw these enterprising tradesmen quickly push back to reclaim their spots in the wake of the royal coach.

They turned into a wide street, climbing steeply toward the castle. Anjell rose up and leaned on the railing, looking back and forth at shops and houses, catching tantalizing glimpses down narrow, twisting alleys, admiring a small plaza devoted to a display of wildly colored silks. In another courtyard she saw great charcoal pits where haunches of meat were roasting on spits, wafting a delectable aroma. Anjell saw the massive bulk of the castle expanding before her eyes, a wide wall, featureless except for numerous imposing towers. A great drawbridge stood open, and an array of trumpeters had already begun a rising fanfare.

In the vicinity of the great gates the street merchants thronged even more densely than in the lower city. Anjell climbed to the top of the railing, leaning farther out to gawk at a seller of exotic birds. Nearby another man displayed several small, furry creatures that cavorted about on leashes.

Suddenly the coach lurched, rocking onto the steep climb before the drawbridge. Her position already precarious, Anjell gasped and tried to seize the railing as she toppled off the back of the carriage onto a sloping sheet of canvas lashed over a cargo compartment. She rolled down this tarp, bouncing as the horses strained, and landed heavily on her rump. Biting back an exclamation of pain, she jumped to her feet and turned to shout after the coach. But then she saw the huge castle gate yawning just beyond. Merchants and pedestrians surrounded her, and she was dazzled by a glittering array of mirrors dangling from the rack of a cart.

In truth, Anjell had been cooped up too long, first in Castle Carillonn and then on the *Gullwind*, and she wasn't quite

ready to get trapped within those lofty walls ahead. She bit
her tongue and looked around, eager to explore—and quite
confident she'd have no problem finding her way back to
something as huge and close by as Castle Corsari. She'd turn
up there eventually, just not yet.

"Are you all right, lass?" asked a kindly old gentlemen,
leaning on a cane and peering forward to study her face.

"Oh, quite—thank you!" Anjell replied brightly, ignoring
the pain that had begun to throb in her rump. "Yes—I was
supposed to get off here!"

The fellow scowled suspiciously, but Anjell had already
skipped past him, darting around the wagon of mirrors and
starting along a street running parallel to the castle wall. First
she stopped to look in a shop window where shiny ceramic
jars, some of which were taller than herself, were displayed.
Next to catch her eye was an open-fronted store where a variety of rich silken gowns dangled from human-sized frames,
which reminded Anjell of the wedding feast in Carillonn—
that was the only time she had seen such opulent attire before.

Another shop offered precious jewelry, displayed behind a
strong iron grille. Anjell's eyes widened at the sight of a
golden necklace interspaced with pendants, each of which was
inset with a brilliant diamond. Next to it was a bracelet that
looked like a solid ring of rubies and emeralds, though when
Anjell tipped her head she saw the platinum circlet linking
the array of gems.

On and on she went, similar splendors meeting her eyes
every time she swiveled her head. The street was crowded
with people, some of whom moved purposefully along, while
others, like Anjell, simply meandered, admiring the goods in
the storefront windows. She came to a swordsmith's shop and
inspected the weapons with a critical eye, deciding that even
the most slender of these blades could not compare to the
digger-forged swords carried by Raine and Rudy.

It was then that she noticed the boy—first because of his
many braids, which flopped like so many snakes around his
shoulders; and second, because he seemed less purposeful
than anyone else on the entire street. Curiosity aroused, Anjell
watched as he scuffed listlessly along the row of shops, uncaring of pedestrians or mounted men—Anjell gasped as an
urgent rider pushed his steed right over the boy, knocking

him down. Seemingly unhurt, the youth climbed to his feet and made a half-hearted effort to dust himself off. He stood in the center of the street, looking away from Anjell, then shook his head in a gesture that made her feel sad. Slouching his shoulders, he started to turn.

Suddenly Anjell feared he would see her watching him. Instinctively she dove into a narrow alley, hiding behind several casks. A crack between the barrels allowed her to keep her eye on him unobserved. Confirming her earlier impression of aimlessness, the lad started slowly back in Anjell's direction, still kicking along the ground, paying little attention to his surroundings.

Then, apparently having come to some decision, he raised his eyes and started forward with more determination, stepping quickly toward the intersection with the castle road. Suddenly his body tensed, and his dark eyes flashed wildly around, coming to rest on Anjell! She shrank back as he tumbled over the casks to squat beside her. Strangely, however, he seemed unaware of her presence as he pressed his eye to another crack between the casks. It occurred to Anjell then that he hadn't been looking at her so much as at her hiding place. Curious, she looked through her own narrow spyhole, watching as a trio of guards in bronze-plated armor ambled past. Only when they had moved beyond earshot did the lad sigh with palpable relief. Then he turned and squinted at Anjell with suspicion. She sensed that he would run like a frightened deer if she made any sudden movement.

"Hi—I'm Anjell Appenfell," she said brightly. "Who are you?"

Scowling, he considered the question. "Darret," he finally replied.

"Hello, Darret. Why are you hiding from the guards?"

"Same ones took Captain Kestrel away, lock him in dungeon. Right quick, too. Tricky scumdogs."

"But what did Captain Kestrel do? Why did he get thrown in the dungeon?" Anjell was instantly intrigued.

"Why? He told truth 'bout monsters in Farkeen, dat's why. Only big scumdog not wanna hear."

"Monsters? You saw *monsters*?"

"Kill de whole city, right quick. Only Captain Kestrel, he sail his big ship away, savin' lotsa people."

"You mean the monsters are already in Dalethica?" Anjell had listened closely to the discussions between her uncle, her friends, and their monarchs; she knew that this was important information.

"Thirty, forty days ago, sure—and comin' here too, I'm thinkin'!"

"But—but *why* was your captain thrown in the dungeon?"

"I told ya—big scumdog, he not wanna hear what we say!"

"When did this happen, that this big scumdog locked the captain up?" Anjell had formed a clear mental picture of the "big scumdog"; she wasn't at all fond of the fellow, and felt quite certain he should be stopped.

"Four, five days ago, I guess. He tried to get me in dungeon too—but I'm too quick, gets away! But first I see him throw poison, kill a couple guys. Still, I sneaked past 'em right quick."

The lad's tone was boastful, but his face remained crestfallen. "Kestrel is good man. I gotta get him out!"

"How can you *throw* poison?" Anjell asked.

Darret described the dark vial, also telling Anjell of the flask in the captain-general's robe—and the drinks he had offered to his henchmen, after the guards had been killed. "Begged like dogs for de stuff!" he declared indignantly.

Anjell's mind was whirling. She understood something of the compulsions of Darkblood, for she had known Takian's brother Garamis and had seen proof of his corruption under its influence. It sounded to her very much as if the power of Darkblood was at work in King Macconal's own castle!

"I'll help you!" Anjell promised. "Yesterday the king wasn't here—but now he is! We've got to go to the castle, tell them what you told me! He'll let Kestrel out!"

"Not de castle!" Darret's eyes widened and he edged away from Anjell, as if she'd suddenly turned into a member of the royal guard.

"They *have* to know! Don't you understand? Those same monsters could be on their way here!"

"We'll see 'em soon enough—I'm not so stupid to go back, get thrown in dungeon!"

"They won't—" Anjell started to protest, then squeaked indignantly as Darret sprang to his feet, leaped over the stack

of barrels, and darted up the city street. By the time she rushed
from their hiding place in pursuit, the lad had already disappeared.

— 2 —

Rudy and Takian took turns straining at the oars, pushing their
little boat faster than the current of the stately River Myn.
They stopped briefly at an abandoned inn on the north bank;
in a few minutes Takian had gathered plenty of food, as well
as small casks of water and wine. Raine lay still between the
benches, eyes closed. Though the Iceman despaired over her
failure to respond to words, even to the clasp of his hand
around hers, he was slightly heartened to see that even the
worst of her cuts had gradually closed, and that some color
had returned to her skin.

Nicodareus was a distant menace again, Rudy learned when
he took a small sip of the precious liquid for himself. Sometimes he couldn't sense the Lord Minion at all. Only once did
he feel the sinister touch of the Eye of Dassadec; but he was
able to pull his awareness away, certain that his location remained unknown to Nicodareus.

Repeatedly Rudy trickled Aura over Raine's lips, trying to
get a few drops down her throat; to his anguished eyes, the
liquid didn't seem to help. He feared that the venom of the
Lord Minion would prove too potent for the magic of Faerine.
Yet he continued to nurse her with the precious stuff—there
was nothing else he could do.

Over the course of several days the river widened around
them, until the far bank became a distant fringe of green—
and then only visible from a standing position on one of the
benches. "We should stick to the left bank," Takian suggested. "That shore leads around to Lanbrij harbor—Inport,
on the Circled Sea."

Rudy, who knew next to nothing about this part of the
world, agreed readily. Soon they noticed the boat rocking to
a rougher swell, and when the Iceman reached over the side
for a taste of water he was startled. "Salt!"

"We're into the bay—no more current to help us," Takian
replied. It was his turn at the oars, and he strained to push

them through the water, keeping the fringe of shoreline visible about a mile away to the left. Raine still lay insensate, so deeply unconscious that Rudy was moved to again check her pulse and touch her forehead, just to reassure himself that she lived.

As gray clouds scudded overhead he noticed that the swells grew larger. The wind whipped, giving modest benefit by blowing from the stern quarter so that at least they didn't have to row into its force. Rudy spelled Takian shortly, and soon the Iceman was exhausted by laboring through the churning surf.

Rudy wondered, somewhat vaguely, if they should look for shelter ashore. The waves rose higher than the gunwales of the boat, and the darkening sky threatened increasing wind and rain. They had no way to protect Raine from the splashes of seawater spilling regularly into the boat—and as the waves rose, whichever man wasn't rowing was forced to bail almost continuously. Yet as the whitecaps whipped higher, spray lashing at his skin, Rudy found himself grinning fiercely, relishing the sensation of elemental power. He saw with startling clarity that Raine was, if not safe on the water, at least in no more danger here than anywhere else. Suddenly he laughed out loud with a feeling of raw exhilaration, a weightless sense of speed, as if he were flying. The boat skipped along, racing with the wind, climbing swells and careening eagerly down descending slopes. Then Takian laughed too, looking past Rudy to the bow of the boat, and the Iceman wondered if they were both losing their minds.

But when he turned to look over his shoulder, he saw Raine sitting up, smiling at him. Her eyes were bright and clear, wet with spray or tears, and the sun-bronzed color had returned to her skin. She wiped the storm-tossed hair from her forehead, leaned forward, and gave him a kiss. Then she pushed him off the seat and took a turn at the oars. All around them glorious, wonderful water surged and rolled—and the three passengers felt the life of that precious liquid and celebrated its chaotic strength. There was no reason to be afraid—Rudy knew then that the tempest offered only hope and sustenance!

The storm chased them along for many hours, through a dark night and into a gray morning. When at last the clouds broke, the sunlight was dazzling on an expanse of blue sea.

Above, slick and pristine and cleaned by the night-long rain, rose the rocky barrier of Lanbrij, crowned by the sandstone bulk of Corsari Castle.

— 3 —

"Sire! Welcome back!" Captain-General Arrante's face split into an unctuous smile as he greeted the carriage in the courtyard of Corsari Castle. Bowing as Jamiesen Macconal emerged, Arrante commanded the heralds to bray another fanfare, while signalmen waved pennants and a rank of the royal guards stood at rigid attention. The wide courtyard was a sea of color, and cheers floated down from the battlements of the castle.

The King of Corsari stepped down from his carriage, every move indicating the royalty that had come to him through a long line of fierce and warlike monarchs. The Queen of Galtigor followed the king down from the wide coach, with Dara Appenfell coming behind.

"Anjell! Come down!" Dara called upward, then scowled in irritation. Her expression turned to alarm as she climbed up the ladder and saw that the upper compartment was empty. "She's gone!"

"Backtrack our route—she must have tumbled off somewhere!" The king immediately barked commands to the men of his mounted escort; the horsemen wheeled about and galloped through the open gates. "They'll have her back before you know it," he promised, though he frowned in concern.

"I'd like to join them—have you an extra horse?" Dara asked urgently.

"Two—I'll come along," Bristyn declared, nearly as anxious about the girl as was Anjell's mother.

The king clapped his hands and two of his courtiers were quick to offer horses, already saddled. The women mounted, Dara with some difficulty, and within moments they were hurrying through the gates. Trying to picture how Anjell had disappeared, Dara discounted the notion that the girl would leap off the carriage of her own accord. It seemed more likely that she had fallen, and the mother's mind was racked with images of her daughter injured, lost in a strange city.

The company of royal guards swiftly vanished down the street, ranging toward the docks and sending merchants scuttling out of the way. In the absence of the king, the peddlers shook their fists and cursed the riders, who did not waste time looking back. The two women rode more slowly, Bristyn leading Dara between the carts—since the peddlers showed no inclination to move yet again. Turning to look down the surrounding streets, Dara noticed the color and teeming activity of the city for the first time. The curtained windows of the coach had insulated those inside from a number of interesting sights—while Anjell, her mother knew, would have been enthralled.

Suddenly she reined back, her eye caught by a waiflike figure in a familiar dress of blue. Looking down a wide avenue parallel to the castle wall, she recognized her daughter. "There she is!" she called to Bristyn, and the pair turned into the street. Anjell stood near a fabric shop, looking back and forth along the street, her face creased in a frown of concentration. Abruptly her eyes met her mother's and she waved absently.

"Anjell!" Dara snapped, relieved to see her daughter unhurt—and irritated by her casual greeting. "We were worried about you! Climb up here—I'm taking you to the castle."

"But, Mama—you can't! Not until I find Darret!"

"Who?"

"Please—it's important, and he's got to be around here somewhere. He ran away from me, out of this alley, and I came out two seconds later but he was already gone. I think he's hiding around here somewhere!"

"Who's Darret?" demanded Dara, nonplused by her daughter's response.

Anjell wasn't listening. Instead, she squinted, turning around in a full circle. Holding a finger to her lips, she approached the open-fronted shop. The place was a wide stall, close beside the street, with numerous wool and cotton fabrics draped on display racks. Anjell walked among the forest of cloth, still looking around. Stopping beside a bolt of red and green plaid, she gestured to Dara and Bristyn, pointing to a grimy fingerprint at the edge of the cloth.

The women dismounted and joined her, and only then did

Anjell lift up the plaid to reveal a smudge-faced, wide-eyed youth crouching behind.

"Come on, Darret," Anjell declared firmly. "I told you—it'll be okay!"

"Who you?" demanded the boy, looking at the two women. Then, apparently realizing that he was caught, he crawled from beneath the cloth and stood, doing his best to swagger as he glared at Dara and Bristyn. "I get away right quick," he warned.

"It's my mother and our friend—she's a queen. And they're both nice—they won't hurt you. Now, we've got to go to the castle so you can tell King Macconal what you saw!"

The girl turned to her mother. "Darret's from Farkeen—a city that got destroyed by minions. But when his friend tried to tell the—I don't know, some scummy guy—about the attack, he was thrown in the dungeon and Darret had to run away, which is how I found him. I was hiding in that alley and he—"

"I think I understand," said Bristyn, gently damming the flow of words. She faced Darret with her hands on her hips. "Anjell's right—you have to come to the palace. We'll see that no harm comes to you."

"I'm gettin' outta here!" the boy insisted, eyes darting around wildly.

"What about your friend—Captain Kestrel?" demanded Anjell sternly. "D'you want to get him out of the dungeon?"

"Y-yes," Darret slowly admitted.

"Then come with us—I told you, we can help!"

Still reluctant, Darret allowed the queen to lift him into her saddle. Anjell climbed up behind Dara, and the women urged their mounts back to the castle gate. By the time they trotted into the courtyard, Jamiesen Macconal and his captain-general had entered the palace, but the king had left a footman with instructions to usher the women into the throne room when they returned.

"His Majesty will be delighted to know that the lass was found safe," assured the fellow, looking askance at the disheveled boy riding with the queen.

Bristyn offered no explanation and the footman asked no questions. He led them into the massive, blockish keep. Darret paled visibly as they passed several guards, but the sentries had either abandoned the search for him or, more likely, never considered the possibility that he would return in such exalted company.

Anjell fell into step beside the boy as their guide led them down a long corridor. Their footsteps scuffed softly on the polished wood of the floor, and when they reached the open doors at the end she saw a great hall lined with carved stone columns, and an ornate wooden throne sitting near the far end. Jamiesen Macconal, the captain-general, and several golden-helmed men-at-arms—apparently ranking officers, to judge from their gilded epaulets and decorative breastplates—stood conversing. Awnro Lyrifell, who was the first to spot the new arrivals, shifted his lute on its strap so that he could wrap Anjell in a hug.

"Ah, my lady," King Macconal said to Dara, smiling warmly. "I see that your search was successful! The lass is unharmed, I trust?"

"Yes, Your Majesty. And thank you for your prompt dispatch of searchers. She apparently fell off the carriage just before we reached the castle."

The king beamed at Anjell, who curtsied gracefully. "I'm sorry, sire, to be a bother," she said politely. "But there's something import—"

"No bother at all—can't have our guests disappearing before we at least get the chance to display our hospitality. Now, if you ladies will excuse me, there are some matters of royal business that require my attention. . . ." With a polite nod, Jamiesen Macconal turned back to his men.

"But, Your Majesty!" Anjell blurted, then clapped a hand over her mouth as the king turned to her with a frown.

"As I said," he told her sternly, "I have matters of state before me."

"Anjell has learned something important—and alarming," Bristyn declared firmly.

"More alarming news? Well, Captain-General Arrante assures me that all is calm. Given that information, you can't expect me to panic, can you?"

"Not given that information, no," replied Bristyn coldly. "But suppose that you have been lied to?"

"How dare you!" cried the captain-general. "Do you challenge the truth—?" He stopped, his eyes widening in shock and fury—for Anjell had just pulled Darret out from behind Bristyn's skirts. "You!" he spat.

"Who is this filthy urchin?" demanded the king with increasing vexation.

"A thief, sire—one condemned to death, who eluded the guards in the palace and escaped into the city. We must thank these ladies for returning him to custody." The captain-general's smile was smooth and oily, but his eyes remained glittering shards of ice.

"He is *not* a thief!" Anjell protested, planting her hands on her hips. She faced the king squarely. "If he was that bad, do you think he would come back here—of his own free will—just to talk to you?"

"Perhaps Your Majesty would be interested in what the lad has to say," Awnro Lyrifell suggested mildly.

Macconal nodded, still scowling. "You came here to speak to me?"

Darret opened his mouth, but no sound emerged.

"Come here lad, speak up," declared the king. He reached out a hand and beckoned Darret toward him. Anjell stepped right beside the boy, until the two children had joined the circle between the king and the captain-general.

"Ask him about the ship captain in your dungeon—the one who brought word that Farkeen has been sacked and destroyed!" Anjell pressed. "Why did the captain-general throw him there in chains when all he did was tell the *truth*?"

"There is no such person," snapped Captain-General Arrante. His eyes bored into Darret with murderous rage, and Anjell saw the officer's hand slip into the pocket of his robe.

"Make him tell you what he's got in there!" demanded Darret, finding his voice and pointing.

"Yes!" Anjell chimed in. "I'll bet it's Darkblood—right from Duloth-Trol! Your Majesty, you can't trust him—he's as bad as Prince Garamis was!"

"Silence!" demanded the captain-general. He pulled an object from his pocket, but it was not a flask—in his fist was a tiny, ink-black vial, which he threw to the floor with a furious gesture.

"Look out—don't breathe!" Darret shouted, tackling Anjell and bearing her, screaming and struggling, to the floor. Skidding across the varnished wood, he pushed her away from the king and his guards. Anjell's eyes stung, and when she drew a breath the air exploded from her lungs in a burst of coughing. Vile and toxic, the cloud lingered in the air, burning the girl's eyes when she tried to blink.

She felt Dara's arms around her, heard her mother and Bristyn also gasping and choking, Awnro shouting that they should get back. It was several moments before Anjell could clear the tears from her eyes. When she could see, she screamed again. King Jamiesen Macconal lay on the floor, his back arched, face twisted by pain, eyes staring, mad with horror and betrayal.

And death. The king's awful stillness, the frozen aspect of his appearance, told her immediately that the monarch was unquestionably, absolutely slain.

"He was murdered!" Anjell gasped, and noticed that the king's three captains also had fallen. "They were all murdered!

"Because of you meddling pests!" Arrante snarled at them. The captain-general had stepped back from the dead men, and now he faced the companions, his face distorted by rage. Reaching into his pocket, he drew forth another of the awful black vials.

"Now see here!" Awnro declared. Lifting his lute, the bard swiveled the instrument toward the assassin. Metal twanged and Arrante stumbled backward, staring stupidly at the steel-shafted dart jutting from his chest. He croaked and gasped, his fist still clenched around the vial, but he couldn't throw it—instead, he toppled backward to sprawl, dead, on the floor.

"Good shot," Bristyn wheezed, still recovering from her own whiff of the gas. She touched the bard on the shoulder. "Thank you."

"I don't get many chances to use it," Awnro said, looking critically at the hole in the end of his lute. "But when I do, it comes in handy."

Anjell turned to Darret. "You saved my life!" she said. "You were right about him being a scumdog, too."

"We've got to call up the guards!" Bristyn declared, waving to several men-at-arms who were already hurrying forward from the far end of the throne room.

"And Captain Kestrel! We get him outta dungeon!" Darret shouted.

"Right quick!" Anjell agreed.

— 4 —

Nicodareus rose from Immersion dripping with Darkblood. He felt vibrant and vital, free of agony and immensely powerful. He had made a promise to Reaper—a promise sealed by the nectar of Duloth-Trol, and thus unbreakable—but it was a task that fitted neatly into the Eye of Dassadec's own mission. He would seize the gate in the First Wall, hold it until the minion horde reached Lanbrij, and then be free to continue his search for the Man of Three Waters.

The Talon of Dassadec remained in a nearby wagon—one that was monstrously oversized, to accommodate the army commander's massive bulk. The serpentine creature would soon wing eastward, toward Carillonn. Lord Minions having no need of pleasantries such as farewells, Nicodareus turned his back upon Reaper and looked toward the unceasing labors of the bovars along the Myn.

The earthen dam extended most of the way across the original river channel, approaching the far bank—or at least, what used to be the far bank. Now the massive waterway, forced from its bed by the ever-growing barrier, flooded the docks of Myntercairn, inundating the part of the city below the northern hills. The terraced towers of great pagodas rose stranded and pathetic in the midst of the flood. By the time the dam was finished, the barrier would extend all the way to those hills, and Myntercairn would become a drowned city, a doomed relic of the past. At the same time minions would charge across the solid bed of the dam, a huge army released to attack relentlessly northward.

Watercraft sallied from the cluster of drowned buildings, long flatboats carrying archers toward the growing dam. As the current of the diverted river raged through the remaining gap, these Myntercairn defenders couldn't hold position off the dam, so quickly did the flow bear them down the river. And those who managed to shoot a volley or two discovered that it took more than a few arrows to distract the bovars.

For Nicodareus, it was enough that some of the humans in the city still lived—he was in need of prey. His body grew smaller, stooping forward as feathers sprouted over his wings and back, bending into the sleek, avian shape of the nighthawk. He became a silent stalker, a sleek and powerful predator bearing cruel death in his talons.

The flooding river glinted below, reflecting a million stars as Nicodareus took flight. He felt the queasiness that was unavoidable when crossing so much water, thankful that the power of Darkslayer sustained him, mockingly arrogant as he thought of the warriors in the Sleepstealer's army. The minions, and even Reaper, would have to wait until the river was dammed before they could cross.

Settling to the rim of a watchtower on one of the villas high above the city, the hunter tucked his wings and watched the world through glittering, far-seeing eyes. In the rooms of this house he saw many warriors, all tense and vigilant. The courtyard was illuminated by numerous fires, while elongated bundles along the villa wall could only be sleeping men.

Fools! The Lord Minion pictured their destruction, when Reaper's army at last crossed and annihilated them, and he wanted to laugh at the ridiculous pride that caused these men to stay here and await that finale. Extending his Sight, he observed that the surrounding manors and estates—the holdings of Myntercairn's lords, which occupied the commanding heights over the city—were all garrisoned. The battle would be savage when the dam was complete, but the minions would prevail.

For now, he had a more immediate need. He could have settled into this courtyard, killed a dozen or a hundred of the humans, and feasted on one of the corpses. Slick with Darkblood as he was, he would be immune to any attacks the humans might raise against him. Yet even so, the hour of his torpor would be fraught with interruption and distraction, objectionable acts by the infuriated survivors among the humans.

Then his Sight was attracted to movement in the brush behind the villa. On the rolling heights, individual sentries paced their routines. In short moments he saw one in particular, who was catching a nap in the protection of a shadowy ravine. Again the nighthawk flew, settling silently to a branch just over the sleeping man's head. That supple limb bent downward under increasing weight, until the talons of Nicodareus came to rest in the man's soft, squirming guts—and the Lord Minion's fangs gulped the sweet, sustaining nectar that drained from his victim's veins. Finally the grasp of the Darkslayer seized him, and Nicodareus collapsed, writhing in the burning grip of agony. When at last the pain lessened, awareness faded until he emerged from torpor sometime around dawn.

Immediately Nicodareus took to the air. The body of the nighthawk was fleet among birds, serving well to carry him northward. With grim pleasure the Eye of Dassadec decided that he would employ it all the way to Lanbrij.

— 5 —

My darkness fell away as suddenly and gloriously as night merges into day. In the end it was Aura, the blessing of Aurianth, that overcame the venom of Nicodareus. Perhaps, too, the surging of seawater aided the cleansing of poison, for I rose to the storm with elation. The dousing of the waves was a new birth, and by straining at the oars, and bailing water from the hull, once again I came of age. I felt acutely, achingly alive as we drew closer to Inport.

Lanbrij was a place I had never seen, but now it offered a multitude of hopes for our future. Primary among these was the thought that from here Rudy and I could commence a journey to Faerine. This undertaking, more than anything else, was an urge that I carried with me from the black depths of the Lord Minion's poison. My Iceman could be a mighty force for good—but that power could only be tapped in Faerine.

Other boats dotted the sea as we drew closer to land. I rowed the last stretch past the breakwater, pushing our little skiff through the crowded harbor. Rudy sat in the stern and I watched his face as we drew near to the dock. His eyes rose to the high walls, barriers across the isthmus. Then his gaze drifted to the south, toward the unseen—but very much perceived—menace lurking beyond the horizon. Watching his face grow tight, I saw his knuckles whiten over the hilt of his sword.

Then I thought of our very desperate need to go to Faerine, and I knew that he was going to decide to stay.

From: *Recollections*, by Lady Raine of the Three Waters

TWELVE

First Wall

A bridge is only as stable as its weakest footing,
and likewise, a wall is as strong as its most
vulnerable gate.
—DIGGERSPEAK PROVERB

— 1 —

"Get me your commander—now!" Bristyn barked orders to
the confused palace guards, several of whom had witnessed
the assassination. The queen's face had regained its color, and
to Anjell she seemed very tall. "There were men working
with the traitor—find his cohorts and arrest them!"

"Over here," Awnro urged his friends, gesturing from the
entryway to an adjacent hall. "The air is easier to breathe."

"And Captain Kestrel," Darret insisted. "We gotta get him
out!"

"We will," Bristyn promised. "You and your Captain
Kestrel just might have given us the time we need." She
whirled toward a guard. "You! Where's your commander?"

"Th-they've sent for him, Your Highness!" he stammered.

Anjell thought that Bristyn didn't look as pretty as she usually did—there was a hardness to the young queen that almost

made the girl a little afraid. Still, she was impressed by the way these men ran around, doing what Bristyn told them.

A few minutes later a slender young nobleman arrived. His beard was clipped to a point, topped by a curved, carefully waxed mustache. The precisely trimmed facial hair couldn't conceal a somewhat boyish appearance, but when he spoke it seemed to Anjell that the man sounded much older than he looked.

"I am Duke Dalston Beymont, High Admiral of the Corsari fleet," he declared, clicking the heels of his shiny boots and inclining his head toward Bristyn. "I believe I have made the acquaintance of the Queen of Galtigor at His Majesty's reception in Carillonn."

"Yes—a far more pleasant occasion than the present one."

"It is true, then—the king is dead?"

"Slain by Captain-General Arrante, who paid for his treachery with his own life. Awnro Lyrifell killed him."

"I had the honor of dispatching the fiend," Awnro admitted with a frown. "Alas, I was too late to save His Majesty."

"That is very much as the guards have described it," the duke agreed.

"The First Wall—does its gate remain open?" asked Bristyn.

"Curiously enough, yes," Beymont stated. "Despite the rumors coming with increasing frequency, the captain-general declined to . . . but that means—!" The duke's eyes widened as he understood the scope of the traitor's intent. "Dellthar!" Duke Beymont's voice snapped out, and a silver-armored officer stepped into view; he had apparently been waiting around the corner. "Take a detachment to the First Wall— gather all the oxen you can get your hands on and start closing the gate. Move, man!"

"Yes, Your Grace—immediately!" Dellthar disappeared again, the clanking of his armor audible as he trotted away, shouting to gather his men.

"There's another thing." Anjell spoke up insistently, as the duke turned back to Bristyn. "A man came here to warn you all, and Arrante threw him in prison. We've got to get him out!"

"The girl is right," Bristyn said firmly. "He brought the only survivors out of Farkeen, a whole galyon of them—plus he escorted a host of smaller boats back here."

"Of course. What's the man's name?" asked the duke.

"Captain Kestrel!" Darret piped up.

The duke snorted—in surprise or amusement.

"Do you know him?" Bristyn asked.

"Perhaps the rogue has a decent side," Beymont declared, shaking his head skeptically. "Yes, I know him—he's the best damned sailor on the Circled Sea, and the most treacherous smuggler! But he's earned himself a pardon, if what you tell me is true."

"It is!" Anjell and Darret chimed together.

Duke Beymont called to another guard, bidding him escort Anjell and Darret to the dungeon, with instructions to free Captain Kestrel. Awnro came along as Darret raced eagerly ahead, urging them to speed. They woke the grimy, stoop-shouldered turnkey from his chair in the guardroom, where he had been slumbering beside a heavy iron door. Grumbling, the scowling jailor raised a massive key, unlocked the door, and started down the narrow stairway revealed beyond. Awnro took a torch from a wall sconce in the guardroom, and the flickering flames provided the only illumination as the two youngsters and the bard followed the guard down these dim corridors.

The dungeons of Castle Corsari proved as damp, dark, and confining as Anjell could have imagined. Stone walls pressed so close that she could touch both sides of the corridor at the same time, and she saw that Awnro and the turnkey had to duck frequently to avoid overhead beams. They moved through a dizzying maze, past numerous doors of rusty iron. Rarely did they hear anything, though the girl fancied more than once that faint groans, or pleading cries, rasped from behind iron bars. The stench of an overflowing latrine reeked from many cells; others smelled even worse. The jailor finally halted at one of the doors, unlocked it, and then stood back with a snort of disgust—as if he'd just as soon leave the visitors in the cell as allow the prisoner to depart.

Kestrel shuffled forward, blinking in the light of the torch. His cheeks were sunken, his skin pasty white—but when he smiled at Darret, Anjell saw the genuine fondness he bore for the boy.

"I had a feeling you'd come for me, lad—it's good to see you!"

Darret sniffled bravely, then stepped forward and wrapped his skinny arms around the sea captain. He stifled his tears after a moment and released Kestrel. "We got to git you some sun, Captain!"

"That would suit me, lad. And who are your fine companions?"

Darret made his introductions as the group hastened through the dungeons, up the stairs, and finally passed the guardroom and entered the open courtyard before the main gates.

"Darret said you saw lots of minions—in Farkeen, or something," Anjell said. "I've seen kroaks and terrions and a stalker, once."

"Shameful things for any mortal eyes, but sadder still for a child's," Kestrel murmured, resting his hand on Darret's shoulder as the girl talked.

"It's because of my uncle Rudy that I got to see them—he's the Man of Three Waters now, because he was trapped under Aurasnow—and stabbed through with a sword of Darkblood! He's trying to find a way to stop these minions—I haven't seen him for a long time." Anjell's voice grew wistful.

The sea captain listened to her tale of adventure with what Anjell thought was remarkable open-mindedness for an adult—he seemed to *believe* her! Of course, that just showed what seeing a whole army of monstrous minions would do to a person's expectations about life.

They joined Dara and Bristyn in the castle courtyard. Kestrel bowed to the queen, then took Dara's hand with a smile. "I've met your charming daughter," he said, "and I see where she gains her delightful nature."

Dara smiled, nonplused. "Thank you, Captain." She nodded at Darret. "Your young friend is a loyal champion."

The halls and the chambers of the great stone citadel grew crowded with grieving subjects of the slain king. The mob was thick in the courtyard too, but Awnro led their little group to a balcony several steps above the ground, where they could momentarily avoid the jostling throng.

Suddenly Bristyn screamed. "Takian!" She raced down the

stairs, forcing herself through the crowd while the other companions shouted and waved from the balcony. Anjell sighted the King of Galtigor's sandy hair, saw Takian's eyes fastened upon his bride. Crying with joy, Bristyn threw herself in his arms, raising her face to meet his kisses. Then Anjell caught sight of a tall figure behind the king, and she glimpsed a head of curling brown hair.

"Uncle Rudy! Look, Mama—Rudy's here too! And Raine! Are we glad to see you!" cried the girl, charging down the steps, pushing her way through milling warriors and nobles. Rudy hugged his niece warmly as Awnro and Dara came quickly behind. The King of Galtigor still embraced his bride with fervor, while the Iceman held his sister-in-law for a long moment, as if reassuring her that he was still alive.

"And this is Darret—and Kestrel. They came on a ship all the way from Farkeen, where the minions first attacked," announced Anjell excitedly, introducing the oddly matched pair.

Rudy held out his hand, clasping the sea captain's callused palm while their eyes met. Kestrel's easy grace belied the lines of age and weather etched across his cheeks. His beard of rusty gray might have been saturated with sea salt, rather then faded from the years. Standing beside his friend, Darret beamed delightedly, braids bobbing like the tentacles of a playful octopus.

"We heard a rumor about the king . . . ?" Takian began, finally holding Bristyn at arm's length.

"It's true—we saw him killed," his bride said.

"Darret saved my life or I would have been poisoned too," Anjell declared. Dara's suddenly pale complexion and quick intake of breath emphasized the truth of her daughter's words. The crowd in the courtyard grew thicker as more and more people flocked into the castle. Cries and wails rose from all sides, a din that grew steadily louder.

"I have a villa in the Low City, just back from the First Gate," Captain Kestrel announced. "There we could get a look at the First Wall, and watch the closing of the gate. Also, I'll wager things are a lot less chaotic there."

"Good idea," Bristyn said. "We should go there and make some plans."

— 2 —

As they departed the castle the companions made their way through crowds of anguished citizens. They had the advantage of walking downhill, but were forced to link hands and arms to stay together. By the time they passed through the lofty Second Gate into the Low City, however, the hilly, winding lanes were much less congested. Kestrel's sprawling adobe brick house, surrounded by a stone wall, occupied the top of a small rise—one of numerous knoblike hills in the Low City of Lanbrij. The reunited travelers were the only people on the road as they climbed the winding street toward the crest.

At the villa, Kestrel was warmly greeted by a dozen servants, all of whom had apparently given him up for dead. Led by a stout, matronly housekeeper, the staff welcomed all the companions effusively before the sea captain took his guests through a large, square courtyard which was enclosed by the three wings of his house. Emerging through a gap in a high hedge, they gathered on an airy veranda with a wide view of Outport harbor, the ocean beyond, and the nearby First Wall. There the massive barrier of the gate slowly creaked in its grooved track, and a long trace of oxen strained at their harness.

Several serving-maids instantly appeared with glasses of a cool fruit drink—a refreshing concoction unlike anything the Halvericans had ever tasted before.

"We don't have much time," Takian began bluntly. "As fast as the minions are traveling, they'll be massing on the other side of that wall within a few days."

"And Corsari stands without a king!" Kestrel groaned.

"At least Duke Beymont seems to command some authority among the men of Lanbrij," Bristyn observed, nodding toward the gates.

"Aye—he's a skilled man, if a bit hard," Kestrel allowed. "He's given the *Black Condor* more than one thorough search—not that I'd ever give myself over to contraband!"

"Ships won't be much use against minions—but alas, the duke will have all he can do on dry land," said Takian.

"How long will it take to close?" Dara wondered aloud,

as they watched the barely perceptible progress of the giant gate.

"The better part of a day, my lady." Kestrel flashed her a smile. "They're the strongest barriers in all Dalethica. Each gate is fifty feet across and twice that high, so heavy it needs two teams of oxen to close. Once shut, they're intended to stay that way for a while—they're lowered into grooves in the ground and become as solid as the wall itself." Kestrel paced, gesturing to the lofty barrier. "We've used them against the Thutan riders, back when they had ambitions of mastering the west—but it's been more than a century since they were last closed. It's worth knowing there's a small door at the foot of the gate—big enough for a single file of men. I imagine that'll stay open until the last of the refugees have reached safety. Otherwise there's no way around, by land."

A steadily increasing number of people streamed northward from the highways of the mainland, seeking protection behind the high wall, filing through the slowly closing gates. Thanks to the barrier of the River Myn, news of the minion incursion actually traveled faster than the horde itself; now people of Myntar Kosh and smaller fiefdoms hastened to the refuge of Lanbrij.

"I hope those gates will stand against the minions. Nothing did in Farkeen," the captain declared grimly. He described the carnage there, and the narrow escape made by the *Black Condor*. "Who knows how many thousands died—all in one, brutal day?"

"It seems that the Nameless One has sent his armies in the same pattern as the Sleepstealer War." Awnro Lyrifell's usually lively voice was flat.

"Aye—and that time Corsari fell to them, I know. But there were no walls then—these were raised by diggers and humans together, at the conclusion of the war," Kestrel explained, pointing to the two walls. The Second Wall was farther away, looming so high that they could see nothing of the castle or the High City beyond. "The same diggers created our canal, linking Inport and Outport."

"I didn't see any canal," Rudy commented. "I thought the Land Bridge was solid all the way to the mainland."

"It is—the canal goes underground, not too far below here as a matter of fact. It's said that the diggers stayed in Lanbrij for a century or more. They had regular barracks down there, in the middle of the canal. Big gathering halls—they even carved out stone kegs, hollows right in the mountain, where they brewed their ale. The taps still work—though the kegs are just big, empty cisterns now.''

"Like the bridges of Carillonn, diggers leaving a mark in Dalethica,'' Rudy mused.

"Faerines . . . allies,'' Raine said, looking directly at the Iceman. "I wonder how things are in Danri's homeland.''

Rudy met her eyes, then looked away as Raine's lips tightened.

"Rudy—what did you learn there . . . at the Academy?'' asked Dara.

The Iceman looked at the frantic preparations going on in the Low City around them: blades grinding against sharpening stones, bellows roaring, and blacksmiths pounding shoes onto nervous horses. In a field below the villa men donned armor and formed companies, while officers shouted orders and placid oxen were lashed into their traces. Rudy sensed the imminence—and awfulness—of the impending battle, and he couldn't answer.

"Rudy must go to Faerine,'' Raine said for him. "That's the only place where he can learn more about his . . . gift.''

"The minions are moving so quickly that I think such a journey would be pointless,'' the Iceman argued, shaking his head. "There's too much to do here for me to flee halfway around the Watershed!''

"You don't have a choice,'' Raine said firmly. She faced the Man of Three Waters squarely. "You know that this struggle will not be over until you're able to master *all* your power!''

"That's impossible!'' Rudy snapped. "Besides, I can't *get* to Faerine! Lanbrij has its own problems, and I can't just keep running away!''

He rose and walked away from the group, angered by a combination of known and unknown threats. The bay and the limitless expanse of ocean spread like a blanket of azure jewels to the distant horizon and beyond. For a moment he was tempted, ready to set out upon the water.

Involuntarily, his gaze shifted to the south. Kestrel's hill was just high enough for him to see over the First Wall, and he looked at the brownish expanse of land and sky that was Dalethica—or this little corner of it, at any rate. Was there a distant murk in that air, or did his eyes deceive him? It didn't matter; if he couldn't see the fires of the minion devastation yet, those blazes would loom in a few days.

Kestrel joined him, drawing a deep breath as he looked out to sea. The captain didn't seem as old as Rudy had first thought; indeed, the physique that the Iceman had first taken to be frail now looked wiry and well-muscled.

"There were times in that dungeon when I thought I might never enjoy this view again. I owe your niece a great deal."

The Iceman laughed softly. "She's a remarkable girl."

Rudy and Kestrel leaned against the parapet. The grizzled sailor rested an elbow on the top of the wall and gazed meditatively at the bay.

"There she is—the *Black Condor*," he drawled. "Sturdiest galyon ever to sail the wide ocean."

"A stout-looking ship," Rudy agreed, impressed by the huge vessel, with her raised forecastle and wheel deck, and four masts jutting proudly into the sky.

"Yes . . . just barely escaped, she did, when the minions came." Kestrel turned to stare into Rudy's face, his eyes clouded by remembered pain. "I don't know how to tell you what it was like—an onslaught that looked like the end of the world."

"I've seen minions of the Sleepstealer—a few at a time," Rudy said grimly. "I can't imagine the horror of a whole army of them."

"But the walls of Lanbrij are high—and the gates are closing," said the seaman, making an attempt at heartiness. "We won't be taken by surprise—and the overfed militiamen of Farkeen are not to be confused with the warriors of Corsari!"

Rudy watched a boat approach the shore of the harbor below the hilltop. He was surprised when the bargelike craft reached the rocks of the shore and continued forward at a steady pace, then disappeared. "The digger canal I mentioned," Kestrel said, chuckling at the Iceman's expression of astonishment. "Runs straight through to the Circled Sea. The barges go this way on the incoming tide; traffic comes the other way when the tide flows out."

"Like the bridges of Carillonn—a remembrance of the Sleepstealer War?"

"Aye. In fact, you can go down there and look around if you want—the canal's a body of water, of course, but there're walkways to either side of it. And a bridge in the middle arcs up near the ceiling. That, you use to cross over to the old digger barracks."

The Low City glowed around them as sunset tinged the aquamarine waters with shades of orange and red. Torchlight flamed in countless windows, marking the luxurious villas that seemingly capped each hill. Because of the rolling topography, this part of Lanbrij seemed like a collection of villages nestled in hollows rather than one large city.

Rudy pictured the horde of monsters bearing down on this place, drawing nearer by the hour to that looming wall. He looked at the men-at-arms, gathering below the wall or marching up the stairs to take positions on the ramparts. The decision was easy and purely instinctive—he wasn't going to leave.

He had no choice but to join these brave men in standing against the Sleepstealer's minions.

— 3 —

Nicodareus killed and feasted north of Myntercairn, absorbing the power of Darkslayer twice more during his flight to Lanbrij. In the body of the nighthawk he made swift progress, soaring far above Dalethica except when he paused to feed, or was subsequently forced to endure his punishment and torpor.

While he flew he watched terror seize the pathetic humans across the world below. Great throngs choked the roads, carts teetering with belongings, mules, oxen, and goats laden as beasts of burden. Channeled by geography, the refugees swept in the same direction as the Lord Minion—toward the bottleneck of the Land Bridge to Corsari.

Finally the isthmus of rock came into view before Nicodareus, a link of brown between bodies of azure water. The Lord Minion extended his Sight to inspect the lofty walls, the great gates, and the blocky, fortified castle. The hawk winged closer, descending as Nicodareus confronted the growing vistas of the Circled Sea and the Great Ocean. The giddy expanses sickened him, so he dove toward the solid bedrock below. As he approached the First Wall, he saw with pleasure that the massive gate still stood open. The traitor Arrante had been successful thus far—and now, the Lord Minion could do the rest.

As a gust of wind slowed his speed, suspending him in the air before the gate, Nicodareus saw movement—humans manning the battlements, bustling around the gate mechanisms on the ground, pressing through the still-open gateway. Streams of people came from across Dalethica, seeking sanctuary behind the walls of Corsari. The Lord Minion circled as the wind died, probing with his far-reaching eyes, watching the teams of oxen labor to turn the mighty capstans. Slowly the massive gate of the First Wall crept shut.

With a shriek of pulse-stopping menace, Nicodareus tucked his wings and dove, shifting form as he neared the ground, expanding to the manlike torso, the arms and legs with taloned paws, obsidian face split by a snarl of fury. The weight of his landing sent a tremor through the ground and the gatehouse. The file of human flotsam scattered, screaming, as horses and oxen bucked, bellowed, and shrilled their terror. Powerful blows of the monster's clublike paws crushed men, women, and children.

The Lord Minion crouched squarely in the middle of the gate. Refugees still outside staggered back, the column quickly disintegrating into panicked flight. Nicodareus reached for the nearest trace of oxen, slicing the cable with a ripping slash of his paw. With a quick blow he killed two beasts at the end of the tether, stampeding the rest into the winding streets of the Low City. In moments he had repeated the process with the other trace of oxen, freeing that capstan as well. The sinews in his limbs stretched like wire as he pulled the mechanism in reverse, straining to restore the gate to a fully opened position.

Several humans, rallied by a posturing nobleman astride a stallion, massed together a hundred paces away. Foolishly, they charged; Nicodareus met them with talon and fang, rending flesh, crushing bone. Still, the men of Lanbrij battled with surprising ferocity, stabbing with lances and swords, shooting arrows and quarrels. Nicodareus killed many, struggling to retain his footing in the press of rampaging humankind. Ultimately, however, the warriors realized that their weapons couldn't penetrate his skin, and they fell back in confusion and dismay. Some of the wounded humans the Lord Minion let live, after breaking their legs in several places. He tossed these wretches into the gatehouse, knowing that they would sustain the Darkslayer if he was forced to remain here for a few days.

Only then did the Lord Minion succumb to his hunger, slaking the craving on the blood of one of his recent victims. He yielded to the oblivion of torpor in the small, dark room containing the capstan mechanism, where he could slumber unobserved.

— 4 —

"A hundred men killed in two minutes' battle!" Duke Beymont's anguish thickened his voice as he paced outside Kestrel's villa. Takian walked beside him, offering such consolation as he could.

"You reacted quickly—made a noble attack."

"I had an elite company standing by, keeping order among the refugees at the gate," declared the distraught nobleman. "By Baracan, no commander could ask for better men! They attacked without hesitation, as many at a time as could crowd into the gate. Armored head to toe, with the strongest lances and sharpest swords in our arsenal. And the monster slew a hundred such!

"And that's not the worst," continued Beymont, relentlessly—as if hypnotized by the horror. "Several of the wounded he kept alive deliberately—he dragged them into the gatehouse. May Baracan spare those brave souls!"

"Where is Nicodareus now?" asked Rudy.

"Inside—he disappeared into the western tower of the gatehouse after the fight."

"Now's the time to strike at him!" the Iceman declared. "He's done this before—there's a period of time after Nicodareus kills when he's . . . I don't know, hibernating or something. I can't say, either, how long it lasts—but it gave us time to get out of Carillonn after the High King was killed.''

''And to escape the Academy, after Pheathers . . .'' Raine added in a fading whisper.

Duke Beymont was shorter than average height, but as he stalked crisply back and forth, a rigid posture and peaked satin hat made him appear taller.

''What's the use of attempting another attack—our weapons don't even break his skin!'' snapped the duke.

''*These* will,'' Raine answered, unsheathing her sword and extending the hilt toward Beymont. The duke took the weapon, slashing it through the air, eyes widening as he felt the lightness, sensed the inner strength of the blade.

''Forged by diggers,'' Takian explained. ''We three bear them—gifts from friends across the Watershed.''

''We should go after him now!'' Rudy urged, gripping the hilt of his own sword. He felt sick at the prospect of facing Nicodareus again, but the right, the *only*, course of action lay clear before him.

''My young Iceman.''

Awnro Lyrifell spoke breezily as he, Dara, and Bristyn sauntered over. Slinging an arm casually about Rudy's shoulders, the bard continued. ''I believe you have heard it before—you're blessed with a unique attribute—a beacon of hope for all mankind. Another fact, perhaps, you *haven't* heard: You have the capacity to behave like a complete fool.''

''What?'' Rudy was more puzzled than angry by Awnro's statement.

''He's right!'' Raine chimed in, with far more vehemence than Rudy cared for.

''Can you think of anything the Lord Minion would like *more* than to have you come walking up to him, offering yourself on a platter, so to speak?'' The bard's tone was genial, but Rudy felt himself shrinking under the verbal barrage. ''Nor can Raine go against him—he recently saw her in your company, and she might provide the link that would lead him to you.''

''*I*—'' Takian stepped forward, ready to volunteer—until Bristyn seized his arm and pulled him roughly about.

''Nor is this a task for the King of Galtigor!'' his wife

snapped. "I didn't get you back again just to lose you two hours later!"

"Her Majesty—and the noble bard, as well—are right," Duke Beymont said, raising a hand to stifle Takian's protests. "We have many swordsmen of tremendous skill among our ranks, any one of whom would willingly volunteer for this task—if he might be permitted use of one of your swords."

"You're welcome to mine," Rudy said, immediately sensing the soundness of the plan—and a little ashamed at the wave of relief he felt. "Some of your men should take casks of water, as well. If they can get above Nicodareus, pour it on him, they might have some chance of hurting the Lord Minion.

Another chilling thought occurred to Rudy. He looked at Takian and Bristyn. "Those casks of Aura—from Taywick? Are they here in Lanbrij?"

"Yes," Bristyn said. "Still stowed aboard the *Searunner*, in the harbor down at Inport."

"There's another chance . . ." Finally Rudy shook his head. "If Nicodareus was doused with Aura, it might kill him—but it might destroy half the city, too."

"You're remembering the legend of Darkenscale—and Darkenheight Pass," Raine guessed.

"Yes!" Awnro interjected. "When a Lord Minion was engulfed by Aura, the resulting explosion ripped apart a mountain range. A trifle drastic under the circumstances, don't you think?"

"Aye," Kestrel said grimly. He looked across from the hilltop to the height of the First Wall, with the gaping slash of the city gate standing wide, revealing the brown terrain of the Lanbrij isthmus beyond.

"Save your Aura," Duke Beymont decided. "But we'll try using water."

"The attack should be made soon," Rudy urged. "There's no way of knowing how long his lethargy will last. And be prepared—he can probably rouse himself to fight."

"I go at once." The duke clicked his heels, turning toward his prancing horse.

"Wait—take my sword, as well," Raine said suddenly. "Two will have a better chance than one."

"Make it three." Takian, too, unbuckled his sword belt and handed the weapon to the grateful duke.

"I will see that they go to the best men we have," he pledged, before mounting his horse and galloping down the hill.

Aided by Kestrel's spyglass, the companions watched Beymont ride to the field below the villa. There he rallied several hundred men. Many filled small casks of water from nearby wells, raising the kegs to their shoulders and starting forward, while tight ranks of armored foot soldiers led the way toward the gate itself. In the forefront three armored men bore the whiplike blades of digger steel.

The gate was a vast, arched opening in the barrier of the First Wall. Towers capped by square ramparts jutted above the top of the wall, bracketing the wide passage. The huge slabs of the gate were almost invisible, drawn fully back into the walls to either side. A file of water-bearing warriors disappeared into each of the two towers of the gatehouse, following which the observers in the villa could only imagine the attack party's progress.

Takian speculated that the heavily laden men were struggling up long flights of stairs. "There are likely to be murder holes in the gatehouse floors—slits where hot oil could be poured on an attacker below. I'm sure they'll work just as well for water, if those fellows are lucky enough to get the upper hand."

The main party of armored men approached the gate itself, rushing through, then charging into the nearby rooms housing the guards' quarters and the capstan machinery. Corsari warriors scrambled like ants around the great structure, but the watchers at the villa heard no cries of alarm, saw nothing that resembled a battle.

The screams came first from the left tower of the gatehouse—hideous shrieks, many cut off in mid-cry. Men spilled out the door at the base of the tower, running for their lives. After a dozen had emerged the door remained open, swinging idly in the breeze, as if all was still within. Rudy remembered with cold horror that nearly a hundred men had started up that tower stair.

Ten minutes later, the same horrible sequence was enacted in the other tower—though nearly half the volunteers escaped, this time. Then Nicodareus glided into view, soaring downward from the overhead archway to land among the warriors within the gate. The Lord Minion pounced back and forth like a great cat, slashing and biting and crushing men to every side. If the digger blades made any difference, the effects weren't obvious from the villa; ultimately the surviving humans had no choice but to flee in abject defeat.

By late afternoon, Beymont, his horse clopping listlessly up the winding road, again made his way to Kestrel's villa. He dismounted despondently, turning to reveal that he brought back only two of the swords.

"The third was lost, destroyed with the brave man who bore it," the duke declared sadly. "The beast was unaware of our arrival. We discovered it at rest, curled in a corner of the machine room. As soon as our first men drew close, the monster awakened, attacking with fury that could not be contested—though many died trying to do so."

"Theirs was the courage of legend," Awnro said, his tone firm. "I know it offers no comfort to the bereaved—but the glory of that attack will linger in song through the ages!"

"And we will resist the beast so long as a man of Corsari can wield a sword or shoot a bow!" the duke asserted. "But it seems any further direct assault is doomed to failure. Here are your weapons."

The Iceman looked at Raine and Takian, and the pair of swords. "You take them," he said quietly, insistently. Without argument his companions armed themselves.

"I see that the monster's back in view," Kestrel declared, standing at the waist-high wall with his spyglass to his eye. As they each took a turn with the glass the companions clearly saw the massive, statuelike figure of Nicodareus, arms crossed upon the obsidian chest, standing directly in the center of the gate.

"What happened in the towers?" asked Raine.

"Apparently he heard the men trying to get the water into position. He came down from above, butchering them on the stairways." The duke's tone was sharp and weary, like the voice of a bitter old man. "Worse, he took even more survivors—crippling them in full view of the rest!"

"And now he's blocking those who come to Lanbrij for

safety," Kestrel added. "How many are trapped on the mainland?"

"Who knows how many thousands?" Beymont said. "And the only way through blocked by that creature!"

"The only *land* route, you mean," corrected the master of the *Black Condor*. "Tide's starting out—I'm going to put to sea, try to bring as many of those folk back behind the walls as I can."

"Can you use some help aboard?" Rudy asked.

"Surely can. Why don't you and Raine come along?"

Beymont brightened slightly at the prospect of useful action. "Good idea—at least we can try to get every one of those refugees over here before the minions arrive. I'll put the Corsari ships to the same task." He looked at Kestrel. "I'm needed here, ashore. Will you take the fleet command?"

Kestrel nodded after a moment's reflection. "Aye, Admiral." His tone was level, but an undeniable spark of irony glinted in his eye.

"In the meantime, we'll have to stand ready to fight for the Low City when the minion army arrives," Duke Beymont continued. "If the Lord Minion can't be dislodged, I intend to meet the horde right inside the gate."

"The Golden Lion Regiment came here on the *Searunner*," Takian told Beymont. "And this is a better place to fight than any I've seen. I place them, and myself, at your disposal."

"That's exactly how *I* feel," Rudy said to Raine, leaning forward to meet her challenging stare. "There's no better place on the Watershed to fight—these walls, the narrow ground. *This* is where the key battle will be fought!"

"I'll grant there'll be a battle—but it's not your fight!" declared Raine.

"It's mine now," Rudy said abruptly, cutting off the debate. "From what I saw at Myntercairn, I'd guess we have no more than a couple of days before that army is marching over the doorstep."

"Another thing," Beymont said, with a meaningful glance at Anjell. "When the minions come, this villa is likely to be on the front lines. I have arranged a spare chamber in the castle—perhaps the Queen of Galtigor and her companions . . ."

"Yes!" Rudy declared, kneeling to confront Anjell's scowl. "You and your mother go to the castle with Queen Bristyn. We'll see you there later!"

"Good idea," Kestrel said. He clapped Darret on the shoulder, his grip harder than his voice. "I'd like you to go up there too, to keep an eye on them for me. Okay?"

"But Captain—"

"I need you to do this for me. Do you understand?" The seaman's voice was soft, and the sternness had melted from his eyes to reveal a naked plea.

"Aye, Captain," Darret said with resignation.

"At least can we stay here until the minions come?" Anjell pleaded. "We'll go to the castle then!" With Kestrel's assent, the other companions agreed.

"To work, then, gentlemen—and ladies," Duke Beymont said with a heel-clicking bow. "And may the gods of light smile upon us!"

And as Rudy accompanied Raine and Kestrel to the waterfront—and Dara kept a firm grip on the squirming Anjell's shoulder—the Iceman once again found himself stepping along with a growing sense of hope.

— 5 —

Anjell found Darret on the veranda of Kestrel's villa, watching the warriors gathering inside the city gate. Duke Beymont's companies—reinforced by Takian's men from Galtigor—assembled in the Low City, forming a barrier across the Land Bridge inside the First Wall. The men-at-arms warily watched the still-open gate, and from the villa Anjell and Darret could see the hulking, bat-winged shape of the Lord Minion.

Turning away with a shiver, Anjell grimaced. "That's Nicodareus—I hate him more than anything!" she said, looking over the crowded surface of Outport.

"Bad scumdog," Darret agreed easily.

"Darret, I've got to talk to you," Anjell declared bluntly, after a few minutes of ship-watching.

"Okay." The boy flopped onto one of the benches and looked at her with his wide eyes.

"It's Rudy. You see, he's got to go to Faerine. Everybody knows it but him—but he's going to find out pretty soon."

"Okay."

Anjell pressed forward impatiently. "Well, he can't just flap his arms and *fly* there!"

"No," Darret agreed seriously. He thought a moment, then squinted shrewdly. "Kestrel could take him, on de *Black Condor*," the boy suggested, cocking an inquiring eyebrow.

"Well, of *course* he could! That's what I'm talking about! You've got to get Captain Kestrel to tell Rudy that—and I'll get Rudy to go."

Darret looked at Anjell with narrowed eyes. "Waitaminit. Do I get to go too?"

"Sure you do!" Anjell promised breezily.

"And what about you? You comin' too?" Darret's manner was casual as he looked out to sea, but he studied the girl out of the corner of his eye. Anjell saw his look and blushed.

"Well, of course!" she declared crossly, stomping her foot in agitation. "I wouldn't miss it for all the Aura in Faerine!"

THIRTEEN

Fires in the Low City

Fighting an army of unlimited numbers is like
mining a pile of sand; one who strives to do
either is inevitably buried.
—DIGGERSPEAK PROVERB

— 1 —

The galyon heeled to starboard, propelled toward Outport by
a strong breeze out of the southwest. Rudy worked his way
among the tired, hungry people crowded on—and below—
the decks. He looked into a multitude of faces and observed
every emotion known to humankind: He saw an old man all
alone, face haunted by sorrow; a young couple, looking toward Lanbrij with hope; a lone woman cradling a babe to her
breast, her face an anguished mixture of love and grief. They
had all come from across Myntar Kosh, fleeing the horde of
minions, leaving everything that had to do with their lives
behind. Now, thanks to Kestrel, they at least had a chance to
survive. For the third time today, the *Black Condor* had taken
hundreds of refugees from the shores of Myntar Kosh, bearing
them across the bay to the safety of Lanbrij and Corsari.

Raine stepped carefully through the exhausted refugees,

reaching Rudy and leaning against the railing. Her fatigue was a spiritual thing, he knew—the Iceman, too, felt the burden of sorrow borne by so many of these people. Yet he was also fascinated by the capabilities of this big ship, impressed by the work the galyon performed, the lives saved. Captain Kestrel himself steered the *Condor* into the harbor, gliding to a rest beside a wide stone quay. Rudy helped secure the gangplank, ushering the numbed, disbelieving folk to shore, trying to ignore the smoke-cloud looming over the mainland.

Beside the *Condor* a sleek, three-masted carrack offloaded her own cargo of displaced humanity, while a trio of caravels crowded against a wooden dock beyond. More than a dozen ships—and countless small boats—had busied themselves over the last few days, carrying thousands of people around the Lord Minion's position in the First Gate. Whether or not the refugees would be safe for long, the Iceman reflected grimly, still remained to be seen.

That danger was on his mind as Kestrel joined him and Raine at the rail, watching the last grateful passengers—a group of children, escorted by several elderly women—make their way down the gangplank to shore.

"You saw that army on the land?" the captain asked.

Rudy nodded, chilled by the recent, vivid memory of the minion horde. The force of inhuman warriors, teeming like ants, had marched into view just an hour ago, clawing onto the isthmus as the galyon departed with this load of survivors. The monsters would reach the First Wall shortly.

"I'm going back for one more trip—to see if there're any more I can bring away."

"The minions are close, now," Raine warned.

"Aye. From the looks of things, you two might want to be finding the king."

"Yes—we'll go and join Takian now," Rudy replied. Raine, her mouth drawn into a tight line, listened silently; she had given up trying to persuade Rudy to remain in relative safety, on the ship. After clasping the captain's hands, wishing him good luck on his trip, the couple debarked and pushed their way through the crowded docks of Outport.

The massive Ocean Tower of the Second Wall stood nearby, plunging to the water line and blocking land access along the shoreline between Outport and the Low City. A wooden catwalk had been erected around the base of the tower, in case the human defenders needed a route of retreat—the scaffold could be easily knocked down in the face of an enemy advance. Now the couple took this walkway on their way to Takian.

"Another two hours till the minions reach the First Gate, at the most," the Iceman muttered.

"Beymont's men have seen the minions from the walls," replied Raine. "The duke's army will be ready for the attack." The rest of the message—"he doesn't need *you*"—remained unspoken, but Rudy clearly felt his lover's rebuke. Clutching the hilt of a heavy cutlass—a weapon loaned to him by Kestrel—Rudy set his jaw firmly, determined to join the King of Galtigor in the line of battle, as stubborn as Raine on this issue.

Duke Beymont's advance companies formed a semicircle around the First Gate. Rudy and Raine found thousands of men with pennants of every color snapping in the breeze; massive ranks of pikemen stood ready beside armored knights on impatient chargers, with long rows of archers arrayed behind the front ranks. Horns blared throughout the army as parties of riders galloped here and there, and the smell of horse overpowered all other odors.

"There's the Golden Lion," Rudy declared, pointing toward the long, brilliant banner of the King of Galtigor. Takian and his regiment occupied a position on the left of the Corsari line. The men of Galtigor stood within the Low City, two hundred paces back from the high wall, alongside thousands more armored men. The army of Corsari, having lost the barrier of the gate, would not give up the Low City without a fight.

"The Iceman!" cried Awnro Lyrifell as the couple reached the line.

"Welcome," Takian said, turning from a conversation with the steel-armored Captain Jaymes. The king's smile was warm, but his eyes were concerned; Rudy knew that Takian shared Raine's worries about the Iceman's presence in the battle.

"Good to see you, sir," came a familiar voice, and Rudy turned to clasp Randart's hand. "We got to the city on horseback a day or so after you," explained the sergeant.

"Just in time for the festivities." He turned to Raine. "Glad to see you're better, my lady."

The sight of Nicodareus, still standing like a statue in that fatal breach, sent a chill down Rudy's spine. He felt the Lord Minion's presence, a dark stain in the air, and took another sip from his flask, making sure he remained screened from the Eye of Dassadec. For now, Nicodareus seemed content to guard the gate; he had obviously suspended his hunt for the Iceman.

Shouts of alarm rose from the top of the wall. Rudy and the men in the Low City couldn't see what was happening, but Takian knew enough of the plan to describe the action: Corsari archers on the rampart showered the advancing minions with arrows. The warriors on the ground could see the missiles whoosh upward from the wall in great volleys, knew they would fall as thick as hail among the hordes. Perhaps the deadly shower would halt the enemy onslaught—at the very least it should make the minions pay for even the initial steps of the attack.

Then dark shapes moved behind Nicodareus, advancing like a tide and sweeping past, waist-high to the Lord Minion. Kroaks trooped through the open gate in a thick wave, each holding a shield over its head. Arrows bristled upward from many of the protective disks, but the minion troops pressed forward with few casualties, the rank expanding through the gate, forming a wide front for attack.

But Duke Beymont didn't give them the chance. Trumpets brayed the call to charge, and heavy lancers galloped. The ground thudded under the beat of metal-shod hooves as a hundred warhorses, each barded from face to knees, surged forward at a run. The Corsari army cheered, roaring encouragement to the grand onslaught of knights.

The first kroaks raised swords against these riders, but vanished beneath crushing hooves. Lances splintered as a dozen minions—including a whip-cracking brutox—were pierced by the steel-headed spears. Now the horsemen drew long-swords, laying about with blades while the horses bucked, kicked, and circled. In moments the entire rank of kroaks had fallen, save for a few miserable survivors scrambling back to the gate.

The Lord Minion met these with deadly rage, beheading two kroaks with a single swipe of his taloned paw. Then Ni-

codareus pounced, more quickly than a cat, more deadly than
the most lethal viper. He flew forty feet through the air, slashing into the knights, felling a pair of the big horses with blows
of hammerlike fists. Talons ripped an armored rider, casting
gory pieces of the man in different directions. Again the Lord
Minion leapt, smashing more horses to the ground, snatching
up a rider by his head. With a flick of his wrist Nicodareus
snapped the man's neck, tossing the corpse with a scornful
gesture into the faces of the dead warrior's comrades.

More minions spilled through the gate, roaring and stomping. Sparks filled the gap as a score of brutox, each bearing
a massive, iron-bladed axe, swept forward. Hundreds of
kroaks followed, and the Lord Minion scattered the last of
the heroic Corsari riders—barely half of whom stumbled back
toward Duke Beymont's position.

"Charge!" Takian bellowed the command, and Rudy
found himself shouting hoarsely as he raced forward with the
Golden Lions. Raine ran to his right, Awnro Lyrifell to his
left, and Rudy was fiercely determined to protect them, to see
them safely through the battle. Abruptly there were kroaks in
front of him, sharp-fanged jaws clacking as the hunched hu-
manoids ducked their heads and charged. His cutlass extended, Rudy lunged forward and stabbed the nearest kroak—
and was surprised when the creature's momentum sent him
stumbling backward. In an instant the Iceman was on the
ground, footsteps pounding around him. He slashed at a sagging black belly, drawing a bellow of pain and driving another
kroak backward.

Something seized him by the shoulder and abruptly he was
standing beside Raine; she released his shirt barely in time to
parry the blow of a lunging kroak. Rudy stabbed again, trying
to remember some of the things Quenidon Daringer had
taught him about the use of a sword. Instead of a natural
extension of his arm, the blade felt like an awkward tool,
reluctant to perform the work that was so desperately needed.
Yet despite the cutlass's weight and its unwieldy shape, the
edge was keen, and quickly grew dark with minion blood.

Rudy chopped, slashed, cursed, and bled in the line of battle. He lost all sense of where he was in relation to the First
Wall or the gate, knew little more than the dangers within
reach of his blade. Vaguely aware, he stumbled back or

rushed forward in concert with the warriors of Galtigor; occasionally Takian's voice rose above the fray, hoarse and unintelligible. For the most part Rudy just tried to follow the examples of Raine and Awnro.

The humans fought with fury and desperation, struggling to kill—and to stay alive. In a welter of sound and fury, the Golden Lion Regiment charged all the way to the massive wall in one sweep, then fell back. Rudy slipped into a ditch, scrambling through mud and blinking the sticky stuff from his eyes. A jolt of pain shot through his leg as he tripped, wrenching his knee. He knew a moment of stark panic, surrounded by murderous kroaks—reflexively he chopped, driving back one of the monsters. With a hacking back slash he cut down another. Then he felt Raine's hand on his arm, pulling him along with the rest of Takian's company.

His cutlass was black with the putrid blood of the minions. Bodies lay everywhere, human and monster collapsing together in death, a thousand morbid poses across the gory length of the field. Rudy's arm grew numb, and his body stung from numerous cuts and scratches. Limping on the twisted knee, he turned and hacked wildly at a kroak that rushed from behind a small building.

Buildings—they were in the Low City now, and it seemed that minions were on the roofs of the houses. Still falling back, the humans fought against a press of enemy warriors that closed in from three sides. Raine stumbled and fell, struck by a rock from above, and Rudy bit back a surge of panic as he leapt over her, slashing at the nearest kroak while she struggled to her feet.

Suddenly they were running again, stumbling over rough ground, fleeing with the surviving men of the Golden Lion. Takian's voice carried, unintelligibly, and the Iceman turned toward the sound, lurching along, conscious of his knee growing weaker. He didn't know why they ran at such a headlong pace, but he knew that if he stopped, if he fell, he was a dead man.

Something looked familiar as they stumbled up a hillside, passed through a gate of latticed iron into the compound of a whitewashed villa. Kestrel's house and courtyard, surrounded by the waist-high wall, would offer some protection against the attackers, and Takian rallied his retreating troops here. Quickly they took positions along the wall, as minions teemed over the entire hillside below.

Rudy saw more kroaks scrambling upward on the neighboring hills. Other villas served as strongholds, though many were already engulfed by flames. These pyres rose into the night sky in billowing clouds of fire and smoke—and it was only as Rudy looked at the contrast that he realized the sun had set.

For an hour the desperate humans battled to hold Kestrel's villa. Minions piled barrels, tree stumps, and bodies against the wall, clambering up and attacking along the length of the barrier. The monstrous troops fell by the dozen and were replaced by the score; men fell alone, or in pairs, and there were none to take the places of the slain.

At the top of the wall Rudy hacked against bestial faces, bloody swords, and taloned paws as snarling kroaks sought to climb over the barrier. The weariness of the long battle, the pain of his wrenched knee and a dozen minor wounds, vanished into a kind of trance—he chopped and slashed relentlessly, hacking the cutlass into kroak skulls, shoulders, and chests.

Abruptly howls of triumph rose from the courtyard as the iron gate crashed inward. Kroaks and brutox spilled into the villa's yard, charging about, crashing through the doors into house and stable. Raine grabbed Rudy's hand, pulling him toward the rear of the compound where a ladder descended into a steep ravine. As he started down, the Iceman's knee collapsed; he skidded to the bottom, landing heavily on the rocky ground. Pain shot through his legs and he rolled to the side.

"Go without me—run!" he groaned, pushing Raine away, sensing the minions surging in greater numbers through the villa.

"Dammit—come on!" Raine snapped, jerking on his arm. Awnro appeared at Rudy's other side, and together they hoisted the Iceman to his feet.

Slipping down the steep slope, lurching awkwardly, the trio joined the survivors of the Golden Lions, abandoning Kestrel's once-splendid house to the invaders.

"Wait," Rudy gasped, pulling his waterskin from his side. Hastily he spilled the liquid into his mouth, feeling the immediate revitalization. He stood, somewhat unsteadily. "I can go on," he insisted.

Then, once again, Rudy ran. At his heels minions barked and snapped, and the air echoed with screams of the wounded. Those who fell into the enemy's hands screamed long and loud before they perished—and it was fear of unspeakable death that kept exhausted troops streaming toward the Second Wall.

Fires flared higher behind them, yellow flames licking into the sky, casting shadows across the battlefield. Creatures flew overhead, and Rudy, remembering the Lord Minion, threw himself to the ground. Terrions winged past, the fires on the ground casting a crimson glow across their reflective bellies and widespread wings. Some of the fliers dove, shrieking, to strike at straggling humans with beak or claws. When Rudy looked back to Kestrel's villa, flames surged upward from all parts of the palatial house. White walls blackened and fell, devoured by insatiable heat, adding brightness to the pall of smoke spiraling into the sky.

Retreating through the night, the men heard shrieks of consuming terror before them. Stumbling onward, Rudy and the rest of the fleeing company came upon the corpses of dozens of men, sundered into gory pieces. Legs and arms lay everywhere, while several pitiful souls had been bent double and left to bleed to death, slowly, from ruptured organs.

One of the victims, groaning weakly, had lost both legs. Now he flailed, barely seeing, toward the Iceman.

"Th—the Lord Minion!" gasped the horribly wounded man, bubbling the words through a froth of blood. Then, with a gagging shudder, he stiffened and died.

Again Rudy moved, not knowing where he ran, dimly aware that they sought safety behind the Second Wall. The Low City was gone and there only remained the hope of escape. He saw an expanse of dark water to the left, knew that they had reached the bluff at the edge of Outport. Starlight flickered on the ocean waters in the far distance; nearby, the surf reflected the angry haze of a burning city.

But at least the minions showed little interest in pursuing so close to the water. The wooden catwalks had been erected for just this possibility, temporary walkways circling the Ocean Tower and allowing the defeated troops a path of retreat. Rudy stumbled along, vaguely aware of a plummeting drop toward the sea off to his left.

In hundreds and thousands, survivors fled the Low City, leaving half of Lanbrij to the minions. Men fled around the catwalks on the girding tower of the Second Wall; other troops filed through the man-sized door at the base of the huge—and secured—Second Gate. For hours the retreat continued, with the men of the Golden Lion among the last humans to depart the Low City.

When the last of the warriors had fled, the catwalks were knocked apart, timbers toppling into the sea. The door in the Second Gate was sealed, barred, and bolted, with massive boulders piled behind it as additional security. The survivors of battle congregated in defeat and confusion behind the Second Wall. Working their way through the mass of exhausted men, Rudy, Raine, and Awnro accompanied Takian toward the gate. Wounded warriors sat beside the road, while others wandered aimlessly, looking for a familiar captain or pennant.

Raine fell behind the others, and when the Iceman slowed to match her pace she took his arm, whirling him around to face her. "Do you see how much good it did to stay and fight?" she blazed at him. "Now do you understand why I wanted you to leave, to get on a ship and sail for Faerine?"

"I told you!" he replied sharply, his own temper flaring. "I *had* to—"

"You had no *right*!" Raine spat back. "What if you had gotten killed—what then? What hope for the world? Just because your ego wouldn't let you miss a battle!"

"Why can't you understand?" Rudy demanded.

"I understand that you're doing everything you can to avoid the quest that's been laid upon you! I heard Kelwyn Dyerston hint at it, and Pheathersqyll came right out and *told* you! You have to go to Faerine!"

"Is it finished, then?" the Iceman asked, slumping. "Is all Dalethica falling to the minions—and I'm to hide in Faerine? *No!* I won't do it!"

"You're *not* hiding! It's your destiny, your fate—and just maybe it will offer the hope of stopping this darkness *before* the world is overwhelmed!"

Still struggling against the bonds of Raine's arguments, unwilling to acknowledge that she was right, Rudy hastened after King Takian and Awnro. He caught up with his companions just below the looming towers of the gate. There they found Duke Beymont badly wounded, his gut sliced by a minion sword. The duke lay on a rude litter, his skin glistening with fever, while frantic retainers stood helplessly around him. Rudy pushed his way through the circle and knelt beside the young nobleman. Beymont's eyes blazed in his pale face, and he held a hand to his side, wincing every time he drew a breath.

"Lost—all is lost!" he groaned, thrashing his head weakly from side to side.

"Not yet," Rudy replied. "The retreat is done, the High City still stands behind the wall."

"Lost . . ." repeated Beymont, his voice barely audible.

"Here—take a drink of this," the Iceman said, offering the waterskin and its precious contents. "The magic of Faerine . . ."

Beymont drank, scarcely acknowledging the Iceman's presence; then he fell back and appeared to sleep. The companions found hot soup being served by a large fire, and settled themselves on some nearby rocks to consume the restorative broth.

"Those casks of Aura, from Taywick—" the King of Galtigor began, breaking a silence that had been punctuated only by the slurping of soup. "They were sent here aboard *Searunner*—they're down on the waterfront. Perhaps we should bring them up here, to help with the wounded."

"That might be a good idea," Rudy agreed absently. His mind wandered, drifting along a current suggested by Takian's words.

Anjell and her mother, together with Bristyn, Kestrel, and Darret found them there. The girl sat beside the King of Galtigor, and Rudy was too tired to notice her whispering into Takian's ear.

The captain shook his head when the others offered consolation on the loss of his villa. "It's just a house. My ship means more to me, and all of our lives still more. I'm glad to see you all—I understand there were many who did not make it to the Second Wall."

"What about the people on the far shore?" Raine asked Kestrel.

"I think we brought the last of 'em over—in any event,

the forest fires are spreading into those coastal woodlands now. I'm afraid it's all over for anyone who's left there."

"But many more are alive because you were there," Dara said, patting Kestrel's arm.

"Perhaps, my lady—though it can't ever be enough." He squeezed Dara's hand. "Still, a man has to do something—and you're kind to say so."

"The battle will rage on, here," Takian declared abruptly. He faced Rudy. "The Second Wall is high and strong—Corsari may hold out for a long time. Now I think it's time we planned for a trip to Faerine. For you and, I think, for Raine."

The Iceman cast an angry glance at Raine. "I told you—I can't keep running from every fight! And this one is far from over!"

"Be realistic, my friend," urged the King of Galtigor, his eyes—and his tone—hard. "Your sword in the line of battle at Lanbrij will not make the difference between winning or losing this fight! Yet the knowledge you might gain in Faerine could prove decisive not only in Corsari but across all the Watershed!"

"You're right about my sword," Rudy declared ruefully. "There's a big difference between knowing how to hold it and knowing how to fight with it."

"And a bigger difference still between fighting with a weapon, and killing with it," Raine declared somberly. "Killing does not come naturally to you."

Rudy heard the regret that underlay her words; in the day's fighting she had shown herself to be a very effective killer indeed. "Thanks—to all of you, for saving my life, frequently," he said in a low tone. He sighed and shook his head, suddenly feeling all the weariness of the long fight. Then, shrugging his shoulders, he looked at Takian frankly. "It doesn't matter whether I plan to go to Faerine—how would I get there?"

"Kestrel will take you!" Darret declared. He blinked when he saw the adults' eyes upon him, but then he puffed out his chest and elaborated. "He can sail *Black Condor* anywhere—and he's not afraid of nuthin'!"

"Thanks for the confidence, lad, though I'm afraid of more than you can know," Kestrel said ruefully. "And sail into the Faerine Sea? It's just not done, by humans at any rate. There's whirlpools, currents of Aura where the watersheds meet in the ocean. They suck down any ship!''

"You said 'humans'—does that mean that Faerine sailors can cross the ocean divides?'' Rudy asked.

"The sylves have been known to sail there, in centuries past,'' admitted Kestrel. The captain looked squarely into Rudy's eyes. "And I believe what these folks tell me—that this task of yours is important to all of us. I'm willing to do what I can to help.''

"Thank you,'' Rudy said, surprised and heartened by the man's offer. At the same time he had a hopeful inkling about those hidden dangers. They would doubtless be caused by surges in Aura, enchanted waters resisting a mingling with the mundane brine of the ocean. If so, it was possible that he would be able to see them, to guide the ship around the dangerous eddies.

"It may be that we can go—*after* we see that Lanbrij is safe,'' the Iceman said. "Then, if you can at least sail me to the coastline of Faerine, I can travel into the realm on foot.''

"You don't have time to waste—you can't wait to see if Lanbrij survives!'' Raine objected, angrily trying to meet Rudy's eyes.

"I'll go—but not yet,'' the Iceman demurred. "There's something else I *can* do here—that might make more of a difference than my sword.''

"What?'' asked Takian, eyes narrowed shrewdly. "Does it have to do with the casks you had me bring down from Taywick Pass?''

"It does.''

"What do you plan to do?'' asked Kestrel, mystified.

"I'm not exactly sure. I'll have to talk to the duke before proceeding. But first I'm going to do a little exploring.'' He looked at Raine, sighed, and extended his hand. Her face softened as she took it and heard him ask, "Care to go for a boat ride?''

Her hooded eyes suddenly brightened in understanding. "Yes,'' she said, nodding gravely. "Yes, I would.''

— 2 —

The little boat drifted through the shadows of the digger canal, riding the incoming tide from the ocean toward the darkened reaches of the watery tunnel. Raine touched a spark to the wick of a lantern, raising the beacon high while Rudy steered, using the oars to hold them between the stone walls.

"There's the bridge!" Raine said, raising the lamp still higher.

A network of rusty girders materialized from the darkness, and Rudy saw a catwalk spanning the canal. "Grab a post— we'll tie up there," he said, and Raine quickly secured them to the bridge piling.

They scrambled onto the smooth, dry walkway running beside the canal. The raised stone surface apparently ran the full length of the tunnel. Rudy felt a familiar twinge, like a touch on the shoulder in a darkened room. Instinctively he sipped a few drops of Aura, feeling the Lord Minion's questing Sight move past him, still seeking. "Soon enough, you'll find me," he murmured—and it was a promise, even if tinged with fear.

Raine still held the lantern as they started into the tunnel that had once connected the diggers' living quarters to the canal. For more than an hour the pair poked and probed through the maze of cisterns, barracks, and drainage systems. Finally satisfied, Rudy led Raine back to the boat, where they untied the rope and rode the ebbing tide back toward the ocean.

It was mid-morning when the small craft shot out of the canal. The *Black Condor* stood at anchor a half mile from shore, and with rapid strokes of the oars Rudy propelled his little boat toward the galyon. Raine caught the rope tossed down from the ship, and within minutes the two of them had climbed aboard.

"We're heading for the harbor," Kestrel said, swinging down from the wheel deck to greet the pair. "Did you find the digger barracks?"

"Yes—the canal is a wonder, like you said."

"Will it work?"

"It might," Rudy said cautiously. "I found the cisterns, and the mechanism still works. That's all I could ask for. Now, *if* we can get the Aura into the cisterns, and *if*—"

"Don't worry about the 'ifs,' " declared the captain, clapping Rudy heartily on the shoulder. "As to the Aura, I have all twenty casks aboard. My crewmen will take them in with the rising tide—they should all be emptied by mid-afternoon.''

''Good. I've marked the cistern with a beam of wood holding the hatch open. Have them pour all the Aura in. Twenty-four hours from now we'll know if it was all a waste. And by the way, the ebbing tide flows at a pretty good clip—it should carry me out of there quickly.''

Kestrel nodded, but his eyes flickered in concern. Rudy's escape was the most dangerous part of the plan, they knew.

''Carry *us* out,'' Raine said firmly.

Rudy turned to his lover, putting his hands on her shoulders and staring into her dark, serious eyes. ''This time I'm not giving in to you. If I survive, it will be in the water—as *part* of the water, perhaps. That's my element—and if you try to come along, you'll be lost for sure.''

''You need my help!'' she insisted.

''I know—I'm finally starting to realize how *much* I need you. But this I do by myself. Or else,'' he threatened, with a tight smile, ''I won't take you on that trip to Faerine you've been harping about!''

For once, Raine gave in, gripping the Iceman's hand firmly as they climbed the ladder to join Kestrel at the helm. From the wheel deck of the galyon, they had a clear view of the minion army sweeping through the Low City. The monsters marched—or swarmed, more accurately—like ants over the rocky terrain of Lanbrij. Plumes of smoke erupted in many places, and the sounds of destruction, of splintering wood and tumbling stone, carried far onto the bay.

The galyon, under jib and a few topsails, eased into the harbor. The longboat was dropped, and several crewmen prepared to ferry Rudy to shore.

''I'll see you on the bay—tomorrow,'' he said to Raine.

''I'll be watching,'' she promised, then pulled him close. As he kissed her, he felt the fear pulling like taut wires inside her body, and he knew that the upcoming hours of waiting would be cruelly hard for her.

But his mind turned unalterably toward the future as he descended the ship's ladder and allowed Kestrel's crewmen to row him to the still-crowded quay. Once ashore, he turned

his back on the waterfront and started up the long hill to the
castle gate, thinking about a colossal gamble.

It was time to talk to Duke Beymont.

— 3 —

The young nobleman was fit and healthy, moving with the
same catlike grace as before his injury, pacing in agitation
atop the highest rampart of the castle gate. Here, Rudy found
him conferring with the King of Galtigor. Dire concerns had
etched lines into the duke's once-youthful features in a remarkably short time, and now he leaned against the wall,
grimacing in despair as he watched the sacking of half his
city.

Yet when Beymont saw Rudy, he surprised the Iceman by
sweeping forward and clasping him on both shoulders. The
duke's eyes clouded with tears, and emotion choked his voice.
"I know that you saved my life," he told Rudy without preamble. "At the same time, you have confounded the wisest
physicians of Corsari. What is this blessing that you have
bestowed upon me?"

"It is not to me, but to the water of Faerine that you owe
your recovery. I'm glad to see you fit and healthy."

"In body, I am," the duke declared, turning to the rampart
with a sigh. "But my spirit aches for Lanbrij. To lose our
city gate before the enemy army is here . . . then all the Low
City, the lives of a thousand brave men, gone in a single day's
battle."

"You have the Second Wall," Takian reminded him.
"And another solid gate—this one sealed and barred!"

"True words, my good king—though they do little to
soothe the sting of our losses. Still, I cannot forget your aid—
and the lives of your own men, perished in the cause of Lanbrij's defense."

"I meant what I said to King Macconal, and I will repeat
it to you: This is a war in which all mankind must stand
together. My men and I were here, so here was where we
would fight."

"Surely you have concerns about your own realm . . . ?"

"Aye," Takian said grimly. "And Carillonn, too—the

marble city stands squarely in the minion's eastward path. We will be taking *Searunner* back to the Ariak shortly, though I will stay as long as I can—and pray for your successful resistance after I depart.''

"I extend my sincerest thanks. I just wish there was some way we might strike at the enemy, to give you some heartening news to carry to the rest of the world.''

"There might be something,'' Takian said quietly. "I think that our Iceman has an idea.''

Beymont turned to Rudy, raising his eyebrows in mute question.

"I do have a proposal,'' Rudy said. "I have to warn you that it may not work at all. If it does, it could alter the face of Lanbrij—but, too, it may save what remains of your city.''

"After your miracle yesterday,'' Beymont said, touching the place where he had been pierced, "I'm willing to listen to anything you have to say. . . .''

— 4 —

Dara met the Iceman in the castle, her face drawn and pale. "I saw the army from the wall today—it was more awful than I imagined in my worst nightmare.''

Rudy nodded grimly as he took his brother's widow in his arms, offering no argument to alter Dara's conclusion. He held her tightly.

"Tomorrow—you'll be going?'' she asked.

"If . . . everything turns out right, yes, I will. But I want you to come too, and Anjell.''

"But . . .'' Dara's objection trailed off.

"Awnro's coming, and we need the two of you. I can't promise that it will be safe—''

"Don't try,'' she told him. "I can see what's happening in the world. But all right . . . if you want us to come, we will.''

"Good—you'll need to get to the dock before dark tonight. I'll join you on the *Condor* tomorrow.'' Giving her a final hug and a kiss on each cheek, Rudy left the widow to make her preparations.

By late afternoon Dara and Anjell had collected their few belongings and said farewell to Bristyn in the castle. Awnro accompanied the Appenfells to the docks just before sunset, and Kestrel and Darret welcomed them all aboard the *Black Condor*.

"We'll be setting out for the sea by tomorrow afternoon," the captain said.

"Thanks, yes," Dara said absently, lost in her own thoughts. As full darkness descended, the young widow tried to remain calm. Taking up the pearl-handled hairbrush that was one of her treasured possessions, she slowly brushed her daughter's hair, as Anjell—for once without fidgeting—sat on the bed in their cabin.

As Dara brushed she was distracted by steady footsteps moving back and forth on the deck. The pacing continued relentlessly, motivated by some anguish that the widow could no longer ignore. Finally, after her daughter fell asleep, she rose and opened the door.

She emerged from her cabin to see Raine pacing the deck, staring in agitation at the city skyline outlined in fire. The younger woman turned, met Dara's gaze, and then turned away—but not before Dara saw her eyes fill with tears.

FOURTEEN

Second Wall and Sea

History is the most commonly accepted version
of a variety of widespread lies.
—SCROLL OF BARACAN

— 1 —

All night the Low City burned, waves of relentless heat singeing the grim-faced men on the Second Wall. The inside of
the castle gate grew warm from the massive conflagrations,
and the pale morning revealed thousands of minions advancing through an ash-strewn wasteland, kicking apart frames of
buildings, fences, and any other structure that had somehow
survived the fires. The brushy hills of the entire Low City
were black and soot-covered, with smoke rising everywhere
and the smell of charcoal heavy in the still air.

The enemy troops, Rudy was relieved to note, stayed well
away from the precipice on the ocean shore of Lanbrij. He
watched from the Second Gate as the horde advanced on the
gentler slopes over the Circled Sea. The minion formations
remained back from the water, save for a few brutox who

advanced far enough to start fires in the shacks and shanties along the Low City waterfront.

Rudy watched as one of the brutox seized a section of wooden scaffold that remained standing near the harbor. The brute stretched out long arms and clasped two poles, one in each hand. In moments the posts were outlined in fire, as were the planks linking the two supports. Flames sizzled along the boards, crackling and popping, and soon the entire structure was engulfed.

The Iceman stood atop the gate with Takian and Duke Dalston Beymont. Men by the hundreds, together with stockpiles of arrows, spears, and water barrels, crowded the ramparts of the tower top and connecting walls. At the outer lip of the rampart numerous charcoal fires glowed, each heating an iron cauldron of bubbling liquid.

The ground just below the wall was clear of obstacles, though Rudy saw several minion corpses there. Arrows still jutted from the bodies; the enemy had been taught a lesson about venturing too close. Still, when the Iceman looked into the ashes of the Low City, even in the twilight of early dawn he saw movement everywhere. Dark swaths of shadow shifted and formed—companies of kroaks, he guessed. Beside these ranks frequent bursts of sparks marked the locations of the brutox.

Rudy again felt the presence of Nicodareus, probing, seeking the Iceman's whereabouts. Immediately he withdrew his own awareness, insuring that the Lord Minion did not touch him, nor even begin to locate him atop the wall.

"Have you considered my . . . suggestion?" Rudy asked the duke.

Beymont looked impassively at the army massed in the ruins of the Low City. "Wait," he said. "Watch for a while."

Silently Rudy nodded. The young duke contemplated a decision perhaps more momentous than any other in the history of humankind—it was not a thing to hurry. Still, Rudy knew that neither would the tide be delayed.

"Look," declared King Takian grimly.

Emerging from the obscurity of dawn, coastal mist, and lingering smoke plodded a file of massive creatures. Each had a broad, bony head, the forehead and skull of which was a blunt plate. The backs of the beasts were protected by dried leather shields, sloping down each flank and meeting in a peak along the brutes' spines. The four-legged minions were lashed into parallel files, and gradually the humans discerned a massive, iron-tipped ram suspended between the twin ranks.

"Awnro said those things are called bovars," Takian said. "They used them to block the Myn—and probably to dam every river and stream between here and the Dry Basin."

The creatures advanced directly toward the gate. Sparking brutox marched at either side, cracking whips and urging the massive beasts forward. More brutox swaggered behind, holding tethers with which they would apparently control the ram.

"Use the oil!" barked Duke Beymont, as the monstrous beasts drew close to the gate.

Immediately Corsari warriors lifted the cauldrons to the wall, dumping bubbling liquid onto the monsters at the gate. The oil splashed over bony heads, pouring onto the leather shields covering the creatures' backs. In the front of the rank, several of the bovars pitched and bucked momentarily, but the whips of the brutox quickly settled them back into their plodding advance; for the most part the searing liquid trickled harmlessly to the ground.

"Arrows—give them a volley," cried the duke, dismayed at the results of the oil. Steel-tipped missiles showered outward from the rampart, aimed at bovar and brutox alike.

Again the heavy protection of the bovars' armor prevented the missiles from even reaching the monsters' skin. Several brutox went down, fatally pierced, while the survivors scrambled back to the rear of the bovar teams. Rudy watched, horrified yet fascinated as a brutox writhed in death throes directly below. The creature bellowed like a bull, kicking and flailing, its body enveloped in a shroud of cascading sparks. The minion's eyes bulged, then exploded outward in a shower of oily fire. Finally the sparks and flames died, and a deflated corpse lay still in the midst of spreading gore.

But now the lead bovars reached the gate. The brutox operating the ram huddled under wooden-roofed wagons fifty paces to the rear, drawing the mighty beam back and then allowing the steel-coated head to smash against the gates. Even through the stone walls and heavy floorboards of the tower, Rudy could feel the impact of the collision. The bovars reared back, and when the ram advanced again it was im-

pelled not just by the tether, but by the coordinated lunge of
the massive haulers. This time the floor creaked underfoot,
and a stone tumbled from the battlements. Once more the ram
struck the Second Gate with massive force. Though it creaked
in protest, the barrier held, and no one voiced the question on
all of their minds: How long could the gates stand against that
assault?

In the increasing light, Rudy saw more and more of the
minion formations come into view. Terrions flew in groups
of five or six, wheeling over the kroaks and brutox. Beyond,
through the gaping hole of the First Wall, he saw still more
of the Sleepstealer's monsters, advancing in a great column
that trailed off the far end of the Land Bridge. The horde
gathered in the Low City, evil waters collecting behind the
dam of the Second Wall—and the ram was an eroding force,
eating away at that lone dike.

There was no sign of the Lord Minion, and when Rudy
took a drink from his flask he felt no specific indication. Nevertheless, the Iceman knew that Nicodareus was out there
somewhere—perhaps he had fed recently, and was now in a
period of recovery.

"Are you prepared?" asked Duke Beymont, joining Rudy
at the rampart, though it was several seconds before his question penetrated the Iceman's concentration.

"Yes . . . but I will await your command."

Beymont drew a deep breath, then looked once more at the
horde teeming through the Low City. "Do it—and may Baracan and Aurianth smile upon you."

"I'll go to the Ocean Tower now," Rudy replied. Shaking
off his uneasiness, he turned to the young nobleman. "You'll
want to get most of your men off the wall beforehand."

"But not too early," Beymont noted. "And there's always
the chance that it won't work. . . ."

"In that case, may the gate of your ancestors stand firm,"
Rudy said. He didn't allow himself to dwell on the prospects
of his own survival; instead he remembered the *Black Condor*,
standing safely offshore.

The duke reached out to the Iceman. "I know what you
risk for us—and together with all my people I thank you.
May we meet again, my friend, on the field of ultimate victory."

"I pray that we will," Rudy said fervently.

Finally, he turned his back on the gatehouse. The time was right—the tide was beginning to ebb. Staying atop the Second Wall, he followed the long rampart to the Ocean Tower. Across the rolling ground of the Low City—now a wreckage-strewn wasteland—stood rank upon rank of kroaks. The nearest of the monsters advanced to within two hundred paces of the wall, in clear view but beyond effective arrow range.

When Rudy was halfway to his destination a brutox cracked a whip in the midst of a massive band of kroaks, sparking across the shoulders of the assembled minions. The kroaks roared and charged, waving swords, stomping hobnailed boots in a stone-crushing cadence. Two dozen bowmen fired from the ramparts in unison, razor-tipped shafts slicing into the kroaks, dropping several to the ground. The remaining minions rushed to the base of the wall, driven by the frenzied roars of the brutox. Again a volley of arrows ripped into the creatures, and more fell. Two missiles struck the brutox, and Rudy watched in awe as the creature plucked the arrows, like pesky thorns, from its flesh. The brute continued to roar at the kroaks, sending the creatures clawing at the base of the massive wall.

Rocks, jugs of oil wrapped in flaming rags, and arrows showered the minions, who had absolutely no chance of reaching the defenders. They bore no ladder, carried no mining equipment, yet they rushed forward and died, apparently more frightened of their master than their enemy.

Finally the brutox fell, its skull crushed by a good-sized boulder. The bloated body twisted in agony, spewing sparks and flames, and immediately the remaining kroaks fled the killing ground at the wall. Less than half of the company survived, and many of the living ultimately reached safety upon hands and knees, or perished under relentless arrows. The brutox erupted, disgorging the vitriol of its body in flaming gouts, adding to the blazes caused by the burning oil. Some dead kroaks were incinerated by the flames, but the blaze quickly faded to ashes, and only a litter of rocks, battered minion corpses, and broken arrows marked the scene of the pointless attack.

Or was it pointless? Rudy realized that the enemy had learned much about the defenses of the wall—the density of

bowmen, and the types of resistance they would meet at the
bottom. The attack could have been some kind of test. The
Iceman took a quick swallow from his waterskin, then stared
into the Sleepstealer's army. Behind at least three ranks of
kroaks he saw a figure that loomed above all the others. The
batlike wings were folded back, but when Rudy focused his
concentration he saw the crimson, burning eyes of the Lord
Minion. The Iceman felt those eyes, seeking, hungry . . .
wanting him. Tearing his gaze away, the Man of Three Waters
shifted his concentration, distracting himself from the presence of his enemy. Now was not the time!

He jogged along the rampart, impelled by a growing sense
of urgency. When he reached the Ocean Tower, he climbed
that lofty pinnacle, where a score of Corsari warriors occupied
the platform, together with a weapon that looked like a large
crossbow mounted on a solid wooden pedestal.

"Sergeant Dalrik, Royal Trebuchet company," declared
one of the warriors. The dark-faced veteran raised his hand
in a quick salute. "My captain said you would be coming,
sir. You'll find everything as you left it, I'm sure."

Nodding his thanks, Rudy crossed the platform, to the large
coils of rope he had placed there earlier. From this rampart
the stone wall plunged straight into the ocean. Two nights
ago, the catwalk down there had led the way to safety; now
nothing stood between the Iceman and the bottom of the tower
wall. He leaned out, seeing the fringe of surf far below. Toward the ruins of the Low City a finger of wave-washed coral
extended along the bottom of the tower.

Gathering one end of the line in a double loop around a
stony battlement, Rudy tied a tight knot for security. Then he
lowered the opposite end toward the ocean, paying out the
rope steadily. When the line touched the waves, he wrapped
the coil several times around the battlement and tied it off
again. Dalrik and the men of his company watched with interest as Rudy clipped a metal ring to his wide leather belt,
then passed the upper end of the rope through the same steel
circlet. After slipping on a pair of stout cowhide gloves, the
Iceman climbed to the wall between a pair of looming battlements and wrapped the rope around his waist. With a wave
to the Corsari troops, he backed over the edge, allowing the

line to race through his hands and around his waist as he skipped backward and down.

For a long time he plunged—in fact, to the watching Sergeant Dalrik it probably seemed interminable. Rudy had rappelled down longer cliff faces in his life, though not often, but even so the smooth, unchanging nature of the tower wall made this descent seem much greater than its actual distance. Occasionally he looked below, watching the surging of the ocean, surprised by the constant roughness of the water, the great heights to which each wave rose as it exploded against the time-smoothed stones at the base of the tower.

The Iceman finally halted his rappel some distance above the high-water mark. Now that he saw the waves surging over the rounded coral his plan seemed more rash than he had earlier believed. Shaking off his doubts, he began to move sideways along the wall, kicking against the stones, swinging back and forth until his momentum carried him over the shelf of treacherous-looking coral. He planted his feet again, resting firmly against the wall, with his rope running at a slight angle from his position up to the loops securing it to the parapet.

Carefully he started to lower himself the last distance, placing one foot firmly before he took his weight off the other. Soon his heels touched the coral, and he watched a large swell carry the surf almost to his feet before he dropped onto a knob of rocklike reef. Releasing the rope, he made his way as quickly as he dared along the rough and treacherously slick surface, bracing himself on the smooth face of the Ocean Tower wall. Once, his right foot skidded, but his left jammed against an irregularity, giving him leverage to retain his balance.

Finally he moved onto the actual rocks of the Lanbrij isthmus, scrambling above the coral and the slick, wave-washed shoreline. The ground dropped steeply to the water, and by traversing along the rugged face he remained below the sight of the gathered minions. He couldn't fully suppress his shudder of apprehension as he realized that he was separated from the mass of the Sleepstealer's army by nothing more than the crest of bluff.

Halfway to his objective, Rudy paused to catch his breath. He saw the *Black Condor*, under partial sail, tacking away from the harbor mouth. Sunlight gleamed from the water out to sea, and in the distance the whitecaps looked gentle, even tranquil. Where the waters reached the shadow of the bluff, however, they became gray and menacing.

All his life Rudy had been taught to scale the vertical cliffs, the sweeping glaciers and treacherous slopes of talus and scree, that surrounded Neshara and framed the grandeur of Halverica. The face he traversed now was lower than any mountain, and held none of the dangers inherent in surfaces of snow or ice. Yet the rock remained constantly wet, sticky with salt in a fashion that made it as dangerous as any ice— since the coating retarded his movement, but offered no advantage in gripping the rock.

His fingers cramped from the tension of clutching the slippery wall, and his legs ached from the steady, measured pace of sideways movement. He traversed the seaside cliff for more than an hour, resting briefly when he came to a foot-wide ledge that gave him space to sit down, and again in a narrow chimney where he could prop his back against one wall, his feet against the other. Then, with no warning, he came around a shoulder of the cliff and saw his destination: the digger canal. The tunnel mouth gaped at the water level, flanked by a series of stone steps that Rudy moved onto gratefully. The current spilled outward quickly, tide rushing from the Circled Sea into the vastness of the ocean. That flow, he knew, would maintain its intensity for at least the next hour.

The canal tunnel was nearly forty feet wide, with most of the space occupied by the trough of deep water running down the center. To either side of the channel the stone walkways allowed someone on foot to walk beside the canal. Now, at high tide, these walks were only a foot or two above the level of the water, though by full ebb they would loom nearly eight feet over the surface. Overhead, the ceiling of the tunnel arched above the water, high enough to allow a small sailboat to pass.

Rudy was acutely conscious of the fact that this was a hallowed, historical place, excavated a thousand years earlier by the diggers who had aided Dalethica in the first Sleep-stealer War. What right had he, a short-lived mortal, even to contemplate the act in which he was now engaged—tampering with something that had withstood the rigors of ten centuries?

No right, he knew—just absolute, dire necessity.

The steep stairway leading down to the walkway extended all the way up the bluff. Rudy jogged upward, toward the top, relieved to see that the minions had shown no inclination to venture down these stairs. Doubtless the restless, surging waters of the ocean distressed them as much as a similar amount of Darkblood might have sickened himself.

Very carefully the Iceman crept up the last stairs, cautiously raising his head to peer over the top step. He saw a full company of kroaks lolling on the ground, no more than a hundred feet away; fortunately, the monsters seemed mostly interested in the gate, which shuddered in the background under the steady onslaught of the ram. Rudy felt a chill of apprehension as he saw that the mighty barrier had already separated slightly, revealing a crack near the top that clearly indicated the progress of the minion assault.

Dropping below the level of observation, the Iceman sat on the damp, chilly stairs and drew his waterskin off his shoulder. He took a long, deep draught of Aura, feeling the enchantment of Faerine spread through his body. He sensed the presence of the Lord Minion near the center of the great army, could feel the creature's hunger, his desire for killing and for vengeance. Climbing again to the top of the stairway, the Iceman reached out with his mind, spearing the Lord Minion with his undeniable presence. Pain shot through Rudy's head, and he reeled backward, confronted by a mental image of fierce, crimson eyes. He swayed weakly, in danger of tumbling down the stairs—and in the grip of total, numbing paralysis.

With howls of warning, the nearby kroaks charged toward the human standing atop the stairs, drawing their swords of dark iron. Rudy struggled in the mental grip of Nicodareus; his gut spasmed, his throat heaved. He retched and vomited onto the ground, and the violent expulsion of bile at last broke the grip of the Lord Minion's will. Dozens of minions pursued as Rudy spun around and staggered down the slick stone stairs. In a few bounds he reached the foot of the cliff and—without pausing to look back at his pursuers—darted into the tunnel, sprinting along one of the stone walkways beside the canal.

He noticed that the water level was lower than it had been

minutes ago, that the current raced through the canal with steadily increasing speed. A hundred steps from the entrance he paused, drawing deep breaths of air as he turned and looked back. A kroak crept around the landing at the bottom of the stairs, peering into the dark tunnel, pressing its back against the wall to stay as far from the water as possible.

Something bellowed and cursed behind the kroak, and the creature—clutching its sword—inched forward. More kroaks crawled into view, and then Rudy saw the sparking trails of a brutox. Even that hulking minion seemed reluctant to get close to the water; the brutox waved kroak after kroak forward without itself venturing into the canal tunnel.

Rudy resumed moving, trotting now instead of sprinting, looking back frequently. The kroaks pressed forward, but only with the greatest reluctance. When the lead minion had penetrated no more than twenty or thirty steps, it ceased moving altogether. It crouched against the wall, eyes fastened on the flowing water, beastlike jowls jabbering pathetic sounds.

The Iceman didn't take the time to envision the Lord Minion's location. Nicodareus would be coming shortly, and Rudy needed to be in position by that time. He drew long, measured breaths as he jogged deeper into the tunnel. When the spill of daylight had faded, Rudy halted long enough to take one of many lanterns from a shelf in the wall. Striking a spark from the flint and steel beside the lamps, he quickly fired the wick and carried his illumination with him as he neared the middle of the tunnel. Overhead was the mass of the Low City, and Rudy felt the weight of rock like a personal load on his shoulders—a pressure that, for a moment, made it difficult to breathe.

Forcing himself to inhale deeply, the Iceman once again started forward. He had not gone ten more steps when he felt, like a blast of chill wind against his back, the evil presence that he awaited. With sickening, fearful certainty, he imagined fiery eyes boring into him, cruel claws seeking his flesh.

Coming fast, sweeping forward on the wings of a nighthawk, Nicodareus dove into the tunnel of the digger canal.

— 2 —

Hatred blinded his eyes and bloodlust fueled the relentless power of his wings as Nicodareus sought the Iceman. The

Lord Minion's prey gleamed like a beacon in the darkness before him, and the Eye of Dassadec was determined that, this time, he would kill—that the taste of his victim's blood would finally be flavored with success, and revenge.

He answered the summons of hate, fixing on the clear mental spoor that marked his quarry. The Man of Three Waters was here! Shifting quickly to this sleek, avian form, Nicodareus had soared after that spoor, despising the fear of the kroaks cowering on the stone steps. At the same time, the voice of reason suggested that the Aurawielder had selected his refuge very carefully. Only Nicodareus, insulated by the power of Darkslayer, could abide the presence of so much water, the steady force of a relentless current.

This same rational awareness made the Lord Minion wonder why he had been attracted so overtly—surely the human had known that he would be noticed! Hesitating slightly, Nicodareus settled to the stone walkway, growing to his full height, seeking further clues. He continued forward, broad, taloned feet stalking over the floor in strides as quick as a human in full sprint. The current flowed sickeningly, the loathsome water rushing barely a few feet away, but the Lord Minion forced himself to concentrate on his prey.

Could this possibly be—the idea was almost too audacious to consider—a *trap*? Nicodareus chortled, the sound a rumbling boil in his belly. In his normal state he would be impervious to any human weapon, and even the crushing force of a massive cave-in would do little more than slow him down—and that only until he shifted his shape into that of some burrowing creature and wormed his way free.

Yet now, Nicodareus was even more potent than normal. The human couldn't know that the Lord Minion had emerged from Immersion in Darkblood barely an hour before the mental image had drawn his attention. The virulent stuff of Duloth-Trol still slicked his skin, protecting his nearly immortal body against all injury. If this was a trap, the Eye of Dassadec resolved, it would only ensnare the one who had laid it—an image that appealed to the Lord Minion's dark sense of irony.

Now the Iceman's presence was a blurred vision in the darkness before him; in fact, it was the flickering glow of a lantern that Nicodareus observed. His Sight probed, saw nothing there, and this was his confirmation—among humans, only the Man of Three Waters could so completely evade his detection.

The Lord Minion loped forward, no longer employing his Sight. Instead, the ordinary vision of his crimson eyes showed his target now. The lanky human shape scrambled frantically along the stone walkway; fear was a palpable stench in the air, bringing an aching hunger to the Lord Minion's belly.

All but trembling in his anticipation, Nicodareus lowered his head, clawed at the stone floor for footing, and sprang after the Man of Three Waters.

— 3 —

Rudy was appalled by the speed of the Lord Minion's approach. The Iceman's feet pounded the stones as he flew toward the center of the tunnel—the tunnel that seemed so much longer than it had during yesterday's reconnaissance. He saw the catwalk ahead of him, girders of rusty iron leading across the canal, into the dark passages of the ancient diggers' quarters. Yet the ground-shaking footsteps of Nicodareus pounded steadily closer. Rudy didn't need to look behind; the sensitivity bred by his drink of Aura focused an awareness of the Lord Minion in a growing circle of heat between the Iceman's shoulder blades.

Straining for air, lumbering toward the high, arched bridge, Rudy knew he wasn't going to make it. He felt Nicodareus reach forward, sensed the talons descending toward the vulnerable flesh of his shoulder. The Iceman dropped the lantern and lowered his head, throwing himself off the walkway, breaking the surface of the water in a clean dive. His momentum carried him forward even against the current, and he kicked toward the far side of the tunnel, remaining underwater as he swam.

His mind suggested that he should be straining for air, but Rudy's lungs felt fresh and powerful. He continued to kick, froglike, swimming under the water until he felt the cold stone of the far side of the canal against his hand. Only then did he raise his head, kicking upward to seize the lip of the walkway, flopping out of the water and bouncing to his feet.

Even in the full darkness he sensed the Lord Minion directly across the canal. Those crimson eyes turned quickly, boring into him, and the Iceman knew that he had been discovered. He spun, pounding toward the entrance to the digger chambers. He bumped into a pillar of iron, recognizing the terminus of the bridge. Here he scrambled up the steps he remembered, darting into the long tunnel that had echoed to digger footsteps during the long course of the canal's excavation. Racing along, Rudy was aware that he could see again, slightly, in the stygian depths.

Aura! Kestrel's men had carted the stuff here yesterday, and apparently one of the casks had enough of a leak to trickle a tiny bit of the liquid into the tunnel. That vague wetness now let the Man of Three Waters see where there was no light.

Nicodareus crossed the canal in a mighty pounce, skidding along the stones as he clawed for traction. In moments he had darted around the corner, flying after the Iceman, once again closing the distance with lightning leaps. Rudy dove past a place he had previously marked, grasping the iron door frame to arrest his headlong flight. With a wrenching tug he slammed shut a heavy metal door, dropping the steel bar into place in a single, fluid movement. The Lord Minion struck the barrier with a resounding crash, denting the metal surface inward and drawing a strident creak as the bar strained unnaturally.

Rudy felt his enemy draw back for another onslaught, but he didn't wait to see the result. Racing up a nearby stairway, crossing a round chamber, he then dropped through a hatch in the floor into another cylindrical vault—the catch basin below the cisterns of the ancient digger keg mechanism. This basin, perhaps fifteen feet in diameter and twice that in depth, stood below the outlets of four great chambers—each connecting by a spout to the basin.

A circular metal door stood open in the wall at the base of the vault. Rudy ducked through the hatchway, then took hold of the large lever on the other side. He pushed the door partially closed, leaning forward to listen for the sounds of the Lord Minion's progress, hearing a clang of metal as Nicodareus wrenched the first door from its hinges. The Eye of Dassadec followed again, unerringly, along the Iceman's path.

When he felt that dire presence at the lip of the cistern

above, Rudy slammed the circular door shut, drawing the bar in place with a latch that held it firmly against its tight-fitting frame. In another moment that door rang with the force of a mighty blow, and the Iceman knew that Nicodareus had leaped into the basin. Muttering a prayer to Aurianth, Rudy found the nearby lever jutting from the wall, seized it with white-knuckled intensity, and pulled. He felt the mechanism work, heard a valve release somewhere above the cistern. Immediately liquid flooded the cistern, surrounding the Lord Minion.

Nicodareus' scream of fury rocked the door on its hinges, but was quickly buried in the rumble of convulsive violence that shook the underground chambers. The Iceman was already gone, racing down the narrow stairway, sprinting past the door the Lord Minion had crushed in his pursuit. The cavern walls rocked around him, and chunks of stone spattered his face and shoulders, but in a dozen desperate steps he reached the walkway beside the canal.

The tide roared outward at full speed now, a white-capped torrent rushing from the Circled Sea to the ocean as the walls and ceiling of the tunnel shuddered under the growing impact. Once more Rudy dove into the water, this time swimming with the current, racing toward the entrance that began to glow like a beacon of hope before him. Water surged as rocks tumbled into the furious flow. A large one struck him between the shoulders, almost driving the air from his lungs, but he kept swimming, mindlessly pulling himself toward that growing circle of daylight. Sometimes he coursed along the surface with powerful strokes, and then he dove, kicking along underwater, avoiding the chaos of shards and debris showering through the air.

Explosive force swelled outward, the force of destruction hurling rock and water—and the Man of Three Waters—away from the chaotic mingling. Then he was through, thrown from the tunnel into the ocean by the swelling force of eruption. He looked skyward, saw pieces of rock the size of houses—of castles!—tumbling lazily through the air, splashing into the brine, raising monstrous waves.

From the crest of one of these mighty breakers he looked back, saw the First Wall of Lanbrij lean toward the growing fissure behind it. One section after another collapsed, disappearing in violence, rocked by continuing explosions. The Low City vanished, ruins tumbling into rubble, spilling into the sea. A huge segment was simply gone, splintered to dust by the violent immersion of a Lord Minion in Aura.

With that destruction went the greatest portion of the Sleep-stealer's host, for the minion army besieging Lanbrij had been almost entirely concentrated within the Low City. A few ter-rions fled, shrieking, toward the mainland; Rudy imagined more shrieks, the shrill cries of dying minions as kroaks and brutox tumbled into the uncaring waves, or were torn to pieces by the powerful explosive force.

Like the explosion that ripped apart Darkenheight Pass, the mixture of Aura and a Lord Minion created an eruption of violence that altered the face of the world, ripping the heart out of the isthmus. Debris showered into the water and over the High City, a stinging rain of dust, gravel, and even boul-ders; along the growing crater, rocky ground continued to collapse. Landslides sent strong currents away from the fir-mament, and turbulent waves rolled Rudy out to sea.

The collapse continued to the base of the Second Wall, and when the waves surged upward the Iceman saw the mighty gate teetering on the brink of destruction. Rudy wondered how many of his men Duke Beymont had kept atop that bar-rier. Certainly the nobleman might have been skeptical of the end result—Rudy himself wasn't prepared for the full scope of the destruction.

Finally the convulsion ran its course, leaving a plunging cliff at the foot of the Second Wall—and numerous notches where the high barrier had cracked and crumbled. Where the ridge of rock had connected Corsari to the mainland there was now gray, storm-tossed water. Settling debris raised a heavy mist, but the haze itself proved transient, wafting away on the evening breeze. The tide still flooded out, now in a great surge that carried Rudy still farther away from the land.

From the crest of another wave Rudy saw the sails of the *Black Condor* as the galyon strove against the tide. The Ice-man dove and swam, feeling the strength thrum through his body. His lungs, nourished by the liquid of Faerine, held air for a very long time, and for more than an hour he stroked tirelessly toward the galyon, until finally the great dark hull loomed overhead. Crewmen lofted a coil of rope through the air and Rudy seized the end, grasping a solid hold and letting the sailors hoist him from the water and bring him to the safety of the deck.

Immediately Raine sprang into his arms, red-eyed, teary—and more beautiful than anything Rudy had ever seen. The wind was strong, filling the sails, urging the ship through the ocean swell—and away from the land.

"To Faerine, my Iceman," his lover said softly, slipping her hands into his. Relief glowed in the flush of her cheeks, the surreal brightness of her eyes. He kissed her with all the fervor of his hope, and all the longing of his love.

Anjell joined in their hug, and Dara and Awnro too, both of them shedding tears of joy. Darret grinned, looking at Lanbrij with an expression of amazement. Then, as Kestrel turned the wheel toward the open sea, Rudy, too, looked back, still unwilling to accept the unbelievable force of the convulsion. Yet the flat expanse of the Circled Sea showed between the two looming cliffs, gray waters shading to blue as the sun broke through the cloud of dust and steam, proving the irreversible truth:

Corsari was now an island.

FIFTEEN

Home to the Rainbow Sky

The happiest feet are striding in the doorway of
their own home.
—DIGGERSPEAK PROVERB

— 1 —

A small cloud floated like a puffball of cotton in the azure
sky. Gusts of wind eddied through the gap called Taywick
Pass, prevailing out of Faerine toward Dalethica in the autumnnal reversal of the typical springtime flow. Breezes became
winds, pressing the cloud northward, trying to push it back
over the rising ground of the pass—for here the mountains
channeled the air like a riverbed directs the flow of water.

Atop the Auracloud the sylvan helmsman rose from his
place near the summit, carrying a small cask to the stern quarter and sprayed shimmering liquid along the bank of whiteness. Rainbow colors formed a prismatic sheet of mist, and
the Auracloud veered smoothly to port, steady on a course to
Spendorial.

The vaporous shape drifted over the streams and valleys of
Faerine. Below, rainbows arced over splashing brooks, and

meadows glowed with emerald viridescence amid copses and groves of tall trees. Danri lounged near the prow of the magical sky-ship, a sense of rising contentment seeping through his body and bones. Nearby, Quenidon Daringer half-slumbered, similarly reclining as the welcoming vistas of their homeland sprawled below, soothing senses and revitalizing spirits.

"This is a sight easier than walkin' home," Danri allowed, sighing as the wind ruffled a crystalline pond, sparkling the surface like an array of diamonds.

"Easier than trying to change the minds of stubborn humans, too." The sylvan captain sighed, shaking his head. "I have a feeling that it will be good to be back among our own kind."

"Aye-uh. You know, once I wouldn't have wanted to spend time with anybody but a digger," Danri remarked. "I have to admit, though, your company has been pleasant over these last months."

"You're only saying that because the alternatives have been humans," Quenidon said with a laugh, before growing serious. "But you're right—it's a shame it took a battle for us to realize how much we, how much *all* Faerines, have in common."

"Even gigants," Danri continued, his tone full of amazement. "I woulda thought my life'd be complete if those galoots stayed out of it altogether—but I was sure glad to see them come down from the mountain and take a stand in our line. Gulatch, Hoagaran—they all looked pretty good to me!"

"Each of us has a role to play in this struggle, my friend. Perhaps the most important piece of knowledge we can take to Spendorial is this conviction: that Faerines must work, must fight together, if we are going to prevail."

"I wonder if the Darkenheight garrison has had any trouble yet?" mused the digger.

"We'll find out soon enough. Even if the minions have attacked, I'll warrant they haven't pushed through. I've commanded both garrisons at different times in the last century, and I can tell you that Darkenheight's a much stronger position than Taywick."

"It'll *have* to be," Danri replied grimly. "Remember, the

Battle of Taywick was fought against *humans*—this time it'll be something worse."

For a moment his mind shifted to darker concerns—to mankind's intransigence, which had set him and Quenidon returning to Taywick Pass with a feeling of failure, and the brutal assassination of Kelwyn Dyerston that had put a dour finale to the mission. The crossing of Dalethica had been trying, since the two Faerines had created a stir wherever they stopped. They had taken to camping outside the towns and villages of men just to avoid the attentions of humankind.

The climb to Taywick had restored some sense of tranquility to the weary travelers. Atop that gap, at the border of their homeland, they found the garrison of Faerine warriors restored. Several sylvan Auramasters were there, and one consented to raise a cloud and sail them to Spendorial. Though Danri was momentarily tempted to start out for Shalemont on foot, he quickly thought better of the notion. Partially, he had come to enjoy Quenidon Daringer's company, but more importantly, it seemed that he could be of real use by going to that great city and spreading his influence among diggers to the cause of Faerine's preparations.

"Look—there's the Auraloch," Quenidon said, pointing to a patch of vivid aquamarine on the horizon. "Spendorial sits on a neck of land between the two rivers that flow into the lake."

"Funny thing—I've seen human cities from Landrun to Carillonn, and never laid eyes on the center of my own realm," said Danri.

"It's been a long time for me," the sylve noted with a touch of wistfulness. "I've been on garrison duty at Taywick for a decade; before that, I spent a score of years at Darkenheight. It will be strange to be among my people in a city instead of a garrison camp."

Danri looked sidelong at his friend, surprised at the longing in Quenidon's tone. "I never thought you missed it that much," he admitted.

"Truth is—I don't. I don't know what's got me so maudlin about it."

"We've had enough sleeping under the stars for a while, I think," Danri remarked.

"You're right there," Quen agreed pensively. "I've always

liked the camaraderie of the army camp, the nights around the watchfires—the responsibility of guarding a border. Up until the humans came to Taywick, it was all sort of a grand game—a contest that I knew was important, but still not real.''

''It's real enough now,'' noted the digger. ''So let's take the chance to enjoy your city a bit, first.'' He noticed with surprise that Quen was barely listening; the sylve's jaw was clenched tightly as he stared at the sylvan capital.

As Danri settled back in his comfortable seat, he allowed his own eyes to turn that way as well. Spendorial rose from its narrow peninsula like a growing thing, elegant curves of crystalline architecture mimicking the brilliance of a blooming garden. The sylves built, Danri knew, with a mixture of crushed stone and Aura. The resulting glassy crystal was malleable when fresh and very strong after it hardened, allowing the sylves to create lofty arches, and high, thin walls. In some places the crystal was stained with shades of rose or yellow or blue; though the material remained translucent, it reflected the sunlight in a sparkling prism of colors.

''That building in the middle—it looks like an enormous rose,'' declared the digger in awe, staring at a structure of sweeping, elegant wings, admiring lofty towers that widened near the top, defying gravity with their fluted curves. ''Those balconies look for all the Watershed like the petals of a gigantic blossom.''

''That's the Palace of Time,'' Quenidon declared. ''Pride of the sylves, and the greatest center of knowledge in all the Watershed.''

The sylve's tone was so quiet that Danri wondered if the edifice held some personal, perhaps unpleasant, memory for his companion. For a moment the digger pondered making an inquiry, but decided to keep his peace. Quenidon pointed toward the open woodland that circled the shore of Auraloch. ''Those are camps there, army camps. Look at the way the tents are lined up.''

''Must be diggers,'' Danri said. ''And there, under the oak grove—it looks like the gigants have come down from the mountains!''

''The peoples of Faerine *have* acknowledged the danger!''

''If only the humans could be so wise,'' Danri mused,

amazed at the numbers of diggers and gigants he saw moving through the woods. Bands of other creatures frolicked nearby, and from the lines of rambunctious dancers he knew that these were sartors. Like their cousins, the goat-footed Faerines had played a major role in the defense of Taywick Pass. Indeed, despite their sometimes playful antics, the sartors had been merciless to their human foes when the enemy had been put to flight. Only the intervention of Danri, Quenidon, and some of the other leaders had prevented the victory from growing into a massacre when the sartors had the defeated humans at their mercy.

"We're sinking!" Danri cried, suddenly alarmed as he perceived the lake waters rising toward them.

Quenidon chuckled. "You didn't want to spend the rest of your life up here, did you?" He indicated the sylvan helmsman, who had removed a lid from an iron pot to reveal a bed of hot coals. With silver tongs the pilot dropped the coals, one after another, through the billowing shape of the Auracloud. As each ember sizzled downward, more of the cloud evaporated, and the remainder continued to settle gently lakeward.

"Couldn't he set us on the land?" groused Danri.

"The lake is easier," Quenidon explained. "The steering of an Auracloud is not a precise science, and the expanse of water allows for a margin of error. Look!" The sylve pointed to several sleek-hulled boats, each propelled by a single oarsman toward the center of the lake. "They're competing for our business. Whoever guesses where the cloud will come down has the privilege of carrying the passengers to shore."

"I still say a nice meadow would do just fine," grumbled the digger.

By the time they could see the individual ripples on the surface of the lake, one of the boats had established a clear lead. The sylvan rower stood gracefully in his narrow hull, raising a pole toward the bottom of the cloud. Danri looked through the clear water, amazed to see schools of large fish swimming far below the surface, while Quenidon took the shaft and pulled the cloudship down to the bobbing watercraft.

"Welcome, esteemed lords!" declared the sylvan boatman, bowing deeply. If he was surprised to see a digger arriving via Auracloud, he made no remark. The helmsman and his two passengers stepped from the cloud to the boat as the last, wispy vapors of their airy craft dissipated across the lake.

With rapid strokes of his oars the sylve propelled his boat across the waters of Auraloch. The skiff floated like a waterbug, seeming to skim the surface without actually getting wet. That was an illusion, of course—when they pulled beside the wooden dock Danri saw the ripples wash away from the narrow hull. The boatman bid them a cheery farewell as the travelers climbed to the dock.

Danri thought that he had never seen such a clean city. Of course, diggers are particular, and Shalemont was not a place of litter or garbage; the sylves, however, apparently spent time actually washing the crystal faces of their buildings! At least, the brilliant sheen of the rounded surfaces suggested a fresh polish of wax. Streets meandered gracefully, curving past the rounded buildings in such a way that a pedestrian usually couldn't see more than two dozen paces in any direction. Though Danri, for practical reasons, preferred the more measured gridwork of a digger—or even a human—city, he found the sweeping curves very attractive to the eye. Fountains splashed at many intersections, and tall bushes of fire-iris and blaze-orange tulipans rose around the fringes of even the smallest houses.

Most of the structures were large, sprawling around gardens, curling upward amidst verdant pines and maples. The glassy crystal was cloudy enough to screen the interiors of the buildings, though Danri sensed that they must be bright and airy places. Balconies abounded, and many smaller apertures allowed the scented breezes and pastoral sounds of the city to waft in and out.

Frequently the rounded shapes of buildings were surrounded by crystal walls no more than waist-high to the digger; these barriers enclosed blooming gardens, paths of crushed white gravel, and placid reflecting pools. Young sylves scampered and chased through the protected yards, often a dozen or more of them at a time.

"Are they all brothers and sisters?" asked Danri, surprised at the gatherings of children. At the same time he thought that these numbers perhaps explained the large residential structures.

Quenidon laughed. "No—cousins, perhaps. Most sylvan

pairs have one or two children, but it's common for many generations to live together in one house. There might be a matriarch or patriarch, and then the families of their two children, and the families of four grandchildren, and so forth— so that when you see twenty little ones playing, chances are they're the offspring of ten sets of parents. They might all live in the same house, of course.''

"I see," said Danri, thinking that his own peace of mind wouldn't last one day in such chaotic surroundings. "How crowded was it for you?"

"I was somewhat alone," the sylve said. "I had but a single brother, half a century younger than myself. My mother had hopes for me . . . things that were not to be." Quenidon cleared his throat awkwardly. "At least, my brother has proven less of a disappointment," he added with uncharacteristic bitterness.

"Do your parents live here still?" asked the digger, regretting his companion's change of mood.

"They're dead, have been for a long time," Quen said, his anger fading to poignant regret. He brightened perceptibly, however, as they emerged from the winding street into an open mall of flowering trees. "Ah—we approach the Palace of Time."

Long reflecting pools lined each side of the walkway, and their route curved toward the looming, petal-shaped wings of the mighty crystal palace. Lush evergreens, three or five heavy-limbed giants to a clump, broke the open grounds with an illusion of thick, enveloping forest.

"Danri! Danri!"

The voice trilled from one of the pine groves, causing the digger to whirl in astonishment.

"Kianna? Is that you?" he demanded, a gruff tone masking the real joy he felt. The twissel flitted into view, buzzing quickly forward on gossamer wings, filmy dress trailing behind. Only Danri's sturdy legs kept him upright as he met her driving embrace with a tender hug of his own. "Ah, little one—I'm glad to see you made it home without me."

"Home?" Kianna sniffed, buzzing in front of the digger's face. "I live up in the valleys, near the Eternal Spring. But everyone seems to be coming to Spendorial these days, so I did too—oh, and I did hope to hear about you. Are you sick of humans yet?''

"Heartily," Danri grumped, as Kianna greeted Quenidon, whom she had previously met only briefly. The digger amended, "Other than a few, like Rudy and Takian and their friends, I think the whole lot of 'em are more bother than they're worth.''

"And Anjell," Kianna reminded him. "How is she? I sort of wondered if she would get to come to Faerine with you.''

"Not while her mother was watching." Danri chuckled. A sudden thought occurred to him. "How did you know you would find me here?''

"Well, I didn't really. But you're *famous* now, you know—after digging into Dalethica and coming to Taywick Pass. Then going *back* to the humans! So we thought you'd be coming to the Palace of Time sooner or later, and we took turns in the garden here, waiting to see if you came along.''

"We? Who's 'we'?''

"Oh, I almost forgot—I met someone here who knows you! A friend from Shalemont. Here she comes now!" Kianna pointed down the flower-lined walkway, away from the palace.

Danri spun, scarcely daring to hope—and then choking out a cry of delight and joy he didn't even try to mask. "Kerri!''

Halting in shock, the diggermaid pressed a hand to her face and blinked. Kerri was even more beautiful than Danri remembered, with lush, curling black hair framing her round face, dazzling the digger with a smile of sunlike brilliance. They ran to each other, and when Kerri held back a moment, remembering Danri's ample supply of digger aloofness, he swept her unabashedly into his arms, squeezing the breath from her lungs. She squealed and hugged him back, and he drew a ragged breath as he relished her sturdy body in his arms, the pressure of her swelling breasts against his chest; the curling hairs on her neck tickled his nose, and he knew only joy.

When Danri finally released the diggermaid, he kept his broad hands around her tiny waist, closing his eyes and absorbing the fragrance of her beautiful hair. Then he looked at her again, swimming in the moistness of her deep, indigo eyes.

"It's been a long time . . . since the Madness took me away," he said gruffly. "By Aurianth, it's good to see you again!"

"You look good, digger," Kerri said, her voice masked by a thickness of its own. "Maybe the Madness agreed with you."

"I had some long years of it—but it's over now," he replied simply. He held her hands, not caring who might see the display of his affection.

"You know," Quenidon said hesitantly. "I should report to the Royal Scion—no doubt he'll want to hear about everything that's happened since the Battle of Taywick. But there's no reason you have to bore yourself with all that—why don't you find some place in the city to sit down and chat? I'll be along as soon as I can make my reports."

"Sure!" Kianna cried, clapping her hands and pleading with Danri. "Kerri's found a place that she said you'd like for sure!"

"The beer is cold, anyway," the diggermaid said with a laugh.

"It's called the Stone Goblet," the twissel explained to Quenidon. "And it's not far away."

"I know the place—your friend has good taste," the sylve replied, clapping Danri on the shoulder. "I'll find you there."

"Agreed," responded the digger. His sylvan companion was already forgotten as, Kerri on one arm and Kianna on the other, Danri started toward the doors of his first Faerine tavern in more years than he wanted to count.

— 2 —

Bidswad snorted into his dirty handkerchief, holding the cloth against his muzzle as minimal protection against the cold. The summits of Darkenheight rose to either side—and if the bleak, looming peaks weren't forbidding enough, the winds scouring through the pass bore the acrid scent of Duloth-Trol. The realm of the Sleepstealer began just a stone's throw away from here, and in the lonely sentry's mind all his troubles could be traced to this accursed notch in what should have been the perfect barrier of the Watershed.

After all, if there were no pass, there would be no need of a Darkenheight garrison. Bidswad would be celebrating autumn with the other sartors, galloping through auburn-tinted woodlands, chasing the does with unfettered delight. Instead, there *was* a Darkenheight Pass, and the garrison *was* needed, and through terrible luck in the sartor lottery Bidswad *was* posted to this Aura-forsaken corner of Faerine for two interminable years. If he lived that long, Bidswad thought glumly. Just his luck—for the first time in ten centuries the Sleepstealer's army might be preparing to attack Faerine, and it had to happen when Bidswad Sartor was on garrison duty!

For a moment the Faerine clutched his spear to his furry chest, shuddering at the prospect of mortal strife. He would stand with his fellows if—or, as he had come to believe, *when*—the minion army rushed the pass. Bidswad knew that he was prepared to fight, even to die in order to hold the dark tide of monsters back from the borders of his enchanted realm. Friends—sartors he had known all his life, and diggers and sylves who had been gambling partners on the long summer afternoons of garrison duty—would be killed in that struggle, but they all accepted the risk, knew that the cost could only be worthwhile. Still, that didn't make his prospective heroics any more palatable.

Bidswad looked down the winding cut of Darkenheight Pass, past the crude huts and tents of the garrison camp. He imagined the comforts and delights of lower Faerine, the food and drink and pleasures awaiting beyond—does, pine-scented groves, glories of fruit and bread and wine!

And, most of all, the fires. The high Bruxrange was a treeless expanse of mountains, and for the warriors garrisoned here there were none of the warming blazes that gave so much life to a camp at a lower elevation—though if Bidswad didn't have guard duty, he could still have been curled up in his fur bedroll, awaiting the minimal warmth of dawn.

Again the sartor looked longingly down the winding canyon, recalling the last doe he had taken, the night before his posting to the heights. She had been a frisky lass who kicked up her hooves most agreeably, and their coupling had driven Bidswad into a memorable frenzy. . . .

Something brought his attention to the cold, bleak surroundings. He looked toward Duloth-Trol, aware that something had moved there. But what?

Light glimmered, like sparks cascading from a grinder's wheel, and Bidswad felt a sudden tension. He remembered ancient rumors: how some of the hulking minions supposedly trailed sparks when they attacked. Abruptly the sparks dripped again, and Bidswad shivered and stared. Should he sound the alarm? The flickers were hundreds of paces away, approaching only slowly.

Bidswad saw movement nearby, and whirled with a gasp, startled, and then relieved to see a digger clumping toward him. Apparently one of the other sentries had come over to take a look.

"Did you see that?" asked Bidswad, starting to turn back to the valley. Something in the digger's eyes stopped him. But they weren't digger eyes. Instead, they swirled with a seductive glow, beautiful, soothing, wondrous. . . .

Bidswad stared, caught by the stalker's hypnotic gaze, for several minutes. His trance ceased only when the brutox arrived and ripped his head off.

— 3 —

"Y'know, I like a place like this—a place with some class. Did you ever think what it would be like to be an innkeeper?"

"Sorry—what was that?" Danri set down his recently emptied goblet and grinned at Kerri, wiping the foam from his mustache as he apologized. "Truth is, I was having such a nice time lookin' at you that I forgot to listen to what you were saying!"

"You digger!" she chided, then leaned over and kissed him. The touch of her lips was pleasing, and it seemed very odd to Danri that once he would have cringed from such a public exhibition of emotions.

"Must be all that time with the humans," he mused, keeping a long arm around Kerri as she settled back in her own chair.

"I was saying that I like it here," Kerri repeated. "A bar doesn't have to be dark and underground in order to be cozy."

Danri, concentrating now, was forced to agree. The Stone Goblet was remarkably airy for a digger pub, with a veranda above the glimmering lake, and windows and doors that seemed to remain constantly open. Still, unlike most of Spendorial's buildings, it had walls of solid stone, and a roof of slate supported by massive, smoke-stained beams.

And true to Kerri's promise, the beer was amply chilled. An unusually muscular sylvan woman waited on their table, but Danri had noticed digger barmaids also clumping about the great room, and a twissel floated behind the long, darkwood bar, diligently scrubbing away any trace of a stain. Several sartors, hooves clopping on the wooden floor, glowered over trays of dirty dishes.

"What was that about being an innkeeper?" Danri asked, swallowing another long draught of sweet ale.

"Just . . . I don't know . . . I thought it might be kind of nice to start a place of my own, you know, cooking and brewing and the lot. 'Course, I'd need some help—but it's a thought that's been on my mind since I left Shalemont."

Danri chuckled, startled by the pleasant picture conjured in his mind. Himself behind the bar, ready hand at the tap, while Kerri cooked, or waited on tables, or met the customers at the door. . . .

"Would only diggers be allowed?" Kianna asked, suddenly frowning.

Kerri laughed and shook her head. Danri thumped a fist on the table. "Any inn that *I* run is going to welcome everyone—twissels, sylves, even gigants and humans!"

"Oh—you're going to have an inn too?" cried the twissel. "That's wonderful!"

"No!" Danri blushed furiously, startled by his own words. "That is, it's Kerri's idea . . . I didn't mean . . ." Abruptly, his thoughts focused and he looked at the diggermaid as if he'd never seen her before. "I *did* mean it! Kerri, will you have me? Can we make that inn together, somewhere?"

"You *have* changed," she said softly, indigo eyes alight with emotion. "And, yes, I will." She snuggled closer to Danri as the digger looked around, his expression of wonder gradually yielding to pure happiness.

"*Now* I understand," Kianna said, with a wink at Kerri.

"How did you two meet, anyway?" asked Danri.

"In Shalemont we heard about the battle at Taywick Pass," Kerri explained. "About Blaze Smelter—how he died a hero."

"Aye," Danri said thickly. "I was with him, there at the end. He spoke of you."

Kerri sniffled, putting her face to Danri's chest for a moment. Her eyes were dry when she looked up. "Some of the diggers that came home after the battle, they told me about Blaze—and said that you were there, too. That you came out of Dalethica with a twissel, and arrived just in time to help win the battle—that you were quite a hero!"

"That'll do for an explanation," he said approvingly.

"They told me that the twissel who'd traveled with you had gone to Spendorial with the sylves, to tell them about humans. So I came here to see if I could find her—"

"And she did, right here outside the Palace of Time!" Kianna concluded. "I told her all about you, and Rudy, and Anjell too, and the duchess and Prince Takian—"

"He's a king, now," Danri interrupted, then shook his head in amazement. "Well, now you've both found me—and you're stuck with me! What should we call our inn?"

"I don't know," Kerri said.

"How about the Inn of Two Waters?" Danri suggested. "Just to show that humans can come in there, too."

"I'd like that!" Kianna voted. "Will Rudy be there? And Anjell?"

Danri chuckled at the twissel's enthusiasm, realizing that he had missed Kianna more than he thought. Before he could reply, however, Kerri caught his attention.

"There's your sylvan friend," the diggermaid announced, pointing toward the door of the Stone Goblet.

"Quenidon—over here! We've got to do some celebrating!" bellowed the digger, nearly toppling his chair as he stood. Only when the sylvan warrior drew close did Danri perceive the grim look in his companion's eye. Quenidon's face was drawn and his hands clenched into fists as he sat down at the table.

"What is it?" Danri asked slowly.

"The Sleepstealer has struck more quickly than we anticipated, sending a mighty army against Darkenheight. His first attack carried the crest of the pass. Every warrior in Faerine

is on the march, trying to stem the tide before it's too late.
I've been given command of the force . . . but I'm going to
need help."

"No!" Kerri declared, her voice a haunted whisper. "No—
they said that the Darkenheight garrison was holding strong,
that there was no danger!"

"The danger is real," replied the sylve grimly. "The garrison has been savaged, and they won't be able to hold for
long. The relief force leaves in a few days."

"You've already done your part!" Kerri said fiercely, laying a hand on Danri's arm. "At Taywick Pass! They don't
need you at Darkenheight too!"

"Yes, love, I think they do," he said, tenderly removing
her hand. "My hammering arm's as strong as anyone's—and
I've fought these vermin before."

"And it's more than your hammer we're needing," Quenidon added. "In all the realm, there are very few of us who
have actually fought, not to mention *led*, in battle."

"That's me," Danri said. He stood, feeling remarkably so-
ber, ready for the job he had to do. The hurt in the diggermaid's eyes pained him greatly, but he could only make a
promise.

"You find us the place, Kerri. And we'll have that inn
together. You'll see."

That pledge seemed to linger in the air between them as
he turned from the table and followed Quenidon Daringer into
the street—and toward the fields of war.

— 4 —

Faerine warriors gathered in a stretch of forested hill country
known as the Suderwild, encamped on heights within sight of
the Auraloch and Spendorial. The Stonebridge, a solid span
of wooden timbers and granite pilings, crossed the deep Aurun River, giving the camp access to the city, but Danri was
so busy once he reached the army that he was afraid he'd
never get a chance to see Kerri before they marched.

Quenidon Daringer labeled the force the Faerine Field
Army, and the troops embraced the name as enthusiastically
as they did their sylvan leader. The victor of Taywick was

the first Faerine commander in a thousand years to fight, and win, a major battle, so Quen was universally regarded as a great hero.

Among the troops forming the army were several hundred golden-helmed sylves of the Royal House—elite warriors, with glowing metal armor and haughty disdain for the lesser troops. The royal company had been provided by the scion, Quen explained to Danri. "I'm to use them as my body-guard!" the sylve spat in disgust. "As if warriors don't have more important work than guarding other warriors!"

"That's the orders of the Royal Scion?" the digger asked, remembering Quen's earlier antipathy toward the sylvan Au-ramaster.

"Yes." The army commander looked at Danri shrewdly, then sighed. "Mussrik Daringer is also my younger brother." At the digger's look of stunned astonishment the sylve went on. "If I had been able to weave an Auracloud—even a *small* one—I'd be the Royal Scion of Spendorial."

"But . . . you're a *prince*?" sputtered the digger.

"It's not the same thing, no—but my father was scion be-fore me, and I am his eldest son."

"Well, shouldn't you command the Royal House sylves or something, then? Why did you spend all that time on the divides?" The digger was completely mystified by his friend's revelation.

"I could have been a noble commander, spending my time at banquets and balls—except I had a bit of a temper back then, a couple of centuries ago it was. After failing my Au-ratest I stormed out of the palace and enlisted in the garrison companies. You might say I've worked my way up the hard way. And speaking of that, some of these recruits need to get started doing the same thing."

Respecting the sylve's privacy, Danri agreed, leaving a vol-ume of questions unasked. There was, in fact, a lot of work to be done: Thousands of untrained warriors were already camped around the banners, hundreds more arriving each hour. From their arrival in the camp, Danri, Quen, and the gigant battle chief, Gulatch, had spent most of their time or-ganizing the newcomers into companies, training them in the rudiments of battle formations and the responses to simple bugle calls. The digger had quickly grown frustrated with these efforts, but continued to bellow himself hoarse as numbers of miners-turned-warriors tried to learn to march in step.

The sartors provided a real challenge, as they seemed incapable of marching without breaking into some kind of dance. Braying like goats, kicking their heels in the air, the creatures scampered chaotically through the camp. When the digger confronted their chief, a big ram named Wattli, the sartor declared that he had come to fight, not to march! He would hear no argument on the point, so the digger left in disgust, stomping over to his own company, the diggers from Shalemont. Here he watched a reasonable demonstration of warriors forming a battle line—at least they all faced the same direction at once!

"Lord Danri?"

"Eh?" He turned from the drill, surprised to see a young digger, chest only half covered with the silken strands of an early beard. "I'm Danri of Shalemont—don't call me 'lord,' though," the older warrior snapped.

"Oh, of course, my lor—that is, sir. I'm Pembroak of Placer—Lord Daringer said I should see if you need a squire. Perhaps I could be of use in that capacity?"

"Squire? By Aurianth, I need *warriors*!" growled Danri, regretting his tone when he saw the hurt look on the youngster's face. "Ah, why not? I'll give you a try, see if it works out. After all, I haven't had time to find myself a shield, sharpen my pick—"

"Consider it done, sir!" cried Pembroak, saluting smartly, before venturing a tentative question. "Er, perhaps you remember my uncle? Hakwan Chiseler, of Shale—"

"Of course I remember Hakwan!" Danri declared. "Why didn't you say you were his kin? Never mind—you're my squire now!"

Later, Danri found his pick sharpened to a needle-like point, his boots oiled, and a horn of cold ale waiting with his supper. Smacking his lips over the precious beverage, he graciously informed the delighted Pembroak that his appointment as squire would last for the duration of the campaign.

"As a matter of fact, I have another task for you," Danri announced, sipping the ale with uncharacteristic patience.

"Anything, sir!"

"I want you to go into the city, carry a message for me. If

you can find the diggermaid Kerri of Shalemont, ask her to meet me at the Aurun bridge tomorrow. At sunset!''

Pembroak vanished immediately, returning around midnight with word that the rendezvous had been arranged. Danri broke away from the next day's drilling in mid-afternoon, clomping down to the broad, wooden-girdered bridge—the only span that crossed the Aurun, since that broad river was too wide for the rainbow bridges that were more common in Faerine. Leaning on the railing, staring idly over the clear waters, Danri waited for his beloved. His eyes drifted frequently toward the road from Spendorial, and he was startled to see a familiar trio approaching—for Kerri was accompanied by Kianna Kyswyllis and Pembroak.

"Kerri!" he cried, sweeping her into his arms. Looking over her shoulder, he saw that Pembroak held a large flat object, wrapped in an oilskin.

"Here—this is for you," Kerri said, sniffling as she stood back to let the squire hand over the package. The digger peeled away the skin to reveal a shield of glimmering steel, with the blue imprint of his pick-tipped hammer emblazoned in the center.

"It's beautiful," he said, moved.

"It's from all the diggers of Shalemont," Kerri explained. "Made from the best steel of the high smelters. Use it well, so that you come back to me!" she added, glaring sternly.

"Aye-uh," he declared. He shifted his gaze to Pembroak. "Do you have some things to do in camp?"

"Right away, sir!" replied the squire, who really did catch on quickly, Danri realized. "C'mon with me?" asked Pembroak, turning to Kianna.

"I think she's going back to the city," Danri interrupted.

"Didn't you know? Quen wants twissels to come along as scouts and stuff." Kianna chirped. "My cousin Garic Hoorkin collected a few dozen—and I'm one!"

"I didn't know *you* were coming!" Danri retorted. "Or I would have sent you back already. This is going to be too dangerous for—"

"Now just a minute, Danri of Shalemont!" The twissel hovered angrily, wagging a finger in the digger's face. "Didn't I fight kroaks before? Do you think you're going to stop me now, when all Faerine is in trouble?"

"No—I just wish . . . I'm glad you're here," Danri finished up, allowing the smug fairy to buzz along with Pembroak toward the camp in the Suderwild.

He stood with Kerri for a time, watching the sun settle toward Auraloch. More recruits marched past, going from the city to the camp. "They seem more somber now than they did even a few days ago," Kerri observed.

"Aye-uh—we're marching tomorrow, and I think they're starting to realize it's not a game anymore."

"*You* understand that, don't you?" the diggermaid said seriously. "That this is deadly serious—and that you *have* to come back to me."

"I understand," he said gravely, speaking the fundamental truth of his life as he kissed her under the stars that started to glimmer into view. "And I'll remember—you just do your part, and find us that inn. Then you can meet me at this same bridge when we come marching back from the war!"

"I *will*," she promised. "I'll find us our inn—and I'll wait for you here!"

Reluctantly, after many more long kisses, they parted. The next day the army would begin its long march, embarking directly on the road toward Darkenheight Pass. The memories of Kerri's smile, of the sweet smell of her hair and the touch of her lips against his skin all burned in Danri's mind as he lay, sleepless, in his tent. Unlike his departure from Shalemont, when he had been in the grip of the Digging Madness, he found that this leave-taking brought a yearning ache to his heart that showed no indication of going away. Before dawn Pembroak gathered up Danri's bedroll and kit, while the elder warrior saw to the marching order of the digger companies.

"Find us that inn, sweetheart," Danri repeated to himself as the Faerine Field Army tromped out of the lowland camp. He could only hope that, across forest and lake, Kerri would know his thoughts. With that wish lingering like a prayer, the digger led his warriors onto the Darkenheight Road.

SIXTEEN

Neambrey

---

*Drackans are the greatest and most aloof
creatures of the Watershed. Like trees over
grass, so are these powerful serpents above the
rest of the mortal world.*
—Songs of Aurianth

— 1 —

A consuming dryness burned Neambrey's throat, yanking him
from dormancy with irresistibly violent urgency. The young
drackan bounced to his feet, then trotted to the Auraspring in
the back of his cave. Slurping eagerly, he drained the bowl-
shaped depression, then raised his wedge-shaped head to look
about for more of the revitalizing draught. He reached the
mouth of the cave in a quick pounce, unleashing his body
like a spring and then gathering his serpentine length into a
hunched bow. His tail lashed back and forth as he peered into
the valley, looking toward the soaring peaks and ridges beyond.

Waterfalls of Aura spilled from those heights, gathering
into streams, silver ribbons coursing through the verdant
brush of the valley floor. Neambrey raced toward the nearest
of the brooks, quickly burying his muzzle in the flow and

drawing deep, sucking gulps—which he immediately coughed out in spluttering gasps, since he'd forgotten about the need to draw breath.

With more patience, Neambrey squatted beside the stream and drank deliberately. His distended belly sagged to the ground, and still the drackan slurped Aura. He belched, a convulsive eruption that stretched his long neck straight out, the burp rumbling wetly from gaping jaws.

More—he needed *more* Aura. The craving was a burning thirst, and Neambrey lowered his muzzle to drink again. Only when his gut was once more bloated, when he was momentarily sated by the volume of liquid within him, did he stop to think, to ponder this unique urge that had brought him so frantically from his cave. Neambrey understood then: He had come to his Time of Thirsting.

The knowledge sent a tremor of excitement through the serpentine body. His tail whipped straight back, and he raised his head, peering about the wide valley, wondering where his quest would take him. It didn't much matter—to be sure, there was Aura everywhere, and Neambrey felt like consuming all of it.

His wings remained stiff and brittle, cramped beneath the hard shell of his youngster's carapace. Ultimately, when he had consumed enough Aura—and spent another few years growing—those membranes would burst free, and he would fly! For now, he could make himself walk, but where? He looked to the summits of the Bruxrange and thought of his sire. Of course, Jasaren was no doubt hibernating, and one generally avoided waking a brown drackan from the depths of dormancy. Though normally a male would swell with pride at the knowledge of his scion's maturation, Neambrey's situation had never been normal. The result of Jasaren's dalliance with a green drackan, the gray-scaled youngster had since been an embarrassing reminder to the mighty brown drackan of poor judgment in a weak moment. With a sigh, Neambrey bent his neck and realized that, for him, there would be no paternal boasting.

His thoughts turned, inevitably, to his mother. Meamare's lair was not so far as the high mountains, and Neambrey would be welcome there—if his maternal parent could be roused from her own hibernation. Still, the green drackans were much less touchy than their brown-scaled cousins. Neambrey could at least venture into Meamare's cave without fear of getting bitten.

But he had another matter to attend to first, Neambrey realized, discovering with some surprise that he was again hugely, desperately thirsty.

— 2 —

The Bruxrange was unlike any part of Faerine Danri had ever seen. Though he had spent his life among the snowy, rugged peaks of the White Range, and the Crown of the World had lofted its dazzling pinnacles in clear view of Shalemont, the digger had never seen mountains so fierce, so relentlessly forbidding.

The border of Duloth-Trol was still many miles away when the diggers, sylves, and gigants of the Faerine Field Army passed from the foothills into the canyonlike valley of the pass road. Soaring ridges of dark rock to the right and left formed barriers as confining as any corridor's walls, and the Faerines passed almost instantaneously from a forest broken by sunlit, bloom-speckled meadows to a damp mountain range of constant shadow. Even for the few hours when the sun passed its zenith, winking from behind the eastern crest and before ducking past the ridge to the west, the rays of warmth failed to penetrate the chill depths of the canyon.

For a fortnight the field army plodded up the valley road, often accompanied by rumbles of distant thunder that reverberated from the heights and echoed in the valleys. The southern sky, over the divide of the Watershed, was a mass of ominous dark clouds, jagged pillars of black that licked tongues of lightning along the crests and high peaks. Violent and malevolent, the storm glowered among the mountain summits, as if awaiting the field army.

Barren of trees, the smooth rock of the Bruxrange was often painted with colorful lichen, or layered with a thick pillow of green moss. Tufts of wildflowers dwelled in small hollows in the bedrock, where the windlash of time had left patches of soil. Despite the lack of forest and glade, the mountain range seemed very much an *alive* place, and Danri soon realized

this was because of all the water. From any given place in
the valley he could look up and see a dozen silvery cascades.
Aura flowed from springs high in the rocky faces, so abundant
at night that it cast its gentle, enchanted illumination throughout the range.

And, led by the resolute example of the diggers, the Faerine
warriors took advantage of this light to march well past sunset, resting for a few hours through the middle of the night.
Chill winds scoured the valleys, and there was no wood for
fires, so these huddled bivouacs were comfortless affairs.
Consequently there was little complaining when it was time
to resume the march. The field army made steady progress,
always climbing, a file snaking toward lofty Darkenheight.

Danri and Quenidon frequently stood to the side of the
stone-bedded road, watching the hard-eyed warriors of Faerine, reflecting upon the differences they saw in their fellow
fighters. The diggers trudged in a wide, blunt column. They
had come from Shalemont, from Placer and Silverhill, from
Forgevalle and the other, smaller villages of the stocky miners. Danri's squire, Pembroak, was typical of these willing
recruits—sturdy and strong, he marched for hour after hour
without faltering or complaint. He polished Danri's shield as
if the brightness of that metal disk would determine the success or failure of the campaign. Several times he even offered
to bear the older digger's hammer—though Danri snorted indignantly at the notion.

The short-legged, bearded warriors marched to battle with
faces as cold as flint, expressions turned inward. If the fear
of death was a real concern to any digger, it was not revealed
in posture, visage, or tone of voice. Without marching songs,
or shouts or boasts, they plodded resolutely toward the task
that lay before them, bearing hammers, picks, broad-bladed
swords, spades, and axes. Many diggers carried their own
unique weapons—hooked poles, long-shafted forks and hal-
berds, and a variety of spears; in addition, the diggers of
Placer were famed for the light, steel-coiled crossbow that
each fighter wore at his side.

Behind the diggers, striding in a long, graceful file, came
the sylves. Each of the slender Faerines wore quivers bristling
with arrows, and most were armed with swords longer and
more slender than the digger blades. Sylves typically dis-

played little emotion, yet to Danri the cultivated aloofness of his Faerine allies wavered with insecurity reflected in the faces of many younger recruits. Eyes wide, the clean-limbed warriors started, deerlike, at any shout of alarm.

Marching sullenly well to the rear, apart from the rest of the army, came the gigants. Both Danri and Quenidon had fought as allies of the battle chief, Gulatch, at Taywick Pass. Still, the big Faerine remained distant and surly; his attitude made it clear that he was here only to fight minions. The prejudices in the gigant's heart apparently erected stronger barriers than any single encounter could overcome—Aurianth knew that the antipathy between digger and gigant was a deeply held tradition. Still, friendly or not, the strapping allies were welcome. Clad in woolly furs, glaring fiercely from tangled beards and manes of unruly hair, a typical gigant towered nearly twice as tall as a lanky sylve. Armed with an assortment of stone-tipped spears, spiked clubs, battered axes and swords of bronze, the gargantuan Faerines were formidable foes in any battle.

Scattered among the bigger Faerines were a number of flitting, winged forms—twissels, such as Kianna and her cousin Garic Hoorkin. These fairies bore short, keen daggers. The winged volunteers primarily served as messengers and scouts, and because twissels could become invisible for short periods of time, they were obviously valuable for reconnaissance.

Only the sartors had been a disappointment. The capricious, goat-footed Faerines had fallen behind on the first days, finally wandering off altogether.

"Are there any signs of sartors down the valley?" Quenidon asked Kianna as the twissel flew up the road to join the leaders.

"Not for miles," said Kianna. "You know how silly they can be—I saw lots of 'em dancing in the lower forest, but I don't think they made it as far as the mountains."

"Figures!" the digger growled, not terribly disappointed.

"We'll make do with those warriors we have," Quenidon assured him gently.

"Are they enough?" wondered Danri, reflecting on the inexperienced troops comprising the Faerine Field Army. The overall force was large, but certain to be outnumbered by the minions.

Quenidon Daringer shrugged. "They have to be, don't they?"

The two veteran warriors turned back toward the heights, trotting along the valley in the wake of the Faerine companies as Kianna buzzed along beside them. Hardened by his years of Madness, further seasoned by his travails in Dalethica, Danri's muscles seemed immune to fatigue. He had found that he could march faster than any digger in the army, and even when they paused periodically for rest he had been uninterested in more than a quick hour or two of sleep. Quenidon, too, seemed to find slumber an unnecessary luxury. The lean sylve's features grew haggard and tight as the weight of command bore him down, but he moved with resolute confidence and showed no sign of succumbing to fatigue.

The hour of sunset came and went as they loped easily along. As usual, the field army stopped for a four-hour rest, then resumed the march before dawn—the twentieth day of the advance up Darkenheight Road. For the current stretch Quenidon and Danri walked with the digger companies at the head of the column, accompanied by Kianna Kyswyllis and Garic Hoorkin. The high springs of Aura in the Bruxrange sent shimmering trickles of illumination down the rocky faces, brightening the night. In fact, Danri had noticed, this Aura-light made the actual contours of the land more apparent than did gray daylight.

"That's an advantage to remember," he pointed out to the army commander. "The minions, like humans, won't see the illumination shed by the Aura—they'll be nearly blind at night."

"Like all humans except Rudy Appenfell," Quenidon reminded him with a chuckle.

"Rudy could see just fine around here," Kianna agreed wistfully.

They shared a moment of quiet melancholy, remembering their friend. "The lad would like these mountains," Danri noted. "He'd be wanting to climb this one and that, to explore in a dozen directions at once."

"I'd like to make those climbs with him," Quenidon said. "There's a serenity in the heights that, I admit, I'm sorely missing right now."

"That may be, and I'm sure the view's pretty up there,"

the digger allowed, "but I'll keep my feet on level ground just the same!"

Danri thought of Kerri and pictured the little inn they would share someday. He surprised himself by imagining Quenidon as a partner in the venture, resolving to speak of the matter to the sylve. For now, he turned to a practical question.

"How much farther to the pass—and the garrison?"

"I don't know—I've been meaning to climb one of these ridges and have a look," the sylve replied. "No more than a few days, I should think."

"I could fly ahead," Kianna suggested, buzzing a few feet off the ground.

Danri looked up the rising course of the valley as sunlight paled the clear sky. The road to Darkenheight Pass was a track across the flat bedrock, fringed by moss, lichen, and clumps of low brush; a curve in the flanking ridges obscured all but the next half mile of the route. A strange unease tugged at the digger, making him wish for a broader vista. The air shimmered oddly around the curve in the valley, almost like heat waves flickering across the mountain. Danri saw the progress of those subtle variations, instantly recognizing the large fliers that almost perfectly matched the rocky background.

"Terrions!" he spat, feeling dire fear at the implications. "But how—?"

"Look—there are minions on the ground, too," the sylve observed grimly.

Stalkers, the first scouts of the minion army, came into sight, gliding along the valley floor, long-limbed bodies concealed by robes of gritty gray. The stalkers saw the diggers and halted, more and more of them slithering forward until perhaps a hundred of the strangely graceful creatures gathered to either side of the roadway. The terrions circled overhead, and Danri counted perhaps a half dozen of the deadly fliers.

"They've come all the way through Darkenheight Pass, completely destroyed the garrison," Quenidon deduced.

"But surely someone would have escaped—we would have heard the news!"

"It depends on how fast they advanced. Do you think anyone could outrun those terrions? Or the stalkers either, for that matter?"

"I killed one of those lizards once," Danri said disgustedly.

"Just in time, too—I looked it in the eyes by mistake, got so dizzy I almost fainted!" As the digger spoke, his mind tried to grasp the scope of disaster. The whole Darkenheight garrison—wiped out? Such a catastrophe wasn't possible! Yet had even a single Faerine survived, he would have carried the alarm down the valley road. This implacable vision of the enemy sent a shiver of apprehension down Danri's spine when he thought of Kerri, or the pastoral homeliness of Shalemont.

Quenidon accepted the implications without visible consternation. "Garic, Kianna—tell the sylves and gigants that we've met the enemy. Have them catch up with us as quickly as they can!"

"Sure!"

"Aye, lord!"

With a buzzing of gossamer wings, the twissels darted back along the roadway. The sylvan captain turned and spoke calmly to the gathered diggers, declaring that the stocky Faerines would stand where they were. A grim chorus of "Aye-uh" signaled the digger agreement with the plan. Pembroak hastened forward, handing Danri his shield and then taking his place beside his leader.

The first companies of kroaks came into view a few minutes later. At first they appeared to be solid blocks of darkness, creeping across the ground like some glacial blanket. Quickly they resolved into individual warriors, advancing at a two-legged trot. Larger monsters hulked among them— the brutox, marked by their furious, sparkling trails and sharp whipcracks of sound. Shimmering terrions wheeled over the Sleepstealer's army, growing bolder as the numbers on the ground increased. Several of the minion fliers dipped through wide circles, swooping toward the diggers, shrieking aggressively.

"Placers!" Danri shouted. "Stand to the center!"

Quickly the warriors from that large mining town clomped over. Unlike their cousins from Shalemont and elsewhere, the Placers disdained heavy metal breastplates, battleaxes, and hammers. Instead, each digger carried a shortsword, his characteristic steel-banded crossbow, and a quiver full of metal-shafted quarrels that could punch through armor at fifty paces.

The terrions swept back and forth, shrill cries ringing

louder with each pass. Danri looked to the diggers of Placer, watched the sergeants-major curse them into curved ranks so that each warrior had a field of fire toward the sky.

"Look for their ripples of movement," the digger commander instructed, once again studying the air. The terrions' camouflage was effective, but not perfect, and as one of the creatures dove insolently close, the metallic twang of digger crossbows echoed through the air. Dozens of quarrels slashed upward, many curving to the valley floor far beyond. A few, however, struck the terrion in both wings, as well as the chest and throat.

The flier uttered a sickly squawk, diving through a frantic arc. Wounded wings folding upward, it smashed to the ground a hundred paces before the rank of digger crossbows. With a twitch of its long neck, the creature died, the body changing to a pale, stony gray amid the green brush on the ground. Shrieking madly, the other terrions dove and banked, but stayed beyond range of the deadly missiles. The steady tromping of the kroaks became audible, the cadence of the minions' march thrumming through air and ground.

"You there—Silverhills!" Quenidon suddenly shouted, attracting the attention of a digger sergeant-major from that town. "Get your company to the left—watch the flank!"

"Aye-uh!" The warrior, barking gruffly through the grizzled tangle of his beard, soon had a hundred sturdy axemen trotting off to the side.

Danri looked to the rear, anxiously seeking some sign of the sylves and gigants—but the road was empty, winding downhill for nearly a mile before a gentle curve of the valley took it out of sight. He spared no more than two seconds for the glance, as a roar erupted from the massed kroaks. The minions surged forward, howling and shrieking in a terrifying frenzy, thrumming the bedrock of the Bruxrange with the pounding impact of their charge. Brutox barked, a deep, chuffing sound booming through the din of the kroaks.

"Stand firm!" shouted Danri, the command echoed by the sergeants-major of the companies. The digger wished for some cover—a clump of boulders, a grove of trees, even a shallow streamlet—but the valley floor was smooth. The low brush crumbled easily underfoot, no impediment to the pounding gait of the minions. A stream ran parallel to their route, a hundred paces from the road, and beyond the trilling waters rose the steep cliff of the valley wall. Though as a desperate measure Faerine survivors could head for water to escape the minions, such a tactic only became relevant when the battle was lost, and Danri refused to consider that possibility.

The kroaks shrilled, pounding closer as Danri's hackles raised in instinctive hatred, the sight of the knobbed foreheads and gaping, brutish jaws infuriating him. "Placers—shoot!" he cried, when the minions were fifty paces away. A volley ripped out and dozens of kroaks tumbled—but the gaps vanished as hundreds more of the hideous minions eagerly pressed forward.

"Good aim!" cheered Pembroak, edging forward to screen Danri from the attackers.

"You, squire!" the veteran digger barked. "Get behind me, and stay there!"

"But—yes, sir." Chagrined, clutching his sword protectively, the youngster did as he was told. The quick crossbows savaged the attackers again at thirty and at ten paces, and then the kroaks and diggers mingled in a chaotic tangle of flailing arms and keen, steel-edged weapons, shields and brutish bodies.

Leaning forward, bracing himself on his short legs, Danri absorbed the impact of the leading kroak with only a single, staggered step backward; at the same time he delivered an overhand hammer blow to the monster's head that killed it instantly. Seeing a Faerine warrior go down, Danri bashed a pair of kroaks aside and straddled the fellow to give him a chance to rise—only to see that the digger had already been stabbed through the back by a minion sword. Cursing, Danri smashed the kroak bearing the bloody blade, then stumbled back to the line, raising his shield against a barrage of kroak assaults. Crouching, he swung his hammer in a low arc, crushing the knee of a howling kroak. The beast fell with a shriek of pain that ceased as the digger's hammer bashed in its skull.

More shouts rose from the battlefield, and Danri dimly realized that he and his fellow diggers were challenging the minions' din with cries of their own. Pembroak whooped nearby, splitting a kroak's skull with a slice of his axe. A focus of battle tightened in Danri's mind. Fighting with inherent skill, propelled by an innate hatred that fueled his determination, the digger struck one deadly blow after another. A pile of kroaks grew before him, and the beasts were forced to clear their dead out of the way—so that more could advance to doom.

Around Danri other diggers took heart, pressing close to his right and left, forming an immovable barrier against the minion advance. Kroaks pushed forward, taking the place of fallen comrades, but the pitch of the creatures' bloodlust subsided visibly. Danri's gore-stained hammer continued to rise and fall with deadly cadence, and abruptly several kroaks stumbled backward, no longer willing to face the savage digger and his killing tool.

"Take it to the ugly scuts—charge!" Danri shouted, scrambling over the gruesome barrier of dead minions to lay about with his weapon. Kroaks yelped and ran in all directions, suddenly desperate to escape. More diggers rushed in, and the whole rank of the enemy fell back. Minions dropped their black steel blades and fled; others turned and slashed at their own comrades, striving to cut their way to imagined safety. A deep, grunted bark abruptly cut through the din, and the blunt-skulled kroaks tumbled to the right and left to reveal a shower of angry sparks. The brutox lunged forward, snakelike whip lashing toward Danri's face—but the digger's shield, raised quickly, blocked the snapping strand.

Danri dodged, bashing at the brutox's brawny thigh, but the monster showed remarkable agility as it skipped to the side. Casting the whip away, the minion drew a massive sword and brought the blade smashing down on Danri's shield, numbing the digger's arm. Tumbling, bringing his hammer down with tremendous force, Danri grunted as he struck a blow on the monster's padded foot—and with a roar, the brute limped backward. The hammer whirled through the air, striking from the right while the steel shield blocked blows from the huge sword. Danri bashed the brutox's hip, and finally the monster fell. Another blow thumped the rounded skull, and the beady, wicked eyes bulged as sparks flew from its gaping mouth and the dying monster writhed on the ground, surrounded by a haze of brightness. It perished in a cascade of burning gore, leaving the acrid scent of a lightning strike lingering in the air.

"Danri—look!" Kianna's voice pierced the din of the melee and the digger whirled in shock, hunching behind his
shield as he saw the twissel hovering beside him.

"Get back from here!" he shouted, appalled. "It's too dangerous!"

"But *look!*" The fairy pointed over his shoulder as Danri
spun back, wary of attacks from behind. Instead he saw
kroaks backing cautiously away, and then bright shafts arcing
overhead, falling among the ranks of the minions, eliciting
shrieks of pain and surprise.

"It's what I was trying to tell you! The sylves are here!"

Danri and the other diggers whooped to see the arrows of
their Faerine allies. Another volley fell among the kroaks;
howling and whining, the minions stumbled back, clawing at
each other in chaotic disarray, fleeing the vengeful fury of the
Faerine Field Army.

                              •

                        — 3 —

Meamare's cave was a passage eroded into a limestone cliff,
remote and well-concealed at the head of a winding gorge.
Neambrey knew the way, and moved steadily upward through
the foothills, pausing every hour or two to fill his belly with
Aura. The young drackan relied on his memory with complete
certainty, trotting, loping, and pacing through narrow, steep-
walled valleys, working his way back into a region of rugged
foothills.

Pausing to drink deeply from a pool, Neambrey then raised
his head, drooling into the mirrorlike waters. He studied a
series of steplike shelves that climbed toward the mouth of a
high, secluded valley—his destination. The liquid in the
young drackan's body sloshed, and the volume of Aura in his
belly slowed him for several minutes. Shortly, however, the
fullness was gone and Neambrey leapt ahead with agility. He
felt the hard shell of his carapace against his spine, constrict-
ing and painful against the rapidly growing wings. Yearning
for flight, he pressed vainly against the cocoon, trying to break
free.

He ceased his struggle only when he scrambled up the last
slope, nearing the looming mouth of Meamare's cave. This

was a special place, Neambrey knew—special not because the matriarch of the green drackans lived there, but because of the Treasure. The mystical object had been guarded by the green drackans for generations, since long before the Sleep-stealer War. Though that conflict had been resolved centuries before Neambrey's birth, Meamare had shared stories that she had learned from her mother—of how the Treasure had been carried to this lofty place, and there guarded from the clutches of deadly minions, irresponsible humans, and dangerous Fa-erines.

Yet Meamare, not the Treasure, occupied the young drackan's mind as he rounded the steep shoulder of a bluff and found the concealed entrance to the cave. Ancient and dark, the shadowy niche proved spacious as soon as one came around a screening pillar of rock; the familiar scent of Mea-mare—

Neambrey froze, alerted by a chilling, startling odor. He found only a musty memory of the soothing, slightly spicy musk of his mother. The overriding presence was a moldy stench, underlaid by a pungent reek suggestive of a kind of swamp-dwelling lizard Neambrey occasionally hunted. Creep-ing inward, the young drackan saw the great form of his maternal parent, recognized the green sail of a mighty wing, the wall-like massif of her giant, scaly flank. But when the young drackan pressed forward, pushing his muzzle into the gap between his mother's wing and her body, he immediately sensed a cool stillness, a depth of torpidity that went beyond even a mature drackan's century-long hibernation. The odor of death assailed him, but he denied the truth, squawking plaintively as he crawled over the great, motionless body.

His squawk turned to a wail then, as he saw the gory wounds where rending violence had been done to the sleeping drackan's neck, almost severing the wise, eternal head. Even before he saw the open, sightless eyes, Neambrey understood.

Meamare, matriarch of the green dragons, was dead—slain in the depths of hibernation by something monstrously, un-speakably evil.

— 4 —

"Hold your pace—steady now, diggers!" cried Danri, forcing his raw voice above the groans of the wounded, bellowing

louder than the sporadic clash of weaponry that still marked
the staggered front of the battle. He cast a quick glance backward, relieved to see that Pembroak followed right behind—
and that Kianna had apparently departed for safer ground to
the rear.

The Faerine rank halted, though a few diggers still pressed
forward, bashing and hacking at kroak stragglers. Even the
most frenzied of the warriors finally halted and, with a few
strong curses hurled after the retreating minions, clumped
back to their kinsmen. Quenidon Daringer held the sylves
back from the digger ranks. The gigants arrived after a little
more time passed, and Gulatch was quick to growl his displeasure at the enemy's escape. The minions ceased their retreat a mile or so away, and now the hulking chieftain was
determined to lead his Faerines in an attack.

"We'll rout them all the way to Darkenheight!" Gulatch
promised, in a tone that suggested Quenidon should consider
the attack plan very carefully—if it was vetoed, the gigants'
violent urges would inevitably be directed at *somebody*.

"Look," declared the sylve patiently. He indicated the
curve of the valley, beyond the minion rank, where more and
more of the Sleepstealer's troops tromped into view. "We
don't even know how big their army is. Best to wait for a
little, get some more information."

"How did they get here so fast?" growled the gigant. "No
word from the garrison at the pass?"

"We have to assume they were overwhelmed, with no survivors," Danri noted grimly. "Then, after the battle, the minions must have moved fast."

"What about now?" Gulatch countered. He gestured to the
company of gigants, formed into ranks behind the digger position. "We should attack before all the minions get here!"

Quenidon shook his head, but his face was sympathetic. "I
admire your warrior's spirit, my ally—but consider this: If we
advance, we move out of the narrow portion of the valley.
The minions already outnumber us—they would have little
difficulty flanking our position, perhaps surrounding the entire
army."

"So we just *wait*?"

"I don't think we'll have to sit around for long," Danri
declared grimly. "Take a look at the enemy."

The Faerines watched the Sleepstealer's army as companies of kroaks marched to the right and left, expanding the broad rank until it spanned the entire valley, at least as far as the shallow stream. A warlike thrumming rose from the minion force, as feet stomped the ground and metal blades clashed against each other in ritual preparation.

"They'll attack again before the day is out," Quenidon deduced.

"Remember that small stream we passed, back down the road a half mile or so?" the digger asked.

Quenidon frowned, then nodded. "Not much of a thing, right?"

"It was mostly dry, but it formed kind of a ditch, the wash from a gulley to the right. And it ran all the way across the valley floor. I suggest we fall back that far, make a stand there."

"It's better than nothing," the sylve agreed. "Gulatch, take your gigants and the sylves back there—the diggers can back up, carefully, when the others are in place." The gigant grudgingly agreed, and quickly the Faerine Field Army withdrew a short distance down the valley. The minions, Danri suspected, hadn't even noticed the movement until the diggers began to retreat—and the enemy showed no stomach for a charge into that front of steel-edged doom.

The gulley was narrow and dry, except for a few muddy spots, and rarely more than three or four feet deep. But, as Danri had suspected, it provided something of a barrier, insuring that the minions couldn't hit the Faerines at full speed. The sylvan commander arrayed the diggers to the right and the sylves to the left, covering the entire extent of the gulley from its emergence below a high cliff to the bank of the stream on the other side of the valley floor. The Royal House sylves and the gigants, unpalatable as it was to Gulatch, would be the reserve.

By the time the plan was made, the pounding from the minion force had attained deafening proportions. Abruptly the monstrous wave swept forward, a dark tide sweeping against the frail-looking shoreline of Faerines. Danri, Quenidon, and their sergeants commanded the troops to stand firm. Despite his bravado, the digger was shaken by the appearance of the charge. Never before had he faced an enemy that seemed to blot out the ground itself—the floor of the valley was a surging mass of kroaks and brutox.

"There—look to the sky!" he shouted, suddenly alert to the danger above. Rippling patterns revealed diving terrions, but sylves and diggers released a shower of arrows that brought three of the creatures plummeting to earth. Five or six more veered away, leaving the battle to the forces on the ground.

The sylvan archers began to shoot as soon as the minions rushed into range—which was nearly five hundred paces for the sleek, spiral-shafted arrows. The graceful bowmen kept up a withering barrage, each warrior shooting a dozen or more arrows into the horde. Knowing the enchanted power of sylvan arrows, Danri suspected that nearly every shot killed one of the minions.

But that carnage still left thousands upon thousands of the enemy alive. The diggers of Placer shot steel quarrels as the enemy roared closer, but these casualties, too, were absorbed without slowing the advance. When the minions reached the other side of the shallow gulley, some of the kroaks tumbled headlong into the depression, only to be buried beneath the pounding feet of their own comrades. Kroaks and brutox clawed and stumbled through the mud and rocks in the ditch, striking upward at the sylves and diggers lining the far edge.

Danri's role as commander vanished immediately, replaced by a dual determination—to protect himself and his fellow diggers, and slay as many of the dark-blooded minions as possible. Here Pembroak proved his worth again, standing beside the older digger and protecting Danri's flank. The veteran warrior fought with cool fury, giving no thought as to what would happen if they were forced away from this ditch—as far as he was concerned, the Faerine Field Army would stand here or perish. The haft of the hammer fit perfectly into Danri's hand, resting there like an old friend. The digger aimed a blow at the first kroak to reach the edge of the gulley, slaying the minion with a smash to the forehead. More of the snarling creatures drove close, and the world became a chaos of noise, movement, violence, and pain.

Black-bladed swords nicked both of Danri's legs, and agony thrummed through his weary shield arm. His shoulders were numb, his grimacing face streaked with sweat and spattered blood, as the fight at the gulley's edge raged on. Dead minions soon choked the bottom of the ravine, but the press of attackers continued—new arrivals stumbled, clawed, and lumbered over the corpses of the slain in order to reach the Faerine defenders.

Rumbling bellows carried across the field and Danri knew that, somewhere, Gulatch and his kinsmen had entered the fray. Risking a glance around, the digger saw that some of the minions had broken through the line at the juncture of the sylvan and digger companies. The monsters raced to expand their breach, but the gigants closed in with relentless fury. Gulatch himself crushed a brutox to the ground with one blow, the minion vanishing in the sparks of its own destruction. In moments the charging troops were slain, the line restored. The monsters still in the gulley held back as if they shared an unheard command to slow the onslaught. The ranks behind ceased their remorseless advance, and gradually a stillness settled over the long and bloody line.

Yet it was not a cessation of the attack, Danri sensed immediately. The kroaks and brutox nearby simply backed a few steps away, avoiding the reach of sword and spear from the Faerine defenders. One brutox, sparks spewing from its claws, pounded its chest furiously and bared long, wicked fangs at the digger. The minion's glittering black eyes fixed Danri with a stare of palpable hatred. Inarticulate rumbles, vaguely hushed, even reverent, rose from the minion hordes. The kroaks shifted and muttered, but didn't advance—instead, the ranks moved slightly sideways, creating a gap in their own formation. Danri heard gasps of horror from the diggers opposite that gap, but at first he couldn't see the cause of their distress.

The horrid appearance of the creature that finally came into view caused bile to rise in Danri's throat. The monstrosity advanced in a rolling gait, lurching upon two stumplike legs, swinging on knuckles dangling from long, apelike arms. The being was larger than a gigant. The digger's revulsion, however, was caused by the sight of the leering, fanged heads— a dozen or more of them, sprouting like vipers, twisting appendages that emerged from a moist aperture in the monster's shoulders. That hole gaped like a wound, as if it had been gored violently, the encircling flesh left to rot and decay.

Danri remembered Awnro's description and knew this must be Phalthak, the Fang of Dassadec. The hideous body was black, slickly wet with Darkblood, and the multitude of snakes were long and supple, each of the wide-open mouths emitting a menacing hiss. The snakes bobbed and weaved, as if inspecting the rank of Faerines for worthy victims. Groaning in despair, Danri wondered how they might combat the immortal horror.

One digger—a burly warrior bearing a massive, gore-streaked axe—bellowed a challenge and rushed forward from the line, aiming that mighty weapon at the Lord Minion's bulging torso. The axe met the slick skin and bounced away without leaving a mark; in the next instant a purple snake-head lashed out, fangs sinking into the digger's cheek.

The Faerine staggered backward, screaming. He fell on his back, kicking wildly, dropping the axe as he flailed. His agonized cries carried the breadth of the valley; the stocky body arched stiffly, and it seemed to Danri that it took a very long time for the miserable fellow to die.

Another voice roared a challenge and a hulking gigant advanced, landing a sideways blow with his heavy club that would have smashed down a house—yet the Lord Minion barely staggered. The monster lashed out with another, longer snake, but the Faerine warrior bashed the fangs aside with his stout stick. The gigant charged in for another blow, raising the club high, but a serpent of bright red lashed forward with lightning speed, biting the fur-covered warrior in the chest.

The big Faerine cried out in pain and pounded at the wound, as if his skin had caught fire—and, indeed, it had. Danri watched in horror as the gigant slumped to the ground, curling into a ball as flames burst from his body. He twitched and writhed, soundless screams emerging with the flames as his mouth gaped. In a few seconds, the Faerine's corpse was nothing more than a twisted, blackened shape.

"Danri—they're getting ready to attack on the other side!" The high-pitched voice broke through the fray, right in the digger's ear.

"Kianna!" he erupted, whirling to see the twissel buzzing beside his shoulder. "I told you to stay back from here!"

"But you should know about this—there's going to be a

big attack. Lots of those sparking ones are coming along the valley wall!''

Cursing, terrified for the fairy's safety, Danri nevertheless followed her pointing finger and looked to the right flank. He saw a formation of brutox limned in a crackling glow, advancing in a great wedge; against them stood a few sylvan recruits, quailing before the monstrous attackers.

''I'm going over there!'' Danri declared. ''Quick—find Quenidon, tell him what's happening!''

''Right!'' Kianna replied. She tucked her head and buzzed into the air, racing over the gulley.

''Not there—look out!'' cried the digger as the Lord Minion stalked out of the ditch, stomping on bodies of diggers and sylves. Two gigants tried to stand at the edge; one fell, screaming, after a single snakebite, and the other dropped his weapon and fled as his comrade's body turned sickly green, then melted into a shapeless ooze.

''Quenidon!'' cried Kianna, spotting the field army commander. Buzzing furiously, she darted toward the sylve, rising well above the lashing heads of the Lord Minion.

A green snake, far longer than any of the others, stabbed upward, tiny fangs puncturing the twissel's calf. Kianna shrieked with a sound that ripped at the core of Danri's heart.

''No!'' bellowed the digger, lunging along the ditch, struggling against Pembroak and the other warriors who seized his arms, trying to restrain his suicidal advance. Kianna's body curled into a tight ball and she dropped to the ground, where more of the Lord Minion's cruel heads hissed forward, biting. She screamed again with shrill, heart-rending power—a sound that would ring in Danri's ears for the rest of his life.

The digger's eyes ran with tears, and he was spared the sight of the tiny corpse bursting into flame, vanishing in an explosion of horrific heat. The grotesque lord of Duloth-Trol stepped over Kianna's shriveled remains, leading the onslaught against a crumbling Faerine position. The minions shouted and howled, and suddenly the Sleepstealer's monsters rushed forward to either side of the Lord Minion.

Danri roared in blind fury, meeting the enemy surge, bashing minions with hammer and shield. Other diggers and sylves fought bravely too, but many fell under the onslaught, and the tenuous line ruptured in several places. Cruel warriors spilled through the breaches, and Faerines whirled to confront a foe that suddenly attacked from every flank. Danri stood firm as a dozen sylves fled to his right. Then several gigants waded backward, fighting to escape the enemy horde, and finally even a company of diggers broke, shouting for their comrades to fall back beside them.

As a creature of a single mind, the Faerine Field Army turned and fled, warriors pounding down the valley floors in a fever of panic. Only Danri tried to stand, straining to kill any minions within reach of his weapon—until finally Gulatch grabbed him around the neck and dragged him away. Only when the digger was half strangled did the gigant let go.

Numbed by horror and disbelief, Danri stumbled along with the rest of his warriors. "Kianna!" He groaned her name aloud, his mind a whirlwind of bright memories overlaid on that bitter end—and his ears ringing with the scream that was as piercing as if the fairy were still alive, and still suffering.

SEVENTEEN

Seas to Faerine

The Watershed's divides extend only across the
fundament. Beyond land the three waters
mingle chaotically, unconstrained by physical
separation.
—CODEX OF THE GUARDIANS

— 1 —

"The straits of Andaran, man—see how they're marked by
yon pillars of rock?"

Rudy followed the direction of Captain Kestrel's pointing
finger, seeing the summits of two peaks piercing the foggy
horizon ahead. "Yes—but those 'pillars' look like full-sized
mountains, to me."

"Aye, indeed. And not a nook or cranny we can seek for
shelter, once we pass between." Kestrel shook his head, grinning as if amused by the notion that the *Black Condor* might
require shelter.

"But this strait is the shortcut to Faerine, isn't it?" Rudy
leaned over the bow rail, looking at the sturdy prow smashing
its way through the waves.

"Shortcut to doom, some say—but aye, if we pass, then
we've clear sailing to the Faerine Sea beyond."

"And you're willing to try?" Rudy forced himself not to think of Raine, of Anjell and Dara, Awnro, Darret and the two dozen crewmen, who were bound by this decision.

"Captain Kestrel'll get us through," Darret piped up, startling the two men, who thought they were alone in the ship's prow. They turned to see the youth grinning down at them from atop the forecastle.

"You rascal—get down from there! If my cabin's clean, then go see Grist about helpin' with supper!" Kestrel barked sternly.

"Aye, sir!" cried the lad, bouncing to his feet and swiping his hand in a salute that verged on mockery, before disappearing behind the small cabin.

"You're willing to take the risk?" Rudy repeated, when once again they were alone.

"Risk? Tell me where in the Watershed is a place without risk," Kestrel replied frankly. "Corsari? I daresay no. And Carillonn? Who knows what'll be there when we get back? To answer your question: Aye, I'm willin' to take the risk."

"What have you heard of the passage? How long will it take?" Rudy knew that the captain had never personally sailed through the strait, though Kestrel had spoken to others who had—and knew third-hand tales of men who had entered the strait, never to be seen again.

"Days—some say eight or ten; others, a fortnight. The wind never varies in direction, always from west to east, but sometimes it's stronger than others. One thing's for sure: It's a one-way passage. The only way to return to Corsari is to sail all the way around Andaran."

"Any regrets?" asked the Iceman.

Kestrel grinned broadly. "Ask me in a fortnight. As for now, I'd say we have about ten more minutes to change our minds. After that, wind and current will take us through the strait, whether we want to go or not. Any regrets for you?"

Reassured by the captain's bold grin, Rudy shook his head. He thought, again, of Raine, Anjell, and Dara, stricken by the full realization that his risks—at least, aboard the ship—would be theirs, too. Yet a conviction had grown with him recently, and he felt serenely, utterly confident that they would arrive in Faerine safely.

"I'd best have a look at those mast-monkeys," Kestrel remarked, as many of his crewmen waited aloft, ready to trim the sails against the increasing force of wind. "You'll get wet, man, if you're determined to stay here."

"Suits me," replied the Iceman as the captain took his leave.

Rudy looked forward, confronting the vast, sweeping expanse of sea. During the past weeks he had found the ocean very much to his liking. Most of the daylight hours he had spent beside the rail, or high on the wheel deck, taking in the limitless vista of water. Generally a thin line of horizon marked the nearest land, and sometimes even this became invisible from the deck. Kestrel told him, though, that the masthead lookouts took care to keep the Watershed itself in view—if the ship was blown into the ocean beyond the sight of land, almost certain doom awaited them.

The familiar, tickling thirst touched Rudy's throat—the craving that had become more and more frequent during the voyage. He hefted the waterskin that was always at his side; the sack was half full, with two more stored in his cabin. The Iceman could only hope they would last until he reached Faerine. Still, days earlier he had given up his fruitless efforts to resist the craving, and now he slung the skin free with an almost thoughtless movement of his hands. Only when he had unstoppered the container and raised it to his lips did he pause.

"Aurianth, Mistress of Magic, I thank you." He murmured what had become a ritual prayer, then allowed a small splash of Aura to trickle into his mouth.

Immediately his senses felt acute, his muscles vibrant. He stared into the misty distance, watched the mountainous summits loom closer. The wind increased, and he perceived the currents of air sweeping across the ocean surface, squeezed and confined by the lofty twin pillars. Waves rolled one after the other, rearing in an endless sequence of powerful, foaming heads, tossing manes of spray like anxious horses in line of battle, poised at the brink of a charge.

Perhaps it was the heightened sensibilities created by the Aura, or merely the bond that continued to grow between them, but somehow he sensed Raine's approach before she came around the corner of the cabin. Rudy dropped a lanky arm around her shoulders, thinking that she had grown more beautiful with every day they spent together.

"You thinking?" she asked, leaning against him.

"No—just being," he admitted. "And the being is better, now that you're here with me."

"I can't get away from you on this ship—not that I've been trying," Raine said with a soft laugh that set his pulse to racing.

He remembered her boyish appearance, brown hair cut short, leather breeches stained with weeks of riding, when he had first met her at the North Shore Wayfarer's Lodge. Even then her smile had captured his imagination, and his heart. Now her hair had grown much longer, and the wind tossed it freely around her sun-browned face. The same high cheekbones framed the mouth that, lately, was so quick to laugh, and impulsively Rudy leaned over and kissed her. She raised her lips to his, and for long moments they remained oblivious to the sea, the ship, and all the rest of the Watershed.

Even as they separated, Rudy's thoughts embraced Raine. He savored the memories of long hours at the ship's rail—and even longer hours within the snug confines of their cabin. Wanting to take advantage of this time, these days of leisure, the Iceman felt a constant desire for Raine's company.

Rudy felt fiercely, vibrantly alive. He remembered the surging waves of the Circled Sea when he, Raine, and Takian had rowed their little boat. The sensation of vitality was the same now, except that the majesty of the ocean—and the capability of the watercraft—were magnified by hundreds. Holding the railing with one hand, Raine with the other, the Man of Three Waters watched and relished the growing fury of the sea.

The strait had at first been obscured by a wall of fog, but as the galyon approached the rearing peaks Rudy saw that the mist wasn't as dense as it had first appeared. The barrier mountains rose like a pair of dark, gaping jaws, and the wind whipped past with increasing frenzy. Pitching and rolling in the curls of tumbling swells, with only the jib and a few topsails unfurled, the galyon plowed into the crests with surging power. The pillars of the strait now loomed to either side, rushing swiftly past.

"Do you want to go to the cabin?" Raine asked, pushing her spray-soaked hair back from her face.

Rudy shook his head, letting the angry needles of flying seawater drive into his face, stinging his skin. He thrilled to each momentary jab of pain, braced himself against the railing as the bow plummeted into a trough between two waves—and then he laughed aloud as the crest surged past his knees. Raine staggered under the impact and again he put an arm around her shoulders, drawing her close. She trembled, from cold or fear, and her reaction startled the Iceman. Rudy felt no danger, no discomfort in this stimulating environment; everywhere was water, and the great expanse of roiling sea welcomed him, carried him rapidly toward his goal.

"Do you want to go below?" he asked, remembering her question.

"No—not yet," Raine replied. "I like watching you out here. You treat it like a contest—you against the storm. And you look so confident I almost believe you could win!"

"Me—*against* the storm?" Rudy shook his head. "It's more like I'm *with* it, a part of the water and the wind."

Another massive swell loomed, though this time the galyon rode easily up a surging slope, then coasted down the descending wave—as if the ship's weight pressed the water into subservience. The roaring, rhythmic power of the gale rose, hurling them forward, and in a flash Rudy saw these forces as the true pulse of the Watershed, even of the gods.

The sounds of wind and crashing waves ruled out conversation, but a part of Rudy's mind acknowledged danger here, for Raine. Reluctantly he turned and took his lover's arm, helping her keep her balance as they stumbled along the pitching deck back to midship. Moving beside the rail he found the waves so violent, the pitching so strong, that Raine was in grave danger of being swept overboard—several times he clutched her with all his strength, holding her as a surge swept past.

Yet it didn't seem strange that for him the water was an empowering, vitalizing force. The sting of spray against his cheeks only excited him, and the frantic pull of a wave washing over him was an embrace of sustenance and strength. Finally they tumbled through the door of their small cabin. Raine, teeth chattering, tore off her soaked clothes and huddled in a heavy woolen blanket. Rudy, equally drenched, stood dripping in the tiny room, listening to the sounds of chaos—and *power*—beyond the sturdy bulkheads.

"Lie with me a moment," Raine said, and he did, wrapping her in his long arms. She curled against him on the tiny bunk, the warmth of her naked body penetrating through his clothes. The ocean's tempo pulsed through the Iceman's veins, and suddenly he and Raine were tearing at his clothes, flinging them away. She clawed at him as he rolled on top of her, and then they coupled desperately, furiously. The pace of the waves was no longer fast enough—they made a cadence of their own, beating faster and faster, overriding the elemental power of the sea with the magic of their own melding.

Afterward, Raine lay in the depths of the fur-covered mattress, but Rudy soon rose and shook himself, stifled in the tiny cabin. He could feel the fury of the sea railing against the galyon, crashing against decks and hatches, and the Iceman could not ignore the summons in that ocean-song. Raine rolled onto her side, murmuring drowsily as he dressed in his sodden clothes. Softly closing the door, he crossed the deck and scrambled up the ladder to join Kestrel on the wheel deck.

Within an hour the galyon was fully caught in the grip of the strait. The wind surged, alternately roaring and wailing, whipping the waters into a frenzy and tilting the ship and its insignificant passengers into the tempest. The current worked to their advantage, serving to divide the stormy surface into a series of broad, rolling swells. Captain Kestrel rapidly acquired a rhythm, and the *Black Condor*, her speed slightly slower than the foam-capped crests, rode the waves under her master's precise sense of timing. The ship reached a peak as the water spilled over it, then rode the dizzying descent for several moments before starting up the next swell.

To port, the cliffs of Andaran remained a looming barrier, jutting upward from the horizon. Immense faces of rock soared a thousand feet into the air, and frequently lofty peaks loomed high above this precipice. Ancient taluses spilled from summits, fanning into wedges of rock, vanishing into wave-tossed chaos.

Off starboard lay the lower terrain of Rockwild, a wilderness of rocky hills and festering swamps according to Kestrel. The topography was for the most part lost in the constant fog of the strait, with only a distant hilly horizon visible, occasionally, under bright sunlight. The captain explained that

sailors used the cliffs of Andaran as their mark, since the
water below them remained deep. Toward Rockwild the
shoreline was harder to see, and in many places gravelly
shoals jutted into the strait, threatening sudden death to any
ship venturing close.

Captain Kestrel remained at the wheel for most of the ten
days in the strait. Rudy stood beside him for much of that
time, proving his worth in the darkest hours of night. It was
then that he could sense the presence of the cliffs, even when
they remained virtually invisible, and the Iceman was able to
guide Kestrel more accurately along his course.

For the full run the wind raged and howled, the current
surged unabated. Timbers creaked, but the masts stood and
the hull held fast against the relentless, smashing waves. Their
emergence from the strait, when it came, was a sudden transition that shocked everyone aboard the galyon. The heights
of Andaran remained visible to the north, but the shoreline of
Rockwild curved sharply away as the strong current settled
gently into a wide bay. Debris carried by that flow—such as
the galyon—inevitably drifted along for the ride.

The sudden silence was strangely liberating, surrounding
the travelers with welcome serenity. Under sunny skies, with
a gentle breeze from the port quarter, Kestrel immediately
sent his men to the top of the masts. Rudy and the other
passengers gazed in wonder at the azure heavens, or into
aquamarine waters that seemed bottomless—and impossibly
clear. The cliffs of Andaran vanished astern, and the Watershed became again a dim line along the western horizon. With
stately grace the galyon followed this shoreline, arcing around
a curve that, over the course of a week, became due south.

For two more weeks the *Black Condor* raced toward the
Faerine Sea. The shoreline to the west vanished altogether,
and Kestrel informed Rudy that they cut across the mouth of
a large, nameless bay. Finally land appeared, and the galyon
skirted a coastline that became increasingly mountainous as
they proceeded. Kestrel veered toward the east, as a spur of
that range extended from Dalethica to form a rugged peninsula jutting into the sea.

"That crest," the captain explained to Rudy and Dara,
pointing to the horizon of the rugged mountain range.
"That'd be the Watershed."

"And where the mountains fall to the sea?" the widow wondered, seeing that the last peaks ended a dozen miles before them.

"That's the Watershed of the ocean, I guess you could say. Beyond lies the Faerine Sea—but as I've told you, the place where the waters meet is said to be death to any ship!"

"You also told me that the Faerines used to sail out of there," Rudy reminded him.

"Aye, then—the death is to any *human* ship!"

The Iceman laughed, but he knew it was an important distinction. As the galyon drew closer to the mountain's end, Rudy scrambled up the rigging into the crow's-nest atop the mainmast. He lashed himself to a spar, taking pleasure in the regal sway of the towering shaft.

Looking ahead, he saw Aura, rainbow colors glowing in a brilliant prism from the sea just before them, and in dozens of places beyond. The waters of magic swirled in a great vortex, spiraling at the tip of the rocky peninsula. Visible as light and color, audible with a deep and thrumming sense of power, the Aura pulsed, spun, and churned, eddying downward with deadly suction. Yet the surface of the enchanted water remained flat and smooth, indistinguishable from a placid sea except for the emanations of power. Those subtle signs, Rudy knew, would be visible to himself alone—and any one of them spelled certain doom for the galyon.

"Stay east!" cried the Iceman, and Kestrel shouted, "Aye," from the wheel. The great ship held steady on her course, skirting the vast whirlpool. The shimmering vortex was a thing of nearly hypnotizing beauty, and Rudy forced his eyes at last to turn away, to watch the mountains of the Watershed fade into the distance. Squinting against the bright sunlight, trying to look beyond the invisible maelstrom, he saw a stretch of turquoise water, while another even larger whirlpool glimmered subtly beyond.

"Due south!"

Again the captain complied with Rudy's order, shifting the rudder as crewmen adjusted the partly trimmed sails. The galyon carved a graceful arc, gliding over a swath of water between the two whirling spirals of Aura. But other perils loomed. Rudy called out more instructions and the galyon turned away from land again, this time veering from a long, jagged line of Aura that stretched like a crevasse gouging a glacier. The stuff of Faerine tumbled into this crack, vanishing somewhere in the unseen depths. Should they cross the obstacle? Certainly, the ship would suffer the same fate as that of any climber who slipped into a glacial crack.

They skirted that danger, though the sailors on deck grumbled superstitiously. To them, one patch of water looked much like another, and the apparently directionless meandering puzzled and disturbed them. Once more Rudy called down, and Kestrel returned to his southerly course. The Iceman saw a whirlpool churning colorfully to port and, far away, another to starboard. Yet as these last obstacles faded toward the stern, he saw an expanse of clear blue water—unmarked by the threats that had screened the meeting place of two seas.

After sunset the moon and stars cast their light from a clear sky, but Rudy—who remained in the crow's-nest—saw that the entire surface of the sea shone with a comforting, benign illumination. This was not the glow of pure Aura, but neither was it the lightless reflectivity of natural water. Instead, he knew that the liquid of magic had somehow blended with the mundane waters of Dalethica, creating a sea of unique beauty and—for now, at least—commendable tranquility.

A rounded crest rose from the horizon before them as dawn colored the eastern sky. From his vantage, Rudy recognized it as an island, and he knew that the Faerine Sea must lie to the west, for the limitless expanse of ocean rolled infinitely toward the east. Calling down his directions, he soon felt the mast lean as the *Black Condor* came around, wind whipping the sails as Kestrel started tacking. After a full day atop the mast, Rudy knew that the dangerous water was behind them, and he descended to the deck with a growing sense of anticipation.

For seven more days they sailed westward, running with the wind or tacking as needed, smoothly crossing the balmy waters of a halcyon sea.

"Look at *that*!" Anjell cried one afternoon, pointing as hundreds of glimmering fish leapt from the water. The humans stared in wonder as silvery gills became wings. The water creatures, suddenly birds, flew for a mile or more before settling back to the sea and vanishing under the surface.

"That's magic! We made it to Faerine!" the girl exclaimed excitedly.

"I don't believe it . . . we're really doing this," Dara murmured in awe.

"Dat's magic?" scoffed Darret, in apparent boredom. Nevertheless, his eyes remained fixed upon the water where the flying fish had disappeared.

Several times monstrous serpents rose, scaly bodies rolling across the surface, wallowing in the gentle waves and, apparently, delighting in the sunlight. Sometimes a great head peered from atop a long neck, deep-set eyes squinting in the direction of the *Black Condor*. But then, with a flip of a massive fin, the creature invariably vanished into the depths. Never did one of the leviathans venture close to the ship, nor exhibit any sign of distress or excitement. Kestrel remarked that this was a good thing, and Rudy was forced to agree—after all, the largest of the beasts had been nearly as long as the galyon.

"I can't believe I'm seeing this with my own eyes," Awnro remarked on a sunny afternoon, strumming his lute on the main deck. The travelers had just watched a particularly monstrous sea-wyrm rise in a great pillar of shimmering scales and water, twist sideways in the air, and fall amid a huge cloud of spray. The waves settled as the serpent, true to form, made no further appearance.

"Seeing it—and gracing it with your song," Dara said, looking up from the sheet of parchment on which she was writing. During the voyage she had taken to keeping "sort of a diary," as she described it, a journal of humans traveling to the realm of magic. Now she set down a description of the sea serpent.

Once more the lute strummed its notes across the sea, but the bard's eyes lingered, with delight, upon the woman beside him. "This is the journey to make a bard's life complete," he declared contentedly, winking at the widow. "And not only because of the destination!"

Finally, on the eighth day of their passage across these enchanted waters, a coastline appeared. Green hills soon emerged in the distance, and the darker shadows of forested vales promised pastoral shelter between the gentle heights. This was the land that was the counterpart to the magical sea, and Rudy felt a tremor of excitement—and a strange, disturbing sense of familiarity—as he recognized the realm.

He had arrived in Faerine. Why, then, did he also have the strong feeling that he had, somehow, come home?

— 2 —

Jasaren crept into the lair, past the massive, slumbering body of the brown drackan. Advancing to the pool of Aura, he crouched beside the spring that was the essential feature of any drackan lair. Leaning over the liquid, Jasaren felt his belly heave in the ritual revulsion that he had come to expect.

Bile tainted with Darkblood rippled up his sinuous throat, propelled by violent convulsions. He retched, spewing inky liquid into the pool. Again and again the venom heaved forth, until his belly was empty—and the pool of Aura foully polluted. The mixture of liquids began to seethe and bubble, producing the caustic stench that would soon bring the big brown out of his hibernation. By then, however, Jasaren would be gone. Indeed, with the emptiness in his belly, a gnawing compulsion once again drew him to the heights of the Watershed.

But surprisingly, as Jasaren emerged from the lair and took wing, he was drawn not toward the border with Duloth-Trol, but toward the valley of the Darkenheight Road. The drackan obeyed the instinct, soaring over ridges, along lofty, barren valleys, until he came to a small box canyon. Here he glided to the ground, extending his neck flat and bowing abjectly before the hulking figure that lurched forward from the shadow of the wall.

"Welcome, my pet," gurgled Phalthak, through the mouth of the silver snake. "Have you served me well?"

"Aye, lord. I have tainted the pools of eleven mighty browns, most of whom have already awakened and drunk. They lie torpid now, awaiting my further command."

"Excellent. And the green drackans?"

"I have slain all I could find—even the one who wanted, once, to be my mate," sneered Jasaren, his jaws curling into a cruel smile. The emotions that once had hindered him were now withered memories of a different creature. "I doubt there is a mature green within a hundred miles."

"That is good, very good indeed." Phalthak rolled closer, rocking back and forth on his blunt, stumpy legs. "Now you must remain alert, ready for my signal. When I call, you will bring the brown drackans, and fly to my aid." The Lord Minion reached the drackan's side, extending several of his serpentine heads to gently touch Jasaren's taut, heaving flank. The coppery scales rippled with anticipation—of pain or pleasure, to the great drackan it mattered not. Finally the silvery snake-head reached out to caress the mighty Faerine's belly, tracing its contours, stroking the trembling flesh before the jaws opened to reveal narrow, glistening fangs.

Then the snake's head bit, puncturing the drackan's skin as Jasaren groaned in ecstasy, relishing the sweet gift of venomous Darkblood.

— 3 —

"It's like a city made of glass!" Anjell gasped. As the galyon rode the tide around a bend in the wide riverway, she pointed to the crystal edifices lining the opposite shore. Curving buildings of many pastel hues glimmered in the sunlight, and bell-shaped towers rose from the midst of colored domes and numerous tall trees. The passengers stood in the bow, watching as the wonders of Faerine rolled past.

"And bridges—like rainbows!" murmured Darret, his voice uncharacteristically hushed.

The ship, after barely a dozen miles of upriver tacking—and aided by an incoming tide—entered a lake of dazzling beauty. The place gleaming across the water, Rudy knew, could only be the sylvan capital of Spendorial.

"It's the end of the voyage, eh?" said Kestrel, lounging comfortably by the rail while Garson guided the galyon across the lake.

"The end . . . or is it the beginning?" wondered the Iceman, as Raine came to stand beside him.

"There are times I thought we'd never get you here," she said.

"I'm glad you didn't stop trying."

With sails trimmed, the galyon floated serenely across the deep lake. Numerous smaller craft dotted the water, and many of these drew closer as fishing boats and ferries all turned to the huge vessel. The galyon's crew furled all canvas but the jib, and the ship crept toward the docks of Spendorial. "Soundings!" ordered Kestrel, observing that his ship was by far the largest vessel on the lake. A crewman in the bow quickly dropped a line, reporting a comfortable and consistent depth as they drew near to the sylvan city.

"Drop anchor—swing out the longboat!" the captain shouted. He turned to Rudy. "See those skinny piers? This ship would crush 'em in an instant. Better to stand offshore on a good chain."

Sylves in great numbers came to stand with quiet dignity on the docks, regarding the galyon curiously. Among the Faerines were diggers and sartors, far more of each than Rudy had expected in this sylvan capital. He was further surprised to see several gigants, standing in the shadows cast by huge elms behind the docks. Smaller forms raced among the sylves, and with a pang Rudy remembered Kianna Kyswyllis. Would he see her, and Danri and Quenidon, now that they had arrived?

The passengers hastened down the ladder to the longboat, as Kestrel took the tiller and two oarsmen rowed Rudy, Raine, and their fellow travelers toward the shore. The boat glided beneath the high arch of a vine-draped dock, entering a placid pond. Small boats rested in flowery slips, while blooming lilies floated along the shore. With a delighted gasp, Dara pointed to a pair of white swans, gliding serenely among the blossoms.

Rudy was more intrigued by the sight of a hulking figure who stepped forward from the shadow of the elms. The crowd of sylves parted, allowing the large, bearded Faerine to advance, his heavy steps causing the wooden catwalk to bounce as he moved onto the dock. The gigant tossed a line to the longboat, then pulled the craft against the piling.

"Hoagaran?" asked the Iceman, recognizing the fiercely bearded chieftain.

"Aye, human," said the gigant, reaching for Rudy's arm and hoisting him up onto the dock. "And welcome."

"Thank you," said the Iceman, looking into Hoagaran's

eyes as he grasped the big hand. "Many things have happened since Taywick Pass."

"In your world—and mine," announced the gigant ominously.

In moments the other travelers had climbed onto the slender wooden dock. A network of bridges and catwalks connected this pier to a dozen others, the entire expanse supported by pilings driven into the gravelly lake bottom. Hoagaran led the companions toward shore, while the crowd stood respectfully back. Still, sylves and all the other Faerines stared with unabashed curiosity.

"You'll be going to the Palace of Time," Hoagaran said, as the docks gave way to the screen of towering elms. Beyond stood small houses of stone and wood, shaded by numerous trees and each surrounded by blooming gardens.

"I—I don't know. Is Quenidon Daringer here, or Danri?" asked Rudy.

"No," Hoagaran replied grimly. "They've gone to fight the minions—with Gulatch and a regiment of gigant warriors."

Rudy's heart quickened, and he felt a stab of alarm. "So it's come here, then, too? War?"

Hoagaran made no answer as they passed beneath the elms to meet several sylves. An elegant figure, nearly as tall as Rudy and draped in golden robes, stepped forward and dipped his head in a polite nod. The richly attired sylve, whom Rudy did not recognize, had silver hair and bright, perceptive eyes.

"Welcome to Spendorial," the sylve intoned. "The Man of Three Waters has been expected for some weeks now."

"I have?" Rudy said, feeling a sudden chill on hearing the familiar-sounding phrase. It was too close to the way he'd been greeted by Pheathersqyll and Kelwyn Dyerston, both of whom had died shortly after meeting the Iceman for the first time.

"On behalf of the Royal House, and High Auramaster Mussrik Daringer, you and your companions are invited to stay in the Palace of Time. Suitable quarters will be provided to meet your every need."

"What marvelous hospitality!" Awnro exclaimed, clapping Rudy on the back. "I see your reputation precedes you!"

"To what do we owe this honor?" inquired the Iceman,

trying to stem his own rising sense of anticipation.

"Your companions will be made comfortable presently. However, the High Patrician Solluel sends his regards to you in particular, sir, and requests the honor of your presence in the Palace of Time—*immediately*."

— 4 —

Neambrey spent a long, miserable night beside the massive corpse of Meamare. He tried to rekindle some of the comfort, the familiarity, that the great drackan had always provided. But the body was lifeless, its shape only a grim reminder of violence and tragedy.

Increasingly Neambrey found himself bothered by the lizardlike stench that pervaded the cave. Padding to the mouth of Meamare's lair, he looked into the small, secluded gorge. Who had done this—who had killed his mother? And why? The unfamiliar odor in the lair gave him his first clue, for it suggested a drackan—though somehow debased, or polluted. Later, as he rose to slurp at the Aurapool, Neambrey discovered a disk of copper-colored shell, and he knew that the attacker had been a large brown drackan.

Turning abruptly, the young drackan looked toward the distant corners of the cave. He didn't know who had done this killing, but he suddenly thought of a possible cause—a thought that sent a tremor through him. Perhaps someone had been seeking the Treasure! Rage infused Neambrey and he pounced to the cave mouth, his eyes glittering coldly at the heights and the valley floor. Nothing moved, but his fury pulsed with a growing determination.

Whirling again, the drackan raced into the depths of his mother's lair, passing through winding tunnels, stopping only briefly to lap at the Aura that puddled in so many places against the walls. He came to the alcove he remembered, skidded to a stop, and poked his nose into the darkened passage.

A solid wall blocked his way, and this was as it should be—the wall moved, he knew, when his mother turned the piece of rock. Only his mother wasn't here ... and *which* piece of rock? Frantically Neambrey scratched at the rough stone wall, prying and twisting and clawing. He didn't feel the catch release, but abruptly the panel swung inward and the drackan crept into a secret, Aura-bright chamber.

The Treasure still stood, jutting importantly upward from the center of a mound of gold coins, surrounded by rubies, emeralds, and diamonds beyond compare. Gowns of the finest silk lay strewn across the bed of coins. A candalabrum flickered, permanently, in myriad colors, dimly illuminating the paintings that leaned against the wall, in which figures leapt and cavorted in real movement!

Neambrey, however, had eyes only for the Treasure, for the mighty sword that rested in its gilded scabbard, hilt upward, partially buried in the heap of coins. In that instant of discovery he felt profound relief, and immediately he backed from the chamber, trying to pull the door shut with a forepaw. But the barrier of stone remained ajar, stubbornly resisting the drackan's attempts to move it. Neambrey pulled and pushed, grunted and strained. He twisted knobs of rock, pressed irregularities in the floor, to no avail.

The door to the Treasure chamber would, unfortunately, remain open.

— 5 —

"You must prepare to meet the Scrying Master," intoned the elderly sylve who escorted Rudy and Raine though the Palace of Time. Walls of transluscent crystal shed gentle, constant illumination, and floors of colored stone—slate, granite, redrock, blue and white quartz—gave each of the many chambers a different feeling of warmth and size.

The other humans had been taken by royal attendants to a palace garden, where they would await word from the Iceman. Raine, at first, had started to go with the others—until Rudy had informed the sylve that she would accompany him into the palace. Opening a silver door, their escort revealed a spacious room, warmed by carpets of fur and furnished with soft, low chairs. A pair of doors led to the right and left—dressing rooms, the sylve explained.

"You will find everything you need in there. Please wash carefully; and do not carry anything, or wear any garments except the silken robes, when you go into the Scrying Master's chamber.''

With an unctuous smile the dignified attendant departed.

"I don't think he's too happy to have humans in here," Raine said with a soft laugh.

"I don't blame him," Rudy said seriously. "When you've lived for three or four centuries, I expect traditions can become pretty entrenched."

"But they *expected* you—and invited you in."

"*Someone* did," Rudy acknowledged. "But I wouldn't be surprised if the Scrying Master raised some eyebrows by doing so. Shall we see what he wants?"

They entered separate dressing rooms, stripped, and washed with spongy, absorbent pads that coated their skin with a light, slightly spicy fragrance. Rudy found a silk robe trimmed in red for himself. Raine donned a smaller garment of white fringed with blue.

The silken robe against his otherwise naked skin felt strange to the Iceman. As he emerged from the dressing room, Raine turned to face him—and Rudy immediately forgot about his meeting with the Scrying Master. She looked stunning, chocolate curls dusting the shoulders of white silk. The trailing fringe of blue lay flat between her breasts, while her hips curved very faintly outward as the robe's fluid material draped toward the floor.

"You're a sight for a Scrying Master—or an Iceman," he said slowly, desire thickening his voice.

"You clean up pretty well yourself," she said wryly.

He wasn't aware of crossing the room, but in seconds Raine was in his arms, that familiar teasing smile on her lips. He kissed her for a long time, and she met his embrace fiercely, hungrily. Blood coursed like Aura through Rudy's veins, and his pulse pounded in his ears when at last they broke apart.

The glow lingered as, reluctantly, he opened the chamber door to discover their sylvan attendant. More corridors followed, until they reached a juncture of many paths. A wide passageway led in one direction, formed not by walls but by clusters of verdant greenery that screened any view down the winding path.

Looking quickly upward, Rudy saw the crystal dome arching overhead and knew that they were still within the walls of the palace. Yet the garden was real—he could smell the dampness of good soil and the mingled scents of many blossoms.

"The Scrying Pool lies within," the sylvan elder announced. For just a moment his aloof façade cracked, and his pale blue eyes met Rudy's dark ones. "May Aurianth be with you—and with us all," he said sincerely.

Raine's hand slipped through Rudy's arm as they started along the winding path. White gravel crunched softly under their bare feet, strangely causing no discomfort. The plantings were odd—many resembled ferns, while some were short, barrel-trunked trees with caplike fringes of broad leaves. They came around a sharp bend and found the pool. Small white boulders fringed the perimeter of the irregular oblong, and in the bays at either end lily pads and cattails sprouted vigorously.

The center of the pool was clear, the outline expanding into a nearly regular circle. Several benches bordered the pond, and taller trees grew all around, leaning inward until they formed a partly shading canopy overhead. The crystal ceiling of the palace loomed a great distance above the tall trees.

"Come here."

Until the sylve spoke, Rudy hadn't even noticed him. Now he saw the slender, white-haired Faerine standing at the very edge of the pool, wearing a robe like the humans'—except that it was trimmed in gold. The sylve stood perfectly still beside the water, his back to the pair as the Iceman and Raine advanced.

Nor did Rudy spend time looking at the tall Faerine—the Scrying Pool captured his full attention. The surface seemed to be alive, so vital was its power, so regular its movement. He saw dots of color form in the center of the circle, and as these spots expanded into rings, each embodied the full spectrum of a rainbow—the outer edge a bloodlike red, while the trailing surface faded into surreal violet. As each ring grew, another dot appeared, expanding into a matching circle, and Rudy realized that the pool pulsed a new ring of color with each beat of his heart.

He was unaware of Raine's hand on his arm, of the sylve or the trees or anything except the mysterious water. The liquid was primarily Aura, though oddly enchanted. Abruptly the pulsing hesitated, and he groaned audibly until it started again, one burst every two heartbeats now. Steadily, over uncounted minutes of staring, the pulsing slowed to three, four, up to six heartbeats between explosions of color. Yet it seemed to the Iceman that each burst was two—or four or six—times more beautiful than any had been at the earlier, hastier pace.

Rudy gradually realized something else: Between the rings of color he discerned more than mere water. A picture evolved there, a scene of confusion—vague images of movement amid rolling clouds of fog. Something resolved itself into a hulking form, and when the Iceman saw sparks trail from its paws he knew it was a brutox. The minion swung a great, black-bladed axe, savage swipes directed at a small figure who wielded a hammer, battling valiantly to hold the monster at bay.

"Danri!" choked the Iceman, with a shiver of fear.

More figures lumbered through the fog, and a pair of kroaks rushed into view. The two beetle-browed minions crouched, swords at the ready, approaching the digger's back.

"Look out!"

Whether the digger heard his warning, Rudy didn't know, but Danri whirled, smashing his hammer into the skull of one kroak. The digger tumbled away, the brutox and surviving kroak in close pursuit. Rudy's hand flailed at his belt, groping for a weapon that wasn't there. He struggled, cursing, and felt the battle engulf him. Only when he gasped for breath and blinked did he realize that he was flat on his back, staring upward, at the drooping fronds of the palms and the crystal sky of the palace.

Raine peered down at him, her eyebrows furrowed in concern. She removed her hand from his chest and gradually the Iceman realized she had thrown him to the ground—doubtless to prevent him from leaping into the Scrying Pool. Finally Rudy turned his attention to the tall sylve, though the fellow still hadn't looked away from the pool.

"What happened?" the Iceman demanded. "I saw Danri—he's in danger! I've got to help him!"

"So it is true . . ." The Scrying Master spoke as though to himself.

"I don't know what you mean!" Rudy snapped, irritated

by the Faerine's aloofness. "But I've got to go!"

"Where?" inquired the sylve, at last turning to face the two humans.

Rudy saw the fellow's face and gasped, unconsciously turning away. He felt Raine's hands tense, though her expression didn't change—nor did she make any sound. Abashed, the Iceman bit back his revulsion and regarded the tall sylve.

From the look of the firm chin, the gracefully high cheekbones, the Scrying Master might once have been handsome. Something had horrifically damaged his face, however—now the nose was a red sore, and the flesh around the eye sockets and forehead a mass of angry, twisted scar tissue.

"Where do you have to go?" repeated the sylve patiently. If he had noticed the Iceman's reaction, he gave no indication. Dimly, Rudy understood that the fellow must be completely blind—he had no openings for his eyes!

"Danri . . . he's in trouble!" Rudy blurted, aware of the hollow sound of his own voice.

"A great many of us are in trouble—and it is clear that you, a being unique in the history of the Watershed, have hope to offer us all."

"I'm a human!" Rudy objected, recognizing the lie even as the words left his lips.

"Forgive me," murmured the sylve dryly. He turned back to the pool, but Rudy sensed that his next question was directed to Raine. "And what did *you* see?"

"A . . . a clear pool. Dazzling fish—silver and gold, and some as bright as rubies, rich as jade. A wonder of gems scattered like pebbles on the bottom of the pool," Raine replied. "It's beautiful—but that's all I saw."

"Danri! He's fighting a brutox, and kroaks!" Rudy shouted. "He's surrounded, trapped!"

"I share your concern," replied the mutilated sylve. "Shall we look again?"

Reluctantly Rudy stood and stared into the water again. He saw the pulses of color, the ringed prisms that had attracted him before. Yet now the circles continued to pulse quickly, once every heartbeat, and the Iceman could see nothing in the gaps between them.

"Slow your breathing," said the Scrying Master quietly.

"Allow your mind to drift free of your body. *See* the pool, but not with your eyes."

Willing himself to be calm, Rudy tried again. Slowly the pulses of color grew brighter and less frequent. It took a long time, but finally they once again burst one to every six heart-beats. And the image of a battlefield became clear. Kroaks lay everywhere, mingled with the bodies of diggers, sylves, and gigants, while fog—or smoke—wafted through the air.

Danri stood now with other Faerine warriors, and Rudy watched tensely as a dozen diggers stood against kroaks three times their number. It was the minions who suffered, and when the Iceman tried to see more of the picture he realized that the small party of diggers was screening the retreat of a large Faerine army. The troops fled a press of minions, falling back along the floor of a valley. A grotesque form advanced among the minions, moving on two legs, rolling with the aid of its rough-knuckled fists. Rudy shuddered at the creature's appearance—the seething snakes, the hideous shape of the body. From Awnro's tales he remembered descriptions of Phalthak, the Fang of Dassadec. As the monstrosity advanced, the stalwart diggers scrambled to get away, once again in full retreat.

"The battle is lost," Rudy declared numbly.

At his words, the images in the pool faded, replaced by the pulses of color. Rudy turned away, confronting the scarred sylve.

"I warned you that there were very many in trouble," the Scrying Master said quietly.

"What can I do about it?" Rudy wondered if here, at last, he might find the answers he had been seeking for so long.

"Well, perhaps you could journey to the Bruxrange. A strapping man like you could no doubt bear a sword well, aiding your friend in his battle against thousands of minions." The sylve's words were dry, his sarcasm very subtle.

In truth, Rudy had once again felt that martial summons. Yet he was forced to acknowledge that his presence on that battlefield would make very little difference to the final out-come. Apparently this realization showed on his face—or, rather, on some deeper level—for the blind sylve's mouth curved into a gently compassionate smile. The expression was strangely soothing to the Iceman, for all that it issued from such a mangled visage.

"You show wisdom and patience, too. I am Larrial Solluel, High Patrician and Scrying Master of Spendorial. I shall try to help you. For now, you must listen very carefully. . . ."

EIGHTEEN

Dark March

A general who is determined only to defend,
never to attack, ultimately confronts a clear
choice: his army's surrender, or its annihilation.
—TOME OF VILE COMPULSIONS

— 1 —

"Where's the damned road?"

"What does it matter—keep movin'!"

"Why bother? Let's fight the bastards here!"

"At least we'd get it over with . . ."

The caustic and despairing remarks, barked halfheartedly by grim-faced diggers, rumbled the discontent of the plodding field army. Danri trudged numbly along with the discouraged warriors, his own mind reeling to the horror around him. His last picture of Kianna, as the twissel cried in the agony of the Lord Minion's venom, burned in his mind, kindling bursts of fury, despair, and hatred in bitter succession.

As the morning's battle became a long afternoon of retreat, Quenidon left the Royal House sylves in the center of the column and joined Danri and the diggers of the rearguard. The sylvan leader encouraged the warriors' griping, telling his fellow commander that disheartened troops drew spirit from shared misery.

Yet Danri barely heard his friend's words. The digger's mind whirled, repeating the guilt-ridden suggestion that he, Danri, had sent Kianna Kyswyllis to die! Hatred for the Lord Minion mingled with self-loathing in such a bitter brew that the digger yearned to stop and fight, to sacrifice himself for no other reason than selfish atonement. Even in the depths of despair he couldn't force himself to such a hopeless task, though it was nearly as difficult to conjure up any reason for encouragement. The Lord Minion had been so remorseless and invincible that, even if the Faerines somehow stood against the horde of minions, Phalthak would ultimately prevail.

"Move up there!" Quen barked at a trailing group of weary diggers. "Or are you trying to scare the minions with your ugly faces?"

"Scare 'em nothin—I'm waitin' to bust a few kroak skulls!" growled a burly digger, glowering at the sylve, obviously willing to accept a substitute. Nevertheless, the stragglers picked up the step, drawing closer to the other Faerines.

Wings buzzed through the air and Danri whirled, gasping in irrational hope—and then grunting in recognition as Garic Hoorkin flew over to him. "They stopped!" declared the male twissel, dropping to the ground, his thin face haggard.

"The minions? How long ago?" asked the digger, groaning inwardly to another surge of guilt—why couldn't this twissel be Kianna?

"A few minutes."

Quenidon appeared at Danri's side. "You say the minions have halted?" asked the sylve.

"Yup. They're all getting lined up."

"What for?" the sylvan commander wondered. "Sustenance? Darkblood, perhaps?"

Danri shrugged. "Want to rest the troops?"

Quenidon shook his head. "Let's keep moving for now— build up the gap between us. Maybe we can allow a rest later, once we know how long the minions stay put."

"I'll go back and keep an eye on them," Garic said, bouncing into the air and starting toward the rear.

"Wait!" Danri's outburst surprised himself. "I mean, be careful," he added gruffly.

"I will—I'll be invisible before I get too close," promised the twissel before buzzing into the night.

Quenidon fell into step beside Danri, speaking with his eyes on the ground. "She was very brave, you know . . . and as much a warrior as any gigant or sylve—or digger."

"I know—but . . ." Danri couldn't articulate his grief.

"And she will be missed, greatly. I'm sorry." The sylve fell silent, striding easily beside the digger, his presence easing a small bit of Danri's heartache. He tried to remember Kianna's courage, her spritely enthusiasm; finally, he found some of these memories taking the place of the horrific image of her death. Yet piercing guilt overwhelmed any further attempt to divert his bleak focus.

Shortly Garic Hoorkin returned out of the gathering darkness. "They're already on the move again," the twissel reported breathlessly. He dropped to the ground and walked beside the sylve and digger, giving his wings a rest. "I got as close as I could. All the minions were lined up at these big wagons—the ones with the iron vats on the back."

"Darkblood," Danri guessed, grimly certain.

"And they're moving again?" pressed Quenidon. "As fast as before?"

"Yep—you've got maybe three miles on them now."

Knowing that, Quenidon ordered a ten-minute rest, giving the Faerine warriors time to chew a little hardtack, drink Aura and water, and sit on the hard ground. But the minions came remorselessly behind, and soon the weary diggers, sylves, and gigants once more shambled from Darkenheight. It was after midnight when Danri looked back and saw the stalkers loping a few hundred paces away. He suspected that terrions flew overhead, but since the fliers were nearly impossible to see against the night sky, he didn't waste time searching. The great mass of kroaks and brutox followed, no doubt within a mile or two. The Faerines could hold that gap for now, but—against the tireless minions—how long could that last?

The field army plodded along, gathered into a rough semblance of companies—though the troops made no effort to form the long, narrow column necessary to follow the Darkenheight Road. Instead, the retreating mob marched in a broad block, giving Danri cause to be thankful for the smooth, unobstructed terrain of the valley floor. The digger scuffed along near the last marchers, wallowing in the well of his dark thoughts.

"At least the minions are out of sight back there," Quenidon noted, his words filtering through Danri's moroseness. "I want to give the troops another rest, for a few minutes."

"Sounds like a good idea," the digger agreed. He looked at the haggard, hunched diggers marching at the rear, knowing that the warriors really needed a night's sleep—but ten minutes was better than nothing. That would serve for the troops, in any event; Danri had no particular preference as to whether he himself walked, fought, or died in the next few hours.

"Feel up to making a little climb?" Quenidon asked, narrowing his eyes to study Danri shrewdly. "I thought maybe we could see up the valley a little farther. And get your mind onto something else."

"Aye-uh." The digger saw that the valley walls sloped gradually here, much more gentle than the canyon cliffs that flanked so much of this accursed road. "That knob to the west, there—looks like it might offer a pretty good view."

"I was thinking the same thing myself." The sylvan commander trotted forward through the ranks, a tireless example of endurance as he cheerfully announced the rest stop. Sylves, diggers, and gigants all slumped wearily to the ground, many falling asleep where they collapsed.

Danri trailed behind Quenidon as the sylve found Gulatch. The big warrior looked up from a gourd of refreshment, listening as bright Aura shimmered through his beard, soaking the gigant's bearskin tunic. "Get the troops going after ten minutes—we won't be back by then, but we'll cut along that ridge and join up with you down the valley."

"Why not send someone else?" asked Gulatch.

"No." The army commander shook his head firmly. "I need to see for myself."

Quen and Danri started up the brush-covered slope. The knob on the ridge was some distance above, but they climbed diagonally away from the minion army, working steadily upward, acutely conscious of time. The Aura-bright valley expanded below them, under a sky brilliant with stars. Aware of the pair's vulnerability on their own, Danri spent a few moments scanning the heavens for signs of roving terrions, but saw no telltale ripples against the starry backdrop. With his relief came the first, grudging acknowledgment that he *did* want to live, if only to deliver revenge against the enemy.

Finally the shoulder leveled off, though the ridge line swept upward into a cliff on one side. A narrow notch allowed them to see into the narrow, secluded valley beyond, but the two commanders' attention centered on the road, and the vista to the south. In the distance the knife-edged crest of the Watershed rose above the tangle of the chaotic Bruxrange. The Faerines could see the cut of the Darkenheight valley, twisting back and forth among the climbing hills, then embarking on a long, exposed slope toward the V-shaped notch of Darkenheight Pass. Swirling in rounded contours, all curves and bowls, the bedrock of the Bruxrange writhed in fantastic shapes, rising into cone-shaped pillars or gliding through long walls as fluidly as silken gowns ruffled by a breeze. Silver trails limned many of the mountain faces, even some of the heights approaching the Watershed itself.

Danri and Quenidon stood in the narrow cut. Wind rushed through the opening, but they took shelter in the lee of several boulders. The minion army was an obvious, dark blot on the landscape, creeping along the valley floor in the wake of the retreating Faerines. The interval might have been a couple of miles at one point, but as the field army paused for its brief rest, the gap had closed to barely a mile. The legion of the Sleepstealer marched relentlessly, sweeping like a tide of ink across the enchanted realm.

"Ten minutes is about the limit for a halt," Quenidon noted grimly.

"Aye-uh—looks like Gulatch is getting them moving again," Danri replied. "We'd best get on—"

He paused abruptly, disturbed by a pungent, vaguely reptilian scent on the wind scouring the high notch. "What's that?" he hissed.

Quenidon was already moving, crouching around the base of the boulder, long sword in hand. The sylve halted with a muffled cry as Danri whirled in disbelief.

A patch of stony ground rose before them. Slitted eyes, pale with a golden gleam, glared above a pair of large, gaping

jaws. The digger stared at the scaly head bobbing in the air,
barely noticing that it was attached to a supple neck. The
fanged mouth widened, revealing a gap large enough to engulf Danri's head.

Then something puffed from that maw, a blast of warm
wind that was not altogether unpleasant. The digger reached
for his hammer, settling into a fighting crouch—but before
Danri drew a full breath he slumped to the ground, embalmed
by darkness.

—— 2 ——

Colors, soft and warm, embraced Rudy in a sensual caress—
yet he remained wary, having learned over the last several
days that this spectral touch was often the prelude to startling,
even terrifying, revelations. He sensed a center to the whirling
prisms, a solid base that drew his attention and his power.

That center was in a deep place, so far away as to be almost
unreachable. It was a mildly sinister sensation, alluring as
well, offering the promise of knowledge and power. The Iceman fell, yielding to that seductive pattern, allowing the summons from the depths to draw him from the physical
boundaries of the Scrying Chamber. Scents of tempting
spices, wafts of seductive incense, surrounded him. He heard
soothing sounds that were not quite music.

"Stop!"

Solluel's voice cut through the haze, jerking Rudy's mind—
and body—back from the depths. The Iceman shook his head,
clearing the foggy residue of the pool, bringing his Aura-
heightened alertness back to his physical surroundings. Only
then did he see that the Scrying Master's mouth was drawn
into a white line, his scarred face twisted by a mixture of
anger and fear.

"What are you trying to do?" demanded Solluel.

"I . . . I don't know! I wasn't trying to do anything—I felt
this presence, drawing my attention . . . I tried to see!"

"You must not look there! Do you understand the danger?"

"No!"

Larrial Solluel drew a breath and sighed. "I believe that

you speak the truth—but you must understand: The Pool of
Scrying is a window into the realms of Dalethica and Faerine
. . . and Duloth-Trol, as well. However, we must not use it to
peer into the Nameless One's domains—lest we give the
Sleepstealer means to insinuate his power among us.''

"Duloth-Trol?'' The Iceman shook his head forcefully.
"But I wasn't . . .'' His objections trailed off as he remembered the subtle temptation, tinged with unmistakable menace.

"The Nameless One seeks to observe you, perhaps even to
attract your interest.'' Solluel's tone was grim, the corners of
his mouth drooping in concentration.

"He was *tempting* me,'' Rudy suggested fearfully. "As if
he wanted to attract me. . . .'' Shivering, he tried to block the
memory of that enticement—but only succeeded in strength-
ening his own fear.

"It is only logical to suspect that the Lord of Duloth-Trol
knows of you. He will seek to turn that knowledge toward
his own ends.''

"How can I escape him?''

"I do not know for certain that you can,'' replied the sylvan
patriarch—not very reassuringly. "But I shall do my best to
help you try.''

Rudy nodded, trying to quell his fears. He didn't know how
long he and Solluel had been isolated within the scrying
chamber; nor would he recognize the passing of the days or
weeks that followed. His life had become a hazily focused
affair, dominated by that deceptively placid pool.

They ate no food, nor did they ever sleep; only the water
of Aura passed their lips. On the elixir of magic their bodies
thrived, and Rudy's mind embarked upon heights of insight
he had never before suspected. Anjell, Danri, even Raine . . .
all his old companions were forgotten. The city and realm
surrounding this splendid palace, sheltering this treasured
pool, vanished from his awareness. Instead, the world was
this garden, this pool—

And this sylve.

Larrial Solluel was a guide as bold, as steadfast and courageous, as any Iceman who had ever made the perilous as-
cent of Faerimont or Trolhorn. The Scrying Master served as
counselor, spiritual anchor, and sometimes adversary to his
human pupil. He challenged and expanded Rudy's knowl-

edge, sometimes mocked the human's confident—but mistaken—assertions. Though their feet never took them more than a dozen paces from the side of the pool, the pair journeyed throughout Faerine, even crossed the Watershed to visit the human lands of Dalethica.

For a time the Iceman watched in horror as the lands west of the River Ariak rose into the pool. The forests of Carrilonn were gone, replaced by a blackened, smoldering wasteland known as Reaper's Horde, the City of One Hundred Bridges. Frequently Rudy found Takian and Bristyn, walking the battlements of the castle or looking westward from a lofty tower. He sensed their distress and longed to offer comfort, to project his voice through the pool—but this, he learned, was impossible.

When tutor and student did not stare into the Scrying Pool, Solluel spoke and Rudy listened, and questioned. The sylve described the techniques of the Auramaster—the raising and steering of an Auracloud, summoning and mastering of wind and rain, the healing of spiritual as well as physical hurts. The human pupil absorbed the information as it was offered, marveling that this mastery of Aura—a thing that sylves spent centuries learning—had been given to him with the gift of Three Waters.

"Auramastery is a rare treasure," Solluel explained. "Even the greatest, the wisest sylves may not be granted proficiency. Destiny might proclaim a son or daughter ready for testing, yet if the talent does not exist, the tutoring is wasted."

"That sounds tragic." The thought of learning a destiny, only to find mortal abilities insufficient for its accomplishment, seemed a fate as bleak as any he could imagine. "How do such failures cope?"

"Failures?" Larrial Solluel cast the Iceman a sly look. "They perform as builders or poets, warriors perhaps. Their lives are not wasted."

Much of the time Solluel did not expound, so much as raise the questions for which the Man of Three Waters had no answers; "What is the origin of Aura?" was his favorite. After some time had gone by, he began to invite Rudy's speculations on answers, and listened intently as the Iceman formulated replies.

"Aura could be the blood of the goddess Aurianth," he

suggested once, after a too-hasty period of reflection.

"Bosh and fairy tales!" snapped Solluel. "There's a *lot* of Aura in Faerine. You'll have to do better than invent some myth."

"Does it ever rain pure Aura? Or do you just find it in the ground, from springs?" asked the human.

"Splendid reply! Remember, questions, always questions! Perhaps later, answers will come; or perhaps not. It is of little import, as long as one is always asking questions!

"And no, pure Aura has never been known to fall from the sky, though mundane waters are mixed with the liquid of magic sometimes only in small proportion."

"Something in the ground separates it, then," Rudy asserted. "But *what*?" he asked quickly, remembering the sylvan sage's lesson. Abruptly he had another idea. "Does the Scrying Pool give answers to this kind of question?"

"I think that you should have a look. To most Auramasters, the pool reveals only that such as you have seen—a view of Faerine and Dalethica, limited to those places open to the sky. However, there are a few among us who have been able to glean more than images—revelations, you might say . . . Some have described the experience as a 'gift of wisdom.' "

"You think that I might be one of these few?"

"I think that you might be *anything*." Solluel's tone was somber, the set of his jaw grim. The scarred forehead turned toward Rudy, and the Iceman had the uncanny sensation that the blind sylve stared into his eyes. "There are times, human, when I see you as a danger—to myself, to Faerine, and to the world. But those times are few, and more often I have beheld you as an image of hope."

"Have you *watched* me?" Rudy asked; the thought gave him an eerie feeling.

"From time to time in the past year, yes. My own dreams first alerted me, and I saw you fall in the avalanche of Aura, witnessed the sword of Darkblood stab you through the heart and create the Man of Three Waters. As I have come to know you, I bear more confidence in the positive outcome."

"Thank you," said the Iceman, touched. He stood and took a drink from the flask of Aura offered by the sage. The sylvan elder's presence was like a physical embrace as Rudy approached the pool, though Solluel elected to remain seated on one of the benches away from the water's edge. The moist air was cool, close against the Iceman's skin, and he inhaled the rich fragrance of flowers before he turned his eyes downward, toward the Aura.

The familiar colors spun from the center of the pool, expanding outward in rings that encircled all of Rudy's awareness. Allowing the colors to soothe him, he relaxed into a state of Aura-focused concentration. Abruptly he fell into a dizzying, spiraling plunge, delightfully giddy and terribly frightened at the same time. Nothing supported him, but neither was he falling. A sense of equilibrium surrounded the physical form of his body, washing him with alternating rings of color, and slowly the Iceman relinquished his fear.

"What is the source of Aura?" he asked, mumbling as if to himself. The question sounded right, and he waited expectantly for an answer.

"What is the destiny of the Man of Three Waters?"

Rudy heard the second question, but for a moment he thought that he himself had asked it. Yet he had made no sound, hadn't even imagined the query before it was voiced.

"What is the destiny of the Man of Three Waters?"

Again came the words, and something . . . some answer within Rudy spilled forth. He whispered, "The Man of Three Waters will master ocean and sky, and his power will smite armies. But he will see killings uncountable—and be helpless to save a single life."

The Iceman's mind reeled, and he knew each word to be a profound truth voiced by himself, prompted from some distant, unknowable source. He was shocked by the import of the words, terrified as he perceived flashes of menace; at the same time he thrilled to the knowledge, the truth, that he *had* a destiny.

"Evil will tempt him, magic will lure him, mankind will mourn him!" He stated the words, the truths that he didn't, couldn't *possibly* know! Yet his tone was unwavering, his jaw set firmly.

"He shall know heartache, and grieve for the loss of his only love!" Rudy's voice grow louder as he struggled now to spit out words he hated to speak; each exploded against his physical will. Suddenly Raine was there, in his vision, and he saw a horrifying picture—her body, broken and bloody, pulseless and pale, lying shattered on a bed of rocks at the foot of a lofty cliff.

And then other images tumbled into his mind, more words that shocked him, which he tried to restrain with all all his strength. The avowal burst forth unbidden, shouted loudly as if it rejoiced in freedom.

"He will face Dassadec in his dark fortress, and banish him or die—for only thus can the Great Betrayal be redeemed!"

The Iceman's blood turned cold, for he was demanding that quest of himself. The very thought was appalling, irrational beyond belief. Yet there was power here, power that could grant him the strength to vanquish anything! He felt a surge of magic rise within him, and again he cried aloud, this time a brazen, animalistic cry of triumph. Only then did he see the source of that power, as darkness once again yawned below him. The sensation of falling returned, bearing him rapidly through the air, but everywhere he saw only black.

When illumination came, it was merely a lessening of utter dark, revealing an image sketched in gray and black. Rudy saw a mountain, rising from a barren plain; streaks of Darkblood lay like ink across that expanse. The sky glowered, thick with clouds, a leaden force pressing on the fortress peak with palpable weight—but no more of a load than the black stone massif could support.

And then Rudy knew that he had seen into Duloth-Trol, an image that promised dire consequences for any Auramaster. The knowledge should have frightened him, perhaps, but instead it caused him a little thrill of pleasure. He probed farther, sensed only utter blackness . . . but a sensation of warmth spread through that murk. He shuddered, suddenly seized by a wave of pure physical ecstasy. The pleasure brought tears to his eyes, and though he sensed danger, he needed to remain a little longer, to soak up this unspeakable delight.

But no—he had to turn away. Again the swelling pleasure spasmed through him, and he wanted to tumble forward, to immerse himself. A small part of his mind resisted, tugging at his consciousness with irritating persistence. He tried to slap this reluctance away, lacked the willpower to tear himself away from the joy—until crimson eyes menaced him from the fog. Turning, Rudy ran, shouting of the danger, feet pounding along the ground until, gradually, the darkness fell away.

At last he shrugged his shoulders and twisted his head, realizing that he hadn't taken a step—he still stood beside the pool. He staggered and dropped to one knee, more tired than he had ever been after a Scrying session. Awareness returned slowly, first in the form of a terrific thirst. He guzzled from the everpresent Auraflask, shaking his head in an effort to restore alertness.

He then turned to look at Solluel, and cried out in alarm. The sylvan Scrying Master lay slumped on the ground, motionless beside his bench. The Iceman knelt and gingerly turned his teacher over, seeing a trickle of bright blood spill from Solluel's mouth.

— 3 —

Danri recognized the sky, pale with the presence of dawn, and immediately remembered the drackan. He groped for his hammer, found it at his belt, and sat up—or, rather, tried to move. Grunting from the exertion, all he could do was close his hand around the wooden haft.

A deep growl rumbled nearby and the digger saw toothy jaws as a drackan leered down at him, gray-green scales rippling along the supple neck, eyes narrowing atop the broad, flat skull. "Do you try to kill me?" rasped a menacing voice, while a forked tongue slithered between curved fangs.

"No . . ." Danri wanted to argue, to declare that he only defended himself, but his tongue lay like a thick, wet rope in his mouth.

The reptilian head drew smoothly back. Even as he cursed his own helplessness, Danri was surprised by the drackan's small size. Though the jaws were long, the mouth at its base was less than a foot wide. From tales and legends heard throughout his life, he had always envisioned drackans as creatures that could swallow a digger in a single gulp. The shadowy impression of his assailant the night before had done little to dispel that notion.

With a monumental effort the digger sat up and studied the serpent. Though it was easily twenty feet long, half of that was tail—the drackan's body was no more massive than that of a draft horse. Four legs supported the belly just above the ground, and those limbs moved with liquid grace as the wyrm twisted and paced. When that snaky neck extended to the side, Danri saw a crusty shell bulge along the drackan's spine. The growth seemed stiff, cracking and flaking like an old snake-skin and apparently too rigid to allow the drackan's torso free movement. Then the head whipped back to face the digger, the mouth looking very dangerous—jaws parted to reveal rows of sharp, inwardly curving fangs above and below.

The eyes belied the drackan's animal-like appearance, glowing with intelligence that the digger found unsettling. Slitted pupils of gold stared from orbs of indigo, a menacing and potent gaze. Pushing himself upward, Danri stood shakily. He saw Quenidon Daringer just beginning to stir nearby. Shaking his head, the digger willed his alertness to return.

"Why do you think I'd want to kill you?" he demanded, glaring at the drackan. His hand gripped the haft of his hammer, just below the head, but for now he kept the weapon in his belt.

The creature thrust his chest forward belligerently, arching the long neck—yet despite the aggressive manner, Danri sensed a hint of uncertainty in the serpent's bearing. The wyrm growled, a dull rumble that Danri felt in his gut.

"Someone killed Meamare," snarled the drackan accusingly.

"Well, it wasn't—!" The digger's angry retort was cut off by a groan from Quenidon Daringer.

The sylve sat up, wincing as he probed at his ribs. "What did you do to us? How did you knock us out?" he asked conversationally.

"How did you do that?" Danri demanded, remembering with chagrin how swiftly they had been felled.

"That was Aurasleep—and at least I was kind enough to let you live," rumbled the drackan, in a tone that struck the digger as surprisingly petulant.

"Who's Meamare?" asked Quenidon. "And why would we kill her?" Lurching unsteadily, the sylve rose to his feet.

"She was my mother," the drackan said, hanging his head, luminous eyes blinking sadly.

Danri glanced around, suddenly alarmed. "Where are we?"

Quenidon looked along the mountain slope, toward a gap in the ridge at their backs. "There's the notch we climbed to—from the *other* side." He turned to the drackan. "You dragged us quite a distance."

Danri suddenly took full note of the dawnlight, and groaned in dismay. "The army!"

"Gulatch started the troops, I'm sure," declared Quenidon. "But we have to get back there!"

"I have not let you go," hissed the drackan, pouncing ahead of the sylve, coiling body and tail to block any attempt by Quen to leave. Danri, taking a closer look at their surroundings, noticed a wide cave mouth in the cliff wall just above them.

"I have questions to ask," continued the serpent, his voice still low and ominous. "Why have you come here, to Meamare's lair?"

"*You* brought us here, remember?" Danri said sharply.

"But why did you climb the mountain beside her lair?"

"We were with the army on the other side—surely you've noticed?" Quenidon replied.

"I saw many lesser Faerines on the road, but they don't bother me. It was you who climbed to the ridge!" The slitted pupils narrowed, as if the drackan sought to penetrate a veil of deception with his shrewd stare.

"Those are more than lesser Faerines," said the sylve coolly. "An army of the Sleepstealer marches there, led by a Lord Minion of Duloth-Trol! Perhaps *they* killed Meamare."

"No." The drackan blinked finally, leathery lids settling over his golden eyes. But the membranes quickly snapped open to stare once again at Quen. "She was killed by a drackan."

Quenidon's eyes widened slightly, but he quickly masked his surprise. "Where is Meamare?"

"This is her lair. She lies within."

The sylve stepped up to the wide cave mouth, then turned to regard the serpent with a sympathetic expression. "Given the circumstances, I think introductions are in order. My name is Quenidon Daringer, of Spendorial." With the supple dignity of his kind, he bowed gracefully.

"I am called Neambrey," the drackan said in a similarly formal tone. The serpentine neck curled downward in a responding bow.

"And Danri, of Shalemont," declared the stocky digger gruffly, regarding the drackan before turning to Quen. "Now—what about the field army? We've got to get out of here!"

"I'd like to see Meamare, first," the sylve declared. "Is that all right with you, Neambrey?"

Reluctantly, the young drackan led them into the cave, arching his head high as he stepped through the entrance. The digger noticed that the lair could have accommodated something much taller even than the drackan—it was a very sizable shelter. Though the passage twisted around, quickly blocking sight of the entrance, fresh Aura trickled along the walls and floor, providing plenty of light.

Approaching a mound on the smooth floor, the drackan mewled softly; the sadness in the sound was unmistakable. Abruptly, Danri realized that the rise was not bedrock, but the still form of a massive creature. Looking closely, he saw a scaly body *much* larger than Neambrey's. Unlike the smaller serpent, the corpse had a pair of huge, limp wings trailing down from the still shoulders. In the soft illumination of Aura the massive creature looked as though she might be sleeping. The body sprawled with tail extended, rear legs coiled underneath. The mighty wings, so unlike the younger wyrm's useless shell, fanned across the ground. Yet the eyes, large as melons, were open—glazed in death—and the drackan's long, forked tongue draped lifelessly from the corner of the great mouth.

"How . . . how did she die?" asked Quenidon gently, awed by the huge body. Even in death, Meamare was a mighty creature. "These are jaw marks," the sylve observed, answering his own question as he indicated the massive wounds, then compared them to the dead drackan's mouth. "Your mother was killed by the bite of a creature even larger than herself—I suspect you're right about another drackan."

Neambrey's head whipped toward the sylve, jaws spread in a snarling grimace. Black hairs bristled around the creature's neck, expanding into a wide collar. The aggression was so sudden that Quenidon leapt backward, drawing his sword.

"It was Jasaren!" Neambrey hissed in fury. "My *sire*! He's the hugest of the browns, and the only one who knows where this cave is!"

"But why?" asked Quenidon, with a grim look at Danri.

The drackan blinked, twisting his long neck toward the cave mouth. Abruptly he whirled away, trotting along the passage, then bounding from the cave altogether. Quenidon stepped after him as Danri watched, mystified.

"He's down at the stream, drinking," reported the sylve.

"Let's get out of here!" urged Danri in a sharp whisper.

"There's no cover—anywhere we go, he'll be able to see us for a mile," Quen argued.

"What about in here?" Danri asked, inclining his head toward the depths of the huge cave. "There are passages leading past Meamare. Maybe one of them has another way out."

"It's worth a try."

Neambrey remained at the stream, body rigid, tail jutting to the rear, caught in the grip of thirst, as the two Faerines ran back into the cave. The cavern twisted and turned around several bends, but the floor was smooth, the going easy. Aura trickled from grooves in the walls, or slicked cave formations with enough wetness to cast a pearly illumination. For some time the pair trotted along, noticing that the cavern grew narrower as they progressed deeper. They had passed a few side passages, but several minutes went by with no suggestion of an alternate route to the outside. Finally the two warriors stopped to catch their breath, leaning on a glowing spire of Aura-slick rock.

"I don't know if we'll find a way out down here," the sylve muttered, between ragged breaths.

"Should we turn back?" Danri asked the question, then stiffened in alarm as he heard sounds from the cavern behind them. Claws rattled over the floor in racing footsteps. "Neambrey!"

They started to run, sensing the pursuing drackan getting closer. If worst came to worst, Danri hoped they could kill the serpent, but a fight would be a risky proposition—and, worse yet, completely unrelated to the *real* threat that brought them to the Bruxrange.

"Up here!" cried Quen, scrambling along a rising sheet of rock to one side. Looking upward, Danri saw the mouth of a side cavern. Surprisingly, a wash of light spilled like a beacon from the aperture, though the brightness was subtly different from daylight or Auraglow. The sylve reached the passage, lunged through the opening—and halted with a gasp of awe. Danri stumbled behind, dodging around the sylve, and then he, too, froze.

The digger looked past the golden coins scattered across the floor, the eternal candelabrum, the gems that dazzled in rainbow colors from all corners of the treasure room. Danri's eyes, like Quenidon's, were fixed upon the mighty sword that jutted, hilt upward, from a vast pile of coins. The crosspiece was gold, with emeralds set at the end of the handgrip. The blade shed the milky glow that filled this chamber and spilled into the cavern beyond, causing Danri's mind to whirl with memories of legends, wondrous tales of the eternal grace of the gods.

"Is it—?" The digger didn't dare speak the word that came to his mind in an onrush of hope.

"It is," Quenidon declared soberly. "We've found an Artifact, thought lost forever. This can only be Lordsmiter, the sword of the gods."

— 4 —

A lone brutox clumped along the new cliff at the edge of the mainland, wondering where the army had gone. For months the minion had guided a team of bovars hauling a huge vat of Darkblood over the wasted expanse of Dalethica. Plodding along under the irresistible pull of instinctive orders, it had drawn closer to Lanbrij, marching day and night.

The brute urged the team forward, following the rutted tracks of the army's progress, bearing his precious and sustaining cargo of Darkblood to support the minion advance. But now those ruts ended at the top of this precipice, and straight below surged a dizzying expanse of water. Half a mile away rose another cliff, with the protecting wall and the city of Lanbrij beyond.

But where was the army?

A few kroaks ambled across the cracked and broken ground, but the brutox didn't even try to get an explanation from them. Instead, it stomped back and forth in growing displeasure, clapping its hands together in showers of angry sparks. Terrions soared low overhead, wailing and crying, but the stupid creatures could not make themselves understood to the brutox.

The lump of black caught the monster's eye. It sat like a chip of coal among the granite of the bedrock, gleaming with a slick, perfect darkness that compelled the brute's attention. The monster reached down, picked up the smooth object—and it felt the compulsion, the command coming from within the thing that was definitely *not* a rock.

Knowing what to do now, the brutox returned to its huge wagon. Climbing up to the driver's bench, the creature scrambled onto the top of the cylindrical iron vat. It twisted off the cover, revealing the thick inky liquid sloshing within.

Finally the brutox took the lump it had found and lowered it, slowly, into the Darkblood. When the thing was fully immersed, the brute let go, and it sank to the bottom of the vat. The minion returned to its bench, cracked the whip, and urged the stupid bovars through a long, gradual turn. Then they started pulling, rolling the great vat across the ground. The brutox felt its mission as a new compulsion, a task to be performed unquestioningly.

Though the journey was long and arduous, and it retraced the steps of its past months' endeavor, the brutox reversed course, willingly returning to Agath-Trol.

NINETEEN

Storms from the Mountain

A tiny voice can make the loudest noise if it
speaks patiently, with wisdom, instead of hastily
and in spite.
—SONGS OF AURIANTH

— 1 —

Neambrey filled the entrance to the treasure room, rearing
above Quenidon and Danri. The drackan hissed, jaws spread
wide, bristles jutting fiercely from his mane. He stabbed his
head at the digger, then whipped around to snap at the sylve.

Quenidon sprang onto the mound of coins, skidding beside
the mighty sword; with a single gesture he seized the hilt and
pulled the weapon free, sending a glittering cascade of gold
across the chamber. The light of the sword pulsed brighter,
forcing Danri to shield his eyes, while the drackan blinked
and reared backward, hissing with wide-open jaws, growling
deeply, menacing.

The sylve raised the sword, holding the hilt in both hands.
His eyes were wide with wonder, but as they came to rest on
the drackan they became hard, accusatory.

"Do you know what this *is*?"

"It is not for you!" the drackan growled.

"Are you *blind*?" Danri said, losing his temper. Hammer upraised, he stepped toward the rearing serpent. "Have you seen the army invading my homeland and yours? This sword gives us a means of fighting that evil! It belongs to all Faerine!"

"It is the *Treasure*! You shall not take it!"

"My friend is right." Quenidon's voice was level now, soothing. "The Sleepstealer's minions are your enemies as much as ours. This blade, Lordsmiter, will aid us to face that evil."

"That is not a drackan concern!" Neambrey spat stubbornly. "You are thieves—and I shall kill you!"

"I fear you are the one who will die," the sylve replied in the same even tone, stepping away from the mound of coins. "Though I would hate to kill you."

"I'm ready to get on with it!" Danri declared—though he remembered the Aurasleep, and watched those powerful jaws warily.

Neambrey's head lashed and the digger threw himself backward, falling onto the coins and barely evading the snapping fangs. Danri rolled to the side, coming up ready to swing. He nodded to Quen, who feinted an attack on the other side of the chamber, and closed in on the drackan. Backing into the entryway, Neambrey lowered his head and shifted the golden eyes between the digger and the sylve. Suddenly he blinked, the focus of those eyes wavering.

"Go! Kill him!" whispered Danri to the sylve, as Neambrey's head bobbed in the digger's direction.

"Wait!" Quenidon held up a hand, advancing cautiously with the great sword clenched in his other fist. "Look."

The drackan's vision had glazed over, the lustrous veneer of golden pupils paling to a corroded bronze. Slowly Neambrey backed from the chamber, looking back and forth along the length of the great cavern beyond. Danri and Quen advanced side by side to the entry, watching as the drackan sniffed the air.

Abruptly Neambrey turned and bounded along the cavern floor, heading deeper into the cave. Danri sniffed, felt the cool moistness on his face even as he heard distant trickling.

"Aura. He's thirsty again," the digger muttered in amazement—and gratitude.

"Let's hope he wants another long drink," Quenidon said
seriously.

"I don't want to wait around and find out," Danri replied.
In another instant the two Faerines were running along the
great cavern, bearing Lordsmiter away from the young
drackan—and hopefully back to an army that had marched
on without them.

— 2 —

Half a day later, Danri and Quenidon reached a tiny notch on
the ridge above the Darkenheight Road. "Good shortcut,"
muttered the digger, as they discovered the field army just
below.

By following the valley of Meamare's cave, and cutting
through a shallow streambed for evasion, they had worked
across the inside of a wide curve followed by the road, seeing
no sign of Neambrey after departing the lair. Now, Danri
looked across the familiar valley and its war-blackened roadway, observing both armies. The minions stretched from directly below them up the winding vale—a thick column of
kroaks and brutox much wider than the road, and extending
at least for the few miles that they could see. The Faerines
were slightly farther down, and, more importantly, the army
was no longer marching, but had drawn into a line.

"Looks like Gulatch is planning to make a stand there,"
Danri noted grimly. "Can't blame him—the troops have to
be just about finished." The weariness of the Faerine warriors
was clearly visible. The companies formed ragged blocks
along the crest of a low moraine. The ridge was steep-sided,
and extended most of the way across the valley; Quenidon
murmured approval of Gulatch's defensive terrain. In the narrower gap between the ridge and the stream, where the ground
was flat and unobstructed, the company of gigants had taken
up a blocking position.

"Let's get down there right away," Quen urged.

"Aye-uh," Danri agreed. They trotted through the gap,
then raced down the slope. Quickly the digger found the shel-

ter of a low ravine that angled toward the field army, and they followed this, skidding and slipping much of the way, to the bottom of the ridge.

"Keep an eye out for terrions," Danri reminded Quenidon. They reached the end of the ravine on the valley floor, loping along at the foot of the field army's moraine. They were greeted at first by gapes of astonishment, then cheers as the Faerines recognized their commanders. At the same time, a roar rose from the minions, and the enemy army launched its attack.

"Lord Danri! Up here! Come on!"

Danri recognized Pembroak's voice and turned toward the steep moraine. With Quenidon following, the digger scrambled to the top of the gravelly ridge at the midpoint of the line, between the sylves and diggers. Warriors cheered and shouted around them, but the two leaders focused on the mass of charging minions.

"There!" Quenidon's keen eyes found the snake-headed Lord Minion. The monstrosity lurched forward, slightly behind the first rank of his troops. Surging masses of kroaks charged to Phalthak's sides, though the minions gave their master a wide berth.

Again the Faerines met the onslaught with arrows, but the barrage lacked the density of earlier volleys—too many sylvan archers had fallen, and those who remained couldn't afford to exhaust their missiles.

The first kroaks reached the foot of the moraine and scrambled upward, only to fall back from the steel of Faerine warriors. More and more of the monsters swept behind, clawing on hands and knees to reach the defenders, howling and snarling furiously. Danri reeled to the putrid scent of Darkblood rising from the howling mob, but he fought with fury and determination. The ridgetop position proved solid, and nowhere did the kroaks and brutox breach the defenders' line.

Deep drumbeats marked the defense of the gigants, a cadence merging into the din of battle. The warriors of Gulatch held firm against large numbers of kroaks, the battle chief wading among the minions, bashing them out of the way. A huge brutox roared and charged, but Gulatch crushed the creature to the ground in a shower of sparks. The big warrior bellowed into the minions' faces, and more gigants threw themselves into the fight, howling and roaring, smashing minions right and left. The screams of wounded monsters mingled with a gruesome spray of Darkblood as gigant axes hacked and clubs bashed. Minions turned and fled, kroaks darting past the whips of the brutox in mad determination to escape.

Quenidon stood at the moraine crest, slashing with Lordsmiter, slaying any minion that came within reach of the blade. The elite warriors of the Royal House fought beside him, golden helmets marking a solid section of the front. A pile of monstrous troops bled at the base of the moraine before Quen's feet, and the sylve clasped the Artifact in both hands, striking with lightning-quick stabs, parrying with instinctive accuracy. Though the blade was stained with black minion blood, the pearly light gleamed through, shedding a halo of white around the sylvan warrior.

The press of the attack lessened for a minute, but as Danri looked across the front, he saw the barrel-shaped body of Lord Minion Phalthak lurching along. Snakes seethed and hissed, darting this way and that, while the grotesque monster rolled from feet to knuckles. Kroaks bellowed a lusty challenge, rallying behind the horrific figure, and even the mighty gigants were helpless to combat the Fang of Dassadec.

"There!" cried the digger, but Quenidon had already seen the danger. The sylve backed out of the line, with Danri racing after.

The moraine petered out a short distance from the stream, and the minions now concentrated their attack in the gap of flat ground. Gulatch stood in the center, club blackened and slick, corpses scattered in a broad circle around his widely spread feet. Other gigants held to his right and left, each defending an area as big as the reach of his weapon, the towering Faerines standing like fence posts in Danri's eyes.

Yet now Phalthak advanced through a gap that opened, as if by magic, in the ranks of his monstrous troops. Several of the serpentine heads bristled stiffly in the air, glittering eyes fixed upon Gulatch. Quenidon and Danri reached the gigant chieftain, the sylve shouting to get their ally's attention. "Stand back—let me face the beast with Lordsmiter!"

Growling, the gigant chieftain refused, but when he cocked his head and saw the glowing blade, his eyes widened in astonishment. The sylve stepped in front and Gulatch made no objection, moving back to stand with Danri just behind Quen.

The monstrosity rolled forward, rearing out of the dust of battle. The bulbous body loomed as high as a gigant's, and no less than a dozen serpents emerged from the oozing pustule of its neck. Snakes of red, green, yellow, black, and orange—as well as others patterned in stripes or spots and diamonds—lashed and whipped, hissing, staring menacingly at the sylve. A fat, viperous head on a body as thick as Danri's thigh drooped over Phalthak's chest, fixing glowing red eyes on Quenidon; another whiplike strand of viridescent green strained higher than all the rest, curling forward at the top to peer down at the Faerine warrior's head.

A crimson snake lashed out like a striking cobra—but the pearly blade of the sword snicked in an even faster crosscut, slicing the member off a foot from the end. The ruby head fell with a thud as the Lord Minion reared back, other heads writhing and squirming. Somehow the grotesque body emitted a howling wail, a sound of mingled pain and fury.

"Look out!" Danri shouted, as the severed head on the ground suddenly sprang toward Queindon's knee. The sylve twisted frantically, bringing the blade down in a whirlwind of precise cuts, leaving the remnant torn and shredded. Even then the digger kept a wary eye on the remains, to be sure that they showed no signs of movement.

Phalthak backed farther away, heads bobbing warily, myriad eyes fixed on that deadly blade. Around him the minion army was poised, waiting, holding its attack in abeyance for the moment. Again came that wail, and Danri had a sudden premonition: The sound was some kind of signal. He looked at his enemy, and saw that several of the Lord Minion's heads were watching the sky.

His own eyes rose to follow, sensing something moving among the clouds of the high valley. Danri squinted and stared, his apprehension swiftly growing into fear.

— 3 —

Neambrey stalked along the bed of the narrow ravine, creeping through the shadows, climbing up the lofty ridge. The

Treasure! It was gone, and the young drackan had lost it. After much searching, Neambrey was forced to admit that the thieves had completely, utterly deceived him. By the time he had slaked his thirst, they had gone from the cave. The faint spoor of their footsteps had led him to a stream of pure Aura, which had further distracted him. Now the trace of scent was gone, blown away by the breeze—and, to make matters worse, Neambrey's wings felt more tightly constrained, more cramped and stiff than ever.

Remembering one important thing about the two lesser Faerines, the drackan finally scaled the ridge near Meamare's lair. The captives had been very concerned about the Darkenheight Road, and had wanted to return to their companions there. Neambrey decided to lope along the crest above that road, seeking the thieves and the Treasure.

Hooking his hard claws into tiny holds, the drackan lifted himself up to the rocky divide at the top of the ridge. Here he moved easily, seeing the valley of Meamare's cave to his left, the Darkenheight Road to his right. Clearly a scourge had moved along that highway—the ground was black, and a palpable stench, like carrion tainted with vile poison, reeked from the blighted landscape. In an hour he covered many miles. To his left wilderness reigned in a tangle of rocky bluffs and well-watered, forested swales, while the long, featureless valley of the road continued on the other side.

A shadow flickered over Neambrey's head and he twisted his neck, shocked to see a wide-winged horror plunging toward the narrow ridge-crest. A brown drackan! With a squawk, the youngster pounced down the steep slope, skidding uncontrollably. The brown wyrm dove, and some instinct halted Neambrey, steering him headlong into a large boulder. The shrieking brown turned its head as it hurtled past. Neambrey saw the gaping jaws, feared an icy blast of Aurafrost.

Instead, the drackan belched a hissing cloud of putrid steam! The gas billowed against the youngster's rock, burning his eyes and nose. He darted backward to avoid the expanding vapors, realizing that the boulder had saved his life. Cringing, Neambrey watched the brown drackan wing along the valley, straining with visible urgency to build up speed—and leaving its young target apparently forgotten.

Neambrey continued on, staying near the crest of the ridge

but now taking care not to silhouette himself. After an hour he came around a broad curve and cast a cautious look into the valley on the other side. The minion horde darkened the flat ground before him. Neambrey squinted into the distance, seeing gigants and smaller warriors in a long line. Something glimmered in the center of the defenders' formation and Neambrey's eyes narrowed—the glow of the Treasure was distinctive, even when it was too far away to see clearly.

But then the drackan was distracted by movement much closer to himself, as winged shadows flickered across the ground. He froze, gawking upward in terror as a rank of brown drackans flew over his head, and banked toward the strife in the valley below.

— 4 —

"Look!" hissed Quenidon Daringer, pointing toward the sky. Danri followed his friend's gesture, his heart like ice.

The drackans came from up the valley, a dozen huge, bronze-colored serpents—most of them larger even than the massive Meamare. Distant at first, the flying monsters swept closer with astonishing speed, diving toward the ground, sweeping along the Darkenheight Road. The brown serpents winged toward the moraine in eerie silence, while the Faerine warriors—still arrayed along that ridge—clutched their weapons against the fresh onslaught.

The lead drackan extended his neck before reaching the Faerine line, expelling a cloud of gas that sizzled into the defenders, searing flesh and igniting leather. Warriors screamed as they died, burned alive by the hissing steam. More of the wyrms spewed searing death, blasting gaps in the army, blistering skin and flesh among helpless Faerines. The cries of the wounded rang piteously through the air, and the overpowering stench of cooked meat had a gruesome and ominous taint.

Then the drackans swept on, climbing, spiraling around for another pass—and leaving hundreds of slain warriors to mark the swaths of deadly steam. The stink of the gas, acrid and sulphurous, still lingered as the minions bellowed. Hundreds of bloodthirsty invaders scrambled up the moraine, spilling through the breaches left by the killing breath.

"Placers—I need your arrows! *Now!*" Danri bellowed, as a pair of brown drackans glided through a half circle, flying low above the stream, banking sharply toward the Faerines, who broke and ran from the crest of the moraine.

A dozen crossbows chucked their bolts, and several of the silver darts struck the lead drackan, drawing an angry bellow. The serpent veered away, straining for altitude, jaws gaping open. The digger captain grimaced, dreading a repeat of the searing explosion that had moments earlier raked the diggers and sylves.

But now the drackans flew on, staying above the reach of the painful arrows—and out of range to deliver that scorching, hissing breath. Three more browns swept into an attacking dive, and Danri flinched instinctively as the big wings gusted downward, nearly striking Faerines when the drackans lurched away. But there was no eruption of killing breath— the only blast was the wind of the creatures' passage.

Kroaks and brutox swarmed over the moraine and flooded onward, while drackans spiraled in the air, content for now that the defending line had been broken. As the field army fled, Danri lumbered along with the retreat, once again despairing of any chance at victory. The deaths of brave Faerines like Kianna, even the Artifact of the gods, didn't seem to be enough to turn the awful tide.

The gap between the armies soon expanded to more than a mile, but the Faerines continued to stumble with weariness. Days of battle and flight had sapped the endurance of even the hardiest warriors, and many of the weak only continued by leaning on the shoulder or arm of a sturdier companion. Twissels floated among them, offering sips from flasks of Aura; the troops swilled the precious liquid without even slowing the pace of their retreat.

"Take as much as you want" offered Garic Hoorkin, buzzing up to eye level as he extended a drink to Danri and Quenidon. "We found a fresh spring back there, and filled all the waterskins. There was a hot spring too, but we got the cold Aura."

"Back where?" asked the digger, who hadn't noticed the place.

"There—oh, now the drackans are going there!" Indignantly the twissel pointed toward a deep notch in the side of the valley. Danri saw several of the brown drackans dip out of their soaring formation, settle to ground before the notch, and creep into the shadows.

"Are you thinking what I am?" Danri asked grimly, turning to Quenidon, watching as more and more of the browns gathered outside the narrow aperture guarding the Auraspring.

"Are they getting the power of the killing steam back? That's my best guess," Quenidon agreed, shaking his head.

"Scatter the companies," Danri suggested. "We'll get all the archers ready, and make sure we don't give them a concentrated target."

"Good tactic," the sylve agreed. They saw to the dispersal of the columns, ordering each warrior to march with space between him and his comrades. It was a grim precaution but, if the drackans struck again, they wouldn't be able to catch scores or hundreds of Faerines in a single, steaming blast.

When the serpents took to the air again, bellies distended by Aura, they flew long, lazy spirals over the minion army, showing no inclination to attack, unsupported, into the hail of arrows and quarrels that would have met them. Yet the minions came on, plodding tirelessly and inexorably in their continued onslaught.

And still, the field army could do nothing but continue its flight.

— 5 —

Rudy told me later that time seemed to stand still for him—he found it hard to believe the true duration of his stay beside the Scrying Pool, in the company of Larrial Solluel. During those days and weeks, he says—and I believed him—neither one of them slept.

For this full month, no one saw the Master Scryer or the Man of Three Waters. I shared a palace room with Dara and Anjell, while Awnro, Darret, and Kestrel returned to the galleon, staying aboard the vessel that reared like a swan over the ducks of the sylvan watercraft. Dara spent much time on her journal of our travels, so Anjell and I explored the city together.

Rumors floated around us. We learned that this was the longest conclave of any young Auramaster—typically, three or four days passed before the newly anointed one emerged. Even the most capable masters had finished the ritual in eight or nine days. Yet as the second and third weeks passed, the sylves came to regard us with steadily growing awe.

Kerri of Shalemont showed us around the splendid city, and we were as much a novelty to the Faerines as they to us. Yet there was little gaiety now among these usually festive people. We heard that an army of minions marched toward the lowlands of Faerine—and Spendorial. Anjell and I both knew that this boded ill for Danri, but we did our best to reassure the increasingly distraught diggermaid.

Refugees arrived, sartors from foothill villages that had been ravaged, twissels bringing reports of constant retreat. It was one of these messengers who told us that Kianna Kyswillis had been slain. The horrifying news cast a pall over each of us, but was especially distressing to Anjell, who lapsed into despondency. Only the company of Darret seemed to offer any hope of consolation. It was not until later that I learned the gruesome manner of the courageous twissel's passing; fortunately, Anjell never heard that tale.

The rest of the army was in desperate condition as well. The Faerine warriors, it was said, marched without rest, sustained only by Aura. Any who fell behind were doomed, while the survivors continued toward the lowlands. As news of the retreat spread, increasing numbers of sylves walked to the Stonebridge, there to wait with worried eyes turned south.

Eventually we saw clouds of smoke on the horizon, and later even heard sounds of distant battle—each a delaying skirmish swiftly resolved, before the smoke clouds advanced again. The wrack drew closer and the smoke billowed higher, ultimately approaching the forests on the far side of Auraloch.

But twenty-nine days after closeting themselves in the garden of the Scrying Pool—and hours before that battle would reach us—Larrial Solluel and Rudgar Appenfell emerged from the Palace of Time.

From: *Recollections*, by Lady Raine of the Three Waters

TWENTY

Auramaster

Through the blessing of love is the power of
magic granted to all.
—SONGS OF AURIANTH

— 1 —

Raine's eyes were bright as she embraced Rudy—but she
quickly stepped back, wrinkling her brow in concern.
"What's wrong?" She stared into his eyes, seeking some sign
of change. "What happened to you in there?"

Accompanied by a stiff and weakened Larrial Solluel, Rudy
emerged from the Palace of Time into bright sunlight, preceded and followed by dozens of sylvan attendants. Raine had
rushed forward from the crowd, and now the Iceman saw
Dara and Awnro waving from the midst of many sylves.

Rudy pulled Raine tightly against his chest, ignoring the
gathered Faerines and humans, the clear sky—which he saw
now for the first time in more than four weeks—and the slight
form of the disfigured Scrying Master.

"What is it?—you're afraid!" Raine whispered, as Rudy's
body tensed.

"No! It's not that—I'm not afraid. I'm confused," the Ice-man replied evasively.

The look on Raine's face showed that she was not convinced, but neither did she press the issue. Rudy held her in the curve of a long arm, turning after Larrial Solluel. Only then did he notice that the gathered sylves had formed a circle around them, expectantly silent.

"What's going on?" he asked the Scrying Master.

"It is customary, when a young sylve is taken into the palace for the Testing, that his family and neighbors will gather upon news of his emergence—to hear of the results and, hopefully, to celebrate."

"Did that happen? Did *I* get tested?" Rudy asked, dumbfounded.

Larrial's mouth twisted into a gentle smile. "You could say that. Many sylves are curious, for we have remained in the chamber far longer than even the most accomplished new Auramaster." The Master of the Scrying Pool turned to face the circle of sylves, clearing his throat formally. Rudy saw looks of curiosity and wonder, and in some cases hints of suspicion or hostility.

"I bring you the first human Auramaster in the history of the Watershed," declared the patriarch, his tone suddenly strong, words booming above the gathered throng. Many sylves gasped, while others gaped at Rudy as if he were some kind of freak.

Perhaps I am, he thought bitterly, even as he waited for Larrial's next words.

"The Iceman of Halverica passed through all the lobes of the pool, even into realms that I myself have never probed. Not only did he exceed the reach of my own power—but when his explorations brought me into danger, it was the human's power, his healing magic, that restored *me*."

"No! What kind of blasphemy is this?" demanded a gaunt sylve, stepping from the crowd to glare at Rudy. "You grow too old for your duties, Solluel—you have allowed the human to deceive you!"

"We shall see, Remarran," said the sage tolerantly. "Let us go to the shore of the lake. Summon the other Auramasters—and see that the coals are fired!"

Mystified, Rudy tried to ask what they were doing, but his

tutor simply smiled pleasantly and escorted him through the winding, flower-lined streets of Spendorial. Despite his mangled, eyeless visage, Solluel delighted in the blossoms, announcing roses, cinnabloom, and lilac as they passed the fragrant gardens, his tutorial steady enough to prevent the Iceman from asking any questions.

"Have you beheld the wonder of the Rainbow Fountain?" asked the patriarch abruptly.

"When I reached Spendorial I was escorted directly to the palace."

"Oh, of course—those were my instructions, as you understand. We didn't have time to allow you a more extended welcome to Faerine."

"But we have time *now*?" the Iceman inquired wryly.

"For this, yes. By the way, notice the autumn honeysuckle there, the sweetness and color. The sun strikes it, does it not?"

"Yes," Rudy replied, amazed at the brilliance of the huge, golden-flowered bush. Long branches draped low, winking and sparkling in the midday sun almost as if weighted with drops of gilded metal.

"I thought so—the full fragrance is only released under direct rays of the sun," replied the Auramaster, nodding at the confirmation.

Rudy was conscious of Raine beside him, and swiftly he took her hand, an unexpected lump of emotion rising into his throat. His life—his *human* life, he realized with a shudder—was coming back to him in its fullness and love.

"Where's Anjell—and Kestrel and Darret?" he asked thickly.

"Anjell's down at the docks. She and Darret have been getting to know the sylvan sailors—and their lake. Kestrel's likely aboard the *Black Condor*; he's been practicing maneuvers with the sylvan boats."

"The lake." Rudy remembered the images from the Scrying Pool—the horde of minions streaming out of the mountains, spreading through the foothills and driving toward this city and its glorious lake.

"Kestrel has helped the sylves to arm a number of their longboats with trebuchets. They've sailed through some maneuvers, the galyon like a goose with a flock of goslings. Still, they might be useful.''

''They will,'' the Iceman declared; he realized by the tightening of Raine's hand that he had spoken with disconcerting conviction. He turned to her. ''I have a lot to tell you . . . travels through the pool, you might say. I know that Takian made it back to Carillonn, that he and Bristyn are well. Also, the city and its bridges still stand.''

Raine gripped his hand even more firmly, conveying her relief at the good news as they emerged from the forested lane into a grassy expanse. The waters of the lake sparkled, setting off a rainbow hue of sails as small Faerine craft scudded about in the light breeze. The *Black Condor* stood at anchor, some distance up the shore beside the tangle of elegant docks.

''Uncle Rudy!'' Anjell's delighted cry drew the Iceman's eyes back to the shore. Trailing her golden braids, his niece raced across the field. Darret loped along, trying to appear nonchalant as he dogged the girl's footsteps.

''I heard you came out of the palace—and I knew you would come here, to the fountain! Is it true what they're saying about you? We're *so* proud! Did you get hungry—they said you didn't ever eat any—''

''Wait!'' Rudy laughed, pulling his niece tight, then waving to Dara as she came along behind the children. ''By Aurianth, it's good to see you. But *what* did you hear about me? And how did you know I'd come to the fountain?''

''How's a person supposed to answer when you ask so many questions together?'' demanded Anjell petulantly. ''But this is where all the Auramasters come after their tests. Didn't you know that?''

''No—but I'm not surprised *you* did,'' he replied, still chuckling.

''Ahem—'' Solluel interrupted softly, shifting his weight awkwardly from foot to foot. The Scrying Master looked uncomfortable for the first time in Rudy's experience. ''It will be some time before the other masters assemble. This might be a good time for you to talk. Why don't we meet at the fountain in a little while?''

''That's fine.'' As Solluel hurried away, Rudy abruptly understood that the sylve had found the humans' strong emotions discomforting.

"Did you hear about the war—that it's come here, too?" Dara asked solemnly.

"I saw," Rudy replied, describing briefly some of the visions of the Scrying Pool. He gave them the good news about Takian and Bristyn. "Danri and Quenidon are still retreating this way with the remnants of the field army."

"Did you hear . . . about Kianna?" asked Anjell, her eyes filling with tears.

"Yes, little one, I did," the Iceman admitted, hugging her and biting back his own tears as she wept softly against him.

"We gonna be ready for de scumdogs!" Darret proclaimed, pounding a fist into his palm and looking across the deceptively peaceful lake. Rudy saw clouds of smoke hanging over the horizon of foothills, and he knew that the minions drew closer with each passing hour. He said little to elaborate on his terse descriptions of the minion campaigns in Dalethica and Faerine, but even the children understood how desperate the situation was.

About the other visions, hints of destinies too dark to contemplate, he said nothing. The image suggesting that Rudy must ultimately confront the Nameless One himself, that Raine would die at the foot of some massive cliff, were things no man should be given to see. He did describe the threat of the drackans, the implacable, killing blasts of steam rending huge gaps in the Faerine ranks. His own awe at the courage of these warriors tightened his voice, and anger hardened his eyes when he spoke of the relentless pursuit. "Aura is the only thing that keeps them going—for a fortnight they've been marching day and night down the Darkenheight Road. Human soldiers would have collapsed days ago—and been massacred."

"How long until they reach the city?" Raine asked, her jaw set grimly.

"At the rate they're marching, a few days at the most."

"I think it's time," Anjell said. "Here comes that poor sylve with those scars on his face."

"Larrial Solluel is not such a poor sylve as you might imagine," Rudy said gently. "He's about the wisest person I've ever met."

"Oh," Anjell replied meekly, curtsying as the Scrying Master reached them.

"The other masters have gathered at the fountain. Will you join us now?"

The companions passed through a ring of tall evergreens, where the scent of pine pressed close and the heavy limbs provided an effective windscreen. The area within was perhaps fifty paces across; it included a fringe of soft grass and a round pool of Aura. The pond, ringed with a border of mossy rocks, was smaller than the Scrying Pool. Rudy assumed that this was the fountain, though he saw no sign of a nozzle, spout, or anything similar within the clear waters. Rainbow colors dappled the surface, swirling gently without rippling the smoothness of the placid pool.

Several dozen sylves stood in a ring around the pool. Each of these wore a white robe similar to Rudy's and Solluel's, and the Iceman assumed that these were the Auramasters. Trying to look relaxed and confident, he ignored the eyes sweeping over him in aloof, skeptical inspection. Several of the sylves were female, as handsome and serene as their male counterparts. Attendants arrived, bearing heavy iron pots containing beds of glowing coals. The braziers, one for each Auramaster, were placed at the edge of the pool, and the robed sylves—and Rudy—advanced to stand before them. Someone handed the Iceman a pair of whiplike wire wands, and he saw that each of the other masters also received the tools. Raine, Anjell, and the Iceman's other companions remained near the trees, together with a number of sylves who had apparently entered the circle to watch.

"Ah, Your Highness—I am delighted you could make it!" Larrial Solluel's tone *was* delighted, though Rudy was mystified as to how the blind Scrying Master had observed the arrival of the tall newcomer. The regal sylve's hair was the yellow of fine-spun gold; his robe seemed to be made of woven silver wire, though it was as fluid as any silken gauze. At least a dozen finely clad sylves, both male and female, stood attentively behind the autocratic figure.

"This is Mussrik Daringer, our Royal Scion—titular chief of Spendorial, and an Auramaster in his own right. Your Highness, Rudgar Appenfell, the Man of Three Waters."

The tall sylve bowed regally. His narrow face, with the

arching eyebrows, reminded Rudy of Quenidon. "Welcome to our realm," declared the scion. "Know, human, that the remarkable journey you commence has captured the hopes of all Faerine."

"Thank you, Your Highness," Rudy replied. "I only seek to follow the course destiny has laid for me."

"Admirable ambition. Should the rumors of your mastery prove true, the Royal House shall insure that you have all the aid we can provide."

With these gracious words, the sylvan princeling and his entourage gathered in the shadows of the encircling pines. Larrial Solluel, meanwhile, advanced to the water's edge and began to chant in a language that Rudy had never heard before—but that he understood as if it had been born in his own heart.

> *"Mistress of Magic, Aurianth,*
> *May it please you to grant*
> *Your power to the masters,*
> *See us, bless us,*
> *Find us worthy*
> *to fly."*

Rudy turned expectantly to the pool. The surface of Aura roiled and bubbled, swirling into a growing vortex. Abruptly the flow turned inward, liquid seething into a violent, rolling boil. Yet there was no steam, and the Iceman knew that if he knelt down he would find the liquid cool and soothing to the touch. This turbulence was created by an unseen source of magic, and still bubbled upward with growing power.

The waters spiraled faster, forming a cone of bright, foaming Aura in the center of the pool. Rising gently, then gathering force and climbing higher, the cone became a pillar, which to Rudy's eyes was like some beautiful, enchanted tree trunk sprouting upward. Suddenly the top of the column exploded, arcing out from the pool, spreading in a curtain of spray toward the gathered masters. As the waters plunged toward the grassy shore they formed separate streams of Aura, fluted spouts of the magical water that poured into the mouths of the iron braziers.

Steam billowed upward from each of the coal-filled kettles,

and now the Auramasters concentrated on their tasks. Each of the robed sylves passed the wire wands through the air, above the mouth of the steaming kettle, and as the white vapor billowed through the rods it took on a solid form, leashed like a giant, gentle balloon to the tether held by the Auramaster.

Rudy was taken by surprise when the Aura spilled into his brazier, and the first explosion of steam hissed away before he could raise his wire tools. Quickly he hoisted the unfamiliar wands, embracing the spume, feeling Aura tug against his pressure. He pulled back and found that the cloud was indeed leashed to the slender rods. Concentrating on gathering every bit of the rising steam, the Iceman took no notice of the other Auramasters. Instead, he caught at the wisps of gas like a weaver pulling threads into a tapestry.

Aura spilled into the brazier in a steady stream, and—though it seemed to Rudy that the coals must long since have been doused—the cloud of steam continued to billow upward. Beads of sweat rose on the Iceman's forehead as, for the first time, he felt the heat generated by the growing enchantment. Despite the discomfort, he held his position, waving the wands back and forth, gathering the billowing Aura into an ever-expanding cloud.

And still the water of magic gushed inward, and the Auracloud of the Iceman grew. Rudy's arms tired, yet he would not lower the wands. Nor did he look at the other Auramasters, so intent was he on the working of his own magic. Gradually, however, he became aware of a pastoral stillness, a silence so serene that it seemed as though he might have been transported to some place far away. With a tremendous effort, he turned to regard Solluel, who had woven his Aura at the brazier next to Rudy's.

The Scrying Master was no longer holding his wands, and his brazier had long ago grown cool. Now his scarred visage was turned toward Rudy, and as the Iceman remembered the ancient sylve's sensitivity to the power of Aura, he suspected that Solluel could see very well the column of enchanted steam still rising from the human's brazier.

Rudy's eyes moved beyond, around the ring of gathered masters, and he realized that all of them had ceased to work their magic. Several Auraclouds hovered overhead, though most of them had been released to drift away when the caster's enchantments had concluded.

Something made Rudy look straight up, and he was shocked by what he saw: The Auraclouds of the sylves were dwarfed by the massive, billowing sky-ship that had gathered over the Iceman's head, spreading over much of the little park, extending over the pond. Rudy reeled with a sense of giddy elation, a touch of awe, and even a glimmer of fear. Drifting on the tether of steam that still rose from the brazier, the huge shape floated above the tops of the pine trees, looming above the other Auraclouds like the *Black Condor* towered above the Faerine longboats.

— 2 —

Neambrey pushed through tangles of brush, waded swamps that sloshed wetly against his belly, and finally worked his way through a series of broken, rock-lined cuts until, by late afternoon, he had found a small and secluded valley. He shuddered, remembering his view of the battle. The theft of the Treasure was awful, but he had begun to wonder if the invasion of the Sleepstealer might not even be worse.

The drackan's thirst was a raw craving in his throat, and though he had drunk many times during the day, it had been hours since he found an ample source of Aura. Now, however, tall and densely needled rustwoods surrounded him, and a pure pool glistened beneath the shady canopy. Some distance away he saw the outlines of a dark entrance against the cliff wall, and he suspected he would even find a cave for his evening's shelter. Trembling from fright and weariness, the young drackan knelt beside the pool and lapped at the Aura, feeling the revitalizing power of Faerine flow through his exhausted sinews.

"Who drinks my pool?"

The demand, made in a deep, bass voice, startled the young drackan so much that he leapt into the air, trying to bound across the pool—but only succeeded in reaching the middle. With a splash he disappeared, coming up spluttering and terrified.

"Out! Get out of there!"

Again came the rumbling, commanding words, and Neambrey hastened to splash his way to the bank, where he shook the droplets from his grayish scales in a rainbow shower. Then, still shivering, he looked around for the speaker.

"Who are you?" bellowed the disembodied voice—but now Neambrey saw a huge shape of the same dark green as the rustwood needles, emerging from around a trunk. The youngster stared into the massive golden eyes of an adult green drackan.

"It is I, Neambrey," he declared weakly. "Greetings, Honored One."

"Hmmph—at least someone taught you manners," grunted the elder. His serpentine neck was fully in view now, and he advanced to reveal his brawny green shoulders and forequarters.

"It was Meamare," the young drackan replied.

"Eh? Meamare?"

"She taught me manners," Neambrey added, thinking that the elder didn't understand. "She is—was—my mother."

"Was? Do you tell me that Meamare is no more?"

"She was killed in her dormancy—by a brown drackan!" the youngster replied in a rush.

"Now see here! I can tolerate a young newtling coming here, even sipping from my well. I don't like that you swam in there, but that, too, I can forgive. But if you think that telling stories about our cousins from the heights—"

"It's not a story!" Neambrey protested. "The brown drackans are helping the Sleepstealer in his war!"

"What?" The adult drackan seemed taken aback. Slowly he blinked his leathery eyelids, masking those golden orbs for several seconds before once again fixing Neambrey with that perceptive, wise gaze. "I do believe that you are telling the truth—at least, such as you believe it to be. But Meamare . . . I find it hard to accept."

"You knew my mother?"

"Aye, as a fledgling not much greater than yourself. I am Verdagon, and I wooed her, and would have won—save for this hulking brown that didn't know enough to stay among his own kind."

"That was Jasaren, my sire. I think it was he who killed Meamare!"

"Your own sire?" Verdagon was skeptical, but not entirely disbelieving. "Even among the browns such an act would be an abomination—though I see by your color that you are a hybrid."

Neambrey was too concerned to feel his usual self-consciousness about his color. "The Lord Minion made the brown drackans join him, and now they're trying to take over all Faerine!"

"This is alarming, to be sure," Verdagon said, trying hard to remain patient. "Now, why don't you just slow down, newtling, and tell me what happened. . . ."

— 3 —

Another digger fell and Danri didn't have the strength to help him. Supporting a limping sylve on his shoulder, grimacing from the pain in his own feet and arms, the digger commander could only mutter a silent prayer for the fellow, hoping he would find the wherewithal to climb to his feet before the stalkers reached him. Danri's hope was not a likely eventuality—the long retreat had sapped these once-hearty Faerines, reducing them to walking skeletons, subsisting on Aura alone.

It had been nearly a fortnight since any of these warriors had slept for more than a few minutes at a time, enjoyed substantial food, or absorbed even a minute's warmth from a fire. Life had become a despairing montage of retreat, brief rests, and bitter skirmishes when stalkers, terrions, or brown drackans closed in, prodding the Faerines back to their increasingly ragged flight.

A day—or two or three days—ago the retreating warriors had spilled from the mouth of their foothill valley, streaming into the woodlands and meadows of lowland Faerine. The minion pursuit remained relentless, and still the survivors of the field army trudged wearily toward Spendorial. Danri had no idea how many of his comrades had collapsed from weariness, abandoning hope, mired in the depths of fatigue and despair. Every warrior who was able to aid a comrade did so, so that most of them shambled along in pairs, the weaker leaning on the shoulders of the stronger. Yet the stronger had grown few as the days went by, and now there were none left to aid the faltering.

Quenidon Daringer joined Danri in the digger's customary position near the rear of the file. Here the roadway meandered through a region of pastoral woods, and for most of this day the minion pursuers had remained out of sight. Yet there was no doubt in Danri's mind—or in any other Faerine's—that they were back there, plodding tirelessly, cruelly delighted by the increasingly frequent victims who lay, utterly exhausted, in their path.

"That's the sartor glade—edge of the Suderwild," Quenidon said, indicating tall elm trees in a hollow beside the road. "It's usually a two days' walk from Spendorial, but at the rate we're going we might reach the Stonebridge by tomorrow morning."

The Stonebridge. That span had come to symbolize life, hope, and freedom to the discouraged Faerines. Here, where the mighty Aurun spilled into Auraloch, where the river was too wide to accommodate a rainbow bridge, the span of stone and timber arched across deep water. The bridge at Spendorial was a solid structure, with stone footings and massive timber beams. The surface was wide enough for two carts to pass in opposite directions—or to allow a column of ten or twelve warriors abreast to march to the promise of safety on the far side. Danri remembered it, too, as the last place he had seen Kerri, and the place where she had promised to meet him—though he desperately hoped that she wouldn't be there. Never would he have imagined that the field army would reach the bridge in the midst of a running battle.

"I wonder how many of us'll still be walkin' by then," Danri questioned dourly.

"Pass the word about how close we are—it may be that a little touch of hope will be enough to get the men through the rest of the day and night."

The digger nodded, realizing that he himself was energized by the knowledge that they at last had a goal that offered some possibility of safety. "Hear that?" he asked the sylve who leaned on his shoulder. The warrior grunted, barely conscious. How long the river might delay the minion advance Danri couldn't even guess, but the thought of a few hours' respite from this relentless pursuit brought a small bounce back to his step—at least he no longer scuffed each heavy boot through the dust of the roadway.

"My lord—let me help." Suddenly Pembroak was there, taking the weight of the exhausted sylve from Danri's shoulder. The digger commander tripped, almost falling, and suddenly realized how fatigued he, himself, had become.

"Thanks," he grunted, looking at the youngster with gratitude. Pembroak, like everyone else, was gaunt and hollow-eyed. His thin beard couldn't conceal the sunken cheeks, the bony outlines of his skull. Still, when he met his commander's gaze, Pembroak's eyes flashed with determination, his jaw jutting belligerently. With warriors like him, Danri thought, they still had a chance.

He noticed more warriors helping, and it gradually dawned on him that there were sartors among the field army, steadily increasing numbers of the horned Faerines. He watched several more sartors come out of the woods, taking the burdens off the shoulders of weary diggers, pacing along with the field army's retreat.

That last afternoon of the march passed like so many of the previous days, in a haze of fatigue and dust. Twissels came through the ranks, offering the sips of Aura that sustained the troops, and Danri greedily drank his share. But after all this time the enchanted liquid could barely quench his thirst—and had little appreciable effect on his consuming fatigue or gnawing hunger.

Marching through the night, the Faerines plodded under the light of the stars and a waxing moon. Though the Auralight was less obvious than it had been in the treeless Bruxrange, the warriors had no difficulty with the darkness. Indeed, because the minions lacked the benefit of enchanted illumination, the retreating field army was able to slightly increase the gap between itself and the pursuing horde.

By dawn, they smelled fresh water and fish, and the warriors knew that the Auraloch could not be far. The road continued to wind through groves of tall, leafy trees, though occasionally enough of a gap appeared for the Faerines to see blue water glinting off to the right. Looking back, Danri saw several stalkers lope into sight. The speedy minion scouts remained a mile or so away, but advanced with visible urgency, suggesting they knew their quarry was on the verge of escape.

"Look out—to the sky!" came the alarm, and immediately the diggers, gigants, and sylves turned their eyes—and weapons—toward the heavens.

A long, coppery shape glided past, partially obscured by the trees. The brown drackan soared near the leafy boughs, but high enough to avoid the danger of arrows from the troops on the ground. Danri growled in impotent rage, hefting his hammer, wishing he could drive it into the draconic head, smash it between the large, slitted eyes.

The huge wyrm made no move to attack, gliding instead with maddening arrogance above the ragged column. Danri turned his fury into strength, resolving grimly to reach the river, cross to safety—and then mount a campaign to obliterate these minions and the treacherous Faerine serpents who were their allies. He watched the drackan as it flapped monstrous wings, gaining speed.

Other shadows flickered past as several more of the browns soared behind their leader. The digger watched tensely, remembering the sudden, roaring attacks, the blasts of killing steam, that had punctuated the retreat on too many occasions to count. Hundreds of Faerines had been burned to death, and dozens more had been clutched in monstrous claws, lofted into the air and dropped amid horrified comrades.

These serpents showed no immediate inclination to attack, though Danri didn't let his vigilance lapse. Still, the drackans—he counted twelve of them by the time the last of the creatures flew over—seemed to have some different purpose today. They flew with uncharacteristic speed in a straight line, trailing the leader unerringly . . .

Toward Spendorial. Would the drackans fly ahead as the first wave of an attack on the sylvan city? Such an onslaught would be horrifying, and could inflict terrible damage. Danri immediately feared for Kerri, but even so, the digger wasn't convinced that this was their intent. During the course of the retreat the big serpents had shown a healthy respect for sylvan archers—surely they wouldn't fly in an unsupported attack against the whole city!

Abruptly the digger had another, more frightening thought—or, at least, a more realistic one. At the same time, the tail end of the Faerine column came around the side of a low hill, revealing the river valley and all of Auraloch before them. The leading end of the field army already advanced across the grassy plain before the bank, approaching the solid span of the Stonebridge—and the long barrier of the Aurun. Thankfully, few Faerines stood on the far side of the bridge; perhaps the city centurions had held back the crowd. To the right was the crystalline purity of the great lake, the shore running roughly parallel to the road. The domes and spires of Spendorial rose from the woodland a few miles beyond the river's mouth—and to all the Faerines that halcyon image offered rest, food, comfort, and safety.

Simultaneously, Danri saw that his worst fear had been realized: The brown drackans dove swiftly toward the bank of the river. A groan of dismay rose as the exhausted warriors sensed the monsters' intent. The leading brown settled to ground at the near end of the Stonebridge. Other drackans landed on the middle of the span, or on the river bank on the far side, while a trio of the huge wyrms dropped into the road, turning to spew steaming blasts of gas into the faces of the Faerines leading the army column. Danri grimaced in helpless fury at the sight of those killing gusts, watching dozens of sylves perish. The survivors fell back across the grassy meadow as the trio of drackans followed the lethal blasts by pouncing aggressively, feinting an attack but ceasing pursuit immediately.

At the bridge the largest brown, a male, reached forward with powerful forepaws, seizing a supporting timber set into the bank. With a wrenching twist he ripped the massive post out of the ground, leaving the bridge sagging as he tossed the beam into the river. Other drackans tore at the supports on the next piling. One of the big serpents abruptly leapt into the air from the middle of the bridge, flapping its wings furiously as the span drooped toward the placid waters of the river.

Another timber came free, ripped by the huge male, and then a whole stretch of bridge tumbled heavily into the water, vanishing beneath the surface. The drackans continued to attack the span with shrieks of cruel glee, like vultures swarming around carrion. More and more of the bridge fell, until only the stone pillars of the footings stood, four useless blocks jutting from the waters.

A roar of triumph came from the minions to the rear, and Danri didn't need to look back to see what was happening—

the trembling in the ground under his threadbare boots told him plenty. The horde charged, the tromp of their footsteps reverberating like drumbeats. The field army no longer had any options: The Faerines were trapped against the deep river and lakeshore, and the enemy surged forward in massive attack.

"Faerines!" Quenidon's cry came over the din of the charge. "We fight here—for the goddess and the Watershed!"

The glow of Lordsmiter rose from the midst of the troops, and cheers rippled outward. Somehow the gaunt shadows of warriors once again raised weapons, shouted in the face of their attackers. Gigants bellowed, diggers hooted and jeered, and sylves whistled and shouted shrill encouragement. More than a few sartors charged along the river bank, joining the line with brayed challenges while the golden helms of the Royal House sylves gleamed on both sides of Quenidon Daringer.

And then the cries and shouts grew to a crescendo of fury; across field and woodland and rocky shore the Faerines stood ready to face kroak and brutox. To the last warrior they knew that there would be no retreat from here—there was only victory, or death.

— 4 —

Twelve bovars clomped stolidly along, trundling the sloshing vat across a land ravaged by war. The brutox wagon driver cracked his whip over the leathery skin of the massive beasts, maintaining a pace through day and night over long, solitary weeks. Other minions passed the wagon, but these servants of the Sleepstealer all marched in the opposite direction— toward battles yet to rage in Dalethica. Only this lone brute pressed against that tide, intuitively sensing a purpose and a destination.

Occasionally kroaks gathered, blocking the wagon, demanding a taste of the sustaining stuff in the great iron vat. The brutox whipped these pests away or, if the kroaks proved unusually stubborn, climbed down from the wagon to kill several of the lesser minions.

Terrions once settled toward the blood vat, screeching of their own hunger, and the brutox stood atop the great wagon and cracked his whip at the sky, finally forcing the fliers to depart in search of easier sustenance. And when stalkers leaped from the ditches beside the road, scrambling up the sides of the vat with quick and stealthy movements, the brutox sprang to the defense, slaying three of the shape-changing minions with quick chops of its heavy sword.

The brutox took little notice as it passed into the desert called the Dry Basin—perhaps because so much of Dalethica had come to resemble the parched wasteland dividing this portion of the human realms from Duloth-Trol. Through this desert trundled the bovars and their precious cargo. The brutox gave little thought to the blackened, coal-like chunk it had placed in the vat; instead, it urged the beasts along with no thought of why it traveled thus.

For more weeks the blackened expanse of Duloth-Trol passed beneath the wagon's huge, stone wheels. Few minions bothered the brutox here, since most of the Sleepstealer's servants were engaged in one of the two great invasions. Yet the brute did not know loneliness, or boredom. Instead it maintained its implacable purpose, now rolling eastward again.

When the towering black mountain took shape across the horizon, sprawling like a great, blunt cone reaching toward the sky—then did the brutox begin to tremble with suppressed excitement. The emotion might have been pleasurable anticipation or terror; certainly the reaction mingled aspects of both, and the minion itself would not have been able to differentiate the two.

It was humbling and gratifying at the same time, thought the brute, to know that it bore a treasure that would be welcomed in Agath-Trol—where, in the deepest bowels of that hulking fortress, the Sleepstealer himself awaited . . .

As the remains of Nicodareus came home.

TWENTY-ONE

Ships On Sky and Water

The power of Auraflight represents the pinnacle
of magical accomplishment—a treasure as
precious as any Artifact of the gods.
—SONGS OF AURIANTH

— 1 —

Captain Direfang stood in his customary position astride the
Dreadcloud's battery deck. The brutox faced into the wind,
relishing the feel of hot air across his skin, the stench of
Darkblood in his nostrils. Above, the mass of the mighty sky-
ship seethed in the air like a sentient being, anxious to run.

"Soon, my glorious steed . . . soon," murmured the brutox,
touching the claws of his right hand to his left, relishing the
explosive release of sparks dripping onto tarry vapor. Six columns of seething bloodsmoke rose from the circular deck, and
each could spit a deadly bolt from the lower surface of the
Dreadcloud. In the stern of the great ship, Direfang knew,
kroaks labored at the three mighty sturmvaults—the gaseous
boilers of Darkblood that propelled the ship into even the
strongest wind. Stalkers slithered and hissed through the hull,
carrying messages, insuring that orders were obeyed, keeping

watch from the upper towers. A score of terrions, too, nested among the billowing summits of the *Dreadcloud*'s triple superstructure. Elsewhere, more than a hundred brutox and a thousand kroaks stood ready as shock troops. They could be lowered to the ground via whirlwinds of Darkblood, spiraling downward from the cloud's belly; alternately, the minions stood ready to defend the ship against any boarder who might somehow hurl himself into the sky.

For the first time in a millennium, Direfang would take the *Dreadcloud* beyond the barrier of the Watershed, striking at targets worthy of this death-dealing sky-ship. The brutox raised his clenched fist, allowing a cascade of sparks to shower audibly from the tips of his stublike claws, and the scent of ozone wafted into the wind as he cocked his head to the side.

"The fueling is completed, my captain," announced a stalker, bowing low and speaking with the throaty lisp of its kind.

"Bring the sturmvaults to full pressure—we will need all of our power to push through the pass."

"Aye, master!" The craven minion bobbed its long, snaky head.

"Remember: Do not spare your chambers—speed is of the essence," declared Direfang, a deeper thrum to his voice underlying the consequences of disobedience.

"Your Greatness may be certain that we sacrifice all considerations against the need to make haste."

"This pleases me. After we reach the pass, power will be diverted forward. I feel certain that we shall have important work for the battery."

The stalker chuckled, a sound that cackled with wet, slurping humor. "The gunners are eager to prove their skill."

"They shall have ample opportunity."

Direfang looked forward again, the slight tilt of his head a gesture of dismissal. Bowing deeply, the stalker departed, passing from the battery deck through a dark hole that gaped, momentarily, in the hull of tarcloud.

With a rumbling shiver, the sky-ship broke free from its gaseous tether, gradually picking up speed as it plunged into a gap between looming heights, the black slopes flanking the Duloth-Trol side of Darkenheight Pass floating serenely by.

Captain Direfang directed the *Dreadcloud*'s course from the bow, preferring the vantage of the deck where he could see the ground before them. Of course, on those occasions when the sky-ship carried a Lord Minion, that powerful being typically usurped this vantage, forcing Direfang to seek the isolation of the high bridge. But for now, he was his own—and this powerful ship's—master. He avoided thinking about the orders that would compel him, upon the conclusion of this voyage, to once again kowtow to one of the Sleepstealer's pets.

Approaching Darkenheight, the *Dreadcloud* rasped against the stone cliffs to right and left, tearing pieces of black vapor away, but the seething sturmvaults kept the great ship plowing ahead, pushing ever higher. With shrieks of elemental protest, sections of cliff cracked and tumbled, scraped by the hull; in the ship's wake, dozens of landslides cascaded from the heights to either side of the steep-walled pass.

Shapes moved along a nearby crest, and with recognition came alarm—Guardians! The creatures moved with deceptive speed. Reaching the lip of the precipice as the great ship moved past, a dozen or more of them sprang onto the *Dreadcloud*.

"Strike them—hold them at bay!" cried the captain. Dozens of brutox charged from the hull, sparking and slashing, chopping into the Guardians with great, black-bladed swords. Direfang cursed as one of the stony attackers knocked two brutox overboard with a quick succession of blows, then grunted in pleasure when a third minion cut one of the Guardian's legs off, kicking the wounded creature after the doomed brutox.

"Captain—more Guardians below!" came the hissed alert from a stalker posted nearby. Direfang saw a score of the creatures in the pass, moving to climb the cliffs and join the attack.

"Use the forward batteries—kill them!" cried the brutox.

Lightning crackled downward, a barrage of six bolts shattering bedrock, singeing the air with the pungent smell of vaporized stone. The first impact blew several Guardians to pieces. Again the battery spit its lethal barrage, blasting through the pass, scattering rocks and stones, raising a blanket of dust that masked all observation. Strong winds quickly cleared the air, and Direfang could see no evidence of life on the ground.

Several Guardians still survived on the *Dreadcloud*, but now dozens of brutox and a hundred kroaks attacked furiously. Terrions joined the skirmish against the boarding party, and Direfang chuckled as the last of the Guardians plunged to its doom. He'd lost a score of brutox, dozens of kroaks, and even a few terrions, but he was well content with the outcome.

Abruptly the ship lurched to a stop, jammed between two enclosing pillars at the summit of the pass. Direfang grimaced against the vista of white snow and Aura spreading beyond, but the brutox knew his goal lay before him. "More power—feed the sturmvaults! Give them all the Darkblood they will consume!" he barked, as a stalker instantly materialized for orders.

Within minutes the hull thrummed to a massive outburst of power. Slowly the great cloud scraped forward, ripping away at the sides of the pass, tearing massive chunks from the sky-ship. A hundred kroaks toppled, screaming, as the hull protecting their assault company was shredded. Direfang felt the tremor, understood the force necessary to propel the great craft through this obstacle. Finally the sky-ship picked up speed, freed to descend the winding route of the Darkenheight valley.

Smoky vapor coiled away from the bulkhead, revealing a leering stalker. The minion bowed as Direfang allowed the sparks from his talons to form a regal cloak around himself.

"I am pleased to report, Captain, that we have passed the Watershed," gurgled the stalker.

"Splendid. Now, set a course—at high speed—for the army of Lord Minion Phalthak."

— 2 —

Neambrey spilled his story to Verdagon in a whirl of description—of brown drackans with breath of killing steam, minions by the tens of thousands marching through Darkenheight, lesser Faerines massacred or fleeing. Only once did the young drackan pause to drink from the Aurapool, and Verdagon waited patiently for Neambrey to lap up as much of the liquid as he desired.

"How long has the Time been upon you?" inquired the elder, when the younger serpent finally raised his drooling mouth from the pool.

"Only a little while," replied Neambrey, realizing with a start that, though he'd been through the most momentous events of his life, all of them had occurred within the last moon cycle.

"I see. Since the Time of Thirsting invariably takes a year or more to run its course, you are in no danger as yet. Now, go on with your story."

Verdagon continued to listen patiently as Neambrey described the brown drackans, and their support of the minion army. "Jasaren led the way—it was he who started the attack!"

"That is the most dire occurence of all," the elder noted grimly. "For it is written: 'The drackans of brown may rise or fall upon darkness, and night may blanket the world.' It is a dire thing warned by this prophecy, one which I convinced myself would never come to be. It would seem I was wrong."

"I fear so, Honored One. I counted twelve browns together with the army—and we know that army came from Duloth-Trol."

"Who, tell me, is this 'we'?" inquired Verdagon archly.

"The digger and the sylve—I told you about them. I thought at first that they might have helped kill Meamare."

"But then you *conversed* with them?"

"We shared the same enemy, after all!" declared the young drackan. He had not yet mentioned the missing Treasure, and still awaited an auspicious time to introduce that distressing piece of news.

"After all? After nothing!" retorted the big drackan, his tone sharp. "We drackans are to have nothing to do with the rest of Faerine—surely you know that! It is written: 'Let the lofty one become low, and he shall be no longer lofty.' We live, we watch and observe and remember. But we do not give diggers the benefit of our wisdom and opinions!"

"Surely you and the other green drackans will help fight the minions?" Neambrey argued. "They'll lay waste to all Faerine if we don't stop them!"

"Oh, they'll be stopped—they always have been before. But it won't be by me, or by any other green drackan!"

"*Why?*" The young drackan's question was a plaintive cry.

"Because . . ." The elder wyrm hesitated, then harrumphed and continued. "Because we drackans fought the minions once, and many of our ancestors gave their lives to send them back through Darkenheight! And when the drackans pursued the minions back to Duloth-Trol, the High Guardians set upon us, slaying many more! Oh, no, newtling—this is not a matter for the drackans. I am surprised at the browns, and if Jasaren comes here, I shall fight him—but it is not in our nature to go looking for strife."

"You don't understand! If we—"

"My dear fledgling, I understand all too well! It is you who are exhibiting ignorance. For it is written: 'As long as the sacred Treasure of the gods is secured, then shall the drackans remain aloof from the world.' "

"It is?" Neambrey asked in dismay.

"The Treasure was entrusted to our ancestors after the War of Worldbirth—it has been our task for millennia to guard it from those who would steal it for their own ends."

Neambrey was disconcerted by this revelation. It seemed a particularly bad time to mention Lordsmiter. "But suppose the Treasure was used not for selfish reasons, but to stop the Sleepstealer? Wouldn't that be all right?" The young drackan posed the question earnestly.

Verdagon chuckled, a deep and rasping sound that did nothing to ease Neambrey's apprehension. "I fear you display the naiveté of youth," the old drackan said condescendingly. "For it is written: 'Let he who has lived for ten centuries wait ten centuries more, and then he shall know the birth of wisdom.' "

Neambrey had never imagined that there were so many writings among drackankind. "Why is it such a mistake to wonder if the Treasure could be used for good?" he pressed.

"Because you do not know the nature of lesser mortals, be they Faerine or human. Give one of them a thing such as Lordsmiter and he will begin to feel invulnerable. Next thing you know he's telling everyone else what to do, and then he tries to make himself some kind of king or something. No, nothing but trouble could come of that!"

"But what if Faerines *find* the Treasure, and then use it in the war?"

"How could they find the Treasure?—it's . . ." For the first time Verdagon's confident manner wavered. "It *was* guarded by Meamare, was it not? But you have told me that she is dead, slain by a brown. Tell me, newtling—" A baleful, slitted eyeball glared into Neambrey's face. The young drackan blinked and gulped, swallowing a large lump down the length of his neck.

"Do you know something about the Treasure? Did the brown drackans take Lordsmiter?"

"No! I mean, I—no, they didn't."

"But the Treasure is missing?" pressed Verdagon.

"Not missing . . . no," replied the young drackan with a firm shake of his head.

"What, then?" Verdagon huffed impatiently. "Is the Treasure still safe in Meamare's cave?"

"No . . . some Faerines have Lordsmiter. I think they're using it to fight the minions."

The big green drackan exhaled very slowly, and for such a long time that Neambrey began to fear for the elder's breath. Finally Verdagon inhaled, with equal deliberation.

"So . . . a legacy of millennia, wasted, shattered, withered away like dust. A trust placed in us by the gods themselves, traditions that have lasted longer than the clans of the Elder Drackans, blighted by twin acts of treachery."

"*Twin* acts?" asked Neambrey nervously. "But the slaying of Meamare—"

"Is but one crime! It took the devious, morally corrupt Faerines to complete the second perfidy. Diggers, I'll bet it was! Thus it is written: 'Never trust a digger.' Perhaps the thieving wretches were in league with Jasaren himself!"

"What? No! I found them, felled them with Aurasleep. Then I dragged—" The young drackan bit his tongue, but it was too late. Neambrey desperately wished that he could, turtlelike, draw in his neck and conceal his head somewhere deep within a hard shell.

"You took the thieves to your mother's lair?" Verdagon's supple neck sagged, as if a great weight had just been laid upon his head.

"Well, I thought maybe they could tell me why she was

killed,'' Neambrey explained, wishing more than ever that he
had working wings—he wanted to be somewhere, *anywhere*,
that was out of this glowering green drackan's sight. ''It was
the sylve who took Lordsmiter,'' he offered helpfully.

''Surely even a newtling such as yourself could overpower
a few lesser Faerines!'' sputtered Verdagon. ''Or did they
trick you? Ensorcel you, perhaps? Those sylves are treacherous, as bad as diggers! Did they magic you?''

''Well, no. I . . . I was thirsty.''

Verdagon sighed long and painfully, nodding as he imagined the scenario. ''And Lordsmiter is . . . *gone*?'' he finally
rasped out.

''Not gone—being used!'' Neambrey retorted, his timidity
fading slightly. After all, the worst was over—wasn't it?
''Used like it was supposed to be used—used for what it was
made for!''

''I can't expect a wyrmling such as yourself to understand
the consequences of what you've done,'' Verdagon said
grimly. ''But there are many of your elders who *will* understand, and who—I'm afraid—may not be so tolerant, nor so
forgiving, as myself.''

''M-many?'' squeaked Neambrey, suddenly feeling very
timid indeed. Verdagon himself seemed neither tolerant nor
forgiving—what would the other elders be like? The young
drackan felt a powerful thirst, but struggled to postpone the
craving for a moment, wondering what Verdagon meant.

Apparently Neambrey would soon know, for the elder
spoke again, ominously. ''I shall summon the Emerald Council to the Grotto. They will decide your fate. May Aurianth
have mercy upon you.''

— 3 —

Hundreds of kroaks surged into view, charging around the
bend of the forest road, pouring over the crest of the hill in
a wave as relentless as any tidal surge. Danri and the rearguard companies had just started down the slope into the river
valley, where the rest of the field army was strung out over
a mile of roadway. The bridge abutments jutted upward from
the riverbed, mocking the efforts of the fleeing Faerines.

"Forward—down the hill!" cried Danri. The roar of attacking minions was a physical assault, but he forced himself to concentrate. The wind bore the scent of the clean lake, and he shuddered with the premonition that it might be the last pleasant odor he inhaled.

The Faerine warriors needed no persuasion. Weariness forgotten for the moment, they streamed toward the broad lakeside meadow near the mouth of the river. Danri saw a blaze of light beside the roadway, where Quenidon Daringer raised Lordsmiter—a rallying point for the field army. Even as the diggers raced toward the commander's position, sylves and gigants formed a line to either side, weapons upraised, preparing to meet the minions for a last battle.

"There—diggers form to the left!" Quenidon's command reached Danri, and the commander from Shalemont veered his lumbering warriors to the side. Sylves fired volleys of arrows, and the deadly showers slowed the minion pursuit. Aggressive cries rose from a new quarter, and Danri was heartened to see another large contingent of sartors rush along the river bank, barking and braying challenges. The goat-footed Faerines formed a solid bulwark at the right end of the arcing line, wielding picks and swords against the minions who drew close to the river bank.

Where that stream met the lakeshore Gulatch bellowed, leading gigants toward the brown drackans around the shattered Stonebridge. Some of the warriors threw rocks at the serpents, while the others brandished clubs, swords, or axes in vengeful fury. But the drackans extended their necks and hooted derisively, dodging the rocks easily. With a great flapping of wings amid the echoes of that wicked, derisive laughter, the creatures took to the air, gliding along the course of the river until they soared over the Auraloch itself.

Quenidon Daringer shouted orders, still forming the ragged troops into the semblance of a battle line. The golden helms of his Royal House sylves gleamed in the center of the line, and these disciplined warriors formed a strong buffer for the rest of the army. The terrain was smooth—here the field army would find neither ditch nor moraine to disrupt the minion charge. A narrow peninsula jutted into the lake behind them, but the spit of land was too small to hold more than a portion of the Faerines—and in any event, it was vulnerable to attack where it joined the shore.

Danri cast one futile look along the lakeshore, but Spendorial was obscured by misty puffs of cloud. Just as well, he thought grimly—he hated the notion that Kerri might watch the battle in which he gave up his life. And in all honesty, he couldn't see any other outcome. The field army would stand bravely, but how long could these weary troops heft their weapons against the teeming, tireless foe?

Before he pulled his eyes away from the deceptively placid vista of the lake, Danri was startled to see a large ship emerge from the misty distance. Huge sails billowed as the vessel, greater than any watercraft Danri had ever seen, sailed toward the river's mouth. Behind came a flotilla of smaller craft, sylvan longboats gliding across the water.

A flicker of hope rose as Danri realized that, just possibly, some of the warriors might be carried to safety if they could hold out until the boats reached them. That brief optimism died as a roar rose from the minions, and the Sleepstealer's warriors, howling fanatically, charged the entire front of the field army. The ground shook beneath the tromp of monstrous feet, and the air rang with the thunderous din of their onrush.

The Faerines had barely completed their line before the first of the lumbering kroaks smashed into them. Diggers and sylves went down in the clash, and Danri himself was knocked off his feet. He scrambled to his knees, blocking a brutox sword with his shield, hammer lashing out from behind the protective barrier to crush the hip and then the skull of the sparking minion. The digger fought desperately, slaying kroaks, smashing the skull of another brutox—then dodging away from the putrid, burning pyre of the creature's corpse.

A kroak lunged toward his blind side, but the minion fell, pierced by a steel-headed spear. The sartor Wattli, who had been so aggressive in the Suderwild camp, now leered at Danri, horned forehead wrinkled into a fierce scowl. Spinning on his hoofed feet, Wattli jabbed the spear into another kroak, sending the minion lurching out of the way.

The line of battle shifted chaotically—once Danri heard minions behind him; then he rushed forward in a counterattack spearheaded by Gulatch. Pembroak charged at Danri's side, wielding his sword with the grim confidence of a veteran warrior. For a time the two diggers fought back to back, felling kroaks that rushed them four or five at a time. Finally Gulatch bashed a gap into the press, and Danri and Pembroak fell back to the relative safety of the Faerine lines.

The din of shrieks grew as more minions charged into the fray. Darkblood was a pungent stink in the air, and the field army was forced grimly, inevitably, toward the marshy river bank and lakeshore. The sun beat down unmercifully, the normally constant autumn breeze fading to nothing, and as Danri's boots slipped on the blood-slick grass the cloying stink of the monsters threatened to suffocate him. Feeling a cloud shadow, the digger was grateful for respite, however brief, from the scorching sun. Sweat stung his eyes and soaked his beard, and his laboring lungs rasped desperately for air.

Nearby Danri saw Quenidon, with Lordsmiter gleaming in his hands, standing in the center of the Faerine position. The sylve was flanked by the warriors of Spendorial's Royal House, and now they faced a spearhead of minions led by many brutox. Lordsmiter struck as the army commander made an immovable bulwark, and in moments the fresh attack was broken, with wounded brutox limping back from the deadly sylves.

The air from the lake smelled moist and deceptively pleasant, but the capricious breeze brought uglier scents too—steaming guts, and that powerful stench of Darkblood. When Danri looked up, he saw the regular outlines of the lone cloud, the tight oblong of whiteness that was surprisingly, unnaturally solid and compact. He wondered wildly if it might be some impossibly massive Auracloud, but he tossed that speculation aside—the vaporous shape was ten or twenty times larger than any enchanted sky-ship he had ever seen.

A fresh wave of kroaks surged, and Danri fought to protect himself against black iron blades. Striking with his hammer, sometimes reversing the weapon to puncture an armored foe with the pick, the digger killed minions before him, right and left, even behind. He met countless blows with his shield, forcing fatigue, weakness, and despair into some distant portion of his mind. Danri's murderous fury frightened even the normally stolid kroaks, so that the brutox overseers had to lash their charges, cursing and bullying them into the reach of the digger's deadly hammer—and still they fell, killed or crippled by the merciless hammer.

Finally three brutox attacked, rushing the stocky digger together. Danri fell back before the rush, thankful as several sylvan arrows whistled over his head to drop the first of the brutes. The digger ducked to the side, bashing the second brutox in the knee, then backhanding the pick of his hammer into the flank of the third minion. Monstrous howls set Danri's ears to ringing as the two survivors whirled, slashing, trailing thick clouds of sparks. Ducking, using the sparks as concealment, Danri rolled between the minions and sprang to his feet with hammer raised. Leaping high, he bashed the weapon against the back of the nearest brutox's skull, dropping the beast with a ground-shaking thud, momentarily blocking the other brutox while stumbling back. Before that minion could pursue, more sylvan arrows hissed, and the monster fell dead.

Surprised, Danri realized that the missiles had come from a very high vantage. Looking upward, he gaped at the spectacle of the massive cloud, which drifted to one side of the battle. Dozens of sylvan archers lined the edge of the cloudship, showering razor-headed shafts into the minion hordes. The shadow of the massive Auracloud covered much of the minion army, and as Danri watched in amazement the whiteness of the enchanted sky-ship darkened to a forbidding gray. Soon rain sifted downward, cooling showers drenching the minions.

Growling, kroaks hunched their heads, trying to get out from beneath the vexing cloud. Many Faerines were also caught in the shower, and they shouted and rejoiced as more enemy troops scattered, falling back from the fight. Danri looked to the lake, hope rising as he saw the four-masted ship tacking closer. Many scores of sylvan longboats also skittered forward, outdistancing the mighty vessel as they raced toward the embattled shore.

"Fall back—form columns!" cried Quenidon Daringer from the center of the army. The command was echoed by sergeants and captains along the ranks, all taking advantage of the temporary respite. Faerine warriors streamed onto the peninsula. Scrub trees clustered in parts of the spit of land, but the ground was dry—and a small company of warriors could hold the neck where the peninsula met the shoreline while the boats drew up onto smooth gravel beaches. Already columns gathered, weary warriors stepping toward the beaches and the waiting boats.

As more minions streamed away, a long rope uncoiled from the rim of the sky-ship, and a slender figure slid down the line. Danri thought this was a sylve until the person dropped from the rope, landing in an easy crouch, then stood and extended an arm to the digger.

"Raine!" Danri spluttered in utter astonishment. "You—you're here!"

In the next instant the digger's jaw dropped and he gaped up at the cloud, an expression of awe creeping across his face. "Our Iceman . . . ?"

Raine nodded, smiling gently. "He's spent the last month in the Palace of Time. But we'll tell stories later—your field army has a problem, I believe."

"Aye-uh." Shrewdly, Danri looked toward the lake, at the flotilla that had grown to a fleet. "There must be a hundred boats out there . . ."

"The rain will only last for another ten minutes or so—why don't you start getting your troops aboard?"

— 4 —

Quenidon's fatigue fell away, banished by fierce exuberance—the field army would survive! The first boats pulled up to the gravel beach, and willing Faerines loaded their weakest comrades into the watercraft. Raindrops still spattered across the sylve's face and he raised his head, exulting in the wetness that had driven the minions away from the field army. Lordsmiter had done much killing today, and now the sylve held the weapon out, let the moisture wash black blood from the blade.

Phalthak had made no appearance during the battle. Indeed, the Lord Minion had avoided all skirmishes since his first encounter with the Artifact. Either fear of the weapon held him at bay or, more likely, the continuing minion victories had rendered his interference unnecessary. Quen noted, too, that the drackans had not returned after savaging the bridge, though the serpents had no doubt gone to consume more hot

Aura, and the army would have to deal with that menace soon
enough. The sylve squinted watchfully into the southern skies,
where a dark overcast, centered around a huge thunderhead,
obscured the far-off view of the mountains themselves; there
was no sign of any drackan in the visible distance.

"Line up there! C'mon, you Faerines—step lively!" he
shouted, as more sylves started onto the narrow peninsula.
The field army's front continued to shrink as more columns
lined up on the beaches. Quen and the sylves of the Royal
House still stood on the shoreline, screening against a renewed minion advance.

Behind, a steady stream of longboats now pulled up to the
beach, each taking a dozen or more weary sylves and diggers
aboard. Warriors stood in the shallow water, helping weaker
comrades. The troops standing by when a boat was filled
pushed it free, and then the oarsman—often with help from
his stronger passengers—strained for the gleaming domes and
towers of Spendorial, just a few miles away. Many hundreds
had been taken away, but a huge number waited patiently for
the returning boats. The longboat of the galyon, meanwhile,
was busy hauling two or three gigants at a time out to the
ship.

The raindrops ceased abruptly. The Auraship remained
overhead, though it had shrunk from its first massive expanse,
and correspondingly the dull gray of the raincloud had light-
ened almost to white. With the cessation of rain, kroaks crept
forward again, urged on by the whips of the brutox. The monstrous warriors halted a hundred paces or more from the Faerines, shouting and stomping furiously, and Quen suspected
they were building up to another attack. The sylve fingered
the hilt of Lordsmiter, ready to fight—yet once again conscious of the sacred Treasure.

Danri came up to the sylvan commander, and Quenidon
blinked in astonishment as he saw Raine beside the digger.
Quickly swallowing his astonishment, Quen gave her a solid
hug. "I won't ask all my questions now," he said with an
easy smile, gesturing to the mud and gore around them. "But
welcome to my homeland."

Embracing him tightly, Raine kissed him on the cheek.
"Come back to the city—we'll tell our tales there."

"Aye-uh! Let's get moving! Half of the army's loaded

up—you're next!" Danri urged, reaching out as if he would seize Quenidon Daringer by the arm.

The sylve shook his head, staring into the digger's eyes, trying to make him understand. "Keep them moving toward the boats—I'm going to hold with my rearguard."

The lead kroaks clomped forward at a measured pace, marching to within fifty paces of the Faerines, but placing their hobnailed boots with care, as if frightened of stepping in a pool of water or Aura. Meanwhile, the keels of another dozen longboats scraped the lakebed beside the beach. "Let's go," repeated Danri, with fervor. "They're not going to charge in the next few minutes."

"Not now—but if we leave here, they will." Quenidon pointed toward the growing mass of kroaks. Some stomped their feet with growing impatience; all brandished weapons, barking and snapping at the Faerines.

"Gulatch, you and Danri see to the rest of the boarding," the sylve barked in his most authoritative commander's tone, as the gigant joined them. "We'll hold the line until everyone else is boarded—then we can make a dash for the last boats."

Danri tried to argue with the sylve, but Quenidon shook off the digger's objections, turning to face him frankly. "The field army will survive—at least, for now. This is more of a miracle than I dared hope for. All that are left, these hundreds of diggers and sylves and gigants, even the sartors—they'll get away. As long as we hold the minions back, they'll reach safety!"

"But so should *you*," Danri pressed. "Fall back, get to the boats quickly—before they attack."

"Soon, when all the others are safe. Not before. Look." Quenidon gestured quickly to the files of weary warriors still lined up on the peninsula, waiting for passage on the boats. "If we sylves don't hold the line here, we're *all* doomed." The army commander fixed Danri with a serious look, then flipped the mighty sword around so that Lordsmiter was extended, hilt first, to the digger.

"I see the cloud up there—and I can guess that it was our human friend who created it. Now, I want you to give Lordsmiter to Rudy," Quenidon declared forcefully.

"But—you *need* it!" objected Danri, eyes widening.

"I have another—a good blade of digger steel. Sadly, its

previous owner has no further use for it. When I see you back in the city, I can explain to Rudy why he must bear Lordsmiter. Now, go!''

"Come on!'' Raine said grimly, taking Danri by the arm, turning her own moist eyes upon Quen. "Hurry to that last boat!'' she pleaded.

"I will—but when you see him, tell Rudy thank you for me—it was that cloud that gave us time to get away.''

"We'll tell him no such thing! You're coming, and you can tell him yourself!'' the digger snapped, shaking his head like a petulant child. He started to bluster and bellow, even reached again as if to hoist the stubborn sylve over his shoulder.

Quenidon looked sternly at his fellow commander, but there was real warmth in his eyes. "From the time that I failed my Auratest and chose the warrior's path I've been preparing for a campaign such as this—a war of survival. And I never thought to lose epic battles, to retreat across half of Faerine. It looked as though my whole army was doomed—my efforts, my whole life a waste! But now, out of the mist and the Aura, they're *saved*! I'll stay until the last of my warriors has been carried to safety—and I stay with the knowledge that the field army will fight again, will stand before Spendorial!'' The normally serene sylve's face tightened with emotion—not despair, nor fear, but genuine joy. Quenidon's tone was so gentle, so tranquil, that Danri could not oppose him. "This is right, Danri. Now go, my digger friend. Please.''

"Hurry up, then,'' Danri croaked, clutching Lordsmiter with both hands. Raine held back her tears with a visible effort, as she took the digger's arm and started toward the boats.

The minions would attack again, Quenidon knew, but he felt well-prepared, warmed by the love of his companions, heartened by the lives that had been saved. He thought of Aurianth in that moment of insight, and knew that she was here with him.

A number of stalkers rushed close, dropping to all fours and sprinting toward the Faerines, then bounding away in a quick feint. "Look alive for the real thing!'' Quen called, his eyes sweeping the lean young faces of the Royal House sylves, knowing they were ready to follow him unquestioningly.

They would have been his personal regiment for all his life had Quen's fate been different—but nevertheless, fate had seen that they now stood ready to die with him. Quenidon knew that he needed these sylves—that the entire army needed them—but he wanted to tell them all to flee, to get on the boats while there was time. He took what slim comfort he could from the fact that even had he ordered them to go, they would not have left him.

Hundreds of kroaks and brutox suddenly stampeded, a surging wave charging in earnest. The spearhead of the attack, a trio of bellowing brutox, rushed toward Quenidon in the center of the line. The sylve met the onslaught with his feet planted, long sword ready, and with a single slash he disemboweled the leading brute in a rush of sparking, oily guts. The putrid stuff quickly burst into flame, forcing the sylvan commander back a few steps. He parried the crushing blow of another brutox, guiding the attacker's heavy blade with a deceptively faulty block. The monster's sword stuck into the soft ground, and before it could pull the weapon free, Quenidon Daringer's steel claimed another victim.

Images and memories flashed through the sylve's mind—Danri's friendship, the love that bound Rudy and Raine and brought them to Faerine, and the hope that the Man of Three Waters might offer to the world. He thought, also, of two gray-haired sylves long forgotten, images long buried—a male and female who bore a weight of crushing disappointment, for their son who was not an Auramaster.

Instead, he had become a warrior. Quenidon glanced back, saw that more of his troops had been carried to safety—but the minions pressed relentlessly, and once again he threw himself into the orchestrated chaos of the battle.

"Retreat—slowly!" he commanded. "Careful—hold the line there!" he cried, as several brutox threatened to break through the left flank. Sylvan swordsmen rushed to replace fallen comrades, and the defenders held.

More kroaks charged, and the sylves met them with steel. The melee pressed along the shore, Quenidon slashing enemies on all sides. The Faerines struggled to stick together, holding amid the piled bodies of their enemies, the sylvan commander slaying a dozen or more as the battle raged again.

So intent was Quenidon on the surrounding minions that

he didn't see the leather-winged serpents gliding low above
the battlefield, veering over the lakeshore. Drackans, bellies
swollen with Aurasteam, dove toward the combat, finally
roaring their presence with a ground-shaking challenge. Three
bronze-colored serpents glided nearly at water level, sweeping
along the shore of the lake toward the small peninsula.

Quenidon cast another look back, seeing the last of the
boats pull away from shore, the tall-masted ship drifting
closer as if to screen the lesser craft. Empty boats surged
forward, drawing near to the beach. Then, much closer, massive jaws gaped as the drackans swooped over the sylvan line.
Dark, sulphurous clouds spewed forth, enveloping sylvan
warriors—and hundreds of kroaks as well. Pain seized Quenidon, unspeakable agony burning away his skin, searing him
to his soul—but almost immediately the torture yielded to
lingering brightness, and the sylve felt Aurianth's presence as
an embrace of purest love.

The serpents swept on as the deadly cloud seethed over the
remnants of the field army's rearguard. The deceptively gentle
lake breeze returned, wafting much of the drackan-breath
away—but for a long time a white plume marked the last
battle and the funeral pyre of a warrior sylve.

TWENTY-TWO

Rains of Darkblood and Doom

When fatigue, hunger, and discomfort align with
the enemy, a warrior's most important ally can
be a measure of time—hours to rest and eat, to
bandage wounds, and to prepare for a
resumption of the campaign.
—SONGS OF AURIANTH

— 1 —

Danri clenched the hilt of Lordsmiter with both hands, straining to pull his fists apart, to wrench the weapon into pieces. His eyes were dry and unblinking, frozen to the place where Quenidon Daringer had died. The galyon on which the digger stood, the presence of Raine and Awnro and Gulatch, were all forgotten, buried by the reality of that blackened patch of battlefield.

His mind was filled with the memory of his warrior friend—by Aurianth, Quenidon deserved to *live*! His army had escaped doom, and the stalwart sylve had seen them through an epic retreat. His death was a cruel, a monstrous, wrong!

"Drackans off the stern!" The cry from the masthead galvanized the digger. Danri hoisted Lordsmiter, grimly seeking the serpents, determined to drive the weapon into a scaly brown body. The wheel deck blocked his view to the rear, so he scrambled up the ladder with Raine and Gulatch hurrying behind.

He found himself on a small, square deck. Looking past a device like a huge crossbow, he saw movement over the lake—there! Three more drackans came in low, their powerful wing strokes touching the surface of the lake while Aurasteam swelled their bellies, threatening imminent explosion. The digger raised the sword and charged the stern, ready to slash the beasts, the menace of the steam forgotten—or ignored.

Gulatch tackled the digger from behind, pinning him to the deck, struggling to block a barrage of kicks and blows. Raine dove in and snatched the sword as Danri landed a punch on the gigant's nose. With a grunt, Gulatch bashed the digger's hand away. "For a friend, I forgive that—once!" the gigant chieftain growled.

"Let me go!" Danri drew back his fist again.

"Say—have a look at Captain Kestrel!" Awnro Lyrifell was there suddenly, remarking in amazement as Danri saw a gray-bearded sailor step up to the great crossbowlike weapon. "Given the circumstances, I think the trebuchet is somewhat more practical than the sword."

The fury within the digger vanished like a fire doused with water. He watched the sea captain swivel and aim the massive trebuchet as the drackans closed. One serpent winged straight toward the ship while the others approached as if to pass on either side. Golden eyes expanded, glowing with palpable hate, while red tongues flicked from the widely spread jaws.

The trebuchet was designed for two men—one to swivel, the other to release the trigger—but the captain easily tilted the frame. Sighting down the length of the long, harpoonlike shaft, he faced the three flying serpents alone. The wyrms flew in grim silence, necks straining toward the galyon, distended guts nearly touching the water. Sweeping closer, the drackans fixed slitted eyes on the ship, and now the digger saw the flaring nostrils, the wickedly curved fangs.

Kestrel squeezed the trigger, a snapping *twang* signaling the release of the steel spring. The shaft shot through the air, straight toward the middle drackan. Instantly the creature twisted, raising a wing and trying to veer away, but the trebuchet was a powerful weapon, and the deadly harpoon flew like a bolt of lightning. The barbed head ripped into that swollen belly, and Aurasteam erupted in a searing cloud, exploding with a scream of escaping pressure. Gory pieces of drackan tumbled, while the leathery wings fluttered to the lake like massive leaves, and a rain of meat and blood left a red slick across the water.

The drackans to either side swerved and careened, flapping frantically. One of the pair lowered his head and belched steam, letting the gas hiss across the lake, boiling the surface. Immediately that serpent surged upward, belly flattened and wings pulling down great scoops of air. The remaining wyrm tried to swerve toward the galyon, but was forced to veer away from the lofty masts and rigging; the last expulsion of steam wafted harmlessly into the air astern of the ship. The pair of drackans banked over the land, joining their comrades in settling to the battlefield.

Again came the warning cry, "More drackans—from starboard!"

Now Danri stepped to the trebuchet, helping Kestrel turn the crank to cock the heavy spring. The captain, teeth clenched and sweat beading on his brow, nodded wordless thanks to the digger while a sailor brought another harpoon. In moments the weapon was reloaded, and Danri crouched to allow Kestrel full freedom of movement.

They saw three drackans diving from lofty skies over the shore. Danri cursed, and pointed out another trio coming in low across the trampled field. But now arrows showered from the great Auracloud, and immediately the low-flying drackans veered away, several shrieking in pain from multiple stings.

The last three serpents were still high above, and they banked through a sharp turn, driving toward the Auracloud. Once again a shower of arrows whistled outward, and the drackans swiftly curled away, straining to climb above the barrage. Once out of range, the wyrms dove for the safety of the minion army.

Wind gusted and Danri became aware of the sails snapping overhead. Slowly, with measured dignity, the galyon moved away from the shore. The digger stared at the brown drackans gathered in the place where Quenidon Daringer had died, at the flapping wings and hideous, snakelike heads, and he trem-

bled with a hatred that blanked out every other emotion he'd
ever felt.

— 2 —

Direfang remained on the battery deck as the *Dreadcloud*
rumbled easily above the Darkenheight Road. The brutox
raised his hands, casting sparks around his shoulders like an
imperial robe as he watched Faerine drift past below. With
his first good look at the enchanted realm he was startled by
the brightness of the snowfields, the putrid verdancy of tundra
and copse. The mountains around him were barren of trees,
but cornices of gleaming white draped the upper elevations.
Grayish-white glaciers swelled in the higher valleys, clinging
to cliffs, probing toward the lowlands. Much of the snow was
mundane, though in places the brute had to squint against the
offensive, sparkling brilliance of Aurasnow.

The stream that had once spilled down the valley had vanished, its bed a streak of dry rocks running beside the road.
Each of the tributaries spilling into the valley had been effectively dammed or diverted—nowhere along this route of attack were the minions forced to march over water. Nor would
the *Dreadcloud* be forced to deplete its substance by flying
across a stream or river—at least, not as long as it followed
the route of the army's march.

Direfang sensed the rumblings of the sturmvaults through
the soft deck under his feet, and he knew that the ship's boiling vats of Darkblood powered the great vessel through the
air with majestic, irresistible force. With every mile of progress it seemed that the air grew warmer. Soon the captain
could see beyond the foothills, across the verdant rises and
lowlands of Faerine. Sunlight sparkled on ponds, streams, and
lakes, reflecting painfully in the minion's eyes—but he forced
himself to look, to examine this hated land. His heart swelled
with the possibility of victory, the knowledge that Darkblood
would rain into these valleys. The streams would flow with
vitriol, and lightning would smite armies and cities as it had
the Guardians.

Now the *Dreadcloud* cruised above a long column of wagons and beasts, and Direfang recognized the bovars and

bloodwagons that made up the rear component of Phalthak's advancing horde. Far ahead he saw the brilliant waters of a large lake, and he suspected that the crystalline blotch of domes and towers beyond must be the sylvan capital of Spendorial.

That city was the ultimate object of Phalthak's attack. Direfang saw many sails across the lake, and he cursed the cowardly use of watercraft—he well knew that the minions could not pursue the Faerines by boat. Still, he also knew that the enemy was not likely to *dwell* upon the water, and the little flotilla seemed like nothing more than a vexing insect, humming around the ears of the great being that was Phalthak's legion.

And then he saw the army, sprawled like a dark blotch across the ground. Tens of thousands of minions had reached the near shore of the lake, gathering where the realm's great river spilled into the lake. The *Dreadcloud* moved over a blackened swath of forest, where many fires still smoldered and thick smoke roiled to all sides. Captain Direfang ordered a halt, and the black sky-ship came to rest, billowing and seething above the mass of Phalthak's army, while the captain stalked through the halls within the dark hull. In the belly of the ship he reached the chamber where several stalkers hissed over a large vat of Darkblood.

The snakelike minions stirred their cauldron frantically, hissing enchantments, eager to please. Still, Direfang entered the chamber with regret, knowing that soon he would have to offer subservience to one of the Sleepstealer's spawn.

— 3 —

The Auracloud reached the shoreline of Spendorial, and Rudy took a last drink of Aura before he settled the great craft onto the elm-dotted parkland. He looked toward the river for one last time, not surprised to see the bovars formed into a column, marching upstream along the far bank. Within a few miles the river spilled from a notch in the rocky foothills—it would be the perfect place for the minions to erect their dam.

The Iceman's eyes rose from the minion army, toward the blackened forests and foothills beyond. At first he thought that

the smoke from countless fires had billowed even higher into
the air, but then he sensed something more purposeful—and
far more dangerous—in the mass of darkness towering in the
southern sky.

It might have been a potent, ominous thunderhead—except
that the perfect blackness of its billowing shape was too
dense, too solid, for any kind of mundane cloud, or even the
pollution of a vast fire. Lightning flashed from the flat un-
derbelly, and the cloud roiled closer, gradually emerging from
the haze of distance. Then Rudy knew that he was watching
the approach of another sky-ship, one many times the size of
his Auracloud, composed of thick, unblemished darkness—a
thing of Duloth-Trol. Thunder rumbled, and the forward ten-
dril of the cloud mass spewed lightning in a fierce barrage.
The shadow of the cloud darkened a great swath of ground,
and as it emerged from the smoke to loom higher and larger,
the shadow gradually embraced most of the minion army.
Here the massive thunderhead halted, a short distance from
the juncture of lake and river, jutting into the sky like a craggy
peak of pure obsidian, gleaming wetly from the internal pulse
of Darkblood.

Rudy guessed that the water prevented the massive ship
from surging forward, from blasting Spendorial with a killing
force of lightning bolts. Despite the shadows, and the soot
tingeing the far shore where the minion army had wreaked its
destruction, the Auraloch glimmered broad and flat and im-
permeable.

Yet when he looked to the Faerine river, Rudy saw a much
more tenuous barrier. The silver ribbon was barely a hundred
paces wide, and from his excursions through the Scrying Pool
the Iceman well knew the damming power of the bovars. He
had seen at least a hundred of the massive brutes with this
army, even beyond the scores needed to haul the wagons of
Darkblood.

His last view was blocked by elms as the Auracloud dissipated onto the grass, gently lowering the sylvan archers of
the Royal House and the human enchanter to the ground.
Raine was waiting for him, and she had brought Danri directly
from the galyon. The digger and the human clasped hands
without speaking for several moments, and Rudy felt a

warmth of friendship—and the pain of shared grief—that tightened his jaw with emotion.

"Welcome—and thanks," Danri said gruffly, at last releasing the Iceman's hand. "I guess you know how bad things are."

"I think so. I saw Quenidon Daringer fall . . . I'm sorry," offered Rudy, knowing his words were no comfort. He felt an awful weight, a load that threatened to crush him. "We came as soon as we could . . . but it wasn't—"

"It wasn't your fault!" the digger replied sharply. "It's to your credit that so many of us survived. But here—Quenidon . . . he asked me to give you this."

The digger extended the mighty sword and Rudy gasped at the bejeweled hilt, the gleaming brightness of the blade, illumination that would not be overwhelmed even in broad daylight. Danri briefly described the recovery of the sacred Artifact, and its effect on the Lord Minion.

Rudy shook his head in amazement. "I've heard of this weapon—it's a great treasure. There are many who could bear it with more skill, and to better effect, than myself!"

"More skill?" Danri chuckled harshly. "I daresay. But when it comes to the one who might have most *need* of it, there can be none better."

"He's right." Raine took the weapon from Danri and wrapped the leather belt around the Iceman's waist, girding the weapon to him in one smooth gesture. "You should wear it—and bear it."

The big sword was surprisingly light, and the hilt fit naturally under Rudy's palm. Still, he couldn't overcome the feeling that he was some kind of imposter, a boy playing the role of warrior.

"Danri!" A diggermaid burst into the crowd, sweeping the bearded warrior into a rib-crushing embrace.

"Kerri!" he moaned, burying his face in her curling hair and muffling his sobs with the strength of his will. He held her very close, and even when he pulled his head up, the two diggers remained firmly clasped in each other's arms.

"By the goddess, you look good, digger," Kerri said, drawing back to gaze at him. She kissed him on both cheeks, then full on the lips.

"And by Aurianth, you don't know how the thought of

you kept me going down that road,'' he declared. ''Memories
of you . . . and hopes for the future . . .''

''I've got some ideas for our inn,'' she said, ''but it wasn't
much fun to think about without you.'' She drew him close
again, and Rudy's own heart ached from the grief in the digger's face when Danri finally pulled away.

''We're not out of danger,'' he said. ''But we're going to
have that inn, you'll see. We just have to wait a little while,
yet.''

''We'll wait as long as we have to.'' Kerri pledged, clasping her digger's arm as he turned to Rudy.

''What did you see from up there?'' Danri asked.

''The minions will start damming the river in a matter of
hours,'' Rudy said grimly. ''Sooner or later the flow will stop
and the army will come. I don't know what I can do *then*.''

''Whatever it is, you won't be doing it alone,'' Danri said
sincerely. The digger looked toward the lake, past the galyon
and the many sylvan boats, over the sparkling waters. He
grimaced fiercely, his chin jutting as if in a personal challenge
to the looming blackness above the distant shore.

— 4 —

The walls of the Grotto soared so high overhead that Neambrey felt like a mouse at the bottom of a tall chimney, gazing
longingly at a distant patch of cloud-studded sky. Nearby the
fountain gushed softly, Aura welling from deep within the
Watershed, rising through a narrow crack in white granite.
The liquid bubbled up for the length of a young drackan's
tail, then spilled outward in a reflective crystalline umbrella.

Mist hung through the Grotto in graceful curtains—not a
cloud fogging the air in uniform obscurity, but tendrils of
vapor draped like garlands from granite ledges and mossy
outcrops. Wisps trailed from numerous Aurafalls, and as the
sun reached its zenith golden rays spilled down into the shaft,
and a hundred rainbows burst into being. Shade-dwelling
blooms of columbine and violet glowed in the brightness, and
the lush moss layered over so much of the white quartz bedrock flared into a radiant emerald blanket.

Neambrey noticed none of the wonders around him. He had

entered through the lone footpath—a damp, shadowy cut between lofty cliffs, so narrow that his tail lashed both walls as
it twitched nervously back and forth. Finally he'd emerged
into the Grotto to find that the elders were already here. The
big drackans had flown, of course, gliding through tight spirals to come to rest on the mossy ledges that staggered the
lower walls of the massive stone cylinder. From here the
green drackans sat in judgment upon their enemies, and upon
those of their number who disobeyed fundamental tribal ten-
ets.

Those such as Neambrey. The young drackan cringed at
the thought. He looked past the spuming fountain to the lowest of the ledges, where luxuriant moss could not conceal the
alabaster whiteness of the granite bedrock. An emerald shape
uncoiled there, slitted eyes of gold blinking slowly as Neambrey crept forward. Verdagon's gaze was not unsympathetic,
but he made no sound, allowing the youngster to look upward,
seeing the occupants of the other ledges. Nearby was Meamare's niche, sadly empty, and as Neambrey's eyes swept
farther he saw other vacant perches. More of the greens than
his mother, it seemed, had met with some mishap—else they
would have heard the mute summons to council, emerging
even from the deepest depths of dormancy to join the conclave.

On her own ledge near Meamare's, Pashra raised the viridescent wedge of her head and nodded slowly. Her eyelids
drooped almost sleepily, but Neambrey sensed that his
mother's cousin, at least, might be willing to hear his story.
Above Pashra, however, Seddiim and Borcanesh huffed suspiciously. The big males stretched their necks, frowning down
at the young malefactor. The other green drackan elders occupied ledges that were higher still, nine in all; most of them
showed a disturbing tendency to mimic the stern expressions
of the angry males.

"Where are the others?" Verdagon asked, his tone grim.
"Know that it is written: 'An ill wind bears no tidings.' I
have been told that Meamare is slain. Is there more news?"

"My sire, Kallafie, was butchered in his dormancy!"
growled Borcanesh. He glowered at Neambrey, as if accusing
the youngster of the crime.

Other greens mumbled menacingly, several reporting that

they, too, had discovered kin or nest mates gruesomely slain.

"It was the brown drackans!" the youngster squawked. He shrank as nine pairs of golden eyes stared, unblinking, downward. "At least, Jasaren killed Meamare—it *had* to be him!"

A terrible thirst gnawed at the young drackan's throat, though he had swilled several gallons of Aura before entering the Grotto. The splashing water was seductive music, but he dared not divert his attention to drink. Miserable, he tried to ignore the craving.

"We have been told that the Treasure was removed from Meamare's lair—Is this true?" Seddiim opened the inquisition with a growled question.

"It—it's true," Neambrey squeaked.

"It has fallen into the hands of the lesser Faerines?" demanded Borcanesh. "This is what has been alleged!"

"At least allow the youngster to answer the questions," Pashra declared sternly, arching an eyebrow at the blustering male. Borcanesh, larger and heavier than his sister by half again, nevertheless drew back his head in the face of her rebuke.

"Now," Pashra said. She allowed herself the hint of an encouraging smile—though a display of teeth by a fifty-foot drackan could not be described as terribly reassuring. Too, her tone with Neambrey was as firm as it had been with Borcanesh.

"I—I guess it began with my Thirsting," Neabrey admitted. He described his awakening, the discovery of Meamare's death, and the intrusion into the Bruxrange by an army of lesser Faerines. He warmed to the tale as he described his ambush of the two Faerine warriors, dragging them to the mouth of the lair, and his harsh accusations when the interlopers emerged from Aurasleep. Borcanesh frowned skeptically, but Seddiim cocked an interested eyebrow, and Pashra continued to look encouraging.

When Neambrey tried to describe the course of his conversations with Danri and Quenidon, however, he found that things became more confusing. The threat of the minion invasion, both as described by his captives and confirmed by his own observations, was a monstrous blight on Faerine— yet until he had seen it himself, Neambrey had been unconcerned. Now he was frustrated to find that the other greens reacted the same way.

The news that the brown drackans had joined with the Sleepstealer was greeted with rumbles of surprise and distress; Neambrey took some slight consolation from the fact that none of the elders disbelieved him on this matter. But when, in conclusion, he was forced to admit that the sylve and the digger had departed in possession of the Treasure, the frowns of the judges grew grim and forbidding. Neambrey described how Quenidon had employed the Artifact, how Lordsmiter had possessed sting enough to drive the Fang of Dassadec back from the line of battle.

"It was only the brown drackans that won the fight," the youngster declared. "If Jasaren and his clan hadn't flown at the Faerines, and killed so many, the minions might have been stopped right in the Darkenheight valley! And Lordsmiter would have helped the Faerines to do it!"

"But the browns came," Verdagon said sternly, "and now the Treasure is lost to us, carried into the lowlands by the fleeing Faerines. Who knows but that it might have been lost on the field, fallen into the hands of the enemy? It is written: 'When a bird is freed, he who opens the cage cannot control the direction of its flight!' "

"I *trust* them!" Neambrey blurted, realizing that this was true—and also that it was the wrong answer for the circumstances. Yet he forged ahead. "Danri is fearless. And Quenidon is a warrior of legend—he knew the sword when he saw it, wielded it like a master. No finer hero could bear the sacred Treasure!"

"Ahem." Pellunia spoke from one of the highest ledges, and the other drackans instantly gave the ancient matriarch their attention. She leaned her neck far over the edge of her notch in the grotto wall, her white-tinged mane surrounding a wrinkled, but still forbidding visage. Now her golden eyes flashed, and Neambrey sensed that her news was not good.

"It is known that I have friends among the twissels," Pellunia began. "Flighty creatures, terribly unwise and short-lived, but friendly and proper just the same. Too, they are useful as sources of information."

"And did they bring you information—recently?" inquired Verdagon patiently.

"Yes, concerning Lordsmiter. It has been . . . there is really no easy way to say this . . . It has been given to, well, to a *human*."

The collective gasps of the elder drackans were not loud enough to quell Neambrey's gasp of dismay. "A human? But—how? And *why*?"

"The sylve, it seems, was killed in battle. Apparently he foresaw his fate, for he consigned the weapon to his companion. It is the digger, apparently, who allowed this human to gain the Treasure."

"But . . . but . . ." Neambrey's objections trailed off dejectedly. His mind reeled with the burden of his guilt. How could he have been so naive, so simple, as to trust a lesser Faerine? A digger, no less! Truly, he deserved whatever fate the elders had in store for him.

"The minions have reached the River Aurun," Pellunia continued. "They will no doubt turn toward our green hills very soon. We must consider the value of fighting them now, before they strike."

Verdagon shook his head, overriding the mutters of agreement from some of the younger males. "If they come, we shall fight—but remember, it is written above all: 'Let the stain of your neighbor's filth be a blight on his home alone!' "

"What do you mean?" Pellunia asked sweetly.

"Enough of that," Verdagon humphed. "I believe the council has heard enough that judgment may be passed. The Treasure is gone, perhaps even beyond the pale of Faerine. Our young clansmate has accepted culpability—"

"And let it be noted that he is only *half* green," Seddiim interjected wickedly. "His father, it is known to all, was brown!"

"Be that as it may, Neambrey has offered the explanation for his actions. How do you, the elders, decide?" Vedagon looked expectantly around the Grotto.

"How long has the wyrmling been Thirsting?" inquired Borcanesh, narrowing his eyes shrewdly as he studied the molting carapace on Neambrey's back.

"Less than a moon cycle," Verdagon replied.

"Banishment to the Stormpeak, then—it's the only choice," growled Seddiim grimly. "If he lives out his year, he'll have plenty of time to swill Aura and sprout his wings."

"Aye, banishment for a year. Ignorance, or foolishness, is no excuse." Borcanesh chimed in with fierce agreement.

"Foolishness is never an excuse," Verdagon noted in his turn. "But young Neambrey is not a fool. Indeed, I sense a reserve of wisdom that, I hope, someday will have the chance to flower. I vote for penance, but not banishment."

Neambrey's heart swelled with the old drackan's words, and his spirits rose further when Pashra echoed Verdagon's vote. But then the tally continued up the walls of the Grotto, past the ledges of other hard-eyed males, and these chimed in with votes for banishment. By the time Pellunia, whose testimony about the sword's fate had doomed Neambrey, cast her own vote—surprisingly enough, for leniency—the issue had been decided. Three drackans wanted Neambrey to serve a time of penance, after which his transgression would be forgotten; but six voted for banishment to the Stormpeak.

That barren summit was the loftiest promontory in the Brux range, a conelike mountain surrounded by sheer cliffs to every side. It was typically used to imprison the greatest enemies of the drackans, green or brown; flying prisoners had their wings clipped. There was no food or water on the summit, and most creatures imprisoned there simply perished.

Some drackan prisoners had been known to become dormant, surviving a year of wasting, then gradually regaining their health upon release. More commonly, the sentenced one shriveled to a skeleton and died, or threw himself from the peak, driven mad by loneliness and inevitable doom.

— 5 —

Stars sparkled overhead, a gem-studded vault of moonless sky arcing over the congregation on the grounds of Spendorial's crystalline palace. Sylves from the city, and the survivors of the field army, and all of those who had awaited their warriors' return had gathered to hear the words of the Royal Scion, and to wonder about the future. Rudy knew that the *Dreadcloud* still loomed in the sky, but he was thankful that the elms of the sylvan parkland were tall enough to block the oppressive shadow from view.

Small fires glowed here and there, sharing warmth with

gathered Faerines—and the few humans who sat with the Iceman on stumps around one of the central blazes. Danri stood nearby, wrapped in thoughts that brought an expression of naked pain to his face. Kerri was with him, clasping his arm, but she was silent now, having exhausted her words, unable to bring him out of his grief. Rudy, too, had failed to pierce the digger's veil of isolation, so he was grateful when Anjell and Dara came over and spoke to Danri.

"We were frightened for you . . . and I'm . . ." Dara spoke softly, her voice catching. "I'm sorry about Quenidon. We missed you both so much since you left Carillonn; now, to see you here, but not Quen . . ." She stopped with a sob and Danri gently patted her shoulder.

"Aye-uh," he said softly. "And thanks."

"We heard about the battles," Anjell said, taking Danri's callused hand in both of hers. "I think you were really brave."

"Thanks to you, too, lass," Danri said, suddenly turning and crossing into the darkness, where he cleared his throat very loudly before clomping back to Rudy and his companions.

Gulatch and Hoagaran had stood back from the fire, but now the gigant battle chief walked over. "Rescued by *humans*," Gulatch growled, glowering down at Raine—who returned his look with a tight smile.

"Pretty fair turnaround, considering that the first time I met you, you were going to throw me into something called the—what was it—the Well of Despair? Wasn't that the place?"

"Yes," snorted Gulatch. If the gigant was embarrassed by the reminder, he made no sign. "It was only the Guardians that saved you and your friends."

"Seems we do a little better when we're all fighting on the same side," Danri said dourly,

"I am sorry about Quenidon Daringer. He was a credit to his people, and to all Faerine—it was an honor to serve under him," Gulatch declared forcefully.

"I reckon I feel the same way—but it should have been me on that shore!" Danri spoke with naked bitterness, clamping his jaw stubbornly.

"Only the gods are entitled to make a judgment like that," retorted the gigant, gently chiding. "It would seem that Au-

rianth has smiled on her children, at least insofar as some of
us were able to escape with our lives. There was a time when
I thought we would all meet our deaths on that shore. The
sylvan warrior's sacrifice was heroic—and it was *not* in
vain."

"Aye," Danri agreed sadly, but his eyes were distant. Rudy
guessed they still lingered on that stained and muddy field,
burning the weight of responsibility—and guilt—into the digger's grieving mind.

Nearby, Awnro tuned his lute very carefully, minutely
tightening the pitch of his highest strings. Dara sat beside him,
her travel journal closed, resting on her lap. Anjell found Darret, and the two children sat, cross-legged, on the ground near
the fire. They were close to a mountain of embers, but both
the fair-haired girl and the boy with the dark braids leaned
forward, as if they couldn't get enough of the warmth.

Rudy looked around expectantly, then realized with a chill
that he had been seeking Quenidon Daringer's face. A wave
of bitterness, as lonely as a distant star, hit him hard. He
leaned against Raine, lowering his face into the comfort of
her curling hair. She tightened her arms around him, and he
drew a deep breath, inhaling her fragrance before he raised
his head and looked at the night.

"We would speak of our kinsman . . . and all the others
who have paid, so dearly, for Faerine." Mussrik Daringer, the
Royal Scion, talked quietly, but his words carried throughout
the quiet night. Rudy couldn't see the sylvan Auramaster, but
his voice was somehow carried by the mist that began to settle
around them. Now the Royal Scion spoke somberly to the
assemblage.

"It is fitting that we gather thus, together—sylves and diggers, sartors and gigants . . . and humans, all united under the
sky of Aurianth. And in Aurianth, we know love, and sometimes because of love we know pain.

"Many of you did not know Quenidon Daringer as my
brother—my *elder* brother," declared Mussrik Daringer.
"For it was his choice to renounce that legacy, to seek his
life's destiny on a different course. Quen's desire was to be
the warrior of Spendorial, to be ready when his service—and
his life—were needed. The legacy he leaves is one of glory,
sacrifice . . . and courage.

"The rank of army commander could have been his by
birth—he desired it, and had been born to the role. Instead
he chose a different path, and became a stranger to those of
us who dwelled in the crystal city. He claimed none of the
power, the status that was his by right, but he perfected his
skills, and his knowledge on his own.

"And when that knowledge was needed, he was there.
Leading by his stalwart example, he marched and fought beside his warriors, and in the end, died with them." A
low chant began among the sylves, wordless rhythm thrumming
through the night, the sound washing over the waters of the
lake.

Awnro murmured quietly, and the sylves fell silent. "The
gods work their schemes, and play their games . . . and Quenidon Daringer had an important role to play." The bard's lute
chimed soft, minor chords, and in the background sylvan
flutes produced a keening accompaniment. Dara sat behind
the bard, her eyes focused on the fire as if she hoped to find
there the answers to a million questions.

"Do you think . . . do you think Quen would say his life
was worth it?" Dara asked, as Awnro settled his lute upon
his knee.

"You know," the bard declared, staring intently into the
fire. "I think he would."

Raine and Rudy stood, hand in hand, a few steps back from
the dying embers. The Iceman felt empty, drained of emotion—and bereft of ideas as well. He wanted to hold Raine,
to bury himself within her, but he knew that that was no real
shelter for himself, or for the world.

Abruptly Rudy discerned a presence behind him.

"Hello, my human friend," said Larrial Solluel, stepping
to the Iceman's side. The master's scarred, unseeing face
swept over the gathering, apparently taking note of everyone
present. "The fire is pleasant against the dark chill of the
night. But we cannot huddle beside its shelter forever, can
we?"

"No, we can't," Rudy agreed solemnly. "But where in
this night do we go?"

"I don't have the answers—not even the Scrying Pool can
give us the knowledge that we need."

"How do we learn, then?"

"I suggest that we start with a prayer."

TWENTY-THREE

The Dam

A dike covering ninety-nine rods of a hundred-
rod gap is exactly as useful as no dike at all.
—DIGGERSPEAK PROVERB

— 1 —

A small Auracloud drifted in the air above Spendorial. From
its rounded crest the Iceman scanned the skies, checking for
drackans and terrions. The minion fliers, however, had shown
no interest in venturing over the lake, and Rudy had observed
the brown wyrms tire visibly during their previous attempt to
attack his sky-ship. He decided the menace was slight for the
time being.

Below, on the still-pristine waters of Auraloch, the *Black
Condor* sailed a monotonous patrol. The galyon, under Kestrel's watchful hand, tacked a course near the enemy-held
shore. The ship remained at least a half mile from land, and
marksmen stood ready at the trebuchet in case the brown
drackans showed inclination to attack, but for the days since
the lakeshore battle the ship had been allowed to conduct its
patrol unmolested.

Drifting closer to the river, the Auracloud scudded through a sky pocked by similar puffs of cumulus. Rudy steered the sky-ship with his mind, having discovered recently that he had no need of the crude braziers and coals employed by the other Auramasters. Now he took a drink of Aura and held the cloud back slightly from the pace of the wind, veering just enough to see the activity in the river valley below.

Raine, who had been watching off the far side of the diminutive cloud, joined the Iceman, and he tried not to let his fear show in his face. The fatal prediction from the pool frightened him to his core and at first he had considered forbidding Raine from riding the cloud, for fear that she would fall. She never would have consented to such a request, he knew—all the more so since he was resolved not to tell her what he had seen—and eventually he had convinced himself that the cloud was safe, since the horrific image had clearly pictured his beloved at the foot of a cliff.

Together they sat on their lofty perch, overlooking so much of Faerine—though the contrast between the two banks of the river was an assault against mortal eyes. The near shore bloomed lush and verdant, forests of broadleaf mingling with flowered meadows and groves of dark evergreen. Even the darkest of these conifers was indisputably vibrant, *alive*. Patches of silver marked ponds, pools, and narrow rivulets—water and Aura mingling, nurturing the myriad lives of Faerine.

On the far bank, and extending to the distant, smudge-limned foothills, spread a wasteland. The sooty, skeletal remains of countless trees marked former forests felled by axe and flame. Now the timber lay scattered, the landscape like a floor covered with charred matchsticks. Ponds and lakes that had once dotted the terrain were now blackened swaths of mud, or straight channels where the minions had gouged drainage ditches. Several tributary creek beds could be seen from the lofty vantage—without exception these were dry, dammed far upstream.

The pressure of Raine's fingers on Rudy's hand became insistent, and he turned to look into her dark eyes—eyes that questioned him with palpable force. He wanted to look away, but her determination—and love—held him spellbound.

"You've got to talk to me . . . tell me what happened in

the palace." Her tone was gentle, but each word had an edge of steel.

"I can't." Rudy shook his head, feeling his hand tremble at remembered images—Raine's shattered, bleeding body; that remorseless precipice of rock . . .

"Dammit—you can, and you will!" She pulled her hand away, roughly spun him by the shoulder until their faces were inches apart. "Was it your future? Did you see something about the war?"

"I can't talk about it—because I love you," Rudy said softly, firmly.

"That's a reason for *telling* me!" Raine retorted. "Do you know what happens to the Watershed? To us?"

"I saw some things about my fate—but that's not what haunts me."

"What *is* it?"

"You have to trust me—it's better left unsaid," Rudy insisted.

"I do trust you—but you have to trust me, as well," retorted his lover. "You have to show me the same kind of faith! Let me know what frightens you—I can help!"

The Iceman shook his head, miserable at the memory, yet unable to defy her any longer. "It was *your* fate I saw, that I have to change!"

Raine rocked backward, eyes wide. She didn't resist as he gathered her into his arms, held her against his chest. Slowly her own arms reached out, wrapping him in a tight, trembling grip.

They remained in that embrace, unspeaking, as the Auracloud wisped farther along the winding course of the Aurun. Rudy guided the ship, the mere thought of a direction being enough to propel them gently. If he concentrated and took a fresh drink of Aura, he could make the cloud go faster, or climb or descend; for now he was content to bob gradually along. He remained alert for drackans, but saw no sign of the brown serpents among the thousands of troops teeming the far shore of the Aurun. Instead his thoughts wrapped Raine tightly to his heart, seeking to hold, to shelter her.

"You were right," she said quietly, squeezing him hard. "Don't tell me any more. But promise me something."

"What?" He responded with firm pressure of his own.

"Don't try to change fate—don't tell me what to do, or not to do. Let me be free to decide. Can you promise that?"

"I—I don't know."

"*Please!*" she whispered, with an urgency that he couldn't deny. Miserably, he nodded assent.

Almost without Rudy's attention the cloud drifted on, until finally his objective came into view. More than half-completed, the dam, an obscenity of fresh dirt and crushed, broken boulders, filled the mouth of the Aurun gorge. The Lord Minion had selected the perfect location for the blockage—the terminus of a narrow channel the river had carved over millennia, through the limestone bedrock of the foothills.

Dozens of huge bovars scraped dirt with their broad skull-shields, scooping piles into the massive bulwark. Other beasts chopped at the limestone with beaklike upper jaws, smashing the bedrock into pebbly gravel. The small stones were then scooped up and carried onto the dam, where they were used to underlay the layer of dirt. The wide Aurun had already been choked to a gap of ten or fifteen yards, a gush of water spuming through the steep-sided crack that remained. On the near side loomed a limestone bluff, a sheer cliff plunging straight to the water's edge. When the dam met this precipice, the river would cease to flow.

From the tenuous vantage of the cloud, high above the contrasted landscape, the minion advance reminded the Iceman of the glaciers that scoured the high valleys of his homeland. There was an irresistible, geological strength to the onslaught that the huge dam only served to underline. "Another day, perhaps two, and the dam'll be done," the Iceman concluded, studying the obstacle as dispassionately as possible.

"Will Danri, will *we* be ready?" Raine asked.

"We can't afford not to be."

"Back to Spendorial, then—to get started?" Raine shook her head in frustration, then nestled against Rudy's side. "At least hold me until we get there."

Grateful that she had spoken no more of the Scrying Pool, his love for her as important to his life as his own heart, Rudy pulled Raine close and started them slowly back toward the city of the sylves.

The Iceman's arms gripped her involuntarily as, once again,

that dread prophecy from the Scrying Pool flashed in his mind. Raine squeezed him back, and for long moments they lay buried in each other's embrace. "Hold me," repeated Raine, her voice taut. "Closer . . ."

Wrapped in the warmth of her touch and the heat of her love, Rudy pressed his beloved into the cloud, feeling the vapor of magic envelop them. Time ceased to pass, or it lasted forever, as they floated through sun-brightened skies. Their clothes came away easily, separating from skin as if the garments had simply evaporated.

Ultimately the soothing warmth gave way to a growing desperation, heat that seared both of them through body and soul. Frantically the Iceman kissed Raine, stroking, touching, teasing, and at last she pulled him to her. She sobbed as he pressed forward, and he never felt the pressure of her fingers raking his back, raising welts and shedding a tiny trickle of blood.

— 2 —

The whirlwind snaked from the bowels of the *Dreadcloud*, swirling toward a blackened patch of land. Direfang rode the cyclone, relishing the power of his mighty ship—but dismayed by the summons that beckoned him landward.

The waters of the Auraloch glittered two miles away, but enough murk and smoke rose from the ruined woodlands to pleasantly mute the sunlight's reflection. Lowering his eyes, Direfang plodded toward the stone-wheeled wagons of Phalthak's train. Four of the great vehicles had been pulled into a square, and it was here that the brute marched, passing between attentive ranks of minions. A brutox subcommander bared his tusks in a grimace as a bobbing stalker ushered Direfang toward a depression in the rocky patch of ground.

Direfang had seen this spot of perfect blackness from the sky, but the brutox had failed to realize how ideal was Phalthak's discovery. The bowl of stone was deep and solid, and the Fang of Dassadec had ordered four wagons of Darkblood drained into this natural tub. Now it made a perfect Immersing place for the privileged leader of the Sleepstealer's army.

The brutox stood at the brink of the Darkblood bath, forcing himself to wait patiently until several of the Fang's snakes emerged. The longest of the serpentine necks thrust upward, the greenish-black snake streaked with Darkblood, staring at the brutox with red, unblinking eyes.

"Greetings, Mighty Lord," declared Direfang, bowing low toward the slick black surface of Phalthak's private bathing pool.

"Yes?" murmured the snake-headed being.

"Your bovars labor well," the captain of the *Dreadcloud* replied, laboring to keep his tone approving and worshipful, knowing that the craven ego of Phalthak needed such encouragements.

"I will observe the action from the foredeck of the *Dreadcloud*," the Lord Minion announced in a whisper than knelled despair within Direfang.

"Aye, Mighty Lord," the brutox agreed, his tone a deep growl.

"The ship is ready to attack immediately?"

"If necessary—though I should refuel for maximum destructive force. The crossing of the pass exhausted some of our reserves."

"I will have my troops burn four vats for you—that will be sufficient?" rasped the green snake.

"More than sufficient, Mighty Lord."

"Good. See to the refueling immediately, then—for tomorrow we smite Faerine!"

— 3 —

Danri peered cautiously around the bole of a heavy-limbed pine, as close as he dared get to the precipice above the river. Out of his view, the limestone cliff dropped straight toward the frothing waters of the Aurun. A few days ago, that plunge had extended a hundred feet. Now, as the nearly complete dam of the minions spanned the gap at the mouth of the gorge, the drop was only half as far—and the water surged through a notch barely five paces wide. Across that torrent, the dam loomed as high as the cliff, and the bovars dumping boulders into the churning flowage labored within a stone's throw of the digger's position.

Admitting a grim admiration for the minions' thoroughness, Danri watched the building of the dam. Many of the large rocks were instantly snatched by the current and carried downstream—indeed, through the ground the digger could feel the thumping, bashing tumbles of cottage-sized boulders. But still other huge stones lodged in place, gradually blocking the flow of the Aurun, each forcing the water to climb a little higher. Finally the large rocks were piled so high that the water merely seeped through the cracks between them, no longer surging over the top. Bovars now carried gravel on their scooplike foreheads, dumping it into the rapidly filling notch, then turning to plod back to the nearby quarries. The gravel showered over the great boulders, filling in the gaps, cutting off still more of the flow.

Around Danri dozens of other diggers, likewise camouflaged in cloaks of mottled brown and green, awaited his signal. Gigants, sartors, and sylvan archers waited farther back in the woods, but Danri was determined to stop the minions at the edge of their dam. He studied the top of the barrier, again conceding the effectiveness of enemy tactics. A shallow slope descended into the water on the upstream side, and a steeper incline plunged down a long face to the drying riverbed, but the top of the massive dam was a flat surface at least twenty paces wide—broad enough to support a heavy column of attacking minions.

Danri crept away from his tree, skirting an outcrop of rock to move downstream from the dam. When he was safe from observation, he crawled to the lip of the gorge and looked down. Many pools of water reflected from the bed of the Aurun, but most of the flow had drained toward the Auraloch, revealing a rocky and irregular bed. In a matter of hours the minions would be able to pick their way across the channel in several places.

Previously Danri had noticed one brutox guiding every ten or twelve bovars on the dam, but now he saw the spark-trailing minions advancing two to the side of each; the enemy commander obviously wanted to smooth out the route of attack. The digger estimated that another two-or three-score loads would raise the gap in the dam flush with the completed section—and with the cliff on the near side of the gorge.

The setting sun cast shadows through the trees, but in the

late twilight Danri watched the last of the bovars dump their loads. Dozens of brutox accompanied these beasts, and now the spark-dripping minions tromped back and forth across the dirt piled onto the dam—smoothing the avenue for the attack. The creatures kept their wicked eyes fixed on the woods as they marched, as if suspecting the presence of the Faerines there.

"Pembroak!" Danri hissed, backing away from his tree. The young digger crawled forward, peering from around a densely needled bush. "Get me a company of sylves, with bows—let's see if we can give these brutes something to worry about!"

Pembroak's eyes flashed at the suggestion, and he bared his teeth in a fierce, warlike grin. In the next instant he was gone, returning a few minutes later at the head of a file of grim-faced sylves.

"Tempting targets," declared their young captain, spying the laboring brutox. He arrayed his arches among the trees, concealed in the shadows. Their targets revealed themselves by the sparks that dripped from their talons, aided further by the fact that they stood silhouetted under a cloudless sky. A half moon provided the Faerines with plenty of illumination.

Danri, meanwhile, crept from tree to tree, quietly gathering his diggers. He explained his plan to each, and he was not surprised at the universal response—warlike snarls, hands clasped around the picks, hammers, and spades that served to arm this hastily organized company.

Sylvan arrows whistled from the woods, barely audible even in the still night. Brutox curses shattered that silence, as several of the minions collapsed. One bellowed furiously, toppling over the rim of the dam, tumbling down the long downstream face to smash into the exposed rocks of the riverbed below. Another brutox fell backward, barely grazed by an arrow but slipping fearfully into the growing reservoir of the dammed Aurun. Danri watched the water for a moment, not surprised to see no sign of the minion's emergence.

Another volley felled more brutox, while many survivors bolted for the far side of the dam. Others crawled away, painfully wounded but still alive, tusks glowing whitely as they turned fear-stricken eyes toward the hidden attackers.

"Go!" Danri barked. Immediately dozens of diggers raced

from the woods, gathering on the freshly packed dirt like laboring ants—or gnawing termites, more accurately. Picks and spades hacked, sending dirt and gravel in a cascade down the long outer face. Danri helped chop loose several embedded stones, but for the most part he kept his eyes on the far bank of the Aurun—and the skies above. Dark shadows moved across the stars sooner than he had expected, as a trio of brown drackans plummeted toward the laboring diggers.

"Off! To the woods!" he cried, shouting to his comrades, waving them toward the tenuous shelter of the trees. Diggers raced toward the limestone ledge, scrambling to get out of the deep notch excavated in a few short minutes of work.

The first drackan soared past, spitting a cloud of hissing steam above the dam. Several diggers perched at the lip of the muddy notch vanished in the killing blast, screaming for interminable moments of agony. The next of the great wyrms dove lower, breathing into the narrow confines of the diggers' excavation, turning the trench into a slippery-sided deathtrap. The third of the mighty drackans arrowed toward the diggers on the far side of the ditch where Danri stood with a few of his stalwart warriors. The digger commander watched the jaws gape, saw the horrific form expand against the star-speckled sky.

"Jump!" someone cried—Pembroak, Danri realized.

The diggers leapt from the top of the dam, some sliding into the muddy notch among the bodies of their companions, others tumbling toward the water on the upstream side. Danri and Pembroak skidded down the front face of the dam, sliding through loose dirt, tumbling over and over. Fighting the vivid memory of the brutox who had died on the rocks below, Danri struggled to stop. With an overhand chop he drove the pick of his hammer into the loose dirt. The tool almost slipped from his grasp, but, seizing the haft with both hands, he jerked his chaotic slide to a halt. Looking over his shoulder, he saw a shape below him, and was relieved that Pembroak, too, had arrested his fall.

Danri saw the pale belly of the drackan as it soared overhead, watched the billowing cloud of hissing gas envelop the top of the dam. Yet he heard no cries, and the digger tried to convince himself that all his troops had jumped out of harm's way before that wyrm had spewed its deadly breath. More shadows flashed across the sky, blanking out the stars in black, broad-winged swaths. Danri saw one of the monsters settling toward him, massive claws extended. He pulled the spike free and scrambled to the side, starting to roll again on the steep surface. The drackan smashed into the dam, claws gouging the dirt where the digger had been, but Danri tumbled below the flying serpent. The drackan slid downward too, twisting away from the dam and pouncing into the air to glide along the drying riverbed, fighting for speed. Finally the big wings pulled through the air and the wyrm banked into a slow, climbing turn.

"Pembroak! Come on!"

The young digger skipped down to Danri, and together they used their picks to make a controlled descent to the riverbed. Hopefully enough water remained to dissuade the minions from charging forward; if not, two diggers had a splendid chance to die fighting.

The bottom of the dam was deserted except for the body of the brutox that had earlier tumbled to its death. Quickly the diggers trotted along the river bank, avoiding the pools of water, sticking close to the Faerine bank. Soon the gorge walls tumbled away, and they had little difficulty scrambling up the muddy embankment and entering the woods.

"Who goes there?" demanded a deep voice, as something dark and huge rose from the shadows of the forest floor.

"Danri of Shalemont, and his squire," the digger replied, thankful to hear the familiar voice. "Gulatch?"

"Aye, digger. How fared the attack on the dam?"

Briefly describing the unsuccessful attempt at sabotage, Danri looked toward the eastern sky. "For some reason they seem to be delaying their attack—maybe waiting for daylight, or for the riverbed to dry. That gives us a few more hours to get ready."

"If they try to cross the riverbed, we'll stop them here," the big Faerine pledged.

Reassured that the lower reach of the defense was as well-guarded as possible, Danri turned back toward the limestone heights with Pembroak trailing behind. The digger captain knew that gigants, sylves, and more of his own kinsmen stood along the two-mile length of the drying Aurun—though whether they would be able to halt a massive minion attack remained very much a question. Still, it seemed to him that the dam was the most vulnerable place, and he would see that his best companies were in position to guard the terminus of that lofty highway.

This time, however, when he looked overhead he saw four or five serpentine shapes, gliding patiently over the dam. There would be no more attacks by the Faerines; from now on, they could only wait for the minion onslaught.

— 4 —

Banishment Peak jutted from the tangled chaos of the Brux-range like some nightmare version of a twisted, stone dagger blade. Indeed, Neambrey—slung like a sack of meal between Seddiim and Borcanesh—viewed the mountain as if it were a murderous knife. A bellyful of Aura sloshed within him, since the elders had allowed him one long drink before they flew; but the effects of the enchanted liquid quickly dissipated with the tension of impending exile.

"No!" cried the young drackan, twisting futilely in the mighty grip of the elders. The pair had to fly banked away from each other, which tended to stretch their unfortunate prisoner awkwardly. Now they clamped firmly down on their squirming charge, and Neambrey could only bray plaintively and cease his struggles.

"This is a tragedy not just for you but for all of drackan-kind!" Seddiim rebuked him. "At least you could try to bear it with dignity!"

"But you're wrong!" Neambrey replied, trying with re-markable success to speak calmly yet forcefully. "The brown drackans have turned against us all—Faerine needs the Trea-sure, now!"

"You're too much of a pup to be making such judgments," Borcanesh snarled. He was very muscular, and almost as big as a brown; now Borc made no effort to treat his young pris-oner gently. "We are creatures of tradition, of dignity and aloofness. You have betrayed all of that! Know that if the choice was mine, your punishment would not be so gentle."

As the barren peak drew closer, Neambrey saw absolutely nothing gentle about it. The summit was a keen edge of stone, sloping steeply from a point. It was perhaps twenty feet long, but only a few inches wide. Steep cliffs plunged for thousands of feet to each side, gradually merging into the upper fans of ancient gray glaciers.

"I *won't* go there!" Neambrey barked, twisting as hard as he could. His stomach was empty, his body fluid, supple, and strong. Aura swelled within him as he fought against this wrong, sensing the injustice not just for him, but for all Faerine! In a flash of clarity the drackan saw his true friends: By Aurianth, it was Quenidon and Danri who saw—and told—the truth, not his fellow drackans! Righteousness flared within the youngster, fueled by massive amounts of Aura—and unable to wait for nature, or tradition.

Perhaps Borc and Sediim relaxed their vigilance because they were so close to depositing Neambrey on the peak. Doubtless, too, he'd been so easily overpowered before they felt sure any further resistance was out of the question. In any event, the prisoner's sudden, desperate twists took the big greens by surprise.

"Scalesplitters!" cursed Seddiim, as Neambrey jerked his shoulder out of the elder drackan's claws.

Half free, Neambrey tumbled to the side, the sudden weight pulling Borcanesh over. The big drackan clung tightly, but sideslipped through the air toward the looming cliff of Banishment Peak—and now they fell below the summit, twisting as Borc tried to avoid a deadly collision.

The big green had no choice but to drop his charge, veering at the last second, grazing a wingtip on the unforgiving granite of the mountainous summit. Borcanesh flipped onto his back and looped through a dive, plummeting dizzily along the magnificent sweep of the cliff. His momentum carried him past the plunging Neambrey, and he was unable to seize the youngster before veering away from the mountain to bank off some of his speed.

Neambrey felt a sensation of joyous, unbelievable freedom. He shouted at the cliff as it swept past—the thought of danger never entered his mind. Exuberantly he strained against the stubby carapace that covered his budding wings—and that bony shell *cracked*!

In a moment of exhilarating power Neambrey unfurled fledgling wings, straining against the wind that swept them upward. He forced the appendages outward, felt the broad membranes catch the air. The rushing mountainside slowed; then the horizon careened across the young drackan's vision as he banked to the side, soaring away from Banishment Peak.

He had wings! Neambrey squawked in triumph, and was startled when the sound that emerged was more of a bellow—it lacked the depth of an adult's cry, of course, but it was much more forceful than a youngster's squeaking exclamations.

Deeper bellows signaled that his elder escorts had witnessed his metamorphosis. Risking a backward glance, Neambrey saw the two diving after his tail. Alarmed by the speed of their advance, Neambrey skittered to the side, stroking his new wings hard as he pulled for altitude. The sensation of flying, it seemed, was inherent to his being—he knew how to balance, how to hold his wings for a glide or beat them for maximum speed.

And he realized that he was much lighter than his two pursuers! Borcanesh plunged past Neambrey in a bellowing rush of talons, fangs, and green scales; the big drackan continued his dive for a long time after the youngster winged past, climbing steadily. Ducking to the side, Neambrey veered away from Seddiim's equally headlong dive, relishing a moment of relative safety as the big serpents struggled to regain altitude.

The young drackan skirted Banishment Peak, dipping into a glacier-lined bowl on the far side and winging desperately for the opposite ridge. Just before he crossed that next horizon he heard a howl from behind, and knew that at least one of the big greens had spotted him. The following valley was more of a plateau—a cliff plunged away from a broad, flat expanse of snowy barrens, while another ridge jutted even higher into the air along the far side of the lofty shelf. Neambrey's shadow pulsed and shimmered across that snowfield as he strove to reach the crest. He glanced back, saw Borcanesh closing in from behind on his left, while Seddiim curled out to prevent any escape to the right.

The barrier of the next cliff rose before Neambrey. As he stroked upward, feeling the chilly winds in his eyes and along his belly, he noticed a black line etched in places along the top of this ridge—the venomous smear of tarfrost. The crest

before him was the Watershed. If he continued on, Neambrey's first flight would take him into the skies of Duloth-
Trol—a dangerous place for even the mightiest drackan.
Terrions of the Nameless One were known to soar among
these heights, and the air itself was reputedly poisonous to
any Faerine who breathed it for more than a few minutes.

Yet Neambrey had, in a very brief time, become a different
drackan from the youngster who had been escorted to banishment. No such fate awaited him—he would die battling these
two elders before he would have his new wings clipped and
allow himself to be returned to that bleak summit. Pulling
sharply upward, he whirled through a tight loop at the top of
the cliff. The ridge of the Watershed was a narrow, slicing
blade of stone, draped with ice on both sides, but standing
out in sharp contrast of black snow against white.

Neambrey came to rest on the summit of the ridge, flapping
his wings for balance. Snapping downward, he tore off chunks
of Auraice with his jaws, swallowing the frozen liquid in long,
rippling gulps. He felt the pressure building and extended his
neck, mouth gaping. Hissing aggressively, he bobbed his head
back and forth between the approaching drackans. Borcanesh
swept upward and the young drackan ducked as the elder
banked along the crest of the ridge, spiraling around for another attack. Seddiim came in more slowly, rising toward the
crest a short distance away from Neambrey. Spreading his
wings, the green drackan lowered himself to the ridgetop,
balancing like a cat as he regarded Neambrey with angry
golden eyes.

"A bold change, wyrmling," Seddiim growled. "And
quick. A pity for you the wings didn't sprout an hour later,
when we'd flown off and left you!"

"I never would have let you put me on that peak!" Neambrey retorted.

Some instinct arose within him. Neck extended, rigid as a
spear, his jaws gaped wide. He blew, expelling the chill of
the Auraice he had eaten, and the blast came out as a whirlwind of frost. Tendrils of deadly cold wrapped around Seddiim's face and the green drackan darted backward, shaking
his head in anger.

"You are growing up too fast, little snake!" The elder's
voice was a furious snarl, his nostrils white with frostbite.

"The coldbreath is a power reserved only for the drackan elders!"

"Like the Treasure is to be kept from Faerines?" snapped Neambrey with heavy sarcasm. "That's always the complaint from you elders—somebody is trying to do something! All you want to do is sit around and talk, and think, and sniff about how much finer you are than any other Faerines!"

"Cease this insolence, wyrmling!" commanded Seddiim, rearing back to tower above the smaller drackan.

Neambrey heard stones skitter loose behind him, and he spun to see Borcanesh land on the other side, also perching on the steep-sided ridge-crest. Flanked by the big serpents, the hybrid lashed his head back and forth, snapping at first one and then the other. He would have chomped another bit of Aurasnow, blasting frosty breath at either one of the elders, except that he would have exposed himself to an attack from one direction or the other.

"You will only force us to hurt you," Borcanesh wheedled, trying the tactic of persuasion; at the same time, Neambrey noticed the big green creep closer by several steps along the ridge-crest. Spinning, the youngster lashed out, snapping his jaws shut on air—but startling Borc so much that the big drackan reared back, teetering precariously.

"You *must* come wi—" Seddiim hissed threateningly, but then choked off his words in a strangled gasp. Staring down the mountainous slope, the drackan growled deep in his chest.

"What is it?" Borcanesh followed his kinsman's gaze, gasping in astonishment when he looked down. "Guardians!"

Several creatures crawled swiftly up the sheer cliff. They were larger than men, though they had arms and legs and heads in a manlike arrangement. They were naked, their bodies a surface of supple, fluid rock. Stonelike fingers seized faint irregularities in the nearly vertical cliff, allowing the Guardians to climb straight up as swiftly as a person might walk across a smooth field.

"Wh-what are Guardians?" Neambrey asked, momentarily forgetting his peril in the face of the ascending beings. He counted five of them—no, six, as another well-camouflaged shape was distinguished by the regular climbing movements.

"They are protectors of the Watershed, aloof from all beings—even from us!" sneered Seddiim. "Perhaps they fear that we are trying to enter Duloth-Trol." The big drackan looked worried but not afraid; he remained squatting on the crest of the ridge, peering downward suspiciously.

"We do not enter the realm of the Sleepstealer!" Borcanesh declared loudly. "Go away!"

You must allow the wyrmling to go. The first Guardian halted thirty feet below. It had no mouth, and made no sound, but all three drackans clearly heard his message.

"Why do you interfere with a matter among drackans?" huffed Borc, his tone belligerent.

We do so when drackans interfere with the defense of the Watershed. Thus you have done, all of you who thwart this wyrmling.

"Why do you say this? The wyrmling has broken clan law—he must be punished!"

He is the only one who knows the real danger. You would do well to listen to him—but that is your concern. Ours is that you release him.

"Do you know what he means?" growled Borcanesh, lowering his head to glower into Neambrey's eyes. "What is this that you know?"

"What I've been telling you!" Neambrey declared. "I *was* right—we've got to help protect Faerine against the Sleepstealer! And it's *good* that the sylve took Lordsmiter, and maybe even that the human has it now!"

Let the young drackan go—he has much to do. And if you are wise, perhaps you will even give some thought to helping him.

The two elder drackans glowered at the Guardian, then turned their fuming expressions on the youngster. Neambrey knew his chance, and knew that he had little time to lose.

"I'm flying to the Aurun valley," the youngster informed them importantly. "You are welcome to come along—but please try to keep up."

With that, he spread his hour-old wings, caught the breeze rising against the border of Faerine, and launched himself into the air.

— 5 —

Rudy maintained his weaving spell for a day and a night, gathering the spray of the mighty fountain, spuming a column of steam to form the largest Auracloud anyone had ever seen. Pausing only long enough for sustaining draughts of Aura, he created a sky-ship long enough to span the entire park, with billowing towers of cumulus rising into three consecutive peaks.

When the Iceman emerged from the ring of pines encircling the fountain Mussrik Daringer was waiting for him. Behind the Royal Scion stood multiple ranks of sylvan warriors, golden helmets burnished to a sunlike brightness. More importantly, each bore a longbow and two quivers of arrows.

"The sylves of the Royal House are eager to avenge my brother, and their other comrades," Mussrik announced. "Two hundred have volunteered."

"They'll have plenty of targets, I can guarantee you that," the Iceman responded. He leaned back to look at the triple-humped cloud. "I'll put them on the central tower, for the most part—and some in the bow." Lowering his gaze, Rudy looked frankly into the sylve's eyes. "And Your Highness, I, too, would like vengeance in Quenidon Daringer's name. He was a friend I'll never forget."

Mussrik nodded. "It occurs to me that you, a human, knew my brother better than I did. Do you find that strange?"

"As strange as a gigant helping a digger, perhaps, or a galyon sailing to Faerine." The Iceman shrugged, but then he saw the truth. "Divides are falling—both to war, and to friendship."

"Let us hope that *one* divide—the Aurun—shall remain intact for a few more days. Good luck, Rudgar Appenfell." The Royal Scion extended a hand, and Rudy clasped it before turning to the embarking of his Auracloud.

The bottom of the cloud mingled with the tops of several of the loftiest elms, and the highest of the great trunks was circled by a spiral flight of steps. The two hundred archers of the Royal House marched to the tree, climbed the stairs, and scrambled onto the cloud.

Anjell and Dara met the Iceman and Raine on the field of grass below the elm. Anjell offered Raine a bouquet of clover she had gathered, then gave her uncle a somber hug.

"Good luck," Dara whispered into Rudy's ear. "May Aurianth fly with you."

"She will!" the Iceman replied. "And you keep an eye from the city."

Dara held up her parchment journal with ink-stained fingers. "I'm going to write down everything I see."

"I wish I could go with you!" Anjell beseeched Rudy.

"No—you're staying in the city, with me!" retorted Dara.

"I can't go on the galyon—or on the cloud! I'm not allowed to go *anywhere*!" wailed the only human girl in Faerine.

Laughing, feeling strangely at ease, Rudy ascended the spiral stairs, supervising a score of gigants who carried along flasks of Aura and extra bundles of arrows. Raine boarded too, climbing to the stern tower, where she and the Iceman would ride. Rudy thought of Danri, somewhere up near the dam, and of Kestrel, Awnro, and Darret aboard the *Black Condor*. He could see the galyon standing off the dock, at anchor for now.

Larrial Solluel arrived in the park shortly. The blind sylve had spent the last days beside the Scrying Pool, but now he ascended the stairs, guided by a young attendant, to the Iceman's Auracloud. The Scrying Master's scarred face looked pallid and unhealthy in the sunlight, but as he spoke to Rudy he bounced vibrantly on the balls of his feet, like a young man eager to run. "The bloodwagons are gathered as you hoped, to the rear of the army. Unfortunately, the *Dreadcloud* remains overhead."

"So I see," Rudy said, as he looked across the lake to the looming black monstrosity. He could feel the violent and destructive power contained within that massive, vaporous shape.

"The minion ranks are drawn up behind the dam," Solleul added. "I believe that the attack will commence within the hour. The army has been in position all morning, but I think they wanted to take the time to fuel their sky-ship."

"When the attack comes, we'll be ready to move," the Iceman declared. He clapped a hand on the scarred sylve's shoulder, surprised to feel the rippling tension in the elder's muscles. "Will you watch us in the pool?"

"No—I will watch from the best vantage of all." With

those words, ignoring the objections that died, barely voiced, in Rudy's throat, the Scrying Master climbed aboard.

And finally the tethers fell away, and the Auracloud of the Iceman was free to fly.

TWENTY-FOUR

Clash of Clouds

Of all the elements of the Watershed, no two
kindle the antipathy of Darkblood mingled with
Aura.
—CODEX OF THE GUARDIANS

— 1 —

Phalthak rode the *Dreadcloud*'s battery deck, padded feet
spread wide-apart as his long green snake extended far over
the vaporous gunwale, looking downward. The Lord Minion
was pleased to see the tangible pillar of dark smoke twisting
with the wind, curling sideways to merge with the hull of the
sky-ship. Below, the bloodwagons were drawn up in a wide
clearing, more than a mile from the shore of Faerine's great
lake. The stone pool he had used for Immersion was still full
of the black liquid, while scores of the wheeled vats and their
bovar haulers had been aligned in neat rows around this rock-
lined bowl.

Three of the wagons had been drawn to the side, the bovar
haulers released from their harnesses, and the iron tanks
parked side by side over a gaping fire hole. Hundreds of
kroaks bore timbers to the pit, tossing them in, steadily boiling

the vats of thick liquid. From each of the tanks an oily column of smoke spewed upward, the plumes merging hundreds of feet in the sky. The combined pillar of gaseous Darkblood continued upward until it vanished into the stern of the *Dread-cloud*.

The Lord Minion's green head curled over the deck again, twisting to fix ruby eyes upon a nearby stalker. "Summon Captain Direfang!" hissed the serpent mouth, flicking a slender tongue.

"Aye, lord!" The stalker all but raced into the hull, returning shortly with the brutox.

Again it was the green head undulating forward, fixing the glowing fire-spots of its eyes upon the lesser minion. "As soon as the vats are capped, make for the dam at full speed."

"Of course, Mighty Lord!" Direfang promised with a sparking salute. "The wind is strong, and will carry us swiftly up the river."

Phalthak looked across the eerie, disorienting expanse of the Auraloch. True to Direfang's observation, wind ruffled the water, sweeping from southeast to northwest in strong, steady gusts. The sky was for the most part clear, though several small puffs of cloud dotted the air over Spendorial—Aura-clouds, perhaps. The Lord Minion's snakes hissed and chortled, sneering at the pathetic little blobs, hoping at least one of them would soon drift near these potent lightning batteries.

Within a few minutes kroaks had sealed the nearly empty vats down below, letting the vaporous umbilical wisp into tattered shreds. Freed of its tether, the *Dreadcloud* drifted slowly inland, borne by the wind until the sturmvaults pulsed and the black cloud picked up speed. Phalthak watched in satisfaction as Direfang guided the ship along the near bank of the river, steadily approaching the earthen dam, casting a broad shadow over both armies. Looking below, the Lord Minion saw the barrier in the end of the Aurun gorge, fanning like a wedge of dirt into the drying riverbed below. That channel was not yet dry enough for the minions to cross, but every hour brought more rocks poking upward from the settling wetness.

The sky-ship came to rest at the dam, sturmvaults anchored over the mass of the minion army while the mighty batteries drifted above the line of the river. From his vantage in the bow, Phalthak could see groves of woods on the far bank, and was coolly certain the forest teemed with diggers and other enemies. Thunder rumbled and boomed in the six black pillars of the battery, and lightning flickered within each vaporous column, ready to explode. Direfang shortly returned to the bow and Phalthak indicated the woods crowning the north side of the river gorge. "When you are done, I do not want to see a single tree left standing."

"It will be an immense pleasure to obey, my lord." The captain bowed, then turned and raised his voice to a bellow, shouting with an outburst of sparks. "Stalkers of the forward battery: Stand to your pillars. Now, fire!"

Bolts of lightning ripped forth from the underside of the massive cloud, six earsplitting crashes in rapid succession. The deck pulsed beneath Phalthak's feet and the Lord Minion felt an electric thrill as jagged thunderbolts slammed into the very crest of the knob, shattering trees and bedrock, cascading debris onto the dam and through the woods. Another sequence of flashes sent a steady barrage of destruction raking across the wooded ground. Tree trunks burst into flames, others splintered into a million shards, and still the killing blasts continued their relentless onslaught, pounding steadily. And even as the battery recharged, the echoes of recent blasts resounded across the lake, rocking the air with continuing, tumultuous noise.

The bombardment first obliterated the grove at the end of the dam—no less than four lethal volleys sizzled into this small stretch of woods, disintegrating ancient roots, pulverizing solid rock. Then Direfang expanded the range of destruction, directing the lethal blasts beyond the bluff. Fires swept through the woods, and blasts of lightning ignited more and more trunks in an ever-wider swath.

Phalthak watched the destruction with fierce pleasure, imagining Faerines blown to pieces, or trapped in the wreckage and slowly burning to death. Many of his fanged jaws twisted into expressions of cruel delight, until one of the kroak gunners broke his mood. The craven minion bobbed forward, too frightened to speak—but obviously seeking the Fang's attention.

"What is it? Talk!"

"Th-there, lord—over the lake!" babbled the terrified kroak, the knobbed forehead bowing low.

"What?" spat Phalthak. The Lord Minion's heads turned, hissing with fury as they saw the white shape gliding over the water, surging toward the near shore. An Auracloud! The Faerine sky-ship was alarmingly big, moving with shocking speed.

"Direfang!" The green head rose stiffly, speaking with the force of command. "Cease the bombardment. We have a new target!"

"Aye, lord!" If the brutox was surprised, he was shrewd enough not to show it.

Immediately the *Dreadcloud*'s batteries grew silent, and the sturmvaults rumbled with thunder of their own, swinging the mighty sky-ship around. Yet now it moved with agonizing slowness, and Phalthak felt a glimmer of apprehension as he remembered the wind—wind that had carried them swiftly up the river, that now bore the Auracloud as if on the wings of an eagle.

— 2 —

Flames kindled by lightning crackled in the branches over Danri's head. The digger's skull rang, and charred splinters showered over him as a huge branch smashed to the ground barely a foot away. Shivering involuntarily, the digger raised his shield over his head and backed up. All around, the woods had been reduced to a tangle of charred deadfalls, splintered trunks, and small, crackling fires. Fortunately, most of the diggers had pulled back with the first blasts. Now, as Danri returned to the front, he could see no sign of the brave scouts who had remained behind.

He looked around cautiously, aware of the loud ringing in his ears—but no longer hearing the explosions or seeing the flashes of lightning. A charred boot jutted from beneath a stump, and the digger grimaced as he stepped over the corpse of a burned, mangled warrior. Danri pushed through the blasted wood seeking survivors, unaware of a forest giant, weakened by fire and lightning, leaning, then falling faster. Still deafened, the digger wasn't aware of the falling tree until a shower of branches brushed his shoulders. He tried to spring away, but a heavy limb pinned his legs, holding him firmly in place.

"Lord Danri! Where are you?" Pembroak's voice was a welcome sound against the background of ringing eardrums and sputtering flames.

"Over here!" the digger croaked, wincing at the pain that shot through his back.

The young warrior scrambled into view, crawling between splintered trunks. "Are you okay? Here—let me help!" Pembroak said. Placing the haft of his axe beneath the limb pinning Danri, he levered it upward for an inch or so—enough to allow the older digger to crawl free.

"Here," said Pembroak, offering Danri a drink of Aura from his half-empty flask. The injured captain drank greedily, feeling the pain soothed from his muscles, the strength and feeling returning to his numbed legs. Stretching his muscles, he massaged bruised thighs, limbering slowly.

A roar exploded from the far side of the gorge as the first rank of kroaks and brutox charged, rushing across the dam. The minions quickly spilled into the shattered forest, and Danri, Pembroak, and the few other digger survivors had no choice but to scramble backward. Diving through the tangled ruin, the Faerines finally reached undamaged forest. Wattli and a band of sartors stood here, and the diggers ceased their retreat to face the onslaught beside their allies. Kroaks fell by the score, and brutox perished among them, but still the tide of death surged onward. More minions rushed across the dam, a steady stream of monsters pounding onto the near side of the river, expanding like floodwaters released from a confining dike.

Danri and Pembroak stood with the sartor chieftain, wielding hammer, sword, and spear in deadly combination. Minions hurled themselves through the tangled wood, only to die beneath the whirling weapons of the Faerines. Even now, when the defenders had gone into battle rested and well fed, weapons repaired and sharpened, replenished with fresh allies like the sartors, their task seemed hopeless. Dozens of minions fell, and still the horde flowed unabated across the dam. What use was strength and rest, Danri wondered in despair, when the enemy would just batter you down again? Nevertheless,

his right hand bashed with the hammer, the left arm raised
his shield against uncountable attacks.

The Faerines held firm for savage minutes, resisting the
increasing pressure of minion numbers. Danri slew two dozen
kroaks by himself; beside him, Wattli felled a score. Faerines
fell too—many of them had survived the long retreat from
Darkenheight only to perish at the gates of their city.

Long shadows fell as leather-winged death soared from the
skies. The drackans dove silently, following their shadows
into the field army with barely an instant's warning. Soaring
at treetop level, formed into a long line, the monsters swept
over the Faerine front with jaws gaping. Steam erupted from
the leader, hissing and lethal, and behind the first drackan
came another, and another, and still more. Scores of brave
warriors died, scalded horribly, falling to the right and left of
each explosive exhalation. In moments the Faerine line broke
once more, and warriors with no lack of courage fled the
battle, railing bitterly against a foe they could not fight.

— 3 —

Rudy's mental hold on the cloud tightened forcefully, and
he felt the showering Aura falling away, pouring toward the
wagons of Phalthak's bloodtrain. As the sky-ship approached
the target, he had observed the square enclosure, black as the
heart of Duloth-Trol, in the rocks. Now he estimated that the
bloodpool was directly below the center of his Auracloud,
under the drops that sprinkled with deceptive beauty toward
the ground.

The waters of Faerine showered into the Darkblood with
an explosion that rocked land and sky, louder than a thun-
derclap. The Auracloud heaved upward, twisted by convulsive
forces, and Rudy's heart froze at the sight of several Royal
House sylves tossed from their lofty vantages on the cloud's
central tower, the golden helmets blinking out of sight as the
warriors plummeted into the smoldering inferno.

The Iceman stood near the stern of his long sky-ship, atop
a low rise in the billowing surface. The sylvan archers were
clustered on the highest mound, amidships, and upon another
large tower in the bow of the Auracloud. Larrial Solluel, the

Iceman knew, rode near the crest of that foremost pillar, while the casks of Aura and bundles of extra arrows were gathered atop the central column. From its entire length the Auracloud shed its rain, and now the explosions spread to the wagons of the bloodtrain. Some of the vats splintered and cracked under the force, spilling more Darkblood onto the ground—where it was exposed to the Aurashower, expanding the destructive force still further.

Rudy looked westward, seeing the *Dreadcloud* tower over the dam, glowering like a shadow above the fires on the far bank of the Aurun. On the other flank he saw the *Black Condor* sailing a stately course, a few hundred paces offshore. The flotilla of Faerine boats, many armed with steel-coiled trebuchets similar to the galyon's powerful armament, skittered and bobbed in the waters around the big ship.

"Drackans!" Rudy spat, suddenly seeing the bronze shapes winging along close to the ground, flying in waves over the minion army on a course for the dam.

"Rudy—look!" Raine's voice was calm but urgent.

The Iceman followed her pointing finger, saw the *Dreadcloud* in the western sky. The mass of darkness surged, abandoning the attack at the dam, striking toward the lake in an obvious effort to save the wagons of precious, sustaining vitriol.

Immediately Rudy urged his Auracloud to move—not in flight, but upward. The great sky-ship rose with regal dignity, still showering into the seething, exploding chaos below—each burst pushing the craft higher, faster. Strong winds still delayed the black cloud's progress, and the Iceman prayed desperately that they could rise above those killing storm batteries. He squinted, watching sylvan archers ready arrows, their keen eyes searching in every direction. He took a long drink from his Auraskin, draining the leather sack, reminding himself that he would shortly have to refill the container from one of the casks amidships.

Still the *Dreadcloud* loomed, closing quickly. Putrid smoke trailed in black tendrils from the stern of the enemy sky-ship, and Rudy sensed the pulsing power of the three huge pillars of black cloud in the stern. They were as perfectly dark as the rest of the monstrous craft, with one difference: A rhymthic, volcanic fire rose in steady cadence within each.

The cloud surface didn't actually glow, but Rudy could see the bursts of crimson heat in the crevices and hollows between billowing lobes of darkness. The central pillar fired first, and the monstrous craft pushed through the skies; then the port and starboard chambers pulsed together, and the towering ship surged farther. Wind whipped the highest summits of the vessel's lofty towers, ripping away pieces of darkness—but these were tenuous, small components. The bulk of the ship pressed ahead relentlessly, and now the Iceman saw ranks of kroaks and brutox standing ready for battle on the dark ship's vaporous decks. Terrions swooped and swirled around the high superstructure, though fortunately these fliers showed no tendency to venture far from their base.

A volley of arrows flicked from the center of the Auracloud, and only then did Rudy see the new threats—more terrions, winging toward his ship with silent, deadly intensity. The minion fliers swept from two directions, a dozen diving from port and an equal number winging swiftly toward the stern. Fortunately the Royal House sharpshooters had been more observant than Rudy, and now they sent a hailstorm of arrows through the air.

The first volleys ripped toward the rear, striking with lethal accuracy. Terrions shrieked and keened, some crumpling while others banked, crippled. More arrows flew, and with the second fusillade all but one of the terrion flight had fallen. The lone survivor tucked its wings and dove, vanishing into the chaos of the disintegrating bloodtrain.

The fliers coming from above swept down one of the Auracloud's pillowy towers, bashing a score of sylves from the sky-ship, crushing the warriors with powerful jaws, or dragging them from the cloud with their talons. One of the creatures swerved toward the stern, diving at Rudy, but Raine stood atop the hummock and she slashed at the monster, driving it away before the Man of Three Waters was threatened. More arrows trailed after the departing terrions, scoring several hits, and Rudy watched the remaining minions bank away from the cloud and continue to dive.

The Iceman's hand came to rest on the pommel of Lordsmiter, and once again the question rang through his mind: *Why me*? Why did he carry this potent weapon, when all around him his comrades and allies battled for their lives?

Perhaps one of those dead sylves could have used it to kill a terrion! Surely the blade would serve better in the hands of some stalwart hero on the front lines!

Abruptly Rudy noticed the *Dreadcloud* again, startled by its proximity. The shadowy form closed in as inexorably as nightfall, filling the sky, blocking out light. The Auracloud still climbed, but not as rapidly as before, and now Rudy strained desperately. He reached for his waterskin, then remembered that it was empty—he had no time!

As he labored for altitude, Rudy saw the lightning pillars tilt back, merging toward the hull of the ship. Black, limitless holes gaped in the underside of the six columns—the holes seemed even darker than the stygian shade of the cloud itself. Higher rose the Auracloud, but Rudy saw the clear peril—he was too slow! The *Dreadcloud* rumbled closer still, bucking the current of the wind, pitching firmly through the smoke-spattered sky. The Iceman concentrated on the need for height, blanking his mind of all distractions. Heeling to the side, the Auracloud rocked in the wind off the lake as the Royal House sylves launched volleys of arrows at the black sky-ship. And still those abyssal holes gaped from the bottom of the batteries.

Sudden heat flared within the wells of darkness, lightning exploding, crackling forth in a series of flaming lances. Rudy *saw* the instantaneous flight of the deadly missiles, watched the forked heads rip, one after another, into his Auracloud amidships. Shrill screams told him that many sylves were hit; at the same time the ship itself hissed into steam, twisting with a violent convulsion. More bolts of lightning ripped the heart out of the sky-ship, blasted Rudy's creation apart, explosions ripping through the moist center of the cloud to tear away the foretower and bow.

Raine tumbled down the slope of the stern tower and the Iceman dove after her in a frenzy, seizing her outstretched hand as the billowing platform rocked chaotically. The central portion of the Auracloud collapsed, scores of sylves tumbling as the vapor dissolved into Aura, spilling as rain and flesh into the continuing ruin of the bloodtrain. The precious casks of liquid also fell, disappearing into the chaos below to trigger a new wave of huge explosions.

Rudy sank his hand into the giving surface of the cloud,

clawing for purchase. At the same time he commanded the
remnant of the ship to rise, and the stern portion of the Auracloud slowly lofted through the air, drawing away from the
seething tumult below. Grasping with her free hand, kicking
with her feet, Raine crawled up the steep side of the cloud
until she reached a pocket of relative safety.

The *Dreadcloud* continued forward inexorably, driving
through the gap where the Auracloud's center had been. The
midsection of Rudy's cloud—the vapor that had dissolved
into rain—reached the ground at the same time, and from
above Rudy watched the black sky-ship tremble and shudder
from the force of the explosions. Large chunks broke from
the stern, careening downward, trailing black vapor.

A tremendous blast erupted and the *Dreadcloud* surged,
twisting and groaning like a ship of timber caught in the grip
of a strong gale. Rudy watched the power chambers in the
stern, saw that only two of them were flashing. The third, to
starboard, showed great rents in its formerly bulbous shape,
and black wisps of cloud trailed away, like smoke, from the
damage.

Only then did the Iceman look down and see the forequarters of his Auracloud. A large portion of the white sky-ship
remained intact, drifting on the other side of the *Dreadcloud*—
though, without Rudy's presence to hold it intact, it steadily
continued to dissolve. Scores of sylves stood atop the remnant, the doomed warriors firing the last of their arrows at
targets on the *Dreadcloud* or the ground below.

The Iceman watched breathlessly, fearing that the bow of
the Auracloud would quickly disintegrate. But it retained its
shape, even as it slowly settled toward the ground, and then
the Iceman knew: Larrial Solluel still lived aboard the remnant of the ship. The Scrying Master's power wasn't sufficient
to control the cloud, which was huge by sylvan standards, but
he held it together as it settled, giving the sylves some chance
at survival.

Yet, with a chill of foreboding, Rudy saw that survival
might not be the blind Auramaster's intention. The remnant
veered toward the minion camp, swerving alongside the looming bulk of the *Dreadcloud*. The enemy ship remained over
the tortured wreckage of the bloodtrain, as if it sought sustenance from the plumes of smoke billowing into the air. Yet

the massive black shape reeled from side to side like a monster in pain, and black vapor trailed from the three great towers of its superstructure.

"No!" The Iceman's cry rang through the air, but quickly vanished into the din of chaos. Rudy watched the white vapor pressing through the smoke, gaining speed, diving purposefully downward.

Kneeling upon the spongy surface, Rudy closed his eyes, exerting all the power of his Auramastery toward the sinking remnant. He tried to touch the cloud, to steer it away from certain disaster, knowing that even a landing in the lake would be preferable to the convulsions and explosions ripping across the ground.

He felt the presence of Larrial Solluel, confirmed his mentor's intentions even as he reacted with instinctive horror. "No!" Rudy shouted again, though he didn't know if he actually articulated the sound.

Leave us. The plea came to his mind, in the Scrying Master's voice, but the Iceman could not obey. He begged Solluel to abandon his plan, but the sylve made no reply; his portion of the Auracloud continued to descend, veering under the belly of the black ship and vanishing from the Iceman's sight. Yet Rudy knew where his sylvan mentor was going, and the human Auramaster fixed his eyes on the twin chambers that still functioned, watched the alternate pulsing of seething bloodfire.

The explosion when Solluel's Auracloud crashed into the bloodtrain was perhaps not quite as violent as one or two of the earlier bursts—but it was placed with absolute precision. Pressure and smoke and steam ripped upward, slashing into the stern of the *Dreadcloud,* tearing away the two sturmvaults in a multitude of smaller eruptions. Stuttering explosions continued to wrack the black hull, and great showers of black rain fell downward—mingled with shrieking kroaks and stalkers. Brutox fell too, each plummeting like a shooting star toward the ground, trailing a long tail of crackling sparks.

Rudy groaned and buried his face in his hands—only Raine's firm grip on his shoulder kept him from toppling forward. "Larrial!" he croaked bitterly.

Frantically Raine pulled him upright, cursing and grunting. "Look!" she spat, pointing to the massive darkness. "Look—

see what he did! And don't waste this chance!''

The *Dreadcloud*, Rudy saw, rocked from side to side, canting violently back and forth. Twisting and spinning through the air, it drifted away from the nearly decimated bloodtrain, moving slowly over the land. By watching carefully, and by comparing it to the plumes of real fires on the ground, Rudy saw the proof.

The enemy ship, for the time being at least, was driven only by the wind.

— 4 —

"Go! Report on the damage! *Immediately!*''

Phalthak needed all of his restraint to avoid slaying Captain Direfang on the spot. The brutox vanished into the hull, no glimmer of spark showing on his cringing figure, while Phalthak's heads bobbed and lashed. The furious Lord Minion kept his footing, with difficulty, on the pitching deck, and when a stalker emerged from the hull, closer to the Fang of Dassadec than it had intended, a red serpent struck from the nest. The stalker screamed as twin fangs punctured its chest, then toppled backward with bright flames bursting from the reptilian body, quickly consuming flesh and Darkblood.

The *Dreadcloud* reeled in the force of the wind, coursing above the ruined bank of the Aurun. The wreckage of the bloodtrain spewed smoke and steam into the air, mocking the successes that Phalthak's army had begun to make on the ground—for, without the reserves of sustaining Darkblood, many of the Lord Minion's troops would have to encamp below, waiting in virtual dormancy until replacement wagons could make their way over Darkenheight Pass.

Yet perhaps the army could still make that camp in the ruins of Spendorial. Already columns of minions poked across the drying riverbed, and the defenders at the dam must surely have been obliterated by the lightning barrage. "What is the status of the sturmvaults?'' the Lord Minion demanded as Captain Direfang scuttled into view again.

"There is a chance . . . a good chance . . . that the starboard chamber can be restored. It will take time, but—''

"Enough prattling. And the other chambers?''

Direfang blinked and squirmed. "They . . . they are gone, lord, simply gone."

Again Phalthak exerted supreme restraint. "How . . . much . . . time—to repair the last chamber?"

"Er, that is not clear. A day, perhaps . . ."

"By that time we'll have blown across half of Faerine!" rasped the Lord Minion.

"B-but, lord—perhaps there is another way . . . perhaps the drackans can hold us, even move the ship! Look, lord—there they fly."

Several of Phalthak's heads turned, following the brutox's extended finger, watching the winged lizards soar past. The drackans flew in twin trios, each in a tight wedge, and for a moment the Lord Minion allowed himself to hope.

Then all of his eyes blazed in fury, and every head whipped toward Direfang. A snake of cobalt blue slithered forward, low along the ground, coiling upward as far as the brutox's bulging belly.

"Fool!" hissed the azure head, extending to flick a forked tongue along Direfang's trembling skin.

"Fool!" echoed the other snakes, a chorus. "Are you so stupid you cannot see that these drackans are *green*!"

— 5 —

Neambrey led the way, Borcanesh and Seddiim flying just behind each of his outspread wings. The gray-scaled drackan—small, but no longer a youngster—dove toward the high dam, arrowing at the four brown shapes perched atop the earthen barrier. His wings were old friends now, and the Aura swelling his belly was a weapon of righteous vengeance.

Elsewhere, Verdagon led Pashra and Messantal in a slanting descent toward the lakeshore. The two groups had split up after making the long flight from the icefields. Their attack plan was aggressive, based on Verdagon's pronouncement of the famed adage: "He who attacks a powerful but sleeping foe must make his first blow count for much."

On the dam, four brown drackans flapped their wings in obvious agitation. Large and sinuous creatures they were, but Neambrey hissed disgustedly as he saw that none of these

wyrms was big enough to be Jasaren. Yet they were all the
enemy, and now they smugly watched their allies surge across
the once-hallowed woodlands of Faerine. The pressure of
Aura swelled in Neambrey's belly, and he could feel the chill
of the snow he and his fellow greens had devoured a few
hours before.

Some premonition warned one of the browns to look upward, bellowing in alarm as he saw the emerald color of the
descending drackans. But the warning came too late—Neambrey raised his head and curled his tail, swooping along the
crest of the dam as Aurafrost exploded from his jaws. The
icy blast swept around the shrieking brown, instantly freezing
the cries in the serpent's rigid, dead throat.

Seddiim blasted his frostbreath across two more browns,
killing both, while huge Borcanesh saved the lethal exhalation
in favor of slamming into the fourth enemy drackan. With a
crushing bite, the big green snapped the neck of his dumb-
struck victim.

Somewhere above, Verdagon, Pashra, and Messantal
soared in great circles, watching for signs of the other browns.
Neambrey looked too, but he didn't see his sire or any enemy
wyrm as he winged steadily upward. He *did* see distressing
signs of war everywhere—a landscape splintered and charred.
Violence had wrenched rocks from the ground, casting monstrous boulders like a child tosses marbles.

Then a bellow exploded like thunder from the far side of
the river, rumbling down from a cloudless sky. Neambrey saw
the widespread wings of a diving horror, a span broader than
any other drackan's—brown or green.

Jasaren had come.

— 6 —

"I have brought this thing, master, as you desired."

You are wise, my brutox, that you know my desires so well.

"Forgive me, O Great One!" The minion, not knowing if
he was being rebuked, flung himself to the black marble floor
of Agath-Trol's vast throne room. Dassadec's presence was
here, though of course the God of Darkness didn't reveal
himself to his abasing follower.

You have the treasure, the shard of darkness you brought from the wreckage of Lanbrij?

"Oh yes, lord! I have it here—carried for thousands of miles immersed in Darkblood. Now only, I bring it forth." The brutox raised the slick black object, which seemed to be a stone about the size of a human's skull, though shaped in more of an oblong. One end of the chunk tapered to a sharp, straight point.

Bring it forward, to the steps of the well.

The brutox trembled slightly at the words, but nevertheless carried the precious object across the broad floor until it stood at the top of a flight of wide stairs. The steps, twelve in number, descended downward to a surface of inky black liquid— the Heart of Darkblood, as every minion knew.

Your reward, brutox, shall be a blessing unlike any other. Raise the treasure before you.

Perhaps the minion had an inkling of its master's desires. In any event, the taloned hands of the brutox, sparking hesitantly, turned the sharp end of the Darkblood block to face its own pounding chest.

Your life, miserable one, shall provide the initial spark that will return my Eye to his throne. Now! Slay yourself! Drive the spike into your worthless heart, and know the glory of my name!

With scarcely a moment's hesitation the brutox pulled the object toward itself, feeling the sharp spike puncture black skin and carve relentlessly into corrupt flesh. The point advanced as if it had a destination in mind, slithering around the brutox's steel-strong ribs, slicing like a wire probe as it found, and entered, the heart.

The brutox grunted and toppled, dead in that instant. The huge corpse rolled over and over, with the spike of the Darkblood treasure still punched through its chest. The body halted its roll halfway to the pool, and the oblong block stuck to its chest began, slowly, to swell. Like a leech approaching the point of bursting, the black remnant of Nicodareus sucked the Darkblood from the dying brutox, until at last the minion was a drained husk, lying like chaff at a grotesque angle on the steeply sloping stairs.

Ultimately, however, the weight of the swollen treasure was enough to dislodge the corpse, and the two denizens of

Duloth-Trol, linked together by death and life, tumbled into
the well and disappeared beneath the dark and oily surface.

For a long time the thing that had been Nicodareus lay
beneath the slick, silent liquid. The corpse of the brutox eventually crumbled and dissolved, leaving the shard of stony
hardness immersed alone in the greatest well of Darkblood in
all Duloth-Trol. The power of the Lord Minion's omnipotent
master flowed through the granite-hard skin, and slowly the
remnant of Nicodareus regained a measure of its earlier vitality.

Gradually the black oblong swelled, distorting grotesquely.
Wings sprouted, wrapping around the rest of the gruesome
shape like smothering blankets—or a leathery eggshell. Arms
and legs extended, and steel-hard talons emerged from the
tips of fingers and toes. The great head took shape once again,
from the beastlike muzzle to the forehead crowned with twin
horns.

And at last, after time uncounted in the blackened depths,
the black eyelids pulled back to reveal the orbs of hatred,
glowing with the red fires of fury. Slowly the thing that was
again Nicodareus rose through the layers of Darkblood—this,
too, being a process that took the passing of many days.

The tips of the batlike wings finally broke the surface of
the well, emerging slick and perfectly black. More of the
wings jutted upward, and then the horns of the Lord Minion's
head came into view. Slowly the crown of the skull rose, and
finally those gleaming, hellish eyes blinked free of their master's liquid, glaring hatefully around the looming chamber of
the throne room.

Nicodareus had returned.

He stepped slowly up the wide, black stone stairs, aware
of a certain irony—many minions had made the journey down
these steps, but he was perhaps the only one of the Sleepstealer's servants to make the march in the opposite direction.

Ah, my pet, my Eye. I see that you have awakened.

"Yes, master," cried Nicodareus, throwing himself flat
upon the floor. He understood only that he must have been
terribly damaged by the human's Aura-trap, and that somehow he—or his remains—had been transported to Agath-Trol.

Nicodareus tried to prepare himself for the punishments his
master certainly had in mind. He remembered earlier wracks,

when his entire body had convulsed with agony, and for just
a moment the Eye of Dassadec wondered if it might not have
been better if he had been left to perish in Landbrij. But this
was a momentary weakness and he banished it forcefully.
Nicodareus had already existed for many millennia, and it was
not the destiny of some pathetically short-lived human to
bring about his expiration.

But as he groveled, face averted, he felt no rivets of burning
agony across his skin, no searing torture wracking his guts;
in fact, there was no pain at all. Instead Nicodareus came to
know something even worse, as Dassadec compelled his powerful lieutenant to crawl abjectly about the mighty throne
room. The dark god summoned kroaks, choosing the weakest
and most malformed specimens of that ignoble race. These
minions spat upon the debased lord, bade Nicodareus wash
their feet, humiliate himself before their gaping, stupid eyes.

With no will of his own, the Lord Minion was forced to
obey Dassadec's will, and he served the miserable kroaks as
a foot-washer, a tailor, even a whore. Every whim of the
creatures Nicodareus granted, with fawning obeisance. The
Sleepstealer granted a sole consolation: Each of the lesser
minions, after serving his role in the punishment, was compelled to march into the Darkblood, consigning his vitality to
that vast pool of the Sleepstealer's power. The disciplining of
Nicodareus was an important task, but Dassadec would not
have witnesses among the kroaks to report their master's humiliation to their comrades through the realm.

Still more minions came, filthy and disgusting mutants,
weaker and more stupid than kroaks, and these Nicodareus
licked clean, tending hideous and eternal sores. He debased
himself ever lower, and with a constant string of new witnesses—until finally the Lord Minion threw himself to the
floor, clawing at his flesh with his own talons. "Please—
torture me, master. Sear me with agony, rip my guts for your
pleasure! But grant me pain, my lord, instead of constant humiliation!"

His only answer was mocking laughter that rumbled like a
thunderstorm. Another wave of deformed wretches trooped
forward to make obscene demands of the lord, and always
the Eye of Dassadec obeyed. Nicodareus was not aware of
the moment when the punishment finally ceased. He became

gradually conscious of a vague nothingness, a surrounding that was not monstrously unpleasant. And then he knew: His debasement had been concluded, and his master would allow him to live to reclaim his throne, and his place among the rulers of the world.

Sitting up, rolling to his hands and knees, the Lord Minion slowly struggled to his feet. He faced the massive dais, looking at the central pillar, seat of his own throne. He would not now presume to climb those spiraling stairs, nor to take that lofty chair; still, he felt confident that one day he would be permitted to do so again.

Now, my Eye, you have been given the chance to serve me again. I have need of your Sight.

"Command, master." Nicodareus trembled to a thrill of elation.

You must again seek for me, locate the Man of Three Waters.

His Sight! The Eye of Dassadec probed immediately, fearful of failure—yet desperate to please his master. Surprisingly he strained only briefly to discover his enemy. "He is in Faerine, master. Yet he does not drink Aura, for I see him without difficulty! Allow me to go, to kill him!"

No—that is a task for one who is not a failure. The words cut through Nicodareus with venomous, doomful import—and all the humiliations of before were as nothing compared to the disgrace he sensed was imminent. *I bid you watch the accomplishment of your cohort, my Fang. . . .*

TWENTY-FIVE

Watershed

There comes a time when prudent decisions,
intricate plans, and the most determined
intentions are overwhelmed by the inexorable
tide of fate.
—SONGS OF AURIANTH

— 1 —

At the edge of the splintered forest beside the dam, Danri spat
in frustration, watching minions advance through the riverbed.
The tireless enemy warriors followed dry, rocky paths through
the trough of the Aurun's course, which by late afternoon had
dried almost completely. In one place near the dam a hundred
kroaks rushed a lone gigant standing against the assault; farther down, many brutox led the way, bashing aside a line of
young sylves. Like a stain of pollution, the minion columns
crossed the drying river and spread through wood and
meadow. Breakthroughs ruptured the line, and clashes and
shouts signaled unseen skirmishes in the forest below. Gradually the roars of triumphant minions overwhelmed the challenges of diggers and gigants.

At the dam, the minions showed no sign of attacking. The
bloody battles fought here had depleted the armies on both

sides, and hundreds of the invaders still occupied the bluff on this end of the dam, preventing the Faerines from setting foot on the earthen barrier. Yet with disaster threatening the whole stretch of line, Danri knew that he had no alternative—the diggers would have to attack again.

"Pembroak! Tell the sergeants—we're gonna have another go. Have the mining company right behind, picks and shovels ready."

"Aye, lord!" pledged the young digger—though Danri noticed, with a pang, that Pembroak's once-youthful features were haggard and lined now, making him look quite a bit older than he had a month earlier.

From somewhere a pair of gigants appeared, and twoscore sylvan archers also slipped through the woods to join the attack force. Wattli led his group of grim-faced sartors who, with bloody blades bare in their hands, took up a position to the right as Danri mustered every warrior on the upper end of the line. The attack force slipped cautiously through the tangles of the ruined forest. Finally the Faerines drew up near the enemy, though in the gathering dusk the brutox sentries showed no sign that they sensed the danger.

"Charge!" Danri's howling cry was echoed by hundreds of throats, and the Faerines rose from the tangle to sweep toward the dam. A snarling brutox lunged at the digger commander and Danri smashed the minion to the ground with a powerful sideswipe. His shield resounded to the strike of a brutox club, but then that minion fell to Wattli's spear. Howling, whooping Faerines, survivors from a dozen companies, raised a frenetic din as they attacked with the pent-up fury of the long campaign.

Hordes of minions stood in their path. The Faerines hacked their way into the enemy ranks, pushing slowly forward—at a horrifying cost in lives. Many fell on both sides, red blood mingling with black across the ground. The minions fought stubbornly, and Danri knew there were too many of them, but he had no choice other than to keep going, keep attacking.

Shadows flickered overhead, and this time it was the minions who were stunned by the appearance of drackans—two green wyrms landing in their midst, clawing and biting to right and left, rending with great claws, roaring over each blood-spattered kill. When the monstrous troops recoiled, the drackans pounced nimbly after, killing more—then leaping into the air as many brutox rushed to counterattack.

The aerial onslaught left the enemy confused and reeling. Shouting hoarsely, Danri bashed a nearby brutox senseless, rushing into the gap left by a green drackan's attack. Remembering the butcheries inflicted by the browns, the digger felt fierce elation to see that gory tide reversed—and in another moment hundreds more Faerines shared that warlike glee, charging through the reeling formations of the enemy. Gigants and sartors halted in the tangled mess of the forest, attacking minions wherever they could be found. The goat-footed Faerines fought viciously, butting with horned heads, hamstringing brutox from behind, kicking and trampling the wounded kroaks that littered the ground in increasing numbers.

The diggers, accompanied by sylvan archers, charged the dam. On that broad surface they found the corpses of four brown drackans, and tumbled the massive bodies down the earthen embankment to jeers and catcalls. Then the diggers set to gouging into the dam, while the sylves kept watch on the skies. The water level was far below, but Danri heartened the workers with a reminder: "Nobody digs like a digger!" In response, dirt and gravel flew in thick showers from the dam, tumbling from both ends of a rapidly growing ditch.

Three brown drackans dove and the sylves shouted a warning. Arrows flew in swift volleys, and the diggers scattered for the edges of the dam or the slight shelter of their shallow trench. Danri squinted upward from the lip of the dam's crest, somewhat heartened to see the flat bellies of these drackans— at least they would breathe no killing steam. And then a pair of emerald shapes slashed in from the right, knocking one of the attackers out of the air and forcing the other two to veer aside. The enraged browns shrieked and dove after the smaller, but more nimble greens.

Danri's heart swelled to the sight of a small gray shape— despite the newly sprouted wings, the digger recognized Neambrey. "Get him!" roared the Faerine commander, cheering as the youngster took a nip of a large brown's wing.

The dam's crest thundered to heavy footsteps, as a monstrous brutox lumbered forward. Thick straps of iron crossed its bulging chest, and it wore a collar and belt of spikes, lethal points jutting a handspan out from the monstrous body. The

monster wore gauntlets on its hands, each tipped with a trio
of hooked blades as long as shortswords. These metal claws
glowed with unnatural heat, and when the brutox touched
them together, a shower of white-hot sparks arced to the
ground.

"Keep digging!" Danri cried, hoisting his shield, raising
the well-worn hammer. He charged, startling the brutox
enough to halt the minion's advance in its tracks. The monstrosity loomed over the digger, and when Danri swung his
weapon, the brute met the blow with all three blades of its
right hand. A jolt of electricity shot down the digger's arm
and he barely held onto his hammer as he tumbled backward,
simultaneously—and instinctively—rolling to the side.

The brutox lunged, stabbing into the dirt where Danri had
been a moment before. The digger bounced to his feet, driving
his hammer at the tusked face, drawing a howl of indignation
as the beast turned away. The minion snarled, bashing a monstrous fist against Danri's shield, striking from right and left
with crackling blades. Smashing each attack aside, the digger
still backed slowly away. He heard the frantic activity of his
miners—picks and shovels biting into the ground, rattling cascades of dirt and soil tumbling down the dam, spilling from
the steadily growing notch.

But again the brutox stepped forward and now the digger
teetered on the brink of the ditch—there was no place left to
retreat. He feinted a charge and the brute grinned cruelly,
spreading its arms as if in invitation. Instead the Faerine warrior inched cautiously to the side, muttering curses as the minion matched him step for step.

Sylves shot arrows at the brute, and the digger flinched as
the missiles whooshed past his ears—yet they struck the iron
bands on the brutox and bounced away. The minion threw
back his brutish head, belching gales of mocking laughter.
Danri cast a quick glance behind, surprised to see that the
trench was already slightly deeper than water level. Pembroak
labored at the wall of dirt holding back the reservoir of the
Aurun.

"Let it go!" shouted Danri to his squire as the brutox
charged forward once again. The digger met the attack with
shield and hammer, grimacing against the pain that shot
through him with each contact. Finally he heard the sound he

awaited and, throwing himself backwards, skidded from the lip of the new ditch, tumbling down the long embankment into rushing water. The flow was already deep and swift, and Danri tumbled heels over head, conscious of the long plunge down the dam's face just a short distance away. He tried to plant his feet but the current pushed him again toward that deadly slide onto the rocks.

"There he is!" Pembroak's voice reached his ears as Danri came up, sputtering—and thankful for the good ropework of a digger sergeant-major. That stalwart warrior had tossed a line, and the digger commander quickly squirmed an arm through the loop. With the support of many companions, the sergeant-major hauled Danri—drenched, but still clutching his shield and hammer—out of the flowage.

The flood increased, the current's pressure ripping away more and more of the loose dirt of the dam—and as it grew wider, more water flooded through the notch. The first waves washed down the long face, swirling into the channel at the bottom and immediately causing the retreat of a hundred kroaks and their brutox leader. Water thundered and surged with growing force, the surface of the dam shifting unsteadily underfoot.

"Faerines—back!" cried Danri, perceiving the danger of a complete collapse. Quickly the diggers and their allies scrambled back to the rocky ground of the bluff, watching water erode the earthen dam.

The restored flow quickly surged out of the eddies at the dam's base, filling in the nearly dry channel, slicing through the minion columns that now fled hastily back to their side of the Aurun. Danri stood beside the dam, not aware that he was cheering as lustily as his warriors.

He thought, with a sudden pang, of Kianna and Quenidon—and then, through his tears, he was able to shout fiercely, triumphantly. It didn't take too much imagination to picture them watching, and relishing, the victory.

— 2 —

Kestrel held the wheel of the *Black Condor*, guiding a course as close as he dared along the mouth of the Aurun. Awnro

Lyrifell and Darret manned the stern trebuchet, holding the swiveling crossbow fixed upon the shore.

"Drackans forgot about us, I guess," Darret suggested, squinting as he scanned the skies over the battlefield.

"They had enough to worry about when their green cousins arrived," Awnro declared with a chuckle. "Aye—that was a fight deserving of a song or two! The first verse is already comin' to me—'when emerald wings fly northward,' or some such."

Darret nodded enthusiastically. "Fast fliers, too. Those greens got de browns right quick."

They all remembered the soaring battles. A masthead lookout had been the first to announce the bright emerald color of the drackan newcomers as one of the big serpents dove against a column of minions in the drying riverbed. Cheers rang upward from the deck as the flying wyrm belched a cloud of whiteness around the monsters, killing a score and coating the rocky attack route with frost. The drackan had landed, biting and clawing among the survivors, and in moments the minions streamed back toward the friendly bank, some even tumbling into pools of standing water in frantic haste.

"Look—dey comin' again!" Darret cried, pointing to the shore.

Shrieks rent the air and massive shapes flew just above the ground, several browns chasing two greens. The emerald wyrms twisted and dodged, staying just out of the browns' reach. The aerial battle shrilled wildly as the massive attackers chased their foes from the treetops into the realms of the clouds, where one of the smaller serpents fell, body cruelly torn. An instant later the other green spun in the air, belching a cloud of white frost, and two browns plummeted, wings frozen by a blast of Aurafrost.

"Look there!" cried Darret. "Dat little gray one teasin' de biggest brown!"

The humans watched in awed fascination as the small serpent spiraled through circles around a frantically bellowing brown. "I saw the little one do that earlier," Awnro remembered. "The big fellow loses his temper, can't seem to catch him."

"Look out!" Darret shouted as the brown's jaws snapped

closed near the youngster's tail. Immediately the gray serpent dove, with his bellowing enemy plunging after; both of the drackans vanished behind the trees of the river bank.

"Now *there's* a target worth my harpoons!" Kestrel said, as another huge form moved along the shore.

Awnro nodded in grim agreement as a bovar, guided by a brutox handler, dumped a pile of dirt into the mouth of the riverbed. "Look's like they're trying to build a dike."

"My shot!" cried the captain. Darret stood back as Kestrel swiveled the massive trebuchet, carefully fixing the crosspiece on the broad flank of the bovar. The sea captain pulled the trigger and the powerful spring sent a jolt through the galyon, casting the heavy missile straight into the monster's flank. With a thunderous bellow the bovar bucked and kicked, knocking the terrified brutox into the lake. The speared beast whirled, staggering toward the river bank, then collapsed with a pathetic grunt.

"Good shooting!"

The high-pitched voice emerged from a large spool of coiled rope, shocking Kestrel with instant recognition.

"Anjell!" cried Awnro, obviously as appalled as the captain when the girl popped up from her hiding place.

"I couldn't see much from in there," she explained seriously. "But I meant what I said—that was a *great* shot!"

"A stowaway!" groaned Kestrel. "You're supposed to be ashore, where it's safe!"

"It's *safe* here!" she retorted.

"Your mother will tack our hides to the wall when she finds out," Awnro declared grimly.

"It's not your fault—I'll tell her that!"

"How'd you get aboard?—we were anchored off the dock. You'd have to have come by boat . . ." Darret began to sidle away as the captain's eyes narrowed, then turned toward the boy. "What do *you* know about this?" Kestrel demanded.

"Me?" Darret's normally cool composure melted, and he turned helplessly to Anjell.

"I told you—it's *my* fault," the girl declared. "But it wouldn't have to be anybody's fault if I was allowed to *do* something once in a while. I couldn't miss everything, could I? I mean, look—isn't it great to see *that* happening?" She pointed along the riverbed, toward the distant barrier of the dam.

"What?" demanded Awnro, as Kestrel's eyes widened in surprise.

"Aye, child—it *is* great," agreed the captain of the *Black Condor*, as white rills burst through the notch and spilled down the face of the dam, surging with whitecapped eagerness along the riverbed. "It's grand to see a pretty river comin' back to life."

"And it's the *minions* who're in danger, not us," Anjell insisted, indicating the verdant bank of the Aurun. A small company of kroaks was trapped there, cut off by the resurgent river. Gigants and sartors closed in from three sides, mercilessly butchering the monsters—and even then the kroaks preferred to fight to the death rather than wade through a barely knee-deep flow. The sylvan longboats moved into the shallow water, chucking harpoons at a few kroaks who tried to slip around the end of the sartor line, and in a few minutes the gory fight was over.

"No retreat for those that got across," Kestrel said. "Look's like the river's comin' back for good." He pointed at the dam, which was couple of miles up the valley from the lake. They watched as the flow widened the notch in the earthen barrier, bringing slabs of mud down the long face, spilling more and more water into the riverbed.

"You know," Awnro mused, wrapping an arm around Anjell's shoulders. "You might be safe here, after all."

— 3 —

Neambrey strained for altitude, winging away from the huge brown. Once more he found Jasaren by recognizing the monster's roaring bellow, and the young hybrid turned his head back to jeer a challenge at his sire. Furious, Jasaren roared, straining to climb higher and faster. His mighty wings swept out, gathering great scoops of air—but the drackan was a heavy, massive creature, and he couldn't close the distance to his smaller foe.

Three times now, in these skies above the battlefield, Neambrey had found Jasaren, had led him on an exhausting

chase back and forth over minion and Faerine positions, and
then evaded his quarry by climbing until Jasaren grew too
tired to pursue. The young drackan vividly remembered Meamare and, looking back at the mighty brown, knew that this
was the killer of his mother—and there was only one way to
make him pay for that crime.

The chomp of massive jaws inches from his tail signaled
Neambrey—he flattened his wings, halting in the air, and then
propelling himself straight down with rapid strokes. He
whisked past Jasaren like a streaking arrow, slashing no more
than a tail's length from the brown's snout. Immediately the
enraged elder twisted in the air, coiling around to follow.

Plunging sleek as a missile, Neambrey watched the ground
rush closer. Abruptly he veered back and forth as if he
couldn't make up his mind, each such twist and turn costing
him valuable speed. Jasaren closed the distance, plunging like
a javelin at the target growing ever larger in his eyes. The
forest rushed dizzyingly at Neambrey when he pulled up, feeling Jasaren's menacing presence once again close on his tail.
Suddenly treetops flashed past, and the gray drackan flew
wildly along the riverbed, almost touching the minions that
now struggled to escape the flooding channel. A quick backward glance showed Jasaren, wings beating furiously, fanged
jaws spread wide and straining forward.

Again Neambrey darted in feigned panic, slowing even
more. Jasaren's jaws snapped, a moment too late to catch the
tail the youngster flicked out of the way. The brown drackan
strained with increasing desperation, putting every ounce of
his strength into speed—hatred blinded him to everything but
his insolent offspring.

But then the dam was there, and the nimble drackan who
was the color of granite rock swept upward, barely skimming
the steeply rising surface. Jasaren tried to climb, too, but he
was heavier, less agile than Neambrey—and by now he was
going much faster. The brown drackan smashed into the
earthen bulwark with bone-crushing force. Neambrey, still
climbing, heard the sound of Jasaren's spine snapping, a sickening, grinding disintegration. The young drackan soared over
the top of the dam, where a hundred diggers stood beside a
long trench. They cheered lustily and Neambrey brayed with

pride, while water spilled down the dam and the River Aurun was reborn.

— 4 —

The black thundercloud towered overhead as Rudy strained to steer his cloud, to rise or veer or simply *move*. But the remnant of the sky-ship drifted on the wind, pivoting slowly away from the lakeshore, crossing the Aurun on the northwest course of the wind. The Iceman knelt upon a low shoulder of the vaporous remnant, racked by thirst—and incapable of affecting their flight.

"Aura . . . ?" he asked, as Raine crawled into view, coming around the side of the cloud.

"Nothing—not a cask or a skin," she said. "There's just you and me—and this." She pressed her hands into the spongy surface, bouncing experimentally. The piece of the once mighty sky-ship was small, though it seemed to hold a steady altitude.

"The rest of them . . . Larrial Solluel, all the Royal House sylves—gone!" Anguish choked Rudy's throat, even as the evidence of Larrial Solluel's accomplishment was clear to him and Raine: The *Dreadcloud* wheeled and pitched, out of control. The stern sections, where the driving pulse of energy had fired so violently, were shredded, and the lightning batteries hadn't fired since the barrage that had destroyed the Auracloud, though many of the columns remained firm on the forward platform.

Barely a long stone's throw of space separated the two vessels, and now the humans crouched in a hollow on the far side of the Auracloud remnant, striving to remain out of sight. Their cloud rotated very slowly, so every few minutes Rudy and Raine crawled a little farther around the fleecy mass, always keeping the vapor of Aura between themselves and the enemy.

"Look—the river's flowing again," Rudy observed.

"The minions are stopped, then—for now," Raine added. "If only Danri and Gulatch are all right . . ."

"The *Dreadcloud*, at least, has a few problems of its own," the Iceman pointed out as the evil ship drifted over the Aurun.

Above the water great portions of the black shape ripped away, vanishing into the air; dozens of minions tumbled, shrieking from the dissipating hull. "Every time it drifts over a lake or river, more of the Darkblood will dissolve!"

"Then let the winds blow," Raine said fervently, looking toward the mountains that rose nearer as they coursed through the air.

"Remember the last time we floated like this, with no way to steer?" Rudy asked as they settled into a fresh niche.

"From Landrun all the way to the Watershed—of course I do," Raine replied, looking curious. "It was your first Auracloud."

"That was half a year ago. You know how the winds blow south in the spring, and north in the fall? I wonder if we're not just floating all the way back?"

"To Dalethica?" Raine wondered aloud. "Perhaps even right through Taywick?"

That notch was the only gap in a thousand-mile range of mountains, and as such was a major passageway for winds. As their cloud drifted over the foothills, a clear sunset etched the distant mountains—and they saw the lone place where the ridge did not extend high into the sky. For a time they huddled in the shelter of the remnant's irregular surface, watching the sun go down in a splendor of lavender clouds and flaring, orange brilliance. They felt warm, even safe. The battlefield was remote, and though the malignant cloud remained near, the lovers were content to lie in each other's arms.

Yet while Rudy held Raine, he fought against a rising tide of panic triggered by the heights beginning to rise around them. The cliff of his Scrying Pool vision, the menace to his beloved's life, could lurk somewhere in these mountains. He should have been able to fly them out of here, to return easily to Spendorial—but because of the lack of Aura he had no control! He feared, more than anything, that his weakness might cost Raine her life.

It was a flicker of movement past one of the bright gaps of sunset that set off real alarm. Rudy stiffened, squinting against the brightness. "Terrions!"

Leaping to his feet, the Iceman pointed to the nearly invisible fliers suddenly swooping toward their cloud. Lordsmiter jumped into his hand as if it had a will of its own, and he slashed upward at the first of the shimmering minions. The blade sliced a long gash in the monster's wing, and the terrion tumbled sideways with a shriek of pain and fury, trying to extend the torn membrane. The leathery skin ripped away, and a keening wail followed the creature all the way to the ground.

Raine tumbled around the side of the cloud, chopping at the jaws of a vicious flier that swept past her. The monster dove away, but not before her digger blade was darkened by a strike against the ridged snout. More of the minions flew around them, shrieking and keening, striking blows with their powerful wings. Jaws snapped audibly as a terrion settled to the cloud's summit and bit at Rudy. Tumbling away, the Iceman rolled past another attacker, then stabbed Lordsmiter deep into the bowels of a third. Gagging at the putrid blood that spattered around him, Rudy whirled back toward the first terrion as the beast launched itself down the slope of the cloud. The Iceman chopped, slicing off a wing and, with a disturbingly humanlike shriek of terror, the creature plummeted.

Twisting away, Raine then darted back to deceive a pursuing terrion; her sword sliced the minion's throat, and it tumbled away from the cloud, straining pathetically to fly—but finally smashing headlong into a hillside. Lordsmiter felt magnificent in Rudy's hand, more perfect than any weapon he'd ever held. He cut and slashed, driving back every terrion he saw. The remaining fliers finally dove away, vanishing beneath the Auracloud, and though Rudy peered over the edge for a long time, he saw no further sign of the deadly avians.

"Look!" Raine's whispered alarm brought his eyes upward, and he saw that again they had swirled into view of the *Dreadcloud*. The once-mighty sky-ship had shrunk dramatically, trailing wisps of black vapor into the air. Like a rudderless rowboat in a roiling stream, the *Dreadcloud* careened through great, spiraling turns. Borne toward the highlands of Taywick, the evil ship drifted over a broad pond—and another section of the vaporous hull disintegrated, tumbling dozens of kroaks to their death. A pair of stalkers fell, too, but these sprouted terrionlike wings and glided back toward Spendorial.

As the *Dreadcloud* continued to dissolve, Rudy saw more minions plunge toward the ground, uttering horrified screams

that reached even the humans' distant ears. Darkness cloaked
them and falling brutox trailed shimmering clouds of sparks
in fantastic pyres.

And still the wind coursed toward Taywick.

— 5 —

Phalthak clutched at the disintegrating stuff of the *Dreadcloud*, hissing furiously as a stalker vanished through the floor
nearby. The Fang's heads lashed and hissed, infuriated by the
knowledge that a craven lackey could sprout wings and escape, while a Lord Minion of the Sleepstealer faced a grim
and dangerous predicament. Alone among the great nobles of
Duloth-Trol, Phalthak was unable to fly—nor did he possess
the power to change shape into some winged creature. Instead, the Fang of Dassadec was now forced to place his trust
in Direfang, hoping that the brutox could restore power to the
lone remaining sturmvault.

More minions tumbled through the hull of the sky-ship,
each time dragging precious Darkblood with them. Their involuntary departure gave the Lord Minion an idea to extend
the life of the dissolving *Dreadcloud*.

"Kroaks and brutox—assemble on the forward deck!"
Phalthak's hissed command penetrated what remained of the
ship, and from the farthest corners, along the smoking passageways, the minions marched to obey. Ultimately the lord
found hundreds of his troops on the foredeck, where four of
the lightning battery pillars had already collapsed and drifted
away; the fifth was tattered, riddled with gaping holes. Only
the sixth, closest to the hull of the ship, remained intact.

"Assemble!" demanded the green snake, and the minions,
cowering away from their master, formed ranks across the
seething, sagging deck

"Now—march! Forward!" snapped the emerald serpent,
hissing wickedly. With fearful glances at the twisting serpents, the lead kroaks stepped reluctantly toward the edge of
the deck. One turned, lunging for the hull, but a black patch
of bulkhead slipped aside to reveal the spark-limned figure of
Direfang. The captain cracked a steel-tipped whip, and the

kroak reacted with instinctive panic, hurling itself from the sky-ship.

"Move, fools! Miserable wretches! *Obey!*" Phalthak's heads shrilled the commands, one after the other, and the minions advanced at a rush, propelled by Direfang's whip on one side and the Lord Minion's venomous serpents on the other. In a steady stream the crew of the *Dreadcloud* trickled from the sky-ship, marking the ship's path along the valley of Taywick with a trail of black, gory assaults against the rocky ground.

As the last members of the minion crew leapt to their deaths, Direfang looked fearfully at his master, but Phalthak ordered the captain to return to his labors at the broken sturm-vault. Considerably lighter, the sky ship solidified into a smaller shape, now capable of bearing its two passengers easily.

It was as Direfang worked that Phalthak felt his master's presence, touching him across the miles from Duloth-Trol.

Phalthak, my many-headed pet: I have a command for you.

"Speak, master!" hissed the green head, writhing around Phalthak's shoulders in an effort to bow low.

My greatest enemy, the Man of Three Waters, rides upon an Auracloud very near to you. I want you to find him, and kill him!

"Aye, lord!"

The victim has been found by my Eye—but Nicodareus has failed me most miserably. It is up to you, glorious Fang, to earn honor for my name.

Phalthak knew that Nicodareus could hear the exchange—there was no other reason for Dassadec to employ such effusive praise—and the Fang took great pleasure in his fellow lord's humiliation. Snakes of every color hissed praise to the name of Dassadec, and chortled at the debasement of the Eye.

The puff of Auracloud still drifted nearby, though after the failure of the terrions, Phalthak had paid little heed to the two human pests. He remembered them well, however, and his heads rose through the murk of Darkblood, seeking, finding the cloud.

At that moment Direfang emerged from the smoky passageway. The snake of cobalt blue turned toward the brutox, while the other heads held their gaze fast to the Auracloud. "Speak!" hissed that azure serpent.

"Good news, Mighty Lord. The sturmvault will yield some power—we can move!"

"Splendid . . ." said the green snake, turning to glare steadily at the sparking brutox. "Take me there, to that cloud of Aura."

"Aye, Mighty Lord—immediately!"

Direfang disappeared into the bowels of the ship. In moments, with a rumble like distant thunder, the cloud of darkness began to drive across the wind.

— 6 —

"Look—it's coming closer." Rudy spoke in measured tones, but underlying tension edged his words with steel.

Raine sat up and nodded. The remains of the *Dreadcloud* moved through the air under power again, looming higher in the sky.

"What's that?" Raine asked, pointing.

Rudy squinted against the backdrop of blackness, staring at the figure he gradually discerned in the bow of the skyship. "Lord Minion Phalthak—the Fang of Dassadec," the Iceman whispered. "I watched him through the Scrying Pool—he's not a sight anyone's likely to forget." The tentacles of hideous heads writhed and twisted above the wet aperture of Phalthak's neck, and his body looked huge and clumsy, but was clearly powerful.

"The terrain looks familiar around here, doesn't it?" Raine suggested with a tight smile, turning from the hideous monster and pointing toward a gap in the mountainous ridge.

Dawn had broken around them, revealing an extent of recognizable mountain peaks. Looking into the distance, Rudy saw the gap in a lofty ridge. Though they came from the opposite direction, the pass looked substantially the same from the south as from the north: The Tor of Taywick rose from the saddle, a spire of rock nearly a thousand feet tall. It was on the flat cap of that pillar that Raine had killed Prince Garamis of Galtigor. There, too, Rudy remembered with a chill, rested the prince's vile weapon: the black-bladed sword of Darkblood, Garamis's talisman from his master, Nicodareus.

"Yes—Taywick Pass," Rudy confirmed. "It's an odd fate that brings us back. . . ." His eyes widened in shock as another memory registered with horrifying effect, and though he turned away from Raine she noticed his fear.

"What is it?"

He thought of lying, of trying to conceal his fear, and knew instantly that any such attempt would fail. Raine's eyes would penetrate the façade, and he would reveal the truth. "The prophecy," he groaned, as the image from the Scrying Pool snapped into focus: the long cliff, with Raine lying bloody at the bottom, was the narrow spire they had climbed together— he had seen her fall from the Tor of Taywick!

"Don't!" Raine cried, but it was already too late. That spire of stone was clearly visible even now, jutting up from the verdant saddle of the pass. "He's coming for us," she observed tightly, bringing Rudy's attention back to the *Dreadcloud*.

Staring around wildly, he tried once more to force his skyship to move, but without Aura his efforts had no effect. They merely drifted, watching the dark cloud close fast. The serpent-headed horror on the foredeck stood still, only the snakes moving as they strained toward the remnant of Auracloud.

"Hold on!" Rudy warned, as the looming hull drove toward them. The black cloud staggered the humans' vessel, rocking them through the sky—but Phalthak leapt with startling agility before the smaller cloud bounced away. Snakes hissed, whipping toward Raine and the Iceman as the Lord Minion's big hands seized their cloudship. A green serpent reached almost to Raine's face, but she bashed it away with her blade, and when a red viper slithered toward her side, she whipped the blade around and it reared back.

The Lord Minion's heads hissed loudly, a physical assault. Some of the snakes stared at the Man of Three Waters while others followed Raine with unblinking intensity. She didn't wait for an attack, instead slashing quickly with her digger steel. The snakes hissed wetly, recoiling from her high blows, but the Lord Minion bashed a forepaw toward the weapon and knocked it from her hand.

Rudy lunged, holding Lordsmiter in both hands, waving the

glowing blade before him. Warily the Lord Minion circled away, heads bobbing and weaving, the many pairs of eyes flaming like embers, blazing even more hotly as they fixed upon the Iceman and his ancient weapon.

Rudy struck, Lordsmiter gouging Phalthak's wrist as the Fang of Dassadec twisted, keening that awful noise. The monster turned with a quick pounce, striking with the green head at Raine. Throwing herself backward, she evaded the fangs by inches, skidding down a slope of the cloud to catch herself in the last pocket before the long fall.

"Raine!" Panicked, Rudy dove after her. At the last moment some silent instinct alerted him and he turned, saw the striking head of cobalt blue. Lordsmiter slashed and the spitting viper flopped free, twisting frantically and then bouncing off the cloud. Phalthak shrieked and drew back, his remaining heads lashing in frenzy.

The Tor of Taywick was near now, the humans' puff of cloud drifting straight toward the spire. Rudy struggled to ignore the horror, railing at the fate that left him powerless to move his vessel, now when he most needed to. Raine struggled up the slope of the cloud, balancing precariously as Rudy frantically gestured for her to stay where she was. Recovering from the loss of his blue snake-head, Phalthak advanced on Rudy once more, lashing at the Iceman with the green snake, red and purple serpents striking to either side. Lordsmiter slashed again, this time cutting off the emerald head—and the rasping hisses exploded with shocking force, gaping mouths assaulting Rudy with a wave of vile, putrid breath.

Again that pearly white blade flashed, carving through hideous flesh, cutting another of the serpents from the beast's shoulders—but missing the hairy chest and the cruel heart that pulsed within. The Auracloud rocked a bit as it nosed gently past the summit of Taywick's tor.

Hissing furiously, the Lord Minion spun, dodging away from Rudy, knocking Raine into the air with a backhand blow. She tumbled to the very edge of the cloud, teetering in the gap between the Auracloud and the Tor of Taywick. "Rudy!" she screamed as the edge of the cloud slipped away. The Iceman lunged, hand outstretched—but the tenuous support of the cloud beneath her was gone.

"No!" he cried, his agonized shout ringing from distant summits as she tumbled free.

Raine had one chance. Twisting in the air, she reached toward the rocky lip of the tor just a few feet away. Her fingers caught that edge, suspending the fall for a moment, but the weight of her body broke the fragile hold. Plummeting without a sound, Raine dropped hundreds of feet alongside the cliff before smashing into a shoulder of the tor. Her body spiraled outward, careening toward rocks far below. Again she bounced, twisting like a rag doll, smashing farther down the steep slope, striking outcrops with bone-crushing impact, finally coming to rest in the talus field at the foot of the cliff.

The Man of Three Waters held the hilt of the sword with loathing, filled with an onrush of rage unequaled in his life. The Fang of Dassadec reared cautiously, as if in fear, and Rudy charged without a care for his own survival. Lordsmiter sought Phalthak's heart as if the weapon had a will of its own, and the human wielder only gave that blade the impetus it required. The Lord Minion swung a hammerlike fist, aiming to bash the sword aside, but the keen edge sliced the monster's hand off at the forearm.

Continuing his relentless drive, Rudy lunged, drew back, then stabbed with all his strength and rage, driving the ancient weapon into the Lord Minion's chest, slicing through the hideous body. Multiple screams of shock and pain faded into a bubbling death rattle as the Iceman pulled the sword free, and Phalthak staggered, writhing, on the edge of the cloud. Rudy trembled, ready to chop and stab again, but then the monster was gone, already dead, plummeting to the rocky ground.

The shred of cloud dissipated on the top of the Tor and Rudy came to rest on that pillar of rock. Shaking, adrenaline still coursing through his bloodstream, he stared numbly downward. Raine lay on her back amid jagged boulders, her body broken, limbs brutally twisted. One foot, at the end of a cruelly shattered leg, rested in a placid pool—one of many springs that dotted the base of the tor.

The image was savagely familiar: Rudy had seen this same picture in the Scrying Pool, when he had dared to seek his destiny. Now Raine was dead, and he alive, looking down at her battered and broken corpse. He shrank to his heels, weary and dizzy and utterly despairing.

Sometime later the Iceman's eyes focused upon something he had never expected to see again: the Sword of Darkblood, once borne by Prince Garamis, traitor to Galtigor and servant of Duloth-Trol. The blade of pure black was sleek and unblemished, the leather-wrapped hilt deceptively smooth and mundane. Rudy and Raine had decided to leave it here, certain that it would never be viewed by mortal man again. Now here he was—a man so arrogant as to seek his own destiny, learning that he couldn't even discard a possession of his hated enemy!

He picked up the blade, sliding it through his belt as he walked to the edge of the platform, numbness slowly yielding to a contained restlessness. Bearing the two weapons, Rudy started down the tor, following the route he and Raine had pioneered a half year before. Placing hands and feet quickly, even recklessly, the Iceman worked his way down the cliff. He moved from ledges to a long chimney, sometimes scaling narrow cracks, always ignoring routine precautions. Though encumbered by two swords, he dropped down the sheer face rapidly.

Rudy had made his decision by the time he reached the bottom, though a part of his mind rejected his intention as obscene, a violation of something treasured—and mourned. Yet when he came upon Raine's crushed, bloody corpse, he knew that he had no choice, no possible alternative.

Standing over the motionless body of his lover, not allowing himself to think, to pause or delay, he drew the blade of Darkblood and thrust it through her still heart—in exactly the place he himself had been stabbed, by this same sword, when he had been carried by an avalanche to the foot of the Glimmercrown.

He withdrew the weapon and cast it aside, repelled by its touch. His stomach heaved in revulsion, but he didn't stop or turn away. Taking Raine's broken body as gently as possible, by the shoulders, Rudy eased her into the pool of Aura until she was covered. Even her face he submerged, gingerly caressing the crushed cheekbones, stroking gentle fingers over her closed eyelids. No bubbles rose from her nostrils or lips— because she did not breathe.

Finally he had done everything he could, tending, caring, watching over a lifeless body. All he could do was settle down to wait, and to pray.

EPILOGUE

Follow a long enough road and you will
eventually return to your own house.
—DIGGERSPEAK PROVERB

Anjell walked along the floating dock of Spendorial's waterfront. She climbed an arching bridge, gazing listlessly at the
dazzling waters, the reed-lined shore, the slender longboats
bobbing gently at anchor. Scuffing her sylvan slippers, which
were a blue softer than the sky's, she tried to snag the silky
material on a splinter of wood, knowing that the smooth surface wouldn't catch. Sighing, she abandoned her efforts, moving with a little more purpose along the pier.

Darret was fishing at the end of the wharf, and he slipped
a worm onto a hook for her as she sat down beside him.
Plopping the bait into the clear water, Anjell tried to concentrate on attracting a fish. Soon, inevitably, her eyes turned
toward the sky.

"Maybe today," she said with a sigh. "Maybe we'll see
them coming back."

"I hope so," Darret agreed, looking sidelong at his friend,
his eyes clouded by concern. "Been a long time."

Anjell nodded stubbornly. " 'Course, I've heard everybody

say that Rudy and Raine got blown up over there, but I know they floated away in the clouds. . . ." The girl's lower lip quivered, but she bit it determinedly. "They're just taking a long time to come back—but they'll be here! You'll see!"

"I believe you!" Darret assured her. "Dat Iceman fly his way back here right quick, one day!"

Anjell nodded solemnly. "I saw Danri and Kerri this morning. He was still kind of grumpy, but at least he's started doing stuff again. They went to look at a place where Kerri thought they might build their inn—up near the river. But first they were visiting that drackan, Neambrey—he's Danri's friend."

The girl hefted her pole, listlessly dangling the worm before a pair of skeptical pan fish.

"Neambrey—he's dat little gray one?"

"Yup—but he's mostly like a green, I mean a *nice* drackan. I like him."

"Good fighter," said the boy approvingly. "Saw him crash de big one into de dam. But why's he stayin' alla time in de forest?"

"I guess drackans don't like cities much—plus, he's helping to keep an eye on all those minions." Anjell wrinkled her nose at the wasteland across the lake, then turned to the precipice at the end of the Aurun gorge. Many Faerine warriors waited and watched there, she knew, keeping an eye on the remnants of the dam—which didn't amount to much of a barrier anymore. Even from here she could see that most of the fill had eroded with the restored current of the river.

"Awnro's up there too, for a few days—since Mama's got so busy."

"She's writin' her story 'bout de battle?"

"Yup. I wish we knew how it ended—the battle, I mean!" Anjell blinked back the tears that suddenly welled in her eyes. She looked across the lake, at the torched and blackened wasteland of the Suderwild. A sudden rush of anger surged upward from her heart—how she *hated* those minions!

The time following the bloody strife had brought a warlike stasis to Faerine. A horde of minions lived, but they huddled on the far bank of the Aurun, making no effort to attack— neither, however, did they show any inclination to retreat. The city of Spendorial still stood, pristine and untouched, once again screened by the great river of Faerine. Fortunately, the minions had made no further effort to rebuild their dam. That was good, of course, but everything else about the war seemed so terribly, utterly *sad*.

Anjell remembered Kianna, and she couldn't stop the tears from spilling down her cheeks. And Quenidon Daringer, about whose bravery the sylves—and Awnro—had already begun to sing. All those trees, the cities and the lives that had been expended . . . and the war wasn't even over yet!

Her eyes wandered, drifting away from the blackened swath to the greener hills to the north. The skies were blue in that direction, perfectly clear except for a single cloud—a puffball of whiteness that set Anjell's heart to pounding. She watched, trying not to let her hopes run wild as the lone white shape drifted closer.

Suddenly she sprang to her feet. "Look! It's an Auracloud! It's got to be Rudy!" she cried, her pole falling unnoticed into the water as she spun to race down the dock.

The regular oblong of cloud drifted along the shore, crossing the direction of the wind. Anjell shouted and waved, and soon it seemed like the entire population of the city had rushed to the lakeside park, seeking to greet the white ship that slowly settled toward the elmstudded swale.

A lanky, brown-haired figure stood at the edge of the cloud, and Anjell screamed in delighted recognition. Then she squinted as she looked beyond her uncle, spying another familiar figure—the slender woman with curly brown hair who came to stand at Rudy's side.

The Auracloud settled to the ground and Rudy and Raine stepped down onto the grass. Anjell raced forward to embrace her uncle, while Danri and Kerri, back from the woods, came up behind. Dara, Darret, and Kestrel also pushed their way through the throng of cheering Faerines.

"Rudy! You're back! And Raine!" cried Anjell, scrutinizing the strangely somber woman who stood beside her uncle. "You took so long—we were *really* worried! Well, some people were, anyway. I always knew you'd be coming back. But why did it take you so long?"

The Man of Three Waters hesitated, looking at Raine and then back at his niece. Anjell was startled by the desperate look in the woman's eyes.

"I was"—Rudy seemed to be searching for the right words—"waiting, at the Tor of Taywick."

Anjell frowned, suddenly concerned by the way her uncle's brow furrowed when he turned to Raine, and by Raine's unsettled, anxious expression. "Is something wrong?" the girl asked hesitantly.

"Wrong? No, but . . ." Rudy spoke slowly, through a smile that was not one of pure joy. "It's just that Raine . . . well, she's changed. . . ."

Finally Rudy took a deep breath, squeezing his lover's hand as he looked straight at Anjell. Raine's face was flushed, and her eyes looked over the crowd toward some distant place. Anjell realized, suddenly, that the woman was frightened.

"She's like me, now," Rudy continued firmly.

"Raine . . . is a Woman of Three Waters."